OVERHEAD IN A BALLOON
AND OTHER STORIES

Mavis Gallant was born in Montreal and worked as a feature writer before giving up newspaper work to devote herself to fiction writing. She left Canada in 1950 and after extensive travel settled in Paris. The author of seven collections of stories, two novels, and numerous essays and reviews, she was made an Officer of the Order of Canada in 1981 in recognition of her contribution to literature. The stories published in this edition first appeared in two separate collections, *Overhead in a Balloon* (1987) and *Home Truths* (1985).

D0830350

ff

MAVIS GALLANT

Overhead in a Balloon and Other Stories

faber and faber

LONDON · BOSTON

First published in Great Britain as *Overhead in a Balloon* in 1987
and *Home Truths* in 1985
by Jonathan Cape Ltd, London
First published in this edition in paperback in 1989
by Faber and Faber Limited
3 Queen Square London WC1N 3AU

Typeset by Goodfellow & Egan Ltd, Cambridge

Printed in Great Britain by
Richard Clay Ltd, Bungay, Suffolk
All rights reserved

Overhead in a Balloon Copyright © 1979, 1981,
1982, 1983, 1984, 1985 by Mavis Gallant; *Home
Truths* Copyright © 1956, 1959, 1963, 1965, 1966,
1968, 1971, 1975, 1976, 1977, 1978, 1981 by
Mavis Gallant.
This edition Copyright © Mavis Gallant, 1989.

'The Assembly' was first published in *Harper's*
magazine and 'With a Capital T' in *Canadian
Fiction Magazine*. All other stories were first
published in *The New Yorker*

*This book is sold subject to the condition that it shall not,
by way of trade or otherwise, be lent, resold, hired out
or otherwise circulated without the publisher's prior consent
in any form of binding or cover other than that in which
it is published and without a similar condition including this
condition being imposed on the subsequent purchaser.*

British Library Cataloguing in Publication Data is available

ISBN: 0-571-15409-3

For G. de D. M.

CONTENTS

OVERHEAD IN A BALLOON

SPECK'S IDEA

S andor Speck's first art gallery in Paris was on the Right
Bank, near the Church of St. Elisabeth, on a street too
narrow for cars. When his block was wiped off the map to
make way for a five-story garage, Speck crossed the Seine to the
shadow of Saint-Julien-le-Pauvre, where he set up shop in a
picturesque slum protected by law from demolition. When this
gallery was blown up by Basque separatists, who had mistaken it
for a travel agency exploiting the beauty of their coast, he
collected his insurance money and moved to the Faubourg Saint-
Germain.

Here, at terrifying cost, he rented four excellent rooms—two
on the loggia level, and a clean dry basement for framing and
storage. The entrance, particularly handsome, was on the street
side of an eighteenth-century *hôtel particulier* built around an
elegant court now let out as a parking concession. The building
had long before been cut up into dirty, decaying apartments,
whose spiteful, quarrelsome, and avaricious tenants were for-
given every failing by Speck for the sake of being the Count of
this and the Prince of that. Like the flaking shutters, the rotting

1

windowsills, the slops and oil stains in the ruined court, they bore a Proustian seal of distinction, like a warranty, making up for his insanely expensive lease. Though he appreciated style, he craved stability even more. In the Faubourg, he seemed at last likely to find it: not a stone could be removed without the approval of the toughest cultural authorities of the nation. Three Marxist embassies installed in former ducal mansions along the street required the presence of armed policemen the clock around. The only commercial establishments anywhere near Speck's—a restaurant and a bookstore—seemed unlikely targets for firebombs: the first catered to lower-echelon civil servants, the second was painted royal blue, a conservative color he found reassuring. The bookstore's name, Amandine, suggested shelves of calm regional novels and accounts of travel to Imperial Russia signed "A Diplomat." Pasted inside the window, flat on the pane, was an engraving that depicted an old man, bearded and mitred, tearing a small demon limb from limb. The old man looked self-conscious, the imp resigned. He supposed that this image concealed a deep religious meaning, which he did not intend to plumb. If it was holy, it was respectable; as the owner of the gallery across the street, he needed to know nothing more.

Speck was now in the parish of St. Clotilde, near enough to the church for its bells to give him migraine headache. Leaves from the church square blew as far as his door—melancholy reminders of autumn, a season bad for art. (Winter was bad, too, while the first chestnut leaves unfolding heralded the worst season of all. In summer the gallery closed.) In spite of his constant proximity to churches he had remained rational. Generations of highly intellectual Central European agnostics and freethinkers had left in his bones a mistrust of the bogs and quicksands that lie beyond reality perceived. Neither loss nor grief nor guilt nor fear had ever moved him to appeal to the unknown—any unknown, for there were several. Nevertheless, after signing his third lease in seven years, he decided to send Walter, his Swiss assistant, a lapsed Calvinist inching toward Rome, to light a candle at St.

Clotilde's. Walter paid for a five-franc taper and set it before St. Joseph, the most reliable intermediary he could find: a wave of post-conciliar puritanism seemed to have broken at St. Clotilde's, sweeping away most of the mute and obliging figures to whom desires and gratitude could be expressed. Walter was willing to start again in some livelier church—Notre Dame de Paris, for instance—but Speck thought enough was enough.

On a damp October evening about a year after this, there could be seen in Speck's window a drawing of a woman drying her feet (Speck permanent collection); a poster announcing the current exhibition, "Paris and Its Influence on the Tirana School, 1931-2"; five catalogues displayed attractively; and the original of the picture on the poster—a shameless copy of Foujita's "Mon Intérieur" re-entitled "Balkan Alarm Clock." In defiance of a government circular reminding Paris galleries about the energy crisis Speck had left the lights on. This was partly to give the lie to competitors who might be putting it about that he was having money troubles. He had set the burglar alarm, bolted the security door, and was now cranking down an openwork iron screen whose Art Nouveau loops and fronds allowed the works inside to be seen but nothing larger than a mouse to get in. The faint, floating sadness he always felt while locking up had to do with the time. In his experience, love affairs and marriages perished between seven and eight o'clock, the hour of rain and no taxis. All over Paris couples must be parting forever, leaving like debris along the curbs the shreds of cancelled restaurant dates, useless ballet tickets, hopeless explanations, and scraps of pride; and toward each of these disasters a taxi was pulling in, the only taxi for miles, the light on its roof already dimmed in anticipation to the twin dots that in Paris mean "occupied." But occupied by whom?

"You take it."

"No, you. You're the one in a hurry."

The lover abandoned under a dripping plane tree would feel a damp victory of a kind, awarding himself a first-class trophy for selfless behavior. It would sustain him ten seconds, until the departing one rolled down the taxi window to hurl her last flint: "You Fascist!" Why was this always the final shot, the coup de grâce delivered by women? Speck's wife, Henriette, book critic on an uncompromising political weekly, had said it three times last spring—here, in the street, where Speck stood locking the iron screen into place. He had been uneasily conscious of his wellborn neighbors, hanging out their windows, not missing a thing. Henriette had then gone away in a cab to join her lover, leaving Speck, the gallery, her job—everything that mattered.

He mourned Henriette; he missed her steadying influence. Her mind was like a one-way thoroughfare, narrow and flat, maintained in repair. As he approached the age of forty he felt that his own intellect needed not just a direction but retaining walls. Unless his thoughts were nailed down by gallery business they tended to glide away to the swamps of imagination, behind which stretched the steamier marshland of metaphysics. Confessing this to Henriette was unlikely to bring her back. There had been something brisk and joyous about her going—her hailing of a taxi as though of a friend, her surprised smile as the third "Fascist!" dissolved in the April night like a double stroke from the belfry of St. Clotilde's. He supposed he would never see her again now, except by accident. Perhaps, long after he had forgotten Henriette, he would overhear someone saying in a restaurant, "Do you see that poor mad intellectual talking to herself in the corner? That is Henriette, Sandor Speck's second wife. Of course, she was very different then; Speck kept her in shape."

While awaiting this sop, which he could hardly call consolation, he had Walter and the gallery. Walter had been with him five years—longer than either of his marriages. They had been years of spiritual second-thinking for Walter and of strain and worry for Speck. Walter in search of the Eternal was like one of those solitary skippers who set out to cross an ocean only to capsize when barely out of port. Speck had been obliged to pluck his assistant out of Unitarian waters and set him on the firm shore of the Trinity. He had towed him to Transubstantiation and back; had charted the shoals and perils of careless prayer. His own aversion to superstitious belief made Speck particularly scrupulous; he would not commit himself on Free Will, for instance, uncertain if it was supposed to be an uphill trudge wearing tight boots or a downhill slide sitting on a tea tray. He would lie awake at night planning Walter's dismissal, only to develop a traumatic chest cold if his assistant seemed restless.

"What will the gallery do without you?" he would ask on the very morning he had been meaning to say, "Walter, sit down, please. I've got something to tell you." Walter would remind him about saints and holy men who had done without everything, while Speck would envision the pure hell of having to train someone new.

On a rainy night such as this, the street resembled a set in a French film designed for export, what with the policemen's white rain capes aesthetically gleaming and the lights of the bookstore, the restaurant, and the gallery reflected, quivering, in European-looking puddles. In reality, Speck thought, there was not even hope for a subplot. Henriette had gone forever. Walter's mission could not be photographed. The owner of the restaurant was in his eighties; the waiters were poised on the brink of retirement. As for the bookseller, M. Alfred Chassepoule, he seemed to spend most of his time wiping blood off the collected speeches of Mussolini, bandaging customers, and sweeping up glass. The fact was that Amandine's had turned out to have a fixed Right Wing viewpoint, which made it subject to attack by commandos wielding iron bars. Speck, who had chosen the street for its upper-class hush, had grown used to the hoarse imprecation of the Left and shriller keening of the Right; he could tell the sob of an ambulance from the wail of a police van. The commerce of art is without bias: when insurance inspectors came round to ask what Speck might have seen, he invariably replied, "Seen where?," to which Walter, unsolicited, would add, "And I am Swiss."

Since Henriette's departure, Speck often ate his meals in the local restaurant, which catered to his frugal tastes, his vegetarian principles, and his desire to be left in peace. On the way, he would pause outside Amandine's, just enough to mark the halt as a comforting bachelor habit. He would glance over the second-hand books, the yellowing pamphlets, and the overpriced cartoons. The tone of the window display seemed old-fashioned rather than dangerous, though he knew that the slogan crowning the arrangement, "Europe for Europeans," echoed from a dark political valley. But even that valley had been full of strife and dissension and muddle, for hadn't the Ur-Fascists, the Italian ones, been in some way against an all-Europe? At least, some of their poets were. But who could take any of that seriously now? Nothing political had ever struck Speck as being above the level of a low-grade comic strip. On the cover of one volume, Uncle Sam shook hands with the Russian Bear over prostrate Europe, depicted as a maiden in a dead faint. A drawing of a spider on a field of banknotes (twelve hundred francs with frame, nine hundred without) jostled the image of a crablike hand clawing away at the map of France. Pasted against the pane, survivor of uncounted assaults, the old man continued to dismember his captive imp. Walter had told Speck he believed the old man to be St. Amand, Apostle of Flanders, Bishop in 430. "Or perhaps," said Walter, after thinking it over, "435." The imp probably stood for Flemish paganism, which the Apostle had been hard put to it to overcome.

From the rainy street Speck could see four or five of Amandine's customers—all men; he had never noticed a woman in the place—standing, reading, books held close to their noses. They had the weak eyes, long chins, and sparse, sparrow-colored hair he associated with low governmental salaries. He imagined them living with grim widowed mothers whose company they avoided after work. He had seen them, or young men like them, staggering out of the store, cut by flying glass, kicked and beaten as they lay stunned on the pavement; his anxious imagination had set them on their feet, booted and belted, the right signal given at last, swarming across to the gallery, determined to make Speck pay for injuries inflicted on them by total strangers. He saw his only early Chagall (quite likely authentic) ripped from its frame; Walter, his poor little spectacles smeared with blood, lambasted with the complete Charles Maurras, fourteen volumes, full morocco; Speck himself, his ears offended by acute Right Wing cries of "Down with foreign art!," attempting a quick counter-stroke with *Significant Minor French Realists, Twentieth Century*, which was thick enough to stun an ox. Stepping back from the window, Speck saw his own smile reflected. It was pinched and tight, and he looked a good twenty years older than thirty-nine.

His restaurant, crammed with civil servants at noon, was now nearly empty. A smell of lunchtime pot roast hung in the air. He made for his own table, from which he could see the comforting lights of the gallery. The waiter, who had finally stopped asking how Henriette was liking Africa, brought his dinner at once, setting out like little votive offerings the raw-carrot salad, the pot-roast vegetables without the meat, the quarter ounce of low-fat cheese, and a small pear. It had long been established that Speck did not wish to be disturbed by the changing of plates. He extracted a yellow pad and three pencils from his briefcase and placed them within the half circle of dishes. Speck was preparing his May-June show.

The right show at the right time: it was trickier than getting married to the right person at any time. For about a year now, Paris critics had been hinting at something missing from the world of art. These hints, poignant and patriotic on the right, neo-nationalist and pugnacious on the Left, wistful but insistent dead Center, were all in essence saying the same thing: "The time has come." The time had come; the hour had struck; the moment was ripe for a revival of reason, sanity, and taste. Surely there was more to art than this sickness, this transatlantic blight? Fresh winds were needed to sweep the museums and galleries. Two days ago there had been a disturbing article in *Le Monde* (front page, lower middle, turn to page 26) by a man who never took up his pen unless civilization was in danger. Its title, "Redemption Through Art—Last Hope for the West?," had been followed by other disturbing questions: When would the merchants and dealers, compared rather unfairly to the money-changers driven from the temple, face up to their share of responsibility as the tattered century declined? Must the flowering gardens of Western European culture wilt and die along with the decadent political systems, the exhausted parliaments, the shambling elections, the tired liberal impulses? What of the man in the street, too modest and confused to mention his cravings? Was he not gasping for one remedy and one only—artistic renovation? And where was this to come from? "In the words of Shakespr," the article concluded, supposedly in English, "That is the qustn."

As it happened, Speck had the answer: say, a French painter, circa 1864-1949, forgotten now except by a handful of devoted connoisseurs. Populist yet refined, local but universal, he would send rays, beacons, into the thickening night of the West, just as Speck's gallery shone bravely into the dark street. Speck picked up a pencil and jotted rapidly: "Born in France, worked in Paris, went his own way, unmindful of fashion, knowing his hour would strike, his vision be vindicated. Cathedral, as this retrospective so eloquently..." Just how does "catholical" come in, Speck wondered, forking up raw carrots. Because of ubiquity, the ubiquity of genius? No; not genius—leave that for the critics. His sense of harmony, then—his discretion.

Easy, Speck told himself. Easy on the discretion. This isn't interior decoration.

He could see the notices, knew which of the critics would write "At last," and "It has taken Sandor Speck to remind us." Left, Right, and Center would unite on a single theme: how the taste of two full generations had been corrupted by foreign speculation, cosmopolitan decadence, and the cultural imperialism of the Anglo-Saxon hegemony.

"The calm agnostic face," Speck wrote happily, "the quiet Cartesian voice are replaced by the snarl of a nation betrayed (1914), as startling for the viewer as a child's glimpse of a beloved adult in a temper tantrum. The snarl, the grimace vanish (1919) as the serene observer of Universal Will (1929) and of Man's responsibility to himself return. But we are left shaken. We have stopped trusting our feelings. We have been shown not only the smile but the teeth."

Here Speck drew a wavy line and turned to the biography, which was giving him trouble. On a fresh yellow page he tried again:

1938—Travels to Nice. Sees Mediterranean.
1939—Abandons pacifist principle. Lies about age. Is mobilized.
1940—Demobilized.
1941—

It was here that Speck bogged down. Should he say, "Joins Resistance"? "Resistance" today meant either a heroic moment sadly undervalued by the young or a minor movement greatly inflated in order to absolve French guilt. Whatever it is, thought Speck, it is not chic. The youngest survivor must be something like seventy-three. They know nothing about art, and never subscribe to anything except monuments. Some people read "Resistance" in a chronology and feel quite frankly exasperated. On the other hand, what about museums, state-subsidized, Resistance-minded on that account? He chewed a boiled leek and suddenly wrote, "1941—Conversations with Albert Camus." I wonder where all this comes from, Speck said to himself. Inspiration was what he meant.

These notes, typed by Walter, would be turned over to the

fashionable historian, the alarming critic, the sound political figure unlikely to be thrown out of office between now and spring, whom Speck would invite to write the catalogue introduction. "Just a few notes," Speck would say tactfully. "Knowing how busy you are." Nothing was as inspiriting to him as the thought of his own words in print on a creamy catalogue page, even over someone else's name.

Speck took out of his briefcase the Directoire snuffbox Henriette had given him about a fortnight before suddenly calling him "Fascist." (Unexpected feminine generosity—first firm sign of adulterous love affair.) It contained three after-dinner tablets—one to keep him alert until bedtime, another to counter the stimulating effect of the first, and a third to neutralize the germ known as Warsaw flu now ravaging Paris, emptying schools and factories and creating delays in the postal service. He sat quietly, digesting, giving the pills a chance to work.

He could see the structure of the show, the sketchbooks and letters in glass cases. It might be worthwhile lacquering the walls black, concentrating strong spots on the correspondence, which straddled half a century, from Degas to Cocteau. The scrawl posted by Drieu la Rochelle just before his suicide would be particularly effective on black. Céline was good; all that crowd was back in vogue now. He might use the early photo of Céline in regimental dress uniform with a splendid helmet. Of course, there would be word from the Left, too, with postcards from Jean Jaurès, Léon Blum, and Paul Éluard, and a jaunty get-well message from Louis Aragon and Elsa. In the first room Speck would hang the stiff, youthful landscapes and the portraits of the family, the artist's first models—his brother wearing a sailor suit, the awkward but touching likeness of his sister ("Germaine-Isabelle at the Window").

"Yes, yes," Speck would hear in the buzz of voices at the opening. "Even from the beginning you can tell there was *something*." The "something" became bolder, firmer in the second room. See his cities; watch how the streets turn into mazes, nets, prison corridors. Dark palette. Opaqueness, the whole canvas covered, immensities of indigo and black. "Look, 1929; he was doing it before What's-His-Name." Upstairs, form breaking out of shadow: bread, cheese, wine, wheat, ripe apples, grapes.

Hold it, Speck told himself. Hold the ripeness. This isn't social realism.

He gathered up the pencils, the snuffbox, and the pad, and put them back in the briefcase. He placed seventy francs, tip included, in a saucer. Still he sat, his mind moving along to the second loggia room, the end room, the important one. Here on the neutral walls would be the final assurance, the serenity, the satire, the power, and the vision for which, at last, the time had come. For that was the one thing Speck was sure of: the bell had rung, the hour had struck, the moment was at hand.

Whose time? Which hour? Yes—whose, which, what? That was where he was stuck.

The street was now empty except for the policemen in their streaming capes. The bookstore had put up its shutter. Speck observed the walls of the three Marxist embassies. Shutters and curtains that once had shielded the particular privacy of the aristocracy—privacy open to servants but not to the street—now concealed the receptions and merry dinner parties of people's democracies. Sometimes at this hour gleaming motorcars rolled past the mysterious gates, delivering passengers Speck's fancy continued to see as the Duchesse de Guermantes and anyone she did not happen to despise. He knew that the chauffeurs were armed and that half the guests were spies; still, there was nothing to stop a foreign agent from having patrician tastes, or from admiring Speck's window as he drove by.

"This gallery will be an oasis of peace and culture," Walter had predicted as they were hanging the first show, "Little-Known Aspects of Post-Decorator Style." "An oasis of peace and culture in the international desert."

Speck breathed germ-laden night air. Boulevard theatres and music halls were deserted, their managers at home writing letters to the mayor of Paris deploring the decline of popular entertainment and suggesting remedies in the form of large cash subsidies. The sluggish river of autumn life congealed and stagnated around millions of television sets as Parisians swallowed aspirin and drank the boiling-hot Scotch believed to be a sovereign defense against Warsaw flu.

A few determined intellectuals slunk, wet, into the Métro on their way to cultural centers where, in vivid translations from the German, actors would address the occasional surly remark to the audience—that loyal, anxious, humorless audience in its costly fake working-class clothes. Another contingent, dressed in Burberry trench-coats, had already fought its way into the Geographical Institute, where a lecture with colored slides, "Ramblings in Secret Greenland," would begin, after a delay owing to trouble with the projection machine, at about nine-twenty. The advantage of slides over films was that they were not forever jumping about and confusing one, and the voice describing them belonged to a real speaker. When the lights went up, one could see him, talk to him, challenge him over the thing he had said about shamanism on Disko Island. What had drawn the crowd was not Greenland but the word "secret." In no other capital city does the population wait more trustfully for the mystery to be solved, the conspiracy laid bare, the explanation of every sort of vexation to be supplied: why money slumps, why prices climb, why it rains in August, why children are ungrateful. The answers might easily come from a man with a box of slides.

In each of the city's twenty administrative districts, Communists, distinguished by the cleanliness of their no-iron shirts, the sobriety of their washable neckties, and the modesty of their bearing, moved serenely toward their local cell meetings. I must persuade Walter to take out membership sometime, Speck thought. It might be useful and interesting for the gallery and it would take his mind off salvation.

Walter was at this moment in the Church of St. Gervais, across the Seine, where an ecumenical gathering of prayer, music, and debate on Unity of Faith had been marred the week before by ugly scuffling between middle-aged latecomers and young persons in the lotus position, taking up too much room. Walter had turned to his neighbor, a stranger to him, and asked courteously, "Is it a string ensemble tonight, or just the organ?" Mistaken for a traditionalist demanding the Latin Mass, he had been punched in the face and had to be led to a side chapel to mop up his nosebleed. God knows what they might do to him tonight, Speck thought.

As for Speck himself, nine-thirty found him in good company, briskly tying the strings of his Masonic apron. No commitment stronger than prudence kept him from being at St. Gervais, listening for a voice in the night of the soul, or at a Communist Party cell meeting, hoping to acquire a more wholesome slant on art in a doomed society, but he had already decided that only the Infinite could be everywhere at once. The Masonic Grand Architect of the Universe laid down no rules, appointed no prophets, required neither victims nor devotion, and seemed content to exist as a mere possibility. At the lodge Speck rubbed shoulders with men others had to be content to glimpse on television. He stood now no more than three feet away from Kléber Schaumberger, of the Alsatian Protestant banking Schaumbergers; had been greeted by Olivier Ombrine, who designed all the Arabian princesses' wedding gowns; could see, without craning, the plume of white hair belonging to François-Xavier Blum-Bloch-Weiler—former ambassador, historian, member of the French Academy, author of a perennially best-selling book about Vietnam called *When France Was at the Helm*. Speck kept the ambassador's family tree filed in his head. The Blum-Bloch-Weilers, heavy art collectors, produced statesmen, magistrates, anthropologists, and generals, and were on no account to be confused with the Blum-Weiler-Blochs, their penniless and mystical cousins, who produced poets, librarians, and Benedictine monks.

Tonight Speck followed the proceedings mechanically; his mind was set on the yellow pad in his briefcase, now lying on the back seat of his car. Direct address and supplication to the unknown were frowned on here. Order reigned in a complex universe where the Grand Architect, insofar as he existed, was supposed to know what he was doing. However, having nowhere to turn, Speck decided for the first time in his life to brave whatever cosmic derangement might ensue and to unburden himself.

Whoever and whatever you are, said Speck silently, as many had said before him, remember in my favor that I have never bothered you. I never called your attention to the fake Laurencin, the stolen Magritte, the Bonnard the other gallery was supposed to have insured, the Maurice Denis notebook that slipped through my fingers, the Vallotton woodcut that got lost between Paris and Lausanne. All I want... But there was no point in his insisting. The Grand Architect, if he was any sort of omnipresence worth considering, knew exactly what Speck needed now: he needed the tiny, enduring wheel set deep in the clanking, churning machinery of the art trade—the artist himself.

Speck came out to the street refreshed and soothed, feeling that he had shed some of his troubles. The rain had stopped. A bright moon hung low. He heard someone saying, "...hats." On the glistening pavement a group of men stood listening while Senator Antoine Bellefeuille told a funny story. Facts from the Bellefeuille biography tumbled through Speck's mind: twenty years a deputy from a rich farming district, twice a Cabinet minister, now senator; had married a sugar-beet fortune, which he inherited when his wife died; no children; his mother had left him majority shares in milk chocolate, which he had sold to invest in the first postwar plastics; owned a racing stable in Normandy, a château in Provence, one of the last fine houses of Paris; had taken first-class degrees in law and philosophy; had gone into politics almost as an afterthought.

What had kept the old man from becoming Prime Minister, even President of the Republic? He had the bearing, the brains, the fortune, and the connections. Too contented, Speck decided, observing his lodge brother by moonlight. But clever, too; he was supposed to have kept copies of files from the time he had been at Justice. He splashed around in the arts, knew the third-generation dealers, the elegant bachelor curators. He went to openings, was not afraid of new movements, but he never bought anything. Speck tried to remember why the wealthy Senator who liked art never bought pictures.

"She was stunning," the Senator said. "Any man of my generation will tell you that. She came down Boulevard Saint-Michel on her husband's arm. He barely reached her shoulder. She had a smile like a fox's. Straight little animal teeth. Thick red-gold hair. A black hat tilted over one eye. And what a throat. And what hands and arms. A waist no larger than this," said the Senator, making a circle with his hands. "As I said, in those days men wore hats. You tipped a bowler by the brim, the other sort you picked up by the crown. I was so dazzled by being near her, by having the famous Lydia Cruche smile at me, I forgot I was wearing a bowler and tried to pick it up by the crown. You can imagine what a fool I looked, and how she laughed."

And of course they laughed, and Speck laughed, too.

"Her husband," said the Senator. "Hubert Cruche. A face like a gargoyle. Premature senile dementia. He'd been kicked by Venus at some time or other"—the euphemism for syphilis. "In those days the cure was based on mercury—worse than the disease. He seemed to know me. There was light in his eyes. Oh, not the light of intelligence. It was too late for that, and he'd not had much to begin with. He recognized me for a simple reason. I had already begun to assemble my Cruche collection. I bought everything Hubert Cruche produced for sixteen years—the oils, the gouaches, the pastels, the watercolors, the etchings, the drawings, the woodcuts, the posters, the cartoons, the book illustrations. Everything."

That was it, Speck remembered. That was why the Senator who liked art never bought so much as a wash drawing. The house was full of Cruches; there wasn't an inch to spare on the walls.

With a monarch's gesture, the Senator dismissed his audience and stepped firmly toward the chauffeur, who stood holding the door of his Citroën. He said, perhaps to himself, perhaps to Speck, thin and attentive in the moonlight, "I suppose I ought to get rid of my Cruches. Who ever thinks about Cruche now?"

"No," said Speck, whom the Grand Architect of the Universe had just rapped over the head. The Senator paused—benevolent, stout. "Don't get rid of the Cruches," said Speck. He felt as if he were on a distant shore, calling across deep cultural waters. "Don't sell! Hang on! Cruche is coming back!"

Cruche, Cruche, Hubert Cruche, sang Speck's heart as he drove homeward. Cruche's hour had just struck, along with Sandor Speck's. At the core of the May-June retrospective would be his lodge brother's key collection: "Our thanks, in particular...who not only has loaned his unique and invaluable...but who also...and who..." Recalling the little he knew of Cruche's obscure career, Speck made a few changes in the imaginary catalogue, substituting with some disappointment "The Power Station at Gagny-sur-Orme" for "Misia Sert on Her Houseboat," and "Peasant Woman Sorting Turnips" for "Serge Lifar as Petrouchka." He wondered if he could call Cruche heaven-sent. No; he would not put a foot beyond coincidence, just as he had not let Walter dash from saint to saint once he had settled for St. Joseph. And yet a small flickering marsh light danced upon the low-lying metaphysical ground he had done so much to avoid. Not only did Cruche overlap to an astonishing degree the painter in the yellow notebook but he was exactly the sort of painter that made the Speck gallery chug along. If Speck's personal collection consisted of minor works by celebrated artists, he considered them his collateral for a rainy, bank-loan day. Too canny to try to compete with international heavyweights, unwilling to burden himself with insurance, he had developed as his specialty the flattest, palest, farthest ripples of the late-middle-traditional Paris school. This sensible decision had earned him the admiration given the devoted miniaturist who is no threat to anyone. "Go and see Sandor Speck," the great lions and tigers of the trade would tell clients they had no use for. "Speck's the expert."

Speck was expert on barges, bridges, cafés at twilight, nudes on striped counterpanes, the artist's mantelpiece with mirror, the artist's street, his staircase, his bed made and rumpled, his still-life with half-peeled apple, his summer in Mexico, his wife reading a book, his girlfriend naked and dejected on a kitchen chair. He knew that the attraction of customer to picture was always accidental, like love; it was his business to make it overwhelming. Visitors came to the gallery looking for decoration and investment, left it believing Speck had put them on the road to a supreme event. But there was even more to Speck than this, and if he was respected for anything in the trade it was for his knack with artists' widows. Most dealers hated them. They were considered vain, greedy, unrealistic, and tougher than bulldogs. The worst were those whose husbands had somehow managed the rough crossing to recognition only to become washed up at the wrong end of the beach. There the widow waited, guarding the wreckage. Speck's skill in dealing with them came out of a certain sympathy. An artist's widow was bound to be suspicious and adamant. She had survived the discomfort and confusion of her marriage; had lived through the artist's drinking, his avarice, his affairs, his obsession with constipation, his feuds and quarrels, his cowardice with dealers, his hypocrisy with critics, his depressions (which always fell at the most joyous seasons, blighting Christmas and spring); and then—oh, justice!—she had outlasted him.

Transfiguration arrived rapidly. Resurrected for Speck's approval was an ardent lover, a devoted husband who could not work unless his wife was around, preferably in the same room. If she had doubts about a painting, he at once scraped it down. Hers was the only opinion he had ever trusted. His last coherent words before dying had been of praise for his wife's autumnal beauty.

Like a swan in muddy waters, Speck's ancient Bentley cruised the suburbs where his painters had lived their last resentful seasons. He knew by heart the damp villa, the gravel path, the dangling bellpull, the shrubbery containing dead cats and plastic bottles. Indoors the widow sat, her walls plastered with portraits of herself when young. Here she continued the struggle begun in the Master's lifetime—the evicting of the upstairs tenant—her day made lively by the arrival of mail (dusty beige of anonymous threats, grim blue of legal documents), the coming and going of process servers, the outings to lawyers. Into this spongy territory Speck advanced, bringing his tactful presence, his subtle approximation of courtship, his gift for listening. Thin by choice, pale by nature, he suggested maternal need. Socks and cufflinks suggested breeding. The drift of his talk suggested prosperity. He sent his widows flowers, wooed them with food. Although their taste in checks and banknotes ran to the dry and crisp, when it came to eating they craved the sweet, the sticky, the moist. From the finest pastry shops in Paris Speck brought soft macaroons, savarins soaked in rum, brioches stuffed with almond cream, mocha cake so tender it had to be eaten with a spoon. Sugar was poison to Speck. Henriette had once reviewed a book that described how refined sugar taken into one's system turned into a fog of hideous green. Her brief, cool warning, "A Marxist Considers Sweets," unreeled in Speck's mind if he was confronted with a cookie. He usually pretended to eat, reducing a *mille-feuille* to paste, concealing the wreck of an éclair under napkin and fork. He never lost track of his purpose—the prying of paintings out of a dusty studio on terms anesthetizing to the artist's widow and satisfactory to himself.

The Senator had mentioned a wife; where there had been wife there was relict. Speck obtained her telephone number by calling a rival gallery and pretending to be looking for someone else. "Cruche's widow can probably tell you," he finally heard. She lived in one of the gritty suburbs east of Paris, on the far side of the Bois de Vincennes—in Speck's view, the wrong direction. The pattern of his life seemed to come unfolded as he dialled. He saw himself stalled in industrial traffic, inhaling pollution, his Bentley pointed toward the seediest mark on the urban compass, with a vanilla cream cake melting beside him on the front seat.

She answered his first ring; his widows never strayed far from the telephone. He introduced himself. Silence. He gave the name of the gallery, mentioned his street, recited the names of painters he showed.

Presently he heard "D'you know any English?"

"Some," said Speck, who was fluent.

"Well, what do you want?"

"First of all," he said, "to meet you."

"What for?"

He cupped his hand round the telephone, as if spies from the embassies down the street were trying to overhear. "I am planning a major Cruche show. A retrospective. That's what I want to talk to you about."

"Not unless I know what you want."

It seemed to Speck that he had already told her. Her voice was languid and nasal and perfectly flat. An index to English dialects surfaced in his mind, yielding nothing useful.

"It will be a strong show," he went on. "The first big Cruche since the nineteen-thirties, I believe."

"What's that got to do with me?"

He wondered if the Senator had forgotten something essential—that Lydia Cruche had poisoned her husband, for instance.

He said, "You probably own quite a lot of his work."

"None of it's for sale."

This, at last, was familiar; widows' negotiations always began with "No." "Actually, I am not proposing to buy anything," he said, wanting this to be clear at the start. "I am offering the hospitality of my gallery. It's a gamble I am willing to take because of my firm belief that the time—"

"What's the point of this show?"

"The point?" said Speck, his voice tightening as it did when Walter was being obtuse. "The point is getting Cruche back on the market. The time has come—the time to...to attack. To attack the museums with Hubert Cruche."

As he said this, Speck saw the great armor-plated walls of the Pompidou Art Center and the chink in the armor through which an 80 x 95 Cruche 1919 abstract might slip. He saw the provincial museums, cheeseparing, saving on light bulbs, but, like the French bourgeoisie they stood for, so much richer than they seemed. At the name "Cruche" their curators would wake up from neurotic dreams of forced auction sales, remembering they had millions to get rid of before the end of the fiscal year. And France was the least of it; London, Zurich, Stockholm, and Amsterdam materialized as frescoes representing the neoclassical façades of four handsome banks. Overhead, on a Baroque ceiling, nymphs pointed their rosy feet to gods whose chariots were called "Tokyo" and "New York." Speck lowered his voice as if he had portentous news. Museums all over the world, although they did not yet know this, were starving for Cruche. In the pause that followed he seemed to feel Henriette's hand on his shoulder, warning him to brake before enthusiasm took him over the cliff.

"Although for the moment Cruche is just an idea of mine," he said, stopping cold at the edge. "Just an idea. We can develop the idea when we meet."

A week later, Speck parked his car between a ramshackle shopping center—survivor of the building boom of the sixties—and a municipal low-cost housing project that resembled a jail. In the space bounded by these structures crouched the late artist's villa, abiding proof in stucco that the taste of earlier generations had been as disastrous as today's. He recognized the shards of legal battle: center and block had left the drawing board of some state-employed hack as a unit, only to be wedged apart by a widow's refusal to sell. Speck wondered how she had escaped expropriation. Either she knows someone powerful, he thought, or she can make such a pest of herself that they were thankful to give up.

A minute after having pushed the gate and tugged the rusted wire bellpull, he found himself alone in a bleak sitting room, from which his hostess had been called by a whistling kettle. He sat down on a faded sofa. The furniture was of popular local design, garnished with marble and ormolu. A television set encrusted with gilt acanthus leaves sat on a sideboard, like an objet d'art. A few rectangular shadings on the wallpaper showed where pictures had hung.

The melancholy tinged with foreboding Speck felt between seven and eight overtook him at this much earlier hour. The room was no more hideous than others he had visited in his professional quest for a bargain, but this time it seemed to daunt him, recalling sieges and pseudo courtships and expenditures of time, charm, and money that had come to nothing. He got up and examined a glass-fronted bookcase with nothing inside. His features, afloat on a dusty pane, were not quite as pinched as they had been the other night, but the image was still below par for a man considered handsome. The approach of a squeaking tea cart sent him scurrying back to the sofa, like a docile child invited somewhere for the first time.

"I was just admiring. . ." he began.

"I've run out of milk," she said. "I'm sure you won't mind your tea plain." With this governessy statement she handed him a cup of black Ceylon, a large slice of poisonous raisin cake, and a Mickey Mouse paper napkin.

Nothing about Cruche's widow tallied with the Senator's

description. She was short and quite round, and reminded Speck of the fat little dogs one saw being reluctantly exercised in Paris streets. The abundant red-gold hair of the Senator's memory, or imagination, had gone ash-gray and was, in any case, pinned up. The striking fact of her person was simply the utter blankness of her expression. Usually widows' faces spoke to him. They said, "I am lonely," or "Can I trust you?" Lydia Cruche's did not suggest that she had so much as taken Speck in. She chose a chair at some distance from Speck, and proceeded to eat her cake without speaking. He thought of things to say, but none of them seemed appealing.

At last, she said, "Did you notice the supermarket next door?"

"I saw a shopping center."

"The market is part of it. You can get anything there now—bran, frozen pizzas, maple syrup. That's where I got the cake mix. I haven't been to Paris for three years."

Speck had been born in France. French education had left him the certainty that he was a logical, fair-minded person imbued with a culture from which every other Western nation was obliged to take its bearings. French was his first language; he did not really approve of any other. He said, rather coldly, "Have you been in this country long?"

"Around fifty years."

"Then you should know some French."

"I don't speak it if I don't have to. I never liked it."

He put down his cup, engulfed by a wave of second-generation distress. She was his first foreign widow. Most painters, whatever their origins, had sense enough to marry French-women—unrivalled with creditors, thrifty hoarders of bits of real estate, endowed with relations in country places where one could decamp in times of need and war.

"Perhaps, where you come from—" he began.

"Saskatchewan."

His tea had gone cold. Tannic scum had collected on its surface. She said, "This idea of yours, this show—what was it you called it? The hospitality of your gallery? I just want to say don't count on me. Don't count on me for anything. I don't mind showing you what I've got. But not today. The studio hasn't been dusted or heated for years, and even the light isn't working."

In Speck's experience, this was about average for a first attempt. Before making for civilization he stopped at a florist's in the shopping center and ordered two dozen roses to be delivered to Mme. Cruche. While these were lifted, dripping, from a plastic pail, he jotted down a warm message on his card, crossing out the engraved "Dr. Sandor Speck." His title, earned by a thesis on French neo-Humanism and its ups and downs, created some confusion in Paris, where it was taken to mean that Speck could cure slipped discs and gastric ulcers. Still, he felt that it gave a grip to his name, and it was his only link with all the freethinking, agnostic Specks, who, though they had not been able to claim affinity by right of birth with Voltaire and Descartes, had probably been wise and intelligent and quite often known as "Dr."

As soon as he got back to the gallery, he had Walter look up Saskatchewan in an atlas. Its austere oblong shape turned his heart to ice. Walter said that it was one of the right-angled territories that so frequently contain oil. Oil seemed to Speck to improve the oblong. He saw a Chirico chessboard sliding off toward a horizon where the lights of derricks twinkled and blinked.

He let a week go by before calling Lydia Cruche.

"I won't be able to show you those roses of yours," she said. "They died right off."

He took the hint and arrived with a spray of pale-green orchids imported from Brazil. Settled upon the faded sofa, which was apparently destined to be his place, he congratulated his hostess on the discovery of oil in her native plain.

"I haven't seen or heard of the place since Trotsky left the

Soviet Union," she said. "If there is oil, I'd sooner not know
about it. Oil is God's curse." The iron silence that followed this
seemed to press on Speck's lungs. "That's a bad cough you've
got there, Doctor," she said. "Men never look after those things.
Who looks after you?"

"I look after myself," said Speck.

"Where's your wife? Where'd she run off to?"

Not even "Are you married?" He saw his hostess as a tough
little pagan figure, with a goddess's gift for reading men's lives.
He had a quick vision of himself clasping her knees and sobbing
out the betrayal of his marriage, though he continued to sit
upright, crumbling walnut cake so that he would not have to eat
it.

"My wife," he said, "insofar as I can still be said to have one,
has gone to live in a warm climate."

"She run off alone? Women don't often do that. They haven't
got that kind of nerve."

Stepping carefully, for he did not wish to sound like a stage
cuckold or a male fool, Speck described in the lightest possible
manner how Henriette had followed her lover, a teacher of
literature, to a depressed part of French-speaking Africa where
the inhabitants were suffering from a shortage of Racine. Unable
to halt once he had started, he tore on toward the edge: Henriette
was a hopeless nymphomaniac (she had fallen in love) who
lacked any sense of values (the man was broke); she was at the
same time a grasping neurotic (having sunk her savings in the
gallery, she wanted a return with fourteen per cent interest).

"You must be thankful you finally got rid of her," said Lydia
Cruche. "You must be wondering why you married her in the
first place."

"I felt sorry for Henriette," he said, momentarily forgetting
any other reason. "She seemed so helpless." He told about
Henriette living in her sixth-floor walkup, working as slave labor
on a shoddy magazine. A peasant from Alsace, she had never
eaten anything but pickled cabbage until Speck drove his Bentley

into her life. Under his tactful guidance she had tasted her first fresh truffle salad at Le Récamier; had worn her first mink-lined Dior raincoat; had published her first book-length critical essay, "A Woman Looks at Edgar Allan Poe." And then she had left him—just like that.

"You trained her," said Lydia Cruche. "Brought her up to your level. And now she's considered good enough to marry a teacher. You should feel proud. You shouldn't mind what happened. You should feel satisfied."

"I'm not satisfied," said Speck. "I do mind." He realized that something had been left out of his account. "I loved her." Lydia Cruche looked straight at him, for once, as though puzzled. "As you loved Hubert Cruche," he said.

There was no response except for the removal of crumbs from her lap. The goddess, displeased by his mortal impertinence, symbolically knocked his head off her knee.

"Hube liked my company," she finally said. "That's true enough. After he died I saw him sitting next to the television, by the radiator, where his mother usually crouched all winter looking like a sheep with an earache. I was just resting here, thinking of nothing in particular, when I looked up and noticed him. He said, 'You carry the seed of your death.' I said, 'If that's the case, I might as well put my head in the oven and be done with it.' 'Non,' he said, 'ce n'est pas la peine.' Now, his mother was up in her room, making lists of all the things she had to feel sorry about. I went up and said, 'Madame,' because you can bet your boots she never got a 'Maman' out of me, 'Hube was in the parlor just now.' She answered, 'It was his mother he wanted. Any message was for me.' I said that if that was so, then all he needed to do was to materialize upstairs and save me the bother of climbing. She gave me some half-baked reason why he preferred not to, and then she *did* die. Aged a hundred and three. It was in *France-Soir*."

The French she had spoken rang to Speck like silver bells. Everything about her had changed—voice, posture, expression.

If he still could not see the Lydia Cruche of the Senator's vision, at least he could believe in her.

"Do you talk to your husband often?" he said, trying to make it sound like a usual experience.

"How could I talk to Hube? He's dead and buried. I hope you don't go in for ghosts, Dr. Speck. I would find that very silly. That was just some kind of accident—a visitation. I never saw him again or ever expect to. As for his mother, there wasn't a peep out of her after she died. And here I am, alone in the Cruche house." It was hard to say if she sounded glad or sorry. "I gather you're on your own, too. God never meant men and women to live by themselves, convenient though it may seem to some of us. That's why he throws men and women together. Coincidence is God's plan."

So soon, thought Speck. It was only their second meeting. It seemed discourteous to draw attention to the full generation that lay between them; experience had taught him that acknowledging any fragment of this dangerous subject did more harm than good. When widows showed their cards, he tried to look like a man with no time for games. He thought of the young André Malraux, dark and tormented, the windblown lock on the worried brow, the stub of a Gauloise sending up a vagabond spiral of smoke. Unfortunately, Speck had been born forty years too late for the model; he belonged to a much reedier generation of European manhood. He thought of the Pope. White-clad, serene, he gazed out on St. Peter's Square, over the subdued heads of one hundred thousand artists' widows, not one of whom would dare.

"So this was the Cruche family home," he said, striking out, he hoped, in a safe direction.

"The furniture was his mother's," said Lydia Cruche. "I got rid of most of it, but there was stuff you couldn't pay them to cart away. *Sa petite Maman adorable*," she said softly. Again Speck heard the string of silver bells. "I thought she was going to hang around forever. They were a tough family—peasants from the west of France. She took good care of him. Cooked him sheep's

heart, tripe and onions, big beefsteaks they used to eat half raw.
He was good-looking, a big fellow, big for a Frenchman. At
seventy you'd have taken him for forty. Never had a cold. Never
had a headache. Never said he was tired. Drank a litre of
Calvados every other day. One morning he just keeled over, and
that was that. I'll show you a picture of him sometime."

"I'd also like to see *his* pictures," said Speck, thankful for the
chance. "The pictures you said you had upstairs."

"You know how I met Hube? People often ask me that. I'm
surprised you haven't. I came to him for lessons."

"I didn't know he taught," said Speck. His most reliable
professional trait was his patience.

"He didn't. I admired him so much that I thought I'd try
anyway. I was eighteen. I rang the bell. His mother let me in. I
never left—he wouldn't let me go. His mother often said if she'd
known the future she'd never have answered the door. I must
have walked about four miles from a tram stop, carrying a big
portfolio of my work to show him. There wasn't even a paved
street then—just a patch of nettles out front and some vacant
lots."

Her work. He knew he had to get it over with: "Would you
like to show me some of your things, too?"

"I burned it all a long time ago."

Speck's heart lurched. "But not his work?"

"It wasn't mine to burn. I'm not a criminal." Mutely, he
looked at the bare walls. "None of Hube's stuff ever hung in
here," she said. "His mother couldn't stand it. We had everything *she* liked—Napoleon at Waterloo, lighthouses, corona-
tions. I couldn't touch it when she was alive, but once she'd gone
I didn't wait two minutes."

Speck's eighteenth-century premises were centrally heated.
The system, which dated from the early nineteen-sixties,
had been put in by Americans who had once owned most of the

second floor. With the first dollar slide of the Nixon era they had wisely sold their holdings and gone home, without waiting for the calamity still to come. Their memorial was an expensive, casual gift nobody knew what to do with; it had raised everyone's property taxes, and it cost a fortune to run. Tenants, such as Speck, who paid a fat share of the operation, had no say as to when heat was turned on, or to what degree of temperature. Only owners and landlords had a vote. They voted overwhelmingly for the lowest possible fuel bills. By November there was scarcely a trace of warmth in Speck's elegant gallery, his cold was entrenched for the winter, and Walter was threatening to quit. Speck was showing a painter from Bruges, sponsored by a Belgian cultural-affairs committee. Cost-sharing was not a habit of his—it lowered the prestige of the gallery—but in a tight financial season he sometimes allowed himself a breather. The painter, who clearly expected Speck to put him under contract, talked of moving to Paris.

"You'd hate it here," said Speck.

Belgian television filmed the opening. The Belgian royal family, bidden by Walter, on his own initiative, sent regrets signed by aides-de-camp on paper so thick it would scarcely fold. These were pinned to the wall, and drew more attention than the show itself. Only one serious critic turned up. The rooms were so cold that guests could not write their names in the visitors' book— their hands were too numb. Walter, perhaps by mistake, had invited Blum-Weiler-Blochs instead of Blum-Bloch-Weilers. They came in a horde, leading an Afghan hound they tried to raffle off for charity.

The painter now sat in the gallery, day after day, smoking black cigarettes that smelled of mutton stew. He gave off a deep professional gloom, which affected Walter. Walter began to speak of the futility of genius—a sure sign of melancholia. Speck gave the painter money so that he could smoke in cafés. The bells of St. Clotilde's clanged and echoed, saying to Speck's memory, "Fascist, Fascist, Fascist." Walter reminded Speck that November was bad for art. The painter returned from a café looking cheerful. Speck wondered if he was enjoying Paris and if he would decide to stay; he stopped giving him money and the gallery became once more infested with mutton stew and despair. Speck began a letter to Henriette imploring her to come back. Walter interrupted it with the remark that Rembrandt, Mozart, and Dante had lived in vain. Speck tore the letter up and started another one saying that a Guillaumin pastel was missing and suggesting that Henriette had taken it to Africa. Just as he was tearing this up, too, the telephone rang.

"I finally got Hube's stuff all straightened out," said Lydia Cruche. "You might as well come round and look at it this afternoon. By the way, you may call me 'Lydia,' if you want to."

"Thank you," said Speck. "And you, of course, must call me—"

"I wouldn't dream of it. Once a doctor always a doctor. Come early. The light goes at four."

Speck took a pill to quiet the pounding of his heart.

In her summing-up of his moral nature, a compendium that had preceded her ringing "Fascist"s, Henriette had declared that Speck appraising an artist's work made her think of a real-estate loan officer examining Chartres Cathedral for leaks. It was true that his feeling for art stopped short of love; it had to. The great cocottes of history had shown similar prudence. Madame de Pompadour had eaten vanilla, believed to arouse the senses, but such recklessness was rare. Cool but efficient—that was the professional ticket. No vanilla for Speck; he knew better. For what if he were to allow passion for painting to set alight his common sense? How would he be able to live then, knowing that the ultimate fate of art was to die of anemia in safe-deposit vaults? Ablaze with love, he might try to organize raids and rescue parties, dragging pictures out of the dark, leaving sacks of onions instead. He might drop the art trade altogether, as Walter kept intending to do, and turn his talents to cornering the onion market. The same customers would ring at election time, saying, "Dr. Speck, what happens to my onion collection if the Left gets in? Shouldn't we try to unload part of it in New York now, just to be on the safe side?" And Speck, unloading onions of his own in Tokyo, would answer, "Don't worry. They can't possibly nationalize all the onions. Besides, they aren't going to win."

Lydia seemed uninterested in Speck's reaction to Cruche. He had expected her to hang about, watching his face, measuring his interest, the better to nail her prices; but she simply showed him a large, dim, dusty, north-facing room in which canvases were thickly stacked against the walls and said, "I wasn't able to get the light fixed. I've left a lamp. Don't knock it over. Tea will be ready when you are." Presently he heard American country music rising from the kitchen (Lydia must have been tuned to the BBC) and he smelled a baking cake. Then, immersed in his ice-cold Cruche encounter, he noticed nothing more.

About three hours later he came downstairs, slowly, wiping dust from his hands with a handkerchief. His conception of the show had been slightly altered, and for the better, by the total Cruche. He began to rewrite the catalogue notes: "The time has come for birth ..." No—"for rebirth. In a world sated by overstatement the moment is ripe for a calm ..." How to avoid "statement" and still say "statement"? The Grand Architect was keeping Speck in mind. "For avouchment," said Speck, alone on the stairs. It was for avouchment that the time had come. It was also here for hard business. His face became set and distant, as if a large desk were about to be shoved between Lydia Cruche and himself.

He sat down and said, "This is going to be a strong show, a powerful show, even stronger than I'd hoped. Does everything I've looked at upstairs belong to you outright? Is there anything which for any reason you are not allowed to lend, show, or sell?"

"Neither a borrower nor a lender be," said Lydia, cutting caramel cake.

"No. Well, I am talking about the show, of course."

"No show," she said. "I already told you that."

"What do you mean, no show?" said Speck.

"What I told you at the beginning. I told you not to count on me. Don't drop boiled frosting on your trousers. I couldn't get it to set."

"But you changed your mind," said Speck. "After saying 'Don't count on me,' you changed your mind."

"Not for a second."

"Why?" said Speck, as he had said to the departing Henriette. "Why?"

"God doesn't want it."

He waited for more. She folded her arms and stared at the blank television set. "How do you know that God doesn't want Hubert Cruche to have a retrospective?"

"Because He said so."

His first thought was that the Grand Architect had granted Lydia Cruche something so far withheld from Sandor Speck: a plain statement of intention. "Don't you know your Commandments?" she asked. "You've never heard of the graven image?"

He searched her face for the fun, the teasing, even the malice that might give shape to this conversation, allow him to take hold of it. He said, "I can't believe you mean this."

"You don't have to. I'm sure you have your own spiritual pathway. Whatever it is, I respect it. God reveals himself according to each person's mental capacity."

One of Speck's widows could prove she descended from Joan of Arc. Another had spent a summer measuring the walls of Toledo in support of a theory that Jericho had been in Spain. It was Speck's policy never to fight the current of eccentricity but to float with it. He said cautiously, "We are all held in a mysterious hand." Generations of Speck freethinkers howled from their graves; he affected not to hear them.

"I am a Japhethite, Dr. Speck. You remember who Noah was? And his sons, Ham, Shem, and Japheth? What does that mean to

you?" Speck looked as if he possessed Old Testament lore too
fragile to stand exposure. "Three," said Lydia. "The sacred
number. The first, the true, the only source of Israel. That crowd
Moses led into the desert were just Egyptian malcontents. The
true Israelites were scattered all over the earth by then. The Bible
hints at this for its whole length. Japheth's people settled in
Scotland. Present-day Jews are impostors."

"Are you connected to this Japheth?"

"I do not make that claim. My Scottish ancestors came from
the border country. The Japhethites had been driven north long
before by the Roman invasion. The British Israelite movement,
which preceded ours, proved that the name 'Hebrides' was
primitive Gaelic for 'Hebrew.' The British Israelites were distinguished pathfinders. It was good of you to have come all the
way out here, Dr. Speck. I imagine you'll want to be getting
back."

After backing twice into Lydia's fence, Speck drove straight to
Galignani's bookshop, on Rue de Rivoli, where he purchased an
English Bible. He intended to have Walter ransack it for contra-
Japhethite pronouncements. The orange dust jacket surprised
him; it seemed to Speck that Bibles were usually black. On the
back flap the churches and organizations that had sponsored this
English translation were listed, among them the National Bible
Society of Scotland. He wondered if this had anything to do with
Japheth.

As far as Speck could gather from passages Walter marked
during the next few days, art had never really flourished, even
before Moses decided to put a stop to it. Apart from a bronze
snake cast at God's suggestion (Speck underscored this for Lydia
in red), there was nothing specifically cultural, though Ezekiel's
visions had a certain surrealistic splendor. As Speck read the
words "the terrible crystal," its light flooded his mind, illuminat-
ing a simple question: Why not forget Hubert Cruche and find
an easier solution for the cultural penury of the West? The
crystal dimmed. Speck's impulsive words that October night,

"Cruche is coming back," could not be reeled in. Senator Bellefeuille was entangled in a promise that had Speck at one end and Lydia at the other. Speck had asked if he might examine his lodge brother's collection and had been invited to lunch. Cruche *had* to come back.

Believing Speck's deliverance at hand, Walter assailed him with texts and encouragement. He left Biblical messages on Speck's desk so that he had to see them first thing after lunch. Apparently the British Israelite movement had truly existed, enjoying a large and respectable following. Its premise that it was the British who were really God's elect had never been challenged, though membership had dwindled at mid-century; Walter could find no trace of Lydia's group, however. He urged Speck to drive to the north of Scotland, but Speck had already decided to abandon the religious approach to Cruche.

"No modern translation conveys the word of Japheth or of God," Lydia had said when Speck showed her Walter's finds. There had been something unusual about the orange dust jacket, after all. He did not consider this a defeat. Bible reading had raised his spirits. He understood now why Walter found it consoling, for much in it consisted of the assurance of downing one's enemies, dashing them against stones, seeing their children reduced to beggary and their wives to despair. Still, he was not drawn to deep belief: he remained rational, skeptical, anxious, and subject to colds, and he had not succeeded in moving Lydia Cruche an inch.

L unch at Senator Bellefeuille's was balm. Nothing was served that Speck could not swallow. From the dining room he looked across at the dark November trees of the Bois de Boulogne. The Senator lived on the west side of Paris—the clients' side. A social allegory in the shape of a city separated Speck from Lydia Cruche. The Senator's collection was fully insured, free from dust, attractively framed or stored in racks built to order.

Speck began a new catalogue introduction as he ate lunch. "The Bellefeuille Cruches represent a unique aspect of Cruche's vision," he composed, heartily enjoying fresh crab soufflé. "Not nearly enough has been said about Cruche and the nude."

The Senator broke in, asking how much Cruche was likely to fetch after the retrospective. Speck gave figures to which his choice of socks and cufflinks lent authority.

"Cruche-and-the-nude implies a definition of Woman," Speck continued, silently, sipping coffee from a gold-rimmed cup. "Lilith, Eve, temptress, saint, child, mother, nurse— Cruche delineated the feminine factor once and for all."

The Senator saw his guest to the door, took his briefcase from the hands of a manservant, and bestowed it on Speck like a diploma. He told Speck he would send him a personal invitation list for the Cruche opening next May. The list would include the estranged wife of a respected royal pretender, the publisher of an influential morning paper, the president of a nationalized bank, and the highest-ranking administrative official of a thickly populated area. Before driving away, Speck took a deep breath of west-end air. It was cool and dry, like Speck's new expression.

That evening, around closing time, he called Lydia Cruche. He had to let her know that the show could go on without her. "I shall be showing the Bellefeuille Cruches," he said.

"The *what*?"

Speck changed the subject. "There is enormous American interest," he said, meaning that he had written half a dozen letters and received prudent answers or none at all. He was accustomed to the tense excitement "American interest" could arouse. He had known artists to enroll in crash courses at Berlitz, the better to understand prices quoted in English.

Lydia was silent; then she said, slowly, "Don't ever mention such a thing again. Hube was anti-American—especially during the war." As for Lydia, she had set foot in the United States once, when a marshmallow roast had taken her a few yards inside North Dakota, some sixty years before.

The time was between half past seven and eight. Walter had gone to early dinner and a lecture on lost Atlantis. The Belgian painter was back in Bruges, unsold and unsung. The cultural-affairs committee had turned Speck's bill for expenses over to a law firm in Brussels. Two Paris galleries had folded in the past month and a third was packing up for America, where Speck gave it less than a year. Painters set adrift by these frightening changes drifted to other galleries, shipwrecked victims trying to crawl on board waterlogged rafts. On all sides Speck heard that the economic decline was irreversible. He knew one thing—art had sunk low on the scale of consumer necessities. To mop up a few back bills, he was showing part of his own collection—his last-ditch old-age-security reserve. He clasped his hands behind his neck, staring at a Vlaminck India ink on his desk. It had been certified genuine by an expert now serving a jail sentence in Zurich. Speck was planning to flog it to one of the ambassadors down the street.

He got up and began turning out lights, leaving just a spot in the window. To have been anti-American during the Second World War in France had a strict political meaning. Any hope of letters from Louis Aragon and Elsa withered and died: Hubert Cruche had been far Right. Of course, there was Right and Right, thought Speck as he triple-locked the front door. Nowadays the Paris intelligentsia drew new lines across the past, separating coarse collaborators from fine-drawn intellectual Fascists. One could no longer lump together young hotheads whose passionate belief in Europe had led them straight to the Charlemagne Division of the Waffen-S.S. and the soft middle class that had stayed behind to make money on the black market. Speck could not quite remember why *pure* Fascism had been better for civilization than the other kind, but somewhere on the safe side of the barrier there was bound to be a slot for Cruche. From the street, he considered a page of Charles Despiau sketches—a woman's hand, her breast, her thigh. He thought of the Senator's description of that other, early Lydia and of the fragments of perfection Speck could now believe in, for he had seen the Bellefeuille nudes. The familiar evening sadness caught up with him and lodged in his heart. Posterity forgives, he repeated, turning away, crossing the road on his way to his dinner.

Speck's ritual pause brought him up to St. Amand and his demon just as M. Chassepoule leaned into his window to replace a two-volume work he had probably taken out to show a customer. The bookseller drew himself straight, stared confidently into the night, and caught sight of Speck. The two greeted each other through glass. M. Chassepoule seemed safe, at ease, tucked away in a warm setting of lights and friends and royal blue, and yet he made an odd little gesture of helplessness, as if to tell Speck, "Here I am, like you, overtaxed, hounded, running an honest business against dreadful odds." Speck made a wry face of sympathy, as if to answer that he knew, he knew. His neighbor seemed to belong to an old and desperate breed, its back to the wall, its birthright gnawed away by foreigners, by the heathen, by the blithe continuity of art, by Speck himself. He dropped his gaze, genuinely troubled, examining the wares M. Chassepoule had collected, dusted, sorted, and priced for a new and ardent generation. The work he had just put back in the window was *La France Juive*, by Édouard Drumont. A handwritten notice described it as a classic study, out of print, hard to find, and in good condition.

Speck thought, A few years ago, no one would have dared put it on display. It has been considered rubbish for fifty years. Édouard Drumont died poor, alone, cast off even by his old friends, completely discredited. Perhaps his work was always being sold, quietly, somewhere, and I didn't know. Had he been Walter and superstitious, he might have crossed his fingers; being Speck and rational, he merely shuddered.

Walter had a friend—Félicité Blum-Weiler-Bloch, the owner of the Afghan hound. When Walter complained to her about the temperature of the gallery, she gave him a scarf, a sweater, an old flannel bed-sheet, and a Turkey carpet. Walter decided to make a present of the carpet to Speck.

"Get that thing out of my gallery," said Speck.

"It's really from Félicité."

"I don't want her here, either," said Speck. "Or the dog."

Walter proposed spreading the carpet on the floor in the basement. "I spend a lot of time there," he said. "My feet get cold."

"I want it out," said Speck.

Later that day Speck discovered Walter down in the framing room, holding a vacuum cleaner. The Turkey carpet was spread on the floor. A stripe of neutral color ran through the pattern of mottled reds and blues. Looking closer, Speck saw it was warp and weft. "Watch," said Walter. He switched on the vacuum; another strip of color vanished. "The wool lifts right out," said Walter.

"I told you to get rid of it," said Speck, trembling.

"Why? I can still use it."

"I won't have my gallery stuffed with filth."

"You'll never have to see it. You hardly ever come down here." He ran the vacuum, drowning Speck's reply. Over the noise Walter yelled, "It will look better when it's all one color."

Speck raised his voice to the Right Wing pitch heard during street fights: "Get it out! Get it out of my gallery!"

Like a telephone breaking into a nightmare, delivering the sleeper, someone was calling, "Dr. Speck." There on the stairs stood Lydia Cruche, wearing an ankle-length fur coat and a brown velvet turban. "I thought I'd better have a look at the place," she said. "Just to see how much space you have, how much of Cruche you can hold."

Still trembling, Speck took her hand, which smelled as if she had been peeling oranges, and pressed it to his lips.

That evening, Speck called the Senator: Would he be interested in writing the catalogue introduction? No one was
better fitted, said Speck, over senatorial modesty. The Senator
had kept faith with Cruche. During his years of disappointment
and eclipse Cruche had been heartened, knowing that guests at
the Senator's table could lift their eyes from quail in aspic to feast
on "Nude in the Afternoon."

Perhaps his lodge brother exaggerated just a trifle, the Senator
replied, though it was true that he had hung on to his Cruches
even when their value had been wiped out of the market. The
only trouble was that his recent prose had been about the capital-
gains-tax project, the Common Market sugar-beet subsidy, and
the uninformed ecological campaign against plastic containers.
He wondered if he could write with the same persuasiveness
about art.

"I have taken the liberty of drawing up an outline," said Speck.
"Just a few notes. Knowing how busy you are."

Hanging up, he glanced at his desk calendar. Less than six
weeks had gone by since the night when, by moonlight, Speck
had heard the Senator saying ". . . hats."

A few days before Christmas Speck drove out to Lydia's with a
briefcase filled with documents that were, at last, working
papers: the list of exhibits from the Bellefeuille collection, the
introduction, and the chronology in which there were gaps for
Lydia to fill. He still had to draw up a financial arrangement. So
far, she had said nothing about it, and it was not a matter Speck
cared to rush.

He found another guest in the house—a man somewhat
younger than he, slightly bald and as neat as a mouse.

"Here's the doctor I was telling you about," said Lydia,
introducing Speck.

Signor Vigorelli of Milan was a fellow-Japhethite—so Speck
gathered from their conversation, which took up, in English, as

though he had never come in. Lydia poured Speck's tea in an offhand manner he found wounding. He felt he was being treated like the hanger-on in a Russian play. He smashed his lemon cupcake, scattering crumbs. The visitor's plate looked cleaner than his. After a minute of this, Speck took the catalogue material out of his briefcase and started to read. Nobody asked what he was reading. The Italian finally looked at his watch (expensive, of a make Speck recognized) and got to his feet, picking up car keys that had been lying next to his plate.

"That little man had an Alfa Romeo tag," said Speck when Lydia returned after seeing him out.

"I don't know why you people drive here when there is perfectly good bus service," she said.

"What does he do?"

"He is a devout, religious man."

For the first time, she sat down on the sofa, close to Speck. He showed her the introduction and the chronology. She made a number of sharp and useful suggestions. Then they went upstairs and looked at the pictures. The studio had been cleaned, the light repaired. Speck suddenly thought, I've done it—I've brought it off.

"We must discuss terms," he said.

"When you're ready," she replied. "Your cold seems a lot better."

Inching along in stagnant traffic, Speck tried one after the other the FM state-controlled stations on his car radio. He obtained a lecture about the cultural oppression of Cajuns in Louisiana, a warning that the road he was now driving on was saturated, and the disheartening squeaks and wails of a circumcision ceremony in Ethiopia. On the station called France-Culture someone said, "Henri Cruche."

"Not Henri, excuse me," said a polite foreigner. "His name was Hubert. Hubert Cruche."

"Strange that it should be an Italian to discover an artist so essentially French," said the interviewer.

Signor Vigorelli explained that his admiration for France was second only to his intense feelings about Europe. His career had been consecrated to enhancing Italian elegance with French refinement and then scattering the result abroad. He believed that the unjustly neglected Cruche would be a revelation and might even bring the whole of Western art to its senses.

Speck nodded, agreeing. The interview came to an end. Wild jungle drums broke forth, heralding the announcement that there was to be a reading of medieval Bulgarian poetry in an abandoned factory at Nanterre. It was then and then only that Speck took in the sense of what he had heard. He swung the car in a wild U-turn and, without killing himself or anyone else, ran into a tree. He sat quietly, for about a minute, until his breathing became steady again, then unlocked his safety belt and got out. For a long time he stood by the side of the road, holding his briefcase, feeling neither shock nor pain. Other drivers, noticing a man alone with a wrecked car, picked up speed. He began to walk in Lydia's direction. A cruising prostitute, on her way home to cook her husband's dinner, finally agreed to drop him off at a taxi stand. Speck gave her two hundred francs.

Lydia did not seem at all surprised to see him. "I'd invite you to supper," she said. "But all I've got is a tiny pizza and some of the leftover cake."

"The Italian," said Speck.

"Yes?"

"I've heard him. On the radio. He says he's got Cruche. That he discovered him. My car is piled up in the Bois. I tried to turn around and come back here. I've been walking for hours."

"Sit down," said Lydia. "There, on the sofa. Signor Vigorelli is having a big Cruche show in Milan next March."

"He can't," said Speck.

"Why can't he?"

"Because Cruche is mine. He was my idea. No one can have my idea. Not until after June."

"Then it goes to Trieste in April," said Lydia. "You could still have it by about the tenth of May. If you still want it."

If I want it, said Speck to himself. If I want it. With the best work sold and the insurance rates tripled and the commissions shared out like candy. And with everyone saying Speck jumped on the bandwagon, Speck made the last train.

"Lydia, listen to me," he said. "I invented Hubert Cruche. There would be no Hubert Cruche without Sandor Speck. This is an unspeakable betrayal. It is dishonorable. It is wrong." She listened, nodding her head. "What happens to me now?" he said. "Have you thought about that?" He knew better than to ask, "Why didn't you tell me about him?" Like all dissembling women, she would simply answer, "Tell you what?"

"It might be all the better," she said. "There'll be that much more interest in Hube."

"Interest?" said Speck. "The worst kind of interest. Third-rate, tawdry interest. Do you suppose I can get the Pompidou Center to look at a painter who has been trailing around in Trieste? It had to be a new idea. It had to be strong."

"You'll save on the catalogue," she said. "He will probably want to share."

"It's my catalogue," said Speck. "I'm not sharing. Senator Bellefeuille...my biography...never. The catalogue is mine. Besides, it would look as if he'd had the idea."

"He did."

"But after me," said Speck, falling back on the most useless of all lover's arguments. "*After* me. I was there first."

"So you were," she said tenderly, like any woman on her way out.

Speck said, "I thought you were happy with our arrangement."

"I was. But I hadn't met him yet. You see, he was so interested in the Japhethite movement. One day he opened the Bible and put his finger on something that seemed to make it all right about the graven image. In Ecclesiastes, I think."

Speck gave up. "I suppose it would be no use calling for a taxi?"

"Not around here, I'm afraid, though you might pick one up at the shopping center. Shouldn't you report the accident?"

"Which accident?"

"To the police," she said. "Get it on record fast. Make it a case. That squeezes the insurance people. The phone's in the hall."

"I don't care about the insurance," said Speck.

"You will care, once you're over the shock. Tell me exactly where it happened. Can you remember? Have you got your license? Registration? Insurance?"

Speck sank back and closed his eyes. He could hear Lydia dialling; then she began to speak. He listened, exactly as Cruche must have listened, while Lydia, her voice full of silver bells, dealt with creditors and dealers and Cruche's castoff girlfriends and a Senator Bellefeuille more than forty years younger.

"I wish to report an accident," Lydia sang. "The victim is Dr. S. Speck. He is still alive—luckily. He was forced off the road in the Bois de Vincennes by a tank truck carrying high-octane fuel. It had an Italian plate. Dr. Speck was too shaken to get the number. Yes, I saw the accident, but I couldn't see the number. There was a van in the way. All I noticed was 'MI.' That must stand for Milan. I recognized the victim. Dr. Speck is well known in some circles...an intimate friend of Senator Antoine Belle-feuille, the former Minister of...that's right." She talked a few minutes longer, then came back to Speck. "Get in touch with the insurance people first thing tomorrow," she said, flat Lydia again. "Get a medical certificate—you've had a serious emo-tional trauma. It can lead to jaundice. Tell your doctor to write that down. If he doesn't want to, I'll give you the name of a doctor who will. You're on the edge of nervous depression. By the way, the police will be towing your car to a garage. They know they've been very remiss, letting a foreign vehicle with a dangerous cargo race through the Bois. It might have hit a bus full of children. They must be looking for that tanker all over Paris. I've made a list of the numbers you're to call."

Speck produced his last card: "Senator Bellefeuille will never allow his Cruches to go to Milan. He'll never let them out of the country."

"Who—Antoine?" said Lydia. "Of course he will."

She cut a cupcake in half and gave him a piece. Broken, Speck crammed the whole thing in his mouth. She stood over him, humming. "Do you know that old hymn, Dr. Speck—'The day Thou gavest, Lord, is ended'?"

He searched her face, as he had often, looking for irony, or playfulness—a gleam of light. There floated between them the cold oblong on the map and the Chirico chessboard moving along to its Arctic destination. Trees dwindled to shrubs and shrubs to moss and moss to nothing. Speck had been defeated by a landscape.

A lthough Speck by no means considered himself a natural victim of hard luck, he had known disappointment. Shows had fallen flat. Galleries had been blown up and torn down. Artists he had nursed along had been lured away by siren dealers. Women had wandered off, bequeathing to Speck the warp and weft of a clear situation, so much less interesting than the ambiguous patterns of love. Disappointment had taught him rules: the first was that it takes next to no time to get used to bad news. Rain began to fall as he walked to the taxi stand. In his mind, Cruche was already being shown in Milan and he was making the best of it.

He gazed up and down the bleak road; of course there were no taxis. Inside a bus shelter huddled a few commuters. The thrust of their lives, their genetic destiny obliged them to wait for public transport—unlike Speck, thrown among them by random adventures. A plastic-covered timetable announced a bus to Paris every twenty-three minutes until five, every sixteen minutes from four to eight, and every thirty-one minutes thereafter. His watch had stopped late in the afternoon, probably at the time of the accident. He left the shelter and stood out in the wet, looking at windows of shops, one of which might contain a clock. He stood for a minute or two staring at a china tea set flanked by two notices: "Hand Painted" and "Christmas Is Coming," both of which he found deeply sad. The tea set had been decorated with reproductions of the Pompidou Art Center, which was gradually replacing the Eiffel Tower as a constituent feature of French design. The day's shocks caught up with him: he stared at the milk jug, feeling surprise because it did not tell him the time. The arrival of a bus replaced this perplexity with one more pressing. He did not know what was needed on suburban buses—tickets or tokens or a monthly pass. He wondered whether the drivers accepted banknotes, and gave change, with civility.

"Dr. Speck, Dr. Speck!" Lydia Cruche, her raincoat open and flying, waving a battered black umbrella, bore down on him out of the dark. "You were right," she said, gasping. "You were there first." Speck took his place at the end of the bus queue. "I mean it," she said, clutching his arm. "He can wait."

Speck's second rule of disappointment came into play: the deceitful one will always come back to you ten seconds too late. "What does it mean?" he said, wiping rain from the end of his nose. "Having it before him means what? Paying for the primary expenses and the catalogue and sweetening the Paris critics and letting him rake in the chips?"

"Wasn't that what you wanted?"

"Your chap from Milan thought he was first," said Speck. "He may not want to step aside for me—a humble Parisian expert on the entire Cruche context and period. You wouldn't want Cruche to miss a chance at Milan, either."

"Milan is ten times better for money than Paris," she said. "If that's what we're talking about. But of course we aren't."

Speck looked down at her from the step of the bus. "Very well," he said. "As we were."

"I'll come to the gallery," she called. "I'll be there tomorrow. We can work out new terms."

Speck paid his fare without trouble and moved to the far end of the bus. The dark shopping center with its windows shining for no one was a Magritte vision of fear. Lydia had already forgotten him. Having tampered with his pride, made a professional ass of him, gone off with his idea and returned it dented and chipped, she now stood gazing at the Pompidou Center tea set, perhaps wondering if the ban on graven images could possibly extend to this. Speck had often meant to ask her about the Mickey Mouse napkins. He thought of the hoops she had put him through— God, and politics, and finally the most dangerous one, which was jealousy. There seemed to be no way of rolling down the window, but a sliding panel at the top admitted half his face. Rising from his seat, he drew in a gulp of wet suburban air and threw it out as a shout: "Fascist! Fascist! Fascist!"

Not a soul in the bus turned to see. From the look of them, they had spent the best Sundays of their lives shuffling in demonstrations from Place de la République to Place de la Nation, tossing "Fascist"s around like confetti. Lydia turned slowly and looked at Speck. She raised her umbrella at arm's length, like a trophy. For the first time, Speck saw her smile. What was it the Senator had said? "She had a smile like a fox's." He could see, gleaming white, her straight little animal teeth.

The bus lurched away from the curb and lumbered toward Paris. Speck leaned back and shut his eyes. Now he understood about that parting shot. It was amazing how it cleared the mind, tearing out weeds and tree stumps, flattening the live stuff along with the dead. "Fascist" advanced like a regiment of tanks. Only the future remained—clean, raked, ready for new growth. New

growth of what? Of Cruche, of course—Cruche, whose hour was
at hand, whose time was here. Speck began to explore his altered
prospects. "New terms," she had said. So far, there had been
none at all. The sorcerer from Milan must have promised
something dazzling, swinging it before her eyes as he had swung
his Alfa Romeo key. It would be foolish to match the offer. By the
time they had all done with bungling, there might not be enough
left over to buy a new Turkey carpet for Walter.

I was no match for her, he thought. No match at all. But then,
look at the help she had—that visitation from Cruche. "Only
once," she said, but women always said that: "He asked if he
could see me just once more. I couldn't very well refuse." Dead
or alive, when it came to confusion and double-dealing, there
was no such thing as "only once." And there had been not only
the departed Cruche but the very living Senator Bellefeuille—
"Antoine"; who had bought every picture of Lydia for sixteen
years, the span of her early beauty. Nothing would ever be the
same again between Speck and Lydia, of course. No man could
give the same trust and confidence the second time around. All
that remained to them was the patch of landscape they held in
common—a domain reserved for the winning, collecting, and
sharing out of profits, a territory where believer and skeptic, dupe
and embezzler, the loving and the faithless could walk hand in
hand. Lydia had a talent for money. He could sense it. She had
never been given much chance to use it, and she had waited so
much longer than Speck.

He opened his eyes and saw rain clouds over Paris glowing
with light—the urban aurora. It seemed to Speck that he was
entering a better weather zone, leaving behind the gray, indefinite mist in which the souls of discarded lovers are said to wander.
He welcomed this new and brassy radiation. He saw himself at
the center of a shadeless drawing, hero of a sort of cartoon strip,
subduing Lydia, taming Henriette. Fortunately, he was above
petty grudges. Lydia and Henriette had been designed by a
bachelor God who had let the creation get out of hand. In the

cleared land of Speck's future, a yellow notebook fluttered and lay open at a new page. The show would be likely to go to Milan in the autumn now; it might be a good idea to slip a note between the Senator's piece and the biographical chronology. If Cruche had to travel, then let it be with Speck's authority as his passport.

The bus had reached its terminus, the city limit. Speck waited as the rest of the passengers crept inch by inch to the doors. He saw, with immense relief, a rank of taxis half a block long. He alighted and strode toward them, suddenly buoyant. He seemed to have passed a mysterious series of tests, and to have been admitted to some new society, the purpose of which he did not yet understand. He was a saner, stronger, wiser person than the Sandor Speck who had seen his own tight smile on M. Chassepoule's window only two months before. As he started to get into a taxi, a young man darted toward him and thrust a leaflet into his hand. Speck shut the door, gave his address, and glanced at the flyer he was still holding. Crudely printed on cheap pink paper was this:

FRENCHMEN!
FOR THE SAKE OF EUROPE, FIGHT
THE GERMANO-AMERICANO-ISRAELO
HEGEMONY!
Germans in Germany!
Americans in America!
Jews in Israel!
For a True Europe, For One Europe,
Death to the Anti-European Hegemony!

Speck stared at this without comprehending it. Was it a Chassepoule statement or an anti-Chassepoule plea? There was no way of knowing. He turned it over, looking for the name of an association, and immediately forgot what he was seeking. Holding the sheet of paper flat on his briefcase, he began to write, as well as the unsteady swaying of the cab would let him.

"It was with instinctive prescience that Hubert Cruche saw the need for a Europe united from the Atlantic to the...That Cruche skirted the murky zone of partisan politics is a tribute to his. . .even though his innocent zeal may have led him to the brink. . .early meeting with the young idealist and future states- man A. Bellefeuille, whose penetrating essay. . .close collabora- tion with the artist's wife and most trusted critic. . .and now, posthumously. . .from Paris, where the retrospective was planned and brought to fruition by the undersigned. . .and on to Italy, to the very borders of. . ."

Because this one I am keeping, Speck decided; this one will be signed: "By Sandor Speck." He smiled at the bright, wet streets of Paris as he and Cruche, together, triumphantly crossed the Alps.

OVERHEAD IN A BALLOON

Aymeric had a family name that Walter at first didn't catch. He had come into the art gallery as "A. Régis," which was how he signed his work. He must have been close to sixty, but only his self-confidence had kept pace with time. His eyes shone, young and expectant, in an unlined and rosy face. In spite of the face, almost downy, he was powerful-looking, with a wrestler's thrust of neck and hunched shoulders. Walter, assistant manager of the gallery, was immediately attracted to Aymeric, as to a new religion—this time, one that might work.

Painting portraits on commission had seen Aymeric through the sunnier decades, but there were fewer clients now, at least in Europe. After a brief late flowering of Moroccan princes and Pakistani generals, he had given up. Now he painted country houses. Usually he showed the front with the white shutters and all the ivy, and a stretch of lawn with white chairs and a teapot and cups, and some scattered pages of *Le Figaro*—the only newspaper, often the only anything, his patrons read. He had a hairline touch and could reproduce *Le Figaro*'s social calendar, in which he cleverly embedded his client's name and his own.

Some patrons kept a large magnifying glass on a table under the picture, so that guests, peering respectfully, could appreciate their host's permanent place in art.

Unfortunately, such commissions never amounted to much. These were not the great homes of France (they had all been done long ago, and in times of uncertainty and anxious thrift the heirs and owners were not of a mind to start over) but weekend places. Aymeric was called in to immortalize a done-up village bakery, a barn refurbished and brightened with the yellow awnings "Dallas" had lately made so popular. They were not houses meant to be handed on but slabs of Paris-area real estate, to be sold and sold again, each time with a thicker garnish of improvements. Aymeric had by now worked his territory to the farthest limit of the farthest flagged terrace within a two-hour drive from Paris in any direction; it had occurred to him that a show, a sort of retrospective of lawns and *Figaros*, would bring fresh patronage, perhaps even from abroad. (As Walter was to discover, Aymeric was blankly unprofessional, with that ignorance of the trade peculiar to its fringe.) It happened that one of the Paris Sunday supplements had published a picture story on Walter's gallery, with captions that laid stress on the establishment's boldness, vitality, visibility, international connections, and financial vigor. The supplement project had cost Walter's employer a packet, and Walter was not surprised that one of the photographs showed him close to collapse, leaning for support against the wall safe in his private office. The accompanying article described mobbed openings, private viewings to which the police were summoned to keep order, and potential buyers lined up outside in below-freezing weather, bursting in the minute the doors were opened to grab everything off the walls. The name of the painter hardly mattered; the gallery's reputation was enough.

Who believes this, Walter had wondered, turning the slippery, rainbow pages. Then Aymeric had lumbered in, pink and hopeful, believing.

He had dealt with, and been dealt with by, Walter's employer, known privately to Walter as "Trout Face." Aymeric showed courteous amazement when he heard just how much a show of that kind would cost. The uncultured talk about money was the gallery's way of refusing him, though a clause in the rejection seemed to say that something might still be feasible, in some distant off-season, provided that Aymeric was willing to buy all his own work. He declined, politely. For that matter, Trout Face was civil, too.

Walter, from behind his employer's back, had been letting Aymeric know by means of winks and signs that he might be able to help. (In the end, he was no help.) He managed to make an appointment to meet Aymeric in a café not far away, on Boulevard Saint-Germain. There, a few hours later, they sat on the glass-walled sidewalk terrace—it was March, and still cold—with Walter suddenly feeling Swiss and insufficient as Aymeric delicately unfolded a long banner of a name. Walter had already introduced himself, much more briefly: "Obermauer." He pointed, because the conversation could not get going again, and said, "That's my Métro station, over there. Solférino."

They had been through some of Aymeric's troubles and were sliding, Walter hoped, along to his own. These were, in order, that for nine years his employer had been exploiting him; that he had a foot caught in the steel teeth of his native Calvinism and was hoping to ease it free without resorting to a knife; that the awfully nice Dominican who had been lending books to him had brusquely advised him to try psychoanalysis. Finally, the apartment building he lived in had just been sold to a chain of health clubs, and everybody had to get out. It seemed a great deal to set loose on a new friend, so Walter mentioned only that he had a long underground ride to work every day, with two changes.

Aymeric replied that from the Notre-Dame-des-Champs station there was no change. That was how he had come, lugging his portfolio to show Walter's employer. "I was too soft with him, probably," Aymeric resumed. His relatives had already turned out to be his favorite topic. "The men in my family are too tolerant. Our wives leave us for brutes."

Leaning forward the better to hear Aymeric, who had dropped to a mutter, Walter noticed that his hair was dyed, pale locks on a ruddy forehead. His voice ran like clockwork, drawling to a stop and then, wound up tight, picking up again, like a refreshed countertenor. His voice was like the signature that required a magnifying glass; what he had to say was clear, but a kind of secret.

Walter said he was astonished at the number of men willing to admit, with no false pride, that their wives had left them.

"Oh, well, they do that nowadays," said Aymeric. "They wait for the children to." To? He must have meant "to grow up, to leave home."

"Are there children?" He imagined Aymeric lingering outside the fence of a schoolyard, trying to catch a glimpse of his estranged children, ducking behind a parked car when a teacher looked his way.

"Grandchildren."

Walter continued to feel sympathy. His employer, back in the days when he had been training Walter to be a gallery instrument as silent and reliable as the lock on the office safe, had repeatedly warned him that wives were death to the art trade. Degas had remained a bachelor. Did Walter know why? Because Degas did not want to have a wife looking at his work at the end of the day and remarking, "That's pretty."

They had finally got the conversation rolling evenly. Aymeric, wound up and in good breath, revealed that he and his cousin Robert and Robert's aged mother occupied a house his family had lived in forever. Actually, it was on one floor of an apartment building, but nearly the whole story—three sides of the court. For a long time, it had been a place the women of the family could come back to when their husbands died or began showing the indifference that amounts to desertion. Now that Paris had changed so much, it was often the men who returned. (Walter noticed that Aymeric said "Paris" instead of "life," or "manners," or "people.") Probably laziness of habit had made him say they had lived forever between the Luxembourg Gardens and the Boulevard Raspail. Raspail was less than a century old, and could scarcely count as a timeless landmark. Still, when Aymeric looked down at the damp cobblestones in the court, out of his kitchen window, he could not help feeling behind him the line of ancestors who had looked out, too, wondering, like Aymeric, if it really would be a mortal sin to jump.

Robert, his cousin, owned much of the space. It was space one carved up, doled out anew, remodelled; it was space on which one was taxed. Sixty square metres had just been sold to keep the city of Paris from grabbing twice that amount for back taxes. Another piece had gone to pay their share in mending the roof. Over the years, as so many single, forsaken adults had tried to construct something nestlike, cushioning, clusters of small living quarters had evolved, almost naturally, like clusters of coral. All the apartments connected; one could walk from end to end of the floor without having to step out to a landing. They never locked their doors. Members of the same family do not steal from one another, and they have nothing to hide. Aymeric said this almost sternly. Robert's wife had died, he added, just as Walter opened his mouth to ask. Death was the same thing as desertion.

Walter did not know what to answer to all this, especially to the part about locks. A good, stout bolt seemed to him a sensible and not an unfriendly precaution. "And lead us not into temptation," he was minded to quote, but it was too soon to begin that ambiguous sort of exchange.

At that moment Walter's employer appeared across the boulevard, at the curb, trying to flag a taxi by waving his briefcase. None stopped, and he moved away, perhaps to a bus stop. Walter wondered where he was going, then remembered that he didn't care.

"I hate him," he told Aymeric. "I *hate* him. I dream he is in danger. A patrol car drives up and the execution squad takes him away. I dream he is drinking coffee after dinner and far off in the night you can hear the patrol car, coming to get him."

Aymeric wondered what bound Walter to that particular dealer. There were other employers in Paris, just as dedicated to art.

"I hate art, too," said Walter. "Oh, I don't mean that I hate what you do. That, at least, has some meaning—it lets people see how they imagine they live."

Aymeric's tongue rested on his lower lip as he considered this. Walter explained that he had to spend another eleven years working for Trout Face if he was to get the full benefit of a twenty-year pension fund. In eleven years, he would be forty-six. He hoped there was still enjoyment to be had at that age.

"When you are drawing retirement pay, I'll be working for a living," Aymeric said. He let his strong, elderly hands rest on the table—evidence, of a kind.

"At first, when I thought I could pull my funds out at any time, I used to give notice," Walter went on. "When I stopped giving notice, he turned mean. I dreamed last night that there was a bomb under the floor of the gallery. He nearly blew himself up digging it out. He was saved. He is always saved. He escapes, or the thing doesn't explode, or the chief of the execution squad changes his mind."

"Robert has a book about dreams," said Aymeric. "He can look it up. I want him to meet you."

About four weeks after this, Walter moved into two rooms, kitchen, and bathroom standing empty between Robert's quarters and his mother's. It was Robert who looked after the practical side of the household and to whom Walter paid a surprisingly hefty rent; but he was on a direct Métro line, and within reach of friendship, and, for the first time since he had left Bern to work in Paris, he felt close to France.

That spring Robert's mother had grown old. She could not always remember where she was, or the age of her two children. At night she roamed about, turning on lights, opening bedroom doors. (Walter, who felt no responsibility toward her, kept his locked.) She picked up curios and trinkets and left them anywhere. Once a month Robert and Aymeric traded back paperweights and snuffboxes.

One night she entered her son's bedroom at two in the morning, pulled open a drawer, and began throwing his shirts on the floor. She was packing to send him on a summer holiday. Halfway through (her son pretended to be asleep), she turned her mind to Aymeric. Aymeric woke up a few minutes later to find his aunt in bed beside him, with her finger in her mouth. He got up and spent the rest of the night in an armchair.

"Why don't you knock her out with pills?" Walter asked him.

"We can't do that. It might kill her."

What's the difference, said Walter's face. "Then shut her up in her own bedroom."

"She might not like that. By the way, here's your phone bill."

Walter was surprised at the abruptness of the deadlock. Aymeric did not so much change the subject as tear it up. Walter could not understand many things—the amount of his telephone bill, for instance. He did most of his calling from the gallery, dialling his parents in Bern with the warm feeling that he was putting one over on Trout Face. He had been astonished to learn that he was supposed to pay a monthly fee for using the elevator. Apparently, it was the custom of the house. Aymeric was turning out to be less of a new religion than Walter had expected. For one thing, he was seldom there. His old life moved on, in an unseen direction, and he did not offer to bring Walter along. He seemed idle yet at the same time busy. He hardly ever sat down without giving the impression that he was trying to get to his feet; barely entered a room without starting to edge his way out of it. Running his fingers through his pale, abundant hair, he said, "I've got an awful lot to do."

Reading in bed one night, Walter glanced up and had the
eerie sight of a doorknob silently turning. "Let me in," Robert's
mother called. Her voice was sweet and pitched to childhood.
"The latch is caught, and I can't use both hands." Walter tied the
sash of the Old England dressing gown his employer had given
him one Christmas, when they were still getting along.

She had put on lipstick and eye-shadow. "I'm taking my
children to Mass," she said, "and I thought I'd just leave this with
you." She opened her fist, clenched like a baby's, and offered
Walter a round gold snuffbox with a cameo portrait on its lid. He
set the box down on a marble-topped table and led her through a
labyrinth of low-ceilinged rooms to Robert's bedroom door,
where he left her. She went straight in, turning on an overhead
light.

By morning, the box had drawn in the cold of the marble, but
it became warm in Walter's hand. He and his employer were
barely speaking; they often used sign language to show that
something had to be moved or hung up or taken down. Walter
seemed to be trying to play a guessing game until he opened his
hand, as Robert's mother had done.

"Just something I picked up," he said, as if he had been
combing second-hand junk stores and was no fool.

"Picked up where?" said his employer, appreciating the
weight and feel of the gold. He changed his spectacles for a
stronger pair, ran his thumb lightly and affectionately over the
cameo. "Messalina," he said. "Look at those curls." He held the
box at eye level, tipping it slightly, and said, "Glued on. An
amateur job. Where did you say you got it?"

"I happened to pick it up."

"Well, you'd better put it back." A bright spot moved on his
bald head as he leaned into the light. "Or, wait; leave it. I'll look
at it again." He wrapped the box in a paper handkerchief and
locked it up in his safe.

"I brought it just to show you," said Walter.

His employer motioned as if he were pushing a curtain aside
with the back of his right hand. It meant, Go away.

Robert was in charge of a small laboratory on the Rue de Vaugirard. He sat counting blood cells in a basement room. Walter imagined Robert pushing cells along the wire of an abacus, counting them off by ten. (He was gently discouraged from paying a visit. Robert explained there was no extra chair.) In the laboratory they drew and analyzed blood samples. Patients came in with their doctor's instructions, Social Security number, often a thick file of medical history they tried to get Robert to read, and blood was taken from a vein in the crook of the arm. The specimen had to be drawn before breakfast; even a cup of coffee could spoil the result. Sometimes patients fainted and were late for appointments. Robert revived them with red wine.

Each morning, Robert put on a track suit and ran in the Luxembourg Gardens, adroitly slipping past runners whose training program had them going the other way. Many of the neighborhood shopkeepers ran. The greengrocer and the Spaniard from the hardware store signalled greetings with their eyes. It was not etiquette to stop and talk, and they had to save breath.

Walter admired Robert's thinness, his clean running shoes, his close-cropped gray hair. When he was not running, he seemed becalmed. He could sit listening to Walter as if he were drifting and there was nothing but Walter in sight. Walter told him about his employer, and the nice Dominican, and how both, in their different spheres, had proved disappointing. He refrained from mentioning Aymeric, whose friendship had so quickly fallen short of Walter's. He did not need to be psychoanalyzed, he said. No analysis could resolve his wish to attain the Church of Rome, or remove the Protestant martyrs who stood barring the way.

Sometimes Robert made a controlled and quiet movement while Walter was speaking, such as moving a clean silver ashtray an inch. No one was allowed to smoke in his rooms, but they were furnished with whatever one might require. Walter confessed that he admired everything French, even the ashtrays, and Robert nodded his head, as if to say that for an outsider it was bound to be so.

Robert got up at five and cleaned his rooms. (Aymeric had

someone who came in twice a week.) He ran, then came back to change and eat a light breakfast before going to work. The first thing he did at five was to put on a record of Mozart's Concerto in C Major for Flute and Harp. He opened his windows; everyone except Walter-the-Swiss slept with them tight shut. The Allegro moved in a spiral around the courtyard, climbed above the mended roof, and became thin and celestial.

Walter usually woke up in the middle of the Andantino. It was much too early to get up. He turned on his side, away from the day. The mysterious sadness he felt on waking he had until now blamed on remoteness from God. Now he was beginning to suppose that people really must be made in His image, for their true face was just as concealed and their true whereabouts as obscure. A long, dangerous trapeze swoop of friendship had borne him from Aymeric's to Robert's side of the void, but all Robert had done was make room for Walter on the platform. He was accommodating, nothing more. Walter knew that he was too old at thirty-five for those giddy, hopeful swings. One of these days he was going to lose momentum and be left dangling, without a safety net.

He could hear music, a vacuum cleaner, and sparrows. The nice Dominican had assured him that God would still be there when his analysis had run its course. From his employer he had learned that sadness was supposed to be borne with every outward sign of elegance. Walter had no idea what that was supposed to mean. It meant nothing.

By the Rondo Allegro, Robert's mother would begin shaking Aymeric awake. Aymeric guided her back to her own apartment and began to boil water and grind coffee for her breakfast. She always asked him what he was doing in her private quarters, and where he had put his wife. She owned a scratched record of "Luna Rossa" sung by Tino Rossi, to which she could listen twelve times running without losing interest. It was a record of the old, breakable kind, and Walter wondered why someone didn't crack it on the edge of a sink. He thought of Farinelli, the castrato who every evening for ten years had to sing the same four tunes to the King of Spain. Nothing had been written about the King's attendants—whether at the end of ten years there were any of them sane.

In his own kitchen, Aymeric brewed lime-flower tea. Later, an egg timer would let him know he was ready for coffee. If he drank coffee too soon, his digestive system became flooded with acid, which made him feel ill. Whenever Robert talked about redistributing the space, Aymeric would remark that he would be dead before long and they could do as they liked with his rooms. His roseate complexion concealed an ashen inner reality, he believed. Any qualified doctor looking at him saw at once that he was meant to be pale. He followed the tea with a bowl of bran (bought in a health-food store) soaked in warm water. After that, he was prepared for breakfast.

When Aymeric was paying a weekend visit to a new patron, in some remodelled village abattoir, he ate whatever they gave him. Artist-in-residence, he had no complaints. On the first evening, sipping a therapeutic Scotch (it lowered blood pressure and made arterial walls elastic), he would tactfully, gradually, drop his chain-link name: he was not only "A. Régis" but "Aymeric Something Something de Something de Saint-Régis." Like Picasso, he said, he had added his mother's maiden name. His hostess, rapidly changing her mind about dinner, would open a tin of foie gras and some bottled fruit from Fauchon's. On Monday, he would be driven home, brick-colored, his psychic image more ashen than ever. Rich food made him dream. He dreamed that someone had snubbed him. Sometimes it was the Archbishop of Paris, more often the Pope.

In a thick, thumbed volume he kept at his bedside, Robert looked up all their dreams. Employer, execution squad, patrol car, arrest combined to mean bright days ahead for someone especially dear to the dreamer. Animals denoted treachery. Walter, when not granted a vision of his employer's downfall, dreamed about dormice and moles. Treachery, Robert repeated, closing the book. The harmless creatures were messengers of betrayal.

Coming up from underground at the Chambre des Députés station (his personal stop at Solférino was closed for repair) one day, Walter looked around. On a soft May morning, this most peaceful stretch of Boulevard Saint-Germain might be the place where betrayal would strike. He crossed the road so that he would not have to walk in front of the Ministry of Defense, where men in uniform might make him say that his dreams about patrol cars were seditious. After a block or so he crossed back and made his way, with no further threats or dangers, to his place of work.

Immersion in art had kept him from spiritual knowledge. What he had mistaken for God's beckoning had been a dabbling in colors, sentiment cut loose and set afloat by the sight of a stained-glass window. Years before, when he was still training Walter, his employer had sent him to museums, with a list of things to examine and ponder. God is in art, Walter had decided; then, God *is* art. Today, he understood: art is God's enemy. God hates art, the trifling rival creation.

Aymeric, when Walter announced his revelation, closed his eyes. Closing his eyes, he seemed to go deaf. It was odd, because last March, in the café, he had surely been listening. Robert listened. His blue gaze never wavered from a point just above Walter's head. When Walter had finished, Robert said that as a native Catholic he did not have to worry about God and art, or God and anything. All the worrying had already been done for him. Walter replied that no one had ever finished with worrying, and he offered to lend Robert books.

Robert returned Walter's books unread. He was showing the native Catholic resistance to religious history and theology. He did not want to learn more about St. Augustine and St. Thomas Aquinas than he had been told years before, in his private school. Having had the great good luck to be born into the only true faith, he saw no reason to rake the subject over. He did not go in for pounding his head on an open door. (Those were Robert's actual words.)

Robert's favorite topic was not God but the administration of the city of Paris, to which he felt bound by the ownership of so many square metres of urban space. He would look withdrawn and Gothic when anyone said, "The city does such a lot for the elderly now." The latest folderol was having old people taken up for helicopter rides, at taxpayers' expense. Robert's mother heard about the free rides while toying with a radio. Robert borrowed his sister's car and drove his mother to the helicopter field near the Porte de Versailles, where they found a group of pensioners waiting their turn. He was told he could not accompany his mother aloft: he was only forty-nine.

"I don't need anyone," his mother said. She unpinned her hat of beige straw and handed it to him. He watched strangers help her aboard, along with three other old women and a man with a limp. Robert raised his hands to his ears, hat and all, against the noise. His mother ascended rapidly. In less than twenty minutes she was back, making sure, before she would tell him about the trip, that he had not damaged her hat. The old gentleman had an arthritic leg, which he had stuck out at an awkward angle, inconveniencing one of the ladies. The pilot had spoken once, to say, "You can see Orléans." When the helicopter dipped, all the old hens screamed, she said. In her own mind, except now and then, she was about twenty-eight. She made Robert promise he would write a letter to the authorities, telling them there should be a cassette on board with a spoken travelogue and light music. She pulled on her hat, and in its lacy shadow resembled her old black-and-white snapshots, from the time before Robert.

One evening, Walter asked Aymeric if Monique de Montrepos, Robert's sister, had ever done anything, any sort of work. He met a drowsy, distant stare. Walter had blundered into a private terrain, but the fault was Aymeric's—never posted his limits. Aymeric told scandalous and demeaning stories about his relatives; Walter thought that half of them were invented, just for the purpose of teasing Walter and leading his speculations about the family astray. And yet Aymeric backed off a simple question, something like, "Does Robert's sister work?"

Finally Aymeric yielded and said Monique could infer character from handwriting. Walter's picture of a gypsy in a trailer remained imprinted even after Aymeric assured him that she worked with a team of psychotherapists, in the clean, glassy rooms of a modern office building in Montparnasse. Instead of dropping the matter, Walter wanted to know if she had undergone the proper kind of training; without that, he said, it was the same thing as analyzing handwriting by mail order.

Aymeric thought it over and said that her daughters were well educated and that one of them had travelled to Peru and got on quite well in Peruvian. This time, Walter had sense enough to keep quiet.

By June, Robert's mother had become too difficult for him to manage alone, and so his sister, Monique, who did not live with her husband, turned her apartment over to one of her daughters and moved in to help. Her name was added to the list of tenants hanging from the concierge's doorknob. Walter asked Aymeric if "Montrepos" was a Spanish name. Walter was thinking of the Empress Eugénie, born Montijo, he said.

One would need to consult her husband, Aymeric replied. Aymeric thought that Gaston de Montrepos had been born Dupuy or Dupont or Durand or Dumas. His childhood was spent in one of the weedier Paris suburbs, in a bungalow called Mon Repos. The name was painted, pale green on a rose background, on an enamel plaque just over the doorbell. Most family names had a simple, sentimental origin, if one cared to look them up. (Walter doubted that this applied to Obermauer.) Monique was a perfect specimen of the paratroop aristocracy,

Aymeric went on. He was referring not to a regiment of grandees about to jump in formation but to a recognizable upper-class physical type, stumping along on unbreakable legs. Aymeric represented a more perishable race; the mother with the spun-out surname had left him bones that crumbled, teeth that dissolved in the gum, fine, unbiddable hair. (There was no doubt that Aymeric was haunted by the subject of hair. He combed his own with his fingers all the while he was speaking. The pale tint Walter had observed last March had since been deepened to the yellow of high summer.) Monique's husband had also carried a look of impermanence, in spite of his unassuming background. Monique's father had at first minded about the name. Some simple names he would not have objected to—Rothschild, for instance. He would have let his only daughter be buried as "Monique de Rothschild" any day. Even though. Yes, even though. Gaston had some sort of patronage appointment in the Senate, checking stationery supplies. He had spent most of his working life reading in the Luxembourg when it was fine, and eating coffee éclairs in Pons on rainy afternoons.

After Gaston Dumas or Dupuy had asked for Monique's hand and been turned down, and after Monique had tried to kill herself by taking port wine and four aspirin tablets, Gaston had come back with the news that he was called Montrepos. He showed them something scribbled in his own hand on a leaf torn off a Senate memo pad.

Well, said her father, if Monique wanted that.

Walter soon saw that it was not true about Monique's stumpy legs. For the rest, she was something like Aymeric—blooming, sound. Unlike him, she made free with friendly slaps and punches. Her pat on the back was enough to send one across the room; a knuckle ground into one's arm was a sign of great good spirits. She kissed easily—noisy peasant smacks on both cheeks. She kissed the concierge for bringing good tidings with the morning mail (a check from Gaston, now retired and living in Antibes); kissed Aymeric's cleaning woman for unpaid favors, such as washing her underclothes. The concierge and the cleaning woman were no more familiar with Monique than with Robert or Aymeric. If anything, they showed a faint, cautious reserve. Women who joke and embrace too easily are often quick to mount a high horse. Of Walter they took the barest notice, in spite of the size of his tips.

Monique soon overflowed two rooms and a third belonging to Robert. She shared her mother's bathroom and Robert's kitchen, striding through Walter's apartment without asking if her perpetual trespassing suited him. In Robert's kitchen she left supper dishes to soak until morning. Robert could not stand that, and he washed and dried them before going to bed. Soon after he had fallen asleep, his mother would come in and ask him what time it was.

"He was her favorite," Monique told Walter. "Poor Robert. He's paying for it now. It's a bad idea to be a mother's favorite. It costs too much later on."

Entering without knocking, Monique let herself fall into one of Walter's cretonne-covered armchairs. She crossed her legs and asked if anyone ever bought the stuff one saw in windows of art galleries. Walter hardly knew how to begin his reply. It would have encouraged him if Monique had worn clothes that rustled. Rustle in women's dress, the settling of a skirt as a woman sat down, smoothing it with both hands, suggested feminine expectancy. Do explain, the taffeta hiss said. Tell about spies, interest rates, the Americans, Elizabeth Taylor. Is Hitler somewhere, still alive? But all that was the far past—his boyhood. He had grown adult in a world where clothes told one nothing. As soon as he thought of an answer, Monique shouted at him, "What? What did you say?" When she made a move, it was to knock something over. In Walter's sitting room she upset a cut-glass decanter, breaking the stopper; another time it was a mahogany plant stand and a Chinese pot holding a rare kind of fern. He offered sponge cakes and watched in distress as she swept the crumbs onto the floor.

"You've got the best space in the house," she said, looking around.

Soon after that remark, after giving himself time to think about it, Walter started locking all his doors.

M onique and Robert began by discussing Walter's apartment, and moved along to the edge of a quarrel.

"In any case," said Robert, "you should be under your husband's roof. That is the law. You should never have left him."

"Nobody left. It's been like this for years." Monique did not mention that she had come here to help; he knew that. He did not say that he was grateful.

"The law is the law," Robert said.

"Not anymore."

"It was a law when you got married," he said. "The husband is head of the family, he chooses the domicile, the wife is obliged to live under his roof, and he is obliged to receive her there. Under his roof."

"That's finished. If you still bothered to go to weddings, you'd know."

"It was still binding when you married him. He should be offering you a roof."

"He can't," said Monique, flinging out her arm and hitting Robert's record-player, which resisted the shock. "It's about to cave in from the weight of the mortgage."

"Well," said Robert, forgetting Gaston for a moment, "he has a lease and he pays his rent regularly. And I am still paying for mending *my* roof." After a pause he said, "Aymeric says Gaston has a rich woman in Antibes."

"I was said to have been a rich young one."

"There is space for you here, always," said Robert instantly. There would be even more, later on. When the time came, they would knock all the flats into one and divide up the new space obtained.

"Look up 'harp' in your dream book," she said. "I dreamed I was giving a concert."

R obert usually got the dream book out on Sundays. The others saved up their weeknight dreams. Aymeric continued to dream he had been slighted. It was a dream of contradiction, and meant that in real life he was deeply appreciated. Robert's mother dreamed she was polishing furniture, which prophesied good luck with the opposite sex. Monique played tennis in a downpour: her affections would be returned. Robert went to answer the doorbell—the sign of a happy surprise. They began each new week reassured and smiling—all but Walter. He had been dreaming about moles and dormice again.

As the summer weather settled in, and with Monique there to care for their mother, Robert began spending weekends out of town. He took the Dijon train at the Gare de Lyon and got off at Tonnerre. Monique found cancelled railway tickets in waste-paper baskets. Walter had a sudden illumination: Robert must be attending weekend retreats in a monastery. That thin, quiet face belonged to a world of silence. Then, one day, Robert mentioned that there was a ballooning club in Tonnerre. Balloons were quieter than helicopters. Swaying in silence, between the clouds and the Burgundy Canal, he had been able to reach a decision. He did not say what about.

He accepted books from Walter to read in the train. They piled up at his bedside as he kept forgetting to give them back. Some he owned up to having lost. Walter could see them overhead, St. Augustine and St. Thomas Aquinas, drifting and swaying. He had no wish to ascend in a balloon. He had seen enough balloons in engravings. Virtually anything portrayed as art turned his stomach. There was hardly anything he could look at without feeling sick. In any case, Robert did not invite him.

Sometimes they watched television together. Aymeric had an old black-and-white set with only two channels. Monique had a

Japanese portable, but the screen was too small for her mother to enjoy. They all liked Walter's set, which had a large screen and more buttons than there would ever be channels in France. One Saturday when Robert was not ballooning, he suddenly said he was getting married. It was just in the middle of "Dallas." They were about a year behind Switzerland, and Monique had been asking Walter, whose occasional trips to Bern kept him up-to-date, to tell them how it would all turn out. Aymeric switched off the sound, upon which Robert's mother went straight to sleep.

Robert said only that his first marriage had been so happy that he could hardly wait to start over. The others sat staring at him. Walter had a crazy idea, which he kept to himself: Would Robert get married overhead in a balloon? "I am happy," Robert said, once or twice. Walter fixed his eyes on the bright, silent screen.

Monique prepared their mother's meals and carried them from Robert's kitchen on a tray. She had to make a wide detour around Walter's locked apartment. Everything was stone cold by the time the old lady had been coaxed to sit down. Their mother had her own kitchen, but she filled the oven with whatever came to hand when she was tidying—towels, a shoebox full of old Bic pens. Once, Monique found a bolster folded in two, looking like a bloated loaf. She disconnected the stove, so that her mother could not turn on the gas and start a fire.

Robert showed them a picture of his bride-to-be. She and Robert stood smiling, with arms linked, both wearing track suits. "Does she run as well as float?" said Aymeric. He turned the snapshot over and read a date and the initial "B."

"Brigitte," said Robert.

"Brigitte what?"

"I don't want anyone driving to Tonnerre for long talks," said Robert. He did say that she taught French grammar to semi-delinquents in a technical high school. She was trying to obtain a transfer to a Paris suburb. There could be no question of the Capital itself: one had to know someone, and there was a waiting list ten years long.

Monique's arrival was followed closely by a new shock from the administrative authorities of Paris: a telephone number old people could call in the summertime, free of charge, in case their families were away and they felt lonely. Robert's mother dialled the number on Aymeric's phone. The woman at the other end— young, from the sound of her—seemed surprised to hear that Robert's mother lived with a son, a daughter, and a nephew, all attentive; had the use of a large television set with plenty of buttons and dials; and still suffered from feelings of neglect and despair. She was afraid of dying alone in the dark. All night long, she tried to stay on her feet.

The young voice reminded her about old people who had absolutely no one, who lived at the top of six steep flights of stairs, who did not dare go down to buy a packet of macaroni for fear of the long climb back. Robert's mother replied that the lives of such people were at the next-to-final stage of hopelessness and terror. Her own meals were brought to her on a tray. She was not claiming more for her sentiments than blind panic.

Aymeric took the telephone out of her hand, said a few words into it, and hung up. His aunt gave him her sweet, steady smile before remarking, "Your poor mother, Aymeric, was nothing much to look at."

W alter, trying to find a place to go for his summer holiday where there would be no reminders of art, fell back on Switzerland and his mother and father. He scrubbed and vacuumed his rooms and put plastic dust sheets over the furniture. Just before calling for a taxi to take him to the airport, he asked Robert if he could have a word with him. He was more than usually nervous, and kept flexing his hands. Terrible things had been said at the gallery that day; Walter had threatened his employer with the police. Robert could not understand the story—something incoherent to do with the office safe. He removed a bundle of clothes fresh from the launderette (he did his own ironing) and invited Walter to sit down. Walter wanted to know if the imminent change in Robert's life and Monique's constant hints about the best space in the house meant that Walter's apartment was coveted. "Coveted" was a heavy word, but Robert finally answered, "You've got your lease."

"According to the law," said Walter, more and more fussed, "you can throw me out if you can prove you need the space." Robert sat quietly, and seemed to be waiting for something else. "I've got to be sure I have a home to come back to—a home I can keep for a long time. This time I really intend to give notice. I don't care about the pension. He's making me an accomplice in crime. I'll stay just until he can train a replacement for me. If he sees I am worried about something else as well, it will give him the upper hand. And then, I'm like you and Aymeric. I feel as if my own family had been living here forever." Robert at this looked at him with a terrible politeness. Walter rushed on, mentioning a matter that other tenants, he thought, would have brought up first. Since moving in, he had painted the kitchen, paved the bathroom with imported tiles, and hung custom-made curtains on rods designed to fit the windows. All this, he said, constituted an embellishment of space.

"Your vacation will do you good," said Robert.

Walter gave Robert his house keys and said he hoped Monique would feel free to use his apartment as a passageway while he was gone. Handing them over, he was reminded of another gesture—his hand, outstretched, opening to reveal the snuffbox.

Their mother had begun polishing furniture, as in some of her dreams. A table in Walter's sitting room was like a pond. Everything else was dusty. The plastic sheets lay like crumpled parachutes in a corner. On Aymeric's birthday, late in August, he and Robert and Monique sat at the polished table eating pastries out of a box. Robert picked out a few of the kind his mother liked and put them aside for her on a plate. They could hear her, in Walter's bedroom, telling City Hall that they had disconnected her stove.

Perhaps because there was an empty chair, Robert suddenly said that Brigitte was immensely sociable and liked to entertain. She played first-class bridge. She had somehow managed to obtain a transfer to Paris after all. They would be getting married in October.

"How did she do it?" Aymeric asked.

"She knows someone."

They fell silent, admiring the empty chair.

"Who wants the last strawberry tart?" said Monique. When no one answered, she cut it in three.

"We will have to rearrange the space," said Robert. He traced lines with his finger on the polished table and, with the palm of his hand, wiped something out.

Aymeric said, "Try to find out what she did with that snuffbox. I wanted to give it to you as a wedding present."

"I'll look again in the oven," Monique said.

"Ask her carefully," said Aymeric. "Don't frighten her. Sometimes she remembers."

Robert went on tracing invisible lines.

Walter came back in September to find his kitchen under occupation, full of rusted sieves and food mills and old graters. On the stove was a saucepan of strained soup for the old woman's supper; a bowl of pureed apricots stood uncovered in the sink. He removed everything to the old woman's kitchen.

I was brought up so soundly, he said to himself. He had respected his parents; now he admired them. At home, nothing had made him feel worried or tense, and he hadn't minded his father's habit of reading the newspaper aloud while Walter tried to watch television. When his father answered the telephone, his mother called, "What do they want?" from the kitchen. His father always repeated everything the caller said, so that his mother would not miss a word of the conversation. There were no secrets, no mysteries. What Walter saw of his parents was probably all there was.

After cleaning his rooms and unpacking his suitcase, Walter called on Robert. He had meant to ask how they had spent their holidays, if in spite of the old lady they had managed to get away, but instead he found himself telling about a remarkable dream he'd had in Switzerland: A large badger had burst into the gallery and taken Walter's employer hostage. Trout Face had said, "You're not getting away with this. I'm not having anybody running around here with automatic weapons." It was not a nightmare, said Walter. He had seen himself, aloof and nonchalant, enjoying the incident.

Robert said he would look it up. That night he made a neat stack of the books Walter had lent him—all that he could still find—and left it outside his locked front door. He wrote on the back of a page torn off a calendar, "Dream of badger taking man hostage means a change of residence, for which the dreamer should be prepared. R." He rewrote this several times, changing a word here and there. In the morning, after starting the record and opening all the windows, he sat down and read his message again. He kept running his finger over the note, as he had traced new boundaries on Walter's table, and seemed to be wondering if there was any point in trying to say the same thing some other way.

LUC AND HIS FATHER

To the astonishment of no one except his father and mother, Luc Clairevoie failed the examination that should have propelled him straight into one of the finest schools of engineering in Paris; failed it so disastrously, in fact, that an examiner, who knew someone in the same ministry as Luc's father, confided it was the sort of labor in vain that should be written up. Luc's was a prime case of universal education gone crazy. He was a victim of the current belief that any student, by dint of application, could answer what he was asked.

Luc's father blamed the late President de Gaulle. If de Gaulle had not opened the schools and universities to hordes of qualified but otherwise uninteresting young people, teachers would have had more time to spare for Luc. De Gaulle had been dead for years, but Roger Clairevoie still suspected him of cosmic mischief and double-dealing. (Like his wife, Roger had never got over the loss of Algeria. When the price of fresh fruit went high, as it did every winter, the Clairevoies told each other it was because of the loss of all those Algerian orchards.)

Where Luc was concerned, they took a practical course,

lowered their sights to a lesser but still elegant engineering school, and sent Luc to a crammer for a year to get ready for a new trial. His mother took Luc to the dentist, had his glasses changed, and bought him a Honda 125 to make up for his recent loss of self-esteem. Roger's contribution took the form of long talks. Cornering Luc in the kitchen after breakfast, or in his own study, now used as a family television room, Roger told Luc how he had been graduated with honors from the noblest engineering institute in France; how he could address other alumni using the second person singular, even by Christian name, regardless of whether they spoke across a ministerial desk or a lunch table. Many of Roger's fellow-graduates had chosen civil-service careers. They bumped into one another in marble halls, under oil portraits of public servants who wore the steadfast look of advisers to gods; and these distinguished graduates, Roger among them, had a charming, particular way of seeming like brothers—or so it appeared to those who could only envy them, who had to keep to "Have I the honor of" and "If Mr. Assistant Under-Secretary would be good enough to" and "Should it suit the convenience." To this fraternity Luc could no longer aspire, but there was still some hope for future rank and dignity: he could become an engineer in the building trades. Luc did not reply; he did not even ask, "Do you mean houses, or garages, or what?" Roger supposed he was turning things over in his mind.

The crammer he went to was a brisk, costly examination factory in Rennes, run by Jesuits, with the reputation for being able to jostle any student, even the dreamiest, into a respectable institute for higher learning. The last six words were from the school's brochure. They ran through Roger Clairevoie's head like an election promise.

Starting in September, Luc spent Monday to Friday in Rennes. Weekends, he came home by train, laden with books, and shut himself up to study. Sometimes Roger would hear him trying chords on his guitar: pale sound without rhythm or sequence. When Luc had studied enough, he buckled on his

white helmet and roared around Paris on the Honda. (The
promise of a BMW R/80 was in the air, as reward or consolation,
depending on next year's results.) On the helmet Luc had
lettered "IN CASE OF ACCIDENT DO NOT REMOVE." "You see,
he does think of things," his mother said. "Luc thinks of good,
useful things."

Like many Parisian students, Luc was without close friends,
and in Rennes he knew nobody. His parents were somewhat
relieved when, in the autumn, he became caught like a strand of
seaweed on the edge of a political discussion group. The group
met every Sunday afternoon in some member's house. Once, the
group assembled at the Clairevoies'; Simone Clairevoie, pleased
to see that Luc was showing interest in adult problems, served
fruit juice, pâté sandwiches, and two kinds of ice cream. Luc's
friends did not paint slogans on the sidewalk, or throw petrol
bombs at police stations, or carry weapons (at least, Roger hoped
not), or wear ragtag uniforms bought at the flea market. A few old
men talked, and the younger men, those Luc's age, sat on a
windowsill or on the floor, and seemed to listen. Among the
speakers the day they came to the Clairevoies' was a retired
journalist, once thought ironic and alarming, and the former
secretary of a minor visionary, now in decrepit exile in Spain.
Extremist movements were banned, but, as Roger pointed out to
his wife, one could not really call this a movement. There was no
law against meeting on a winter afternoon to consider the false
starts of history. Luc never said much, but his parents supposed
he must be taking to heart the message of the failed old men; and
it was curious to see how Luc could grasp a slippery, allusive
message so easily when he could not keep in mind his own
private destiny as an engineer. Luc could vote, get married
without permission, have his own bank account, run up bills. He
could leave home, though a course so eccentric had probably not
yet occurred to him. He was of age; adult; a grown man.

The Clairevoies had spent their married life in an apartment
on the second floor of a house of venturesome design, built just
after the First World War, in a quiet street near the Bois de

Boulogne. The designer of the house, whose name they could never recall, had been German or Austrian. Roger, when questioned by colleagues surprised to find him in surroundings so bizarre, would say, "The architect was Swiss," which made him sound safer. Students of architecture rang the bell to ask if they might visit the rooms and take photographs. Often they seemed taken aback by the sight of the furniture, a wedding gift from Roger's side of the family, decorated with swans and sphinxes; the armchairs were as hard and uncompromising as the Judgment Seat. To Roger, the furniture served as counterpoise to the house, which belonged to the alien Paris of the nineteen-twenties, described by Roger's father as full of artists and immigrants of a shiftless kind—the flotsam of Europe.

The apartment, a wedding present from Simone's parents, was her personal choice. Roger's people, needing the choice explained away, went on saying for years that Simone had up-to-date ideas; but Roger was not sure this was true. After all, the house was some forty years old by the time the Clairevoies moved in. The street, at least, barely changed from year to year, unless one counted the increasing number of prostitutes that drifted in from the Bois. Directly across from the house, a café, the only place of business in sight, served as headquarters for the prostitutes' rest periods, conversations, and quarrels. Sometimes Roger went there when he ran out of cigarettes. He knew some of the older women by sight, and he addressed them courteously; and they, of course, were polite to him. Once, pausing under the awning to light a cigarette, he glanced up and saw Luc standing at a window, the curtain held aside with an elbow. He seemed to be staring at nothing in particular, merely waiting for something that might fix his attention. Roger had a middle-aged, paternal reflex: Is that what he calls studying? If Luc noticed his father, he gave no sign.

Simone Clairevoie called it the year of shocks. There had been Luc's failure, then Roger had suffered a second heart attack, infinitely more frightening than the first. He was home all day on convalescent leave from his ministry, restless and bored, smoking on the sly, grudgingly walking the family dog by way of moderate exercise. Finally, even though all three Clairevoies had voted against it, a Socialist government came to power. Simone foresaw nothing but further decline. If Luc failed again, it would mean a humble career, preceded by a tour of Army duty—plain military service, backpack and drill, with the sons of peasants and Algerian delinquents. Roger would never be able to get him out of it: he knew absolutely no one in the new system of favors. Those friends whose careers had not been lopped sat hard on their jobs, almost afraid to pick up the telephone. Every call was bad news. The worst news would be the voice of an old acquaintance, harking back to a foundered regime and expecting a good turn. Although the Clairevoies seldom went to church now—the new Mass was the enemy—Simone prayed hard on Christmas Eve, singling out in particular St. Odile, who had been useful in the past, around a time when Roger had seemed to regret his engagement to Simone and may have wanted to break it off.

Soon after the New Year, however, there came a message from the guidance counsellor of the Jesuit school, summoning the Clairevoies for "a frank and open discussion."

"About being immortal?" said Roger to Simone, recalling an alarming talk with another Jesuit teacher long ago.

"About your son," she replied.

A card on his door identified the counsellor as "F.-X. Rousseau, Orientation." Orientation wore a track suit and did not look to Roger like a Jesuit, or even much like a priest. Leaning forward (the Clairevoies instinctively drew back), he offered American cigarettes before lighting his own. It was not Luc's chances of passing that seemed to worry him but Luc's fragmented image of women. On the Rorschach test, for instance, he had seen a ballet skirt and a pair of legs, and a female head in a fishing net.

"You brought me here to tell me what?" said Roger. "My son has poor eyesight?"

Simone placed her hand on Father Rousseau's desk as she might have touched his sleeve. She was saying, Be careful. My husband is irritable, old-fashioned, ill. "I think that Father Rousseau is trying to tell us that Luc has no complete view of women because Luc has no complete view of himself as a man. Is that it?"

Father Rousseau added, "And he cannot see his future because he can't see himself."

It was Roger's turn to remonstrate with Luc. Simone suggested masculine, virile surroundings for their talk, and so he took Luc to the café across the street. There, over beer for Luc and mineral water for Roger, he told Luc about satisfaction. It was the duty of children to satisfy their parents. Roger, by doing extremely well at his studies, had given Luc's grandparents this mysterious pleasure. They had been able to tell their friends, "Roger has given us great satisfaction." He took Luc on a fresh tour of things to come, showing him the slow-grinding machinery of state competitive examinations against which fathers measured their sons. He said, Your future. If you fail. A poor degree is worse than none. Thousands of embittered young men, all voting Socialist. If you fail, you will sink into the swamp from which there is no rising. Do you want to sell brooms? Sweep the streets? Sell tickets in the Métro? Do you want to spend your life in a bank?

"Not that there is anything wrong with working in a bank," he corrected. Encrusted in his wife's family was a small rural bank with a staff of seventeen. Simone did not often see her provincial cousins, but the bank was always mentioned with respect. To say "a small bank" was no worse than saying "a small crown jewel." Simone, in a sense, personified a reliable and almost magical trade; she had brought to Roger the goods and the dream. What had Roger brought? Hideous Empire furniture and a dubious nineteenth-century title Simone scarcely dared use because of the Communists.

Only the word "Socialist" seemed to stir Luc. "We need a good little civil war," he declared, as someone who has never been near the ocean might announce, "We need a good little tidal wave"—so Roger thought.

He said, "There are no good little civil wars." But he knew what was said of him: that his heart attacks had altered his personality, made him afraid. On a November day, Roger and his father had followed the coffin of Charles Maurras, the nationalist leader, jailed after the war for collaboration. "My son," said Roger's father, introducing Roger to thin-faced men, some wearing the Action Française emblem. Roger's father had stood for office on a Royalist platform, and had come out of the election the last of five candidates, one an impertinent youngster with an alien name, full of "z"s and "k"s. He was not bitter; he was scornful and dry, and he wanted Roger to be dry and proud. Roger had only lately started to think, My father always said, and, My father believed. As he spoke, now, to Luc about satisfaction and failure, he remembered how he had shuffled behind the hearse of a dead old man, perhaps mistaken, certainly dispossessed. They got up to leave, and Roger bowed to an elderly woman he recognized. His son had already turned away.

In order to give Luc a fully virile image, Simone redecorated his room. The desk lamp was a galleon in full sail with a bright red shade—the color of decision and activity. She took down the photograph of Roger's graduating class and hung a framed poster of Che Guevara. Stepping back to see the effect, she realized Guevara would never do. The face was feminine, soft. She wondered if the whole legend was not a hoax and if Guevara had been a woman in disguise. Guevara had no political significance, of course; he had become manly, decorative kitsch. (The salesman had assured her of this; otherwise, she would never have run the risk of offending Roger.) As she removed the poster she noticed for the first time a hole drilled in the wall. She put her eye to it and had a partial view of the maid's bathroom, used in the past by a succession of *au pair* visitors, in Paris to improve their French and to keep an eye on a younger Luc.

She called Roger and made him look: "Who says Luc has no view of women?"

Roger glanced round at the new curtains and bedspread, with their pattern of Formula 1 racing cars. Near the bed someone—Luc, probably—had tacked a photo of Hitler. Roger, without saying anything, took it down. He did not want Luc quite that manly.

"You can't actually see the shower," said Simone, trying the perspective again. "But I suppose that when she stands drying on the mat...We'd better tell him."

"Tell Luc?"

"Rousseau. Orientation."

Not "Father Rousseau," he noticed. It was not true that women were devoted guardians of tradition. They rode every new wave like so much plankton. My father was right, he decided. He always said it was a mistake to give them the vote. He said they had no ideas—just notions. My father was proud to stand up for the past. He was proud to be called a Maurrassien, even when Charles Maurras was in defeat, in disgrace. But who has ever heard of a Maurrassienne? The very idea made Roger smile. Simone, catching the smile, took it to mean a sudden feeling of tolerance, and so she chose the moment to remind him they would have an *au pair* guest at Easter—oh, not to keep an eye on Luc; Luc was too old. (She sounded sorry.) But Luc had been three times to England, to a family named Brunt, and now, in all fairness, it was the Clairevoies' obligation to have Cassandra.

"Another learner?" Roger was remembering the tall, glum girls from northern capitals and their strides in colloquial French: That is my friend. He did not sleep in my bed—he spent the night on the doormat. I am homesick. I am ill. A bee has stung me. I am allergic and may die.

"You won't have to worry about Cassandra," Simone said. "She is a mature young woman of fifteen, a whole head taller than Luc."

Simone clipped a leash to the dog's collar and grasped Roger firmly by the arm. She was taking two of her charges for a walk, along streets she used to follow when Luc was still in his pram.

On Boulevard Lannes a taxi stopped and two men wearing white
furs, high-heeled white boots, and Marilyn Monroe wigs got out
and made for the Bois. Roger knew that transvestites worked the
fringe of the Bois now, congregating mostly toward the Porte
Maillot, where there were hotels. He had heard the women in
the café across the street complaining that the police were not
vigilant enough, much the way an established artisan might
grumble about black-market labor. Roger had imagined them
vaguely as night creatures, glittering and sequined, caught like
dragonflies in the headlights of roving automobiles. This pair was
altogether real, and the man who had just paid the taxi-driver
shut his gold-mesh handbag with the firm snap of a housewife
settling the butcher's bill. The dog at once began to strain and
bark.

"Brazilians," said Simone, who watched educational television in the afternoon. "They send all their money home."

"But in broad daylight," said Roger.

"They don't earn as much as you think."

"There could be little children playing in the Bois."

"We can't help our children by living in the past," said
Simone. Roger wondered if she was having secret talks with
Father Rousseau. "Stop that," she told the barking dog.

"He's not deliberately trying to hurt their feelings," Roger
said. Because he disliked animals—in particular, dogs—he tended
to make excuses for the one they owned. Actually, the dog was an
accident in their lives, purchased only after the staff psychologist
in Luc's old school had said the boy's grades were poor because
he had no siblings to love and hate, no rivals for his parents'
attention, no responsibility to any living creature.

"A dog will teach my son to add and subtract?" said Roger.
Simone had wondered if a dog would make Luc affectionate and
polite, more grateful for his parents' devotion, aware of the many
sacrifices they had made on his behalf.

Yes, yes, they had been assured. A dog could do all that.

Luc was twelve years old, the puppy ten weeks. Encouraged to find a name for him, Luc came up with "Mongrel." Simone chose "Sylvestre." Sylvestre spent his first night in Luc's room— part of the night, that is. When he began to whine, Luc put him out. After that, Sylvestre was fed, trained, and walked by Luc's parents, while Luc continued to find school a mystery and to show indifference and ingratitude. Want of thanks is a parent's lot, but blindness to simple arithmetic was like an early warning of catastrophe. Luc's parents had already told him he was to train as an engineer.

"Do you know how stiff the competition is?" his mother asked.

"Yes."

"Do you want to be turned down by the best schools?"

"I don't know."

"Do you want to be sent to a third-rate school, miles from home? Have you thought about that?"

Roger leaned on Simone, though he did not need to, and became querulous: "Sylvestre and I are two old men."

This was not what Simone liked to talk about. She said, "Your family never took you into consideration. You slept in your father's study. You took second best."

"It didn't feel that way."

"Look at our miserable country house. Look at your Cousin Henri's estate."

"His godmother gave it to him," said Roger, as though she needed reminding.

"He should have given you compensation."

"People don't do that," said Roger. "All I needed was a richer godmother."

"The apartment is mine," said Simone, as they walked arm in arm. "The furniture is yours. The house in the country is yours, but most of the furniture belongs to me. You paid for the pool and the tennis court." It was not unpleasant conversation.

Roger stopped in front of a pastry shop and showed Simone a chocolate cake. "Why can't we have that?"

"Because it would kill you. The specialist said so."

"We could have oysters," Roger said. "I'm allowed oysters."

"Luc will be home," said Simone. "He doesn't like them."

Father Rousseau sent for the Clairevoies again. This time he wore a tweed jacket over a white sweater, with a small crucifix on one lapel and a Solidarność badge on the other. After lighting his cigarette he sat drumming his fingers, as if wondering how to put his grim news into focus. At last he said, "No one can concentrate on an exam and on a woman. Not at the same time."

"Women?" cried Simone. "What women?"

"Woman," Roger corrected, unheard.

There was a woman in Luc's life. It seemed unbelievable, but it was so.

"French?" said Roger instantly.

Father Rousseau was unable to swear to it. Her name was Katia, her surname Martin, but if Martin was the most common family name in France it might be because so many foreigners adopted it.

"I can find out," Simone interrupted. "What's her age?"

Katia was eighteen. Her parents were divorced.

"That's bad," said Simone. "Who's her father?"

She lived in Biarritz with her mother, but came often to Paris to stay with her father and brother. Her brother belonged to a political debating society.

"I've seen him," said Simone. "I know the one. She's a terrorist. Am I right?"

Father Rousseau doubted it. "She is a spoiled, rich, undereducated young woman, used to having her own way. She is also very much in love."

"With Luc?" said Roger.

"Luc is a Capricorn," said Simone. "The most levelheaded of all the signs."

So was Katia, Father Rousseau said. She and Luc wrote "Capricorn loves Capricorn" in the dust on parked cars.

"Does Luc want to marry her?" said Simone, getting over the worst.

"He wants something." But Father Rousseau hoped it would not be Katia. She seemed to have left school early, after a number of misadventures. She was hardly the person to inspire Luc, who needed a model he could copy. When Katia was around, Luc did not even pretend to study. When she was in Biarritz, he waited for letters. The two collected lump sugar from cafés but seemed to have no other cultural interest.

"She's from a rich family?" Simone said. "And she has just the one brother?"

"Luc has got to pass his entrance examination," said Roger. "After he gets his degree he can marry anyone he likes."

" 'Rich' is a relative term," said Simone, implying that Father Rousseau was too unworldly to define such a thing.

Roger said, "How do you know about the sugar and 'Capricorn loves Capricorn' and how Luc and Katia got to know each other?"

"Why, from Katia's letters, of course," said Father Rousseau, sounding surprised.

"Did you keep copies?" said Simone.

"Do you know that Luc is of age, and that he could take you to court for reading his mail?" said Roger.

Father Rousseau turned to Simone, the rational parent. "Not a word of reproach," he warned her. "Just keep an eye on the situation. We feel that Luc should spend the next few weeks at home, close to his parents." He would come back to Rennes just before the examination, for last-minute heavy cramming. Roger understood this to be a smooth Jesuitical manner of getting rid of Luc.

Luc came home, and no one reproached him. He promised to work hard and proposed going alone to the country house, which was near Auxerre. Simone objected that the place had been unheated all winter. Luc replied that he would live in one room and take his meals in the village. Roger guessed that Luc intended to spend a good amount of time with Cousin Henri, who lived nearby, and whom Luc—no one knew why—professed to admire. Cousin Henri and Roger enjoyed property litigation of long standing, but as there was a dim, far chance of Henri's leaving something to Luc, Roger said nothing. And as Simone pointed out, meaning by this nothing unkind or offensive, any male model for Luc was better than none.

In the meantime, letters from Katia, forwarded from Rennes, arrived at the Paris apartment. Roger watched in pure amazement the way Simone managed to open them, rolling a kitchen match under the flap. Having read the letter, she resealed it without trace. The better the quality of the paper, the easier the match trick, she explained. She held a page up to the light, approving the watermark.

"We'll need a huge apartment, because we will have so many children," Katia wrote. "And we'll need space for the sugar collection."

The only huge apartment Simone could think of was her own. "They wish we were dead," she told Roger. "My son wishes I were out of the way." She read aloud, " 'What would you be without me? One more little Frenchman, eternally studying for exams.' "

"What does she mean by 'little Frenchman'?" said Roger. He decided that Katia must be foreign—a descendant of White Russians, perhaps. There had been a colony in Biarritz in his father's day, the men gambling away their wives' tiaras before settling down as headwaiters and croupiers. Luc was entangled in a foreign love affair; he was already alien, estranged. Roger had seen him standing at the window, like an idle landowner in a Russian novel. What did Roger know about Russians? There were the modern ones, dressed in gray, with bulldog faces; there were the slothful, mournful people in books, the impulsive and slender women, the indecisive men. But it had been years since Roger had opened a novel; what he saw were overlapping images, like stills from old films.

" 'Where are you, where are you?' " read Simone. " 'There is a light in your parents' room, but your windows are dark. I'm standing under the awning across the street. My shoes are soaked. I am too miserable to care.'

"She can't be moping in the rain and writing all at the same time," said Simone. "And the postmark is Biarritz. She comes to Paris to stir up trouble. How does she know which room is ours? Luc is probably sick of her. He must have been at a meeting."

Yes, he had probably been at a meeting, sitting on the floor of a pale room, with a soft-voiced old man telling him about an older, truer Europe. Luc was learning a Europe caught in amber, unchanging, with trees for gods. There was no law against paganism and politics, or soft-voiced old men.

At least there are no guns, Roger told himself. And where had Simone learned the way to open other people's letters? He marvelled at Katia's doing for his son what no woman had ever done for him; she had stood in the rain, crying probably, watching for a light.

Ten days before Easter, Cassandra Brunt arrived. Her father was a civil servant, like Roger. He was also an author: two books had been published, one about Napoleon's retreat from Moscow, the other about the failure of the Maginot Line and the disgraceful conduct of the French officer class. Both had been sent to the Clairevoies, with courteous inscriptions. When Simone had gone over to England alone, to see if the Brunts would do for Luc, Mrs. Brunt confided that her husband was more interested in the philosophy of combat than in success and defeat. He was a dreamer, and that was why he had never got ahead. Simone replied that Roger, too, had been hampered by guiding principles. As a youth, he had read for his own pleasure. His life was a dream. Mrs. Brunt suggested a major difference: Mr. Brunt was no full-time dreamer. He had written five books, two of which had been printed, one in 1952 and one in 1966. The two women had then considered each other's child, decided it was sexless and safe and that Luc and Cassandra could spend time under the same roof. After that, Luc crossed the Channel for three visits, while Simone managed not to have Cassandra even once. Her excuse was the extreme youth of Cassandra and the dangers of Paris. Now that Cassandra was fifteen Mrs. Brunt, suddenly exercising her sense of things owed, had written to say that Cassandra was ready for perils and the French.

Roger and Simone met Cassandra at the Gare du Nord. The moment he saw her, Roger understood she had been forced by her parents to make the trip, and that they were ruining her Easter holiday. He marvelled that a fifteen-year-old of her size and apparent strength could be bullied into anything.

"I'll be seeing Luc, what fun," said Cassandra, jackknifed into the car, her knees all but touching her chin. "It will be nice to see Luc," she said sadly. Her fair hair almost covered her face.

"Luc is at our country residence, studying with all the strength of his soul," said Simone. "He is in the Yonne," she added. Cassandra looked puzzled. Roger supposed that to a foreigner it must sound as though Luc had fallen into a river.

There had been no coaxing Luc, no pleading; no threat was strong enough to frighten him. They could keep the BMW; they could stop his allowance; they could put him in jail. He would not come to Paris to welcome Cassandra. He was through with England, through with the Brunts—through, for that matter, with his mother and father. Katia had taken their place.

"We'll have her in Paris for a week, alone," Simone had wailed. Luc's argument was unassailable; alone, he could study. Once they were all there, he would have to be kind to Cassandra, making conversation and showing her the village church. Simone put the blame on Mrs. Brunt, who had insisted in a wholly obtuse way on having her rights.

"How are your delicious parents?" she asked, turning as well as the seat belt allowed, seeming to let the car drive itself in Paris traffic.

"Daddy's at home now. He's retired from the minstrel."

"The ministry," said Simone deeply. Cassandra's was the only English she had ever completely understood. "My husband has also retired from public service. It was too much for his heart. He is much younger than Mr. Brunt, I believe."

"Daddy was a late starter," said Cassandra. "But he'll last a long time. At least, I hope so."

Like the dog bought to improve Luc's arithmetic; like the tropical fish Simone had tended for Luc, and eventually mourned; like the tennis court in which Luc had at once lost interest and on which Roger had had his first heart attack, so Cassandra fell to Luc's parents. With Simone, she watched television; with Roger, she walked uphill and down, to parks and museums.

"What was your minstrel?" she asked Roger, as they marched toward the Bois.

"Years ago, when there was a grave shortage of telephones, thanks to President de Gaulle—" Roger began. "Do you recall that unhappy time?"

"I'm afraid I'm dreffly ignorant."

"I was good at getting friends off the waiting list. That was what I did best."

He clutched her arm, dragging her out of the way of buses and taxis that rushed from the left while Cassandra looked hopelessly right.

"You like the nature?" he said, letting Sylvestre run free in the Bois. "The trees?"

"My mother does. Though this is hardly nature, is it?"

Sylvestre loped, snuffling, into a club of dusty shrubbery. He gave a yelp and came waddling out. All Roger saw of the person who had kicked him was a flash of white boot.

"You have them in England?" said Roger.

"Have what?"

"That. Male, female. Prostitutes."

"Yes, of course. But they aren't vile to animals."

"You like the modern art?" Roger asked, breathless, as they plodded up the stalled escalators of the Beaubourg museum.

"I'm horribly old-fashioned, I'm afraid."

Halfway, he paused to let his heart rest. His heart was an old pump, clogged and filthy. Cassandra's heart was of bright new metal; it beat more quietly and regularly than any clock.

Above the city stretched a haze of pollution, unstirring, all of an even color. The sun suffused the haze with amber dye, which by some grim alchemy was turned into dun. Roger saw through the haze to a forgotten city, unchanging, and it was enough to wrench the heart. A hand, reaching inside the rib cage, seemed to grasp the glutted machine. He knew that some part of the machine was intact, faithful to him; when his heart disowned him entirely he might as well die.

Cassandra, murmuring that looking down made her feel giddy, turned her back. Roger watched a couple, below, walking hand in hand. He was too far away to see their faces. They were eating out of a shared paper bag. The young man looked around, perhaps for a bin. Finding none, he handed the bag to the girl, who flung it down. The two were dressed nearly alike, in blue jackets and jeans. Simone had assured Roger that Katia was French, but he still saw her Russian. He saw Katia in winter furs, with a fur hat, and long fair hair over a snowy collar. She removed a glove and gave the hand, warm, to Luc to hold.

"I'm afraid I must be getting lazy," Cassandra remarked. "I found that quite a climb."

The couple in blue had turned a corner. Of Luc and Katia there remained footsteps on lightly fallen snow.

"This place reminds me of a giant food processor," said Cassandra. "What does it make you think of?"

"Young lovers," Roger said.

Cassandra had a good point in Simone's eyes: she kept a diary, which Simone used to improve her English.

"The Baron has sex on the brain," Simone read. "Even a museum reminds him of sex. In the Bois de Boulogne he tried to twist the conversation around to sex and bestiality. You have to be careful every minute. Each time we have to cross the road he tries to squeeze my arm."

When Cassandra had been shown enough of Paris, Simone packed the car with food that Luc liked to eat and drove south and east with the dog, Roger, and Cassandra. They stopped often during the journey so that Cassandra, who sat in the back of the car, could get out and be sick. They found Luc living like an elderly squatter in a ground-floor room full of toast crusts. It was three in the afternoon, and he was still wearing pajamas. Inevitably, Cassandra asked if he was ill.

"Katia's been here," said Simone, going round the house and opening shutters. "I can tell. It's in the air."

Luc was occupying the room meant for Cassandra. He showed no willingness to give it up. He took slight notice of his parents, and none whatever of their guest. It seemed to Roger that he had grown taller, but this was surely an illusion, a psychological image in Roger's mind. His affair, if Roger could call it that, had certainly made him bolder. He mentioned Katia by name, saying that one advantage of living alone was that he could read his mail before anyone else got to it. Roger foresaw a holiday of bursting quarrels. He supposed Cassandra would go home and tell her father, the historian, that the French were always like that.

On the day they arrived, Simone intercepted and read a letter. Katia, apparently in answer to some questioning from Luc, explained that she had almost, but not entirely, submitted to the advances of a cousin. (Luc, to forestall his mother, met the postman at the gate. Simone, to short-circuit Luc, had already picked up the letters that interested her at the village post office.) Katia's near-seduction had taken place in a field of barley, while her cousin was on leave from military service. A lyrical account of clouds, birds, and crickets took up most of a page.

Roger would not touch the letter, but he listened as Simone read aloud. It seemed to him that some coarse appreciation of the cousin was concealed behind all those crickets and birds. Katia's blithe candor was insolent, a slur on his son. At the same time, he took heart: If a cousin was liable for Army duty, some part of the family must be French. On the other hand, who would rape his cousin in a barley field, if not a Russian?

"You swore Katia was French," he said, greatly troubled.

He knew nothing of Katia, but he did know something about fields. Roger decided he did not believe a word of the story. Katia was trying to turn Luc into a harmless and impotent bachelor friend. The two belonged in a novel of the early nineteen-fifties. (Simone, as Roger said this, began to frown.) "Luc is the good, kind man she can tell stories to," he said. "Her stories will be more and more about other men." As Simone drew breath, he said quickly, "Not that I see Luc in a novel."

"No, but I can see you in the diary of a hysterical English girl," said Simone, and she told him about Cassandra.

Roger, scarcely listening, went on, "In a novel, Katia's visit would be a real-estate tour. She would drive up from Biarritz with her mother and take pictures from the road. Katia's mother would find the house squat and suburban, and so Luc would show them Cousin Henri's. They would take pictures of that, too. Luc would now be going round with chalk and a tape measure, marking the furniture he wants to sell once we're buried, planning the rooms he will build for Katia when the place is his."

All at once he felt the thrust of the next generation, and for the first time he shared some of Simone's fear of the unknown girl.

"The house is yours," said Simone, mistaking his meaning. "The furniture is mine. They can't change that by going round with a piece of chalk. There's always the bank. She can't find *that* suburban." The bank had recently acquired a new and unexpected advantage: it was too small to be nationalized. "Your son is a dreamer," said Simone. "He dreams he is studying, and he fails his exams. He dreams about sex and revolutions, and he waits around for letters and listens to old men telling silly tales."

Roger remembered the hole drilled in the wall. An *au pair* girl in the shower was Luc's symbol of sexual mystery. From the great courtesans of his grandfather's time to the prettiest children of the poor in bordellos to a girl glimpsed as she stood drying herself—what a decline! Here was the true comedown, the real debasement of the middle class. Perhaps he would write a book about it; it would at least rival Mr. Brunt's opus about the decline of French officers.

"She can't spell," said Simone, examining the letter again. "If Luc marries her, he will have to write all her invitations and her postcards." What else did women write? She paused, wondering.

"Her journal?" Roger said.

In Cassandra's journal Simone read, "They expect such a lot from that poor clod of a Luc." That night at dinner Simone remarked, "My father once said he could die happy. He had never entertained a foreigner or shaken hands with an Englishman."

Cassandra stared at Roger as if to say, Is she joking? Roger, married twenty-three years, thought she was not. Cassandra's pale hair swung down as she drooped over her plate. She began to pick at something that, according to her diary, made her sick: underdone lamb, cooked the French way, stinking of garlic and spilling blood.

At dawn there was a spring thunderstorm, like the start of civil war. The gunfire died, and a hard, steady rain soaked the tennis court and lawn. Roger got up, first in the household, and let the dog out of the garage, where it slept among piles of paperbacks and rusting cans of weed killer. Roger was forty-eight that day; he hoped no one would notice. He thought he saw yellow roses running along the hedge, but it was a shaft of sunlight. In the kitchen, he found a pot with the remains of last night's coffee and heated some in a saucepan. While he drank, standing, looking out the window, the sky cleared entirely and became soft and blue.

"Happy birthday."

He turned his head, and there was Cassandra in the doorway, wearing a long gypsy skirt and an embroidered nightshirt, with toy rings on every finger. "I thought I'd dress because of

Sunday," she explained. "I thought we might be going to church."

"I could offer you better coffee in the village," said Roger. "If you do not mind the walk." He imagined her diary entry: "The Baron tried to get me alone on a country road, miles from any sign of habitation."

"The dog will come, too," he assured her.

They walked on the rim of wet fields, in which the freed dog leaped. The hem of Cassandra's skirt showed dark where it brushed against drenched grasses. Roger told her that the fields and woods, almost all they could see, had belonged to his grandparents. Cousin Henri owned the land now.

Cassandra knew; when Simone was not talking about Luc and Katia and the government, she talked about Cousin Henri.

"My father wants to write another book, about Torquemada and Stalin and, I think, Cromwell," Cassandra said. "The theme would be single-mindedness. But he can't get down to it. My mother doesn't see why he can't write for an hour, then talk to her for an hour. She asks him to help look for things she's lost, like the keys to the car. Before he retired, she was never bored. Now that he's home all day, she wants company and she loses everything."

"How did he write his other books?" said Roger.

"In the minstrel he had a private office and secretary. Two, in fact. He expected to write even more, once he was free, but he obviously won't. If he were alone, I could look after him." That was unexpected. Perhaps Luc knew just how unexpected Cassandra could be, and that was why he stayed away from her. "I don't mean I imagine my mother not there," she said. "I only meant that I could look after him, if I had to."

Half a mile before the village stood Cousin Henri's house. Roger told Cassandra why he and Henri were not speaking, except through lawyers. Henri had been grossly favored by their mutual grandparents, thanks to the trickery of an aunt by marriage, who was Henri's godmother. The aunt, who was very rich as well as mad and childless, had acquired the grandparents' domain, in their lifetime, by offering more money than it was worth. She had done this wicked thing in order to hand it over, intact, unshared, undivided, to Henri, whom she worshipped. The transaction had been brought off on the wrong side of the law, thanks to a clan of Protestants and Freemasons.

Cassandra looked puzzled and pained. "You see, the government of that time..." said Roger, but he fell silent, seeing that Cassandra had stopped understanding. When he was overwrought he sounded like his wife. It was hardly surprising: he was simply repeating, word for word, everything Simone had been saying since they were married. In his own voice, which was ironic and diffident, he told Cassandra why Cousin Henri had never married. At the age of twenty Henri had been made trustee of a family secret. Henri's mother was illegitimate—at any rate, hatched from a cuckoo's egg. Henri's father was not his mother's husband but a country neighbor. Henri had been warned never to marry any of the such-and-such girls, because he might be marrying his own half sister. Henri might not have wanted to: the such-and-suches were ugly and poor. He had used the secret as good reason not to marry anyone, had settled down in the handsomest house in the Yonne (half of which should have been Roger's), and had peopled the neighborhood with his random children.

They slowed walking, and Cassandra looked at a brick-and-stucco box, and some dirty-faced children playing on the steps.

"There, behind the farmhouse," said Roger, showing a dark, severe manor house at the top of a straight drive.

"It looks more like a monastery, don't you think?" said Cassandra. Although Roger seemed to be waiting, she could think of nothing more to say. They walked on, toward Cassandra's breakfast.

On the road back, Roger neither looked at Cousin Henri's house nor mentioned it. They were still at some distance from home when they began to hear Simone: "Marry her! Marry

Katia! Live with Katia! I don't care what you do. Anything, anything, so long as you pass your exam." Roger pushed open the gate and there was Simone, still in her dressing gown, standing on a lawn strewn with Luc's clothes, and Luc at the window, still in pajamas. Luc heaved a chair over the sill, then a couple of pillows and a whole armful of books. Having yelled something vile about the family (they were in disagreement later about what it was), he jumped out, too, and landed easily in a flower bed. He paused to pick up shoes he had flung out earlier, ran awkwardly across the lawn, pushed through a gap in the hedge, and vanished.

"He'll be back," said Simone, gathering books. "He'll want his breakfast. He really is a remarkable athlete. With proper guidance, Luc could have done anything. But Roger never took much interest."

"What was that last thing he said?" said Cassandra.

"Fools," said Simone. "But a common word for it. Never repeat that word, if you want people to think well of you."

"Spies," Roger had heard. In Luc's room he found a pair of sunglasses on the floor. He had noticed Luc limping as he made for the hedge; perhaps he had sprained an ankle. He remembered how Luc had been too tired to walk a dog, too worn out to feed a goldfish. Roger imagined him, now, wandering in muddy farmyards, in shoes and pajamas, children giggling at him—the Clairevoies' mooncalf son. Perhaps he had gone to tell his troubles to that other eccentric, Cousin Henri.

Tears came easily since Roger's last attack. He had been told they were caused by the depressant effect of the pills he had to take. He leaned on the window frame, in the hope of seeing Luc, and wept quietly in the shelter of Luc's glasses.

"It's awfully curious of me," said Cassandra, helping Simone, "but what's got into Luc? When he stayed with us, in England, he was angelic. Your husband seems upset, too."

"The *Baron*," said Simone, letting it be known she had read the diary and was ready for combat, "the *Baron* is too sensible. Today is his birthday. He is forty-eight—nearly fifty."

Roger supposed she meant "sensitive." To correct Simone might create a diversion, but he could not be sure of what kind. To let it stand might bewilder the English girl; but, then, Cassandra was born bewildered.

Luc came home in time for dinner, dressed in a shirt and corduroys belonging to Cousin Henri. His silence, Roger thought, challenged them for questions; none came. He accepted a portion of Roger's birthday cake, which, of course, Roger could not touch, and left half on his plate. "Even as a small child, Luc never cared for chocolate," Simone explained to Cassandra.

The next day, only food favored by Luc was served. Simone turned over a letter from Katia. It was brief and cool in tone: Katia had been exercising horses in a riding school, helping a friend.

The Clairevoies, preceded by Luc on the Honda, packed up and drove back to Paris. This time Cassandra was allowed to sit in front, next to Simone. Roger and the dog shared the back seat with Luc's books and a number of parcels.

They saw Cassandra off at the Gare du Nord. Roger was careful not to take her arm, brush against her, or otherwise inspire a mention in her diary. She wore a T-shirt decorated with a grinning mouth. "It's been really lovely," she said. Roger bowed.

Her letter of thanks arrived promptly. She was planning to help her father with his book on Stalin, Cromwell, and Torquemada. He wanted to include a woman on the list, to bring the work in line with trends of the day. Cassandra had suggested Boadicea, Queen of the Iceni. Boadicea stood for feminine rectitude, firmness, and true love of one's native culture. So Cassandra felt.

"Cassandra has written a most learned and affectionate letter," said Simone, who would never have to see Cassandra again. "I only hope Luc was as polite to the Brunts." Her voice held a new tone of maternal grievance and maternal threat.

Luc, who no longer found threats alarming, packed his books and took the train for Rennes. Katia's letters seemed to have stopped. Searching Luc's room, Simone found nothing to read except a paperback on private ownership. "I believe he is taking an interest in things," she told Roger.

It was late in May when the Clairevoies made their final trip to Rennes. Suspecting what awaited them, Simone wore mourning—a dark linen suit, black sandals, sunglasses. Father Rousseau had on a dark suit and black tie. After some hesitation he said what Roger was waiting to hear: it was useless to make Luc sit for an examination he had not even a remote chance of passing. Luc was unprepared, now and forever. He had, in fact, disappeared, though he had promised to come back once the talk with his parents was over. Luc had confided that he would be content to live like Cousin Henri, without a degree to his name, and with a reliable tenant farmer to keep things running.

My son is a fool, said Roger to himself. Katia, who was certainly beautiful, perhaps even clever, loved him. She stood crying in the street, trying to see a light in his room.

"Luc's cousin is rich," said Simone. "Luc is too pure to understand the difference. He will have to learn something. What about computer training?"

"Luc has a mind too fluid to be restrained," said Father Rousseau.

"Literature?" said Simone, bringing up the last resort.

Roger came to life. "Sorting letters in the post office?"

"Machines do that," said Father Rousseau. "Luc would have to pass a test to show he understands the machine. I have been wondering if there might be in Luc's close environment a family affair." The Clairevoies fell silent. "A family business," Father

Rousseau repeated. "Families are open, airy structures. They take in the dreamy as well as the alert. There is always an extra corner somewhere."

Like most of her women friends, Simone had given up wearing jewelry: the streets were full of anarchists and muggers. One of her friends knew of someone who had had a string of pearls ripped off her neck by a bearded intellectual of the Mediterranean type—that is, quite dark. Simone still kept, for luck, a pair of gold earrings, so large and heavy they looked fake. She touched her talisman earrings and said, "We have in our family a bank too small to be nationalized."

"Congratulations," said Father Rousseau, sincerely. When he got up to see them to the door, Roger saw he wore running shoes.

It fell to Roger to tell Luc what was to become of him. After military service of the most humdrum and unprotected kind, he would move to a provincial town and learn about banks. The conversation took place late one night in Luc's room. Simone had persuaded Roger that Luc needed to be among his own things—the galleon lamp, the Foreign Legion recruiting poster that had replaced Che Guevara, the photograph of Simone that replaced Roger's graduating class. Roger said, somewhat shyly, "You will be that much closer to Biarritz."

"Katia is getting married," said Luc. "His father has a riding school." He said this looking away, rolling a pencil between thumb and finger, something like the way his mother had rolled a kitchen match. Reflected in the dark window, Luc's cheeks were hollowed, his eyes blazing and black. He looked almost a hero and, like most heroes, lonely.

"What happened to your friends?" said Roger. "The friends you used to see every Sunday."

"Oh, that...that fell apart. All the people they ever talked about were already dead. And some of the parents were worried. You were the only parents who never interfered."

"We wanted you to live your own life," said Roger. "It must have been that. Could you get her back?"

"You can do anything with a woman if you give her enough money."

"Who told you a thing like that?" In the window Roger examined the reflected lamp, the very sight of which was supposed to have made a man of Luc.

"Everyone. Cousin Henri. I told her we owned a bank, because Cousin Henri said it would be a good thing to tell her. She asked me how to go about getting a bank loan. That was all."

Does he really believe he owns a bank, Roger wondered. "About money," he said. "Nothing of Cousin Henri's is likely to be ours. Illegitimate children are allowed to inherit now, and my cousin," said Roger with some wonder, "has acknowledged everyone. I pity the schoolteacher. All she ever sees is the same face." This was not what Luc was waiting to hear. "You will inherit everything your mother owns. I have to share with my cousin, because that is how our grandparents arranged it." He did not go on about the Freemasons and Protestants, because Luc already knew.

"It isn't fair," said Luc.

"Then you and your mother share my share."

"How much of yours is mine?" said Luc politely.

"Oh, something at least the size of the tennis court," said Roger.

On Luc's desk stood, silver-framed, another picture of Simone, a charming one taken at the time of her engagement. She wore, already, the gold earrings. Her hair was in the upswept balloon style of the time. Her expression was smiling, confident but untried. Both Luc and Roger suddenly looked at it in silence.

It was Simone's belief that, after Katia, Luc had started sleeping with one of her own friends. She thought she knew the one: the Hungarian wife of an architect, fond of saying she wished she had a daughter the right age for Luc. This was a direct sexual compliment, based on experience, Simone thought. Roger thought it meant nothing at all. It was the kind of empty declaration mothers mistook for appreciation. Simone had asked

Roger to find out what he could, for this was the last chance either of them would ever have to talk to Luc. From now on, he would undoubtedly get along better with his parents, but where there had been a fence there would be a wall. Luc was on his own.

Roger said, "It was often thought, in my day, mainly by foreigners who had never been to France, that young men began their lives with their mother's best friend. Absurd, when you consider it. Why pick an old woman when you can have a young one?" *Buy* a young one, he had been about to say, by mistake. "Your mother's friends often seem young to me. I suppose it has to do with their clothes—so loose, unbuttoned. The disorder is already there. My mother's best friends wore armor. It was called the New Look, invented by Christian Dior, a great defender of matronly virtue." A direct glance from Luc—the first. "There really was a Mr. Dior, just as I suppose there was a Mr. Mercedes and a Mr. Benz. My mother and her friends were put into boned corsets, stiff petticoats, wide-brimmed, murderous hats. Their nails were pointed, and as red as your lampshade. They carried furled parasols with silver handles and metal-edged handbags. Even the heels of their shoes were contrived for braining people. No young man would have gone anywhere near." Luc's eyes met Roger's in the window. "I have often wondered," said Roger, "though I'm not trying to make it my business, what you and Katia could have done. Where could you have taken her? Well, unless she had some private place of her own. There's more and more of that. Daughters of nice couples, people we know. Their own apartment, car, money. Holidays no one knows where. Credit cards, bank accounts, abortions. In my day, we had a miserable amount of spending money, but we had the girls in the Rue Spontini. Long after the bordellos were closed, there was the Rue Spontini. Do you know who first took me there? Cousin Henri. Not surprising, considering the life he has led since. Henri called it 'the annex,' because he ran into so many friends from his school. On Thursday afternoons, that was." A slight question in Luc's eyes. "Thursday was our weekly holiday, like Wednesdays for you. I don't suppose every Wednesday—no, I'm sure you don't. Besides, even the last of those places vanished years ago. There were Belgian girls, Spanish girls from Algeria. Some were so young—oh, very young. One told me I was like a brother. I asked Cousin Henri what she meant. He said he didn't know."

Luc said, "Katia could cry whenever she wanted to." Her face never altered, but two great tears would suddenly brim over and course along her cheeks.

The curtains and shutters were open. Anyone could look in. There was no one in the street—not even a ghost. How real Katia and Luc had seemed; how they had touched what was left of Roger's heart; how he had loved them. Giving them up forever, he said, "I always admired that picture of your mother."

Simone and Roger had become engaged while Roger was still a lieutenant in Algeria. On the night before their wedding, which was to take place at ten o'clock in the morning in the church of Saint-Pierre de Chaillot, Roger paid a wholly unwelcome call. Simone received him alone, in her dressing gown, wearing a fine net over her carefully ballooned hair. Her parents, listening at the door, took it for granted Roger had caught a venereal disease in a North African brothel and wanted the wedding postponed; Simone supposed he had met a richer and prettier girl. All Roger had to say was that he had seen an Algerian prisoner being tortured to death. Simone had often asked Roger, since then, why he had tried to frighten her with something that had so little bearing on their future. Roger could not remember what his reason had been.

He tried, now, to think of something important to say to Luc, as if the essence of his own life could be bottled in words and handed over. Sylvestre, wakened by a familiar voice, came snuffling at the door, expecting at this unsuitable hour to be taken out. Roger remarked, "Whatever happens, don't get your life all mixed up with a dog's."

A PAINFUL AFFAIR

Grippes' opinion remains unchanged: He was the last author to have received a stipend from the Mary Margaret Pugh Arts Foundation, and so it should have fallen to him—Henri Grippes, Parisian novelist, diarist, essayist, polemical journalist, and critic—to preside at the commemoration of the late Miss Pugh's centenary. (This celebration, widely reported in Paris, particularly in publications that seemed to have it in for Grippes, took place in a room lent by the firm of Fronce & Baril, formerly drapers and upholsterers, now purveyors of bluejeans from Madras. The firm's books reveal that Miss Pugh was the first person ever to have opened a charge account—a habit she brought from her native America and is thought to have introduced into France.) But the honor did not fall to M. Grippes. The Pugh Memorial Committee, made up of old-age pensioners from the American Embassy, the Chase Manhattan Bank (Paris), the French Ministry for Culture, and other intellectual oatcakes, chose instead to invite Victor Prism, winkling him with no trouble out of his obscure post at a university in the North of England. Prism's eagerness to get away from England whatever the season, his willingness to travel under foul conditions, for a trifling sum of money, make him a popular feature of subsidized gatherings throughout the Free World. This is still the way Grippes sees things.

Prism, author of *Suomi Serenade: A Key to the Kalevala*, much praised in its day as an outstandingly skillful performance, also thinks Grippes should have been chairman. The fact that the Pugh centenary celebration coincided with the breakup of the M. M. Pugh Investment Trust, from which the Foundation—and, incidentally, M. Grippes—had drawn considerable funds over the years, might have made Grippes' presence in the chair especially poignant. It could also have tested his capacity for showing humility—an accommodation already strained more than once. Think of Grippes, Miss Pugh's youthful protégé, fresh from his father's hog farm in Auvergne, dozing on a bed in her house (a bed that had belonged to Prism a scant six months before), with Rosalia, the maid, sent along every half hour to see how he was getting on with Chapter 2. Think of Grippes at the end, when Miss Pugh's long-lost baby brother, now seventy-something—snappy Hong Kong forty-eight-hour tailoring, silk shirt from Bangkok, arrogant suntan—turned up at her bedside, saying, "Well, Maggie, long time no see."

"She died in his arms," wrote Grippes, in an unusually confidential letter to Prism, "though not without a struggle."

Prism says he had been promised Miss Pugh's library, her collection of autograph letters (Apollinaire to Zola), her matching ormolu-mounted opaline urns, her Meissen coffee service, her father's cufflinks, her Louis XVI period writing table, and the key to a safe-deposit vault containing two Caillebottes and a Morisot. The promise was not kept, but no trick of fortune could possibly erode his gratitude for earlier favors. He still visits Miss Pugh's grave, in a mossy corner of Passy Cemetery, whenever he happens to be in Paris. He leaves a bunch of anemones, or a pot of chrysanthemums, or, when the cost of flowers is really sky-high, merely stands silently with his head bowed. Sunshine flows upon the back of his neck, in a kind of benison. Seeing how the rich are buried imbues him with strengthened faith. He receives the formal promise of a future offered and accepted—a pledge he once believed existed in art. He thinks of Grippes, in his flat across the Seine, scribbling away amid Miss Pugh's furniture and his tribe of stray cats.

Grippes says he visits Miss Pugh's grave as often as he is able. (He has to find someone to stay with the cats.) Each time he goes to the cemetery he gets caught up in a phalanx of mourners shuffling behind a creeping hearse. The hearse parks close to some family mausoleum that is an architectural echo of the mansions that lined Avenue du Bois before it became Avenue Foch. Waiting for the coffin to be unloaded, the mourners stare at one another's collars. Grippes reads inscriptions on tombstones, some of which indicate with astonishing precision what the occupant expected to find on the other side. In this place, where it is never spring, he is conscious of bare branches, dark birds cawing. The day takes on a grainy texture, like a German Expressionist film. The only color glows from the ribbons and rosettes some of the mourners wear on their lapels. (Among the crumbs flicked in Grippes' direction was Miss Pugh's Legion of Honor, after her brother had been assured it would not fetch one franc, his floor price, at auction.) There is nothing extravagant or dangerous about these excursions. They cost Grippes a Métro ticket each way—direct line, Montparnasse-Trocadéro, no awkward change, no transfer, no flight along underground corridors pursued by a gang of those savage children of whom even the police are afraid.

Prism thinks that Grippes started showing signs of infantile avarice and timidity soon after Miss Pugh's death, which left him homeless. For a time Grippes even thought of moving to London. He sent Prism a letter suggesting they take a flat together and live on their memories. Prism responded with a strange and terrifying account of gang wars, with pimps and blackmailers shot dead on the steps of the National Gallery. In

Paris, Prism wrote, Grippes could be recognized on sight as a literary odd-jobs man with style. No one would call him a climber—at least, not to his face. Rather, Grippes seemed to have been dropped in early youth onto one of those middling-high peaks of Paris bohemia from which the artist can see both machine-knit and cashmere blazers hanging in Boulevard Haussmann department stores and five-thousand-franc custom tailoring. In England, where caste signs were radically different, he might give the false impression that he was a procurer or a drug pusher and be gunned down at a bus stop.

After reading this letter, Grippes got out a map of London and studied it. It looked crowded and untidy. He cashed in about half the bonds Miss Pugh had made over to him in her lifetime and bought four rooms above a cinema in Montparnasse. While he was showing the removal men where to place Miss Pugh's writing table, a cat came mewing at the door and he let it in.

Grippes denies the imputation of avarice. When Prism gave his famous lecture in Brussels, in 1970, "Is Language a Deterrent?," Grippes travelled by train to hear him, at his own expense. He recalls that Prism was wearing a green corduroy suit, a canary-yellow V-neck sweater, and a tie that must have been a souvenir of Belfast. On his return to Paris, Grippes wrote a lighthearted essay about *le style Anglais*.

J ust before the centennial, Prism was interviewed on French television: eighteen minutes of Victor Prism, at a green baize table, with an adulating journalist who seemed to have been dipped in shellac. Prism's French had not deteriorated, though it still sounded to Grippes like dried peas rattling in a tin can. "The fact is," he said, rattling, "that I am the only person who knew Miss Pugh well—apart from her devoted servant Rosalia, that is. All raise hands, please, who remember Rosalia. (*Camera on studio smiles*) I am the person who called on Miss Pugh after she was evicted from her beautiful house and transported by ambulance to a nursing home in Meudon. She never quite understood that she had bought a house but not the land it stood on. (*Sympathetic laughter*) The last time I saw her, she was sitting up in bed, wearing her sapphire earrings, drinking a bottle of Veuve Clicquot. I have forgotten to say that she was by now completely bald, which did not make her in the least self-conscious. (*Immense good will*) I was obliged to return to England, believing I was leaving Miss Pugh in radiant health and in trusted hands." (*Audience delight*)

A heavily edited version of Grippes' answer appeared in *Le Figaro*, under the heading "A Painful Affair: Further Correspondence." Mr. Prism had neglected to mention the date of Miss Pugh's transfer to the nursing home: 10 May, 1968. Clouds of tear gas. Cars overturned in Paris streets. Grippes' long-awaited autobiographical novel, *Sleeping on the Beach*, had appeared the day before. His stoic gloom as he watched students flinging the whole of the first edition onto a bonfire blazing as high as second-story windows. Grippes' publisher, crouched in his shabby office just around the corner, had already hung on the wall the photograph of some hairy author he hoped would pass for Engels. The glow from the bonfire tinged bogus Engels pink, investing him with the hearty tone that had quit the publisher's cheeks when, early that morning, a delegation representing what might well turn out to be a New Order had invaded the premises. Grippes, pale trenchcoat over dark turtleneck, hands clenched in trenchcoat pockets, knew he was aging, irreversibly, minute by minute. Some of the students thought he was Herbert Marcuse and tried to carry him on their shoulders to *Le Figaro*'s editorial offices, which they hoped he would set on fire. The melancholia that descended on Grippes that evening made him unfit to help and sustain an old lady who was said to be spending all her time sulking under a bedsheet and refusing to eat. He managed to be with Miss Pugh at the end, however, and distinctly heard her say something coherent about the disposal of her furniture. As for *Sleeping on the Beach*, it was never reprinted, for the usual craven reasons.

Prism says that even before the Pugh Investment Trust filed its bankruptcy petition before a Paris court, the dismantling of Miss Pugh's house had been completed, with the wainscoting on the staircase stripped and sold to a tearoom and what remained of the silver, pictures, and furniture brought under the hammer. (Grippes and Rosalia had already removed some of the better pieces, for safety.) Her will was so ambiguous that, to avoid litigation, Miss Pugh's brother and the Trust split the proceeds, leaving Prism and a few other faithful friends of hers in the cold. Grippes is suspected of having gold ingots under the bed, bullion in the bathtub, gold napoleons in his shoes. The fact is (Grippes can prove it) that Miss Pugh's personal income had been declining for years, owing to her steadfast belief that travel by steamship would soon supersede the rage for planes. "Her private investments followed her convictions as night follows day," writes Grippes, with the cats for company. "And, one day, night fell."

Prism discovered that some of the furniture removed for safety was in the parlor of Rosalia's son, permanent mayor and Mafia delegate of a town in Sicily. He at once dispatched an expert appraiser, who declared the whole lot to be fake. It may have been that on a pink marble floor, against pink wall hangings, in a room containing a bar on which clockwork figures of Bonaparte and Josephine could be made to play Ping-Pong, Miss Pugh's effects took on an aura of sham. Still, the expert seemed sincere to Prism. He said the Boulle chest was the kind they still manufacture on the Rue du Faubourg Saint-Martin, scar with bleach, beat with chains, then spend years restoring.

About a month after the funeral, a letter appeared in *Le Matin de Paris*, signed "Old-Style Socialist." The writer recalled that some forty years before, a Miss Pugh (correctly spelled) had purchased from an antique dealer a wooden statue said to represent St. Cumula, virgin and martyr. (A brief history of Cumula followed: about to be forced into marriage with a pagan

Gaul, Cumula painted herself purple and jumped into the Seine, where she drowned. The pagan, touched by her unwavering detestation of him, accepted Christian baptism, on the site of what is now the Paris Stock Exchange.) Miss Pugh had the effigy restored to its original purple and offered it to the Archbishop of Paris. After several coats of paint were removed, the carving was found to be a likeness of General Marchand, leader of the French Nile Expedition. The Archbishop declined the present, giving as his reason the separation of church and state. "Old-Style Socialist" wondered what had become of the carving, for even if General Marchand stood for nineteenth-century colonial policy at its most offensive, history was history, art was art, and it was easily proved that some persons never ceased to meddle in both.

Prism believes Grippes might have had some talent to begin with but that he wasted it writing tomfool letters. He thinks a note that came in the mail recently was from Grippes: "Dear Ms. Victoria Prism, I teach Creative Journalism to a trilingual class here in California (Spanish/Chinese/some English). In the past you have written a lot of stuff that was funny and made us laugh. Lately you published something about the lingering death of a helicopter pilot. Is this a new departure? Please limit your answer to 200 words. My class gets tired." The letter had an American stamp and a Los Angeles postmark, but Prism has known Grippes to spend days over such details.

Grippes says that Prism's talent is like one of those toy engines made of plastic glass, every part transparent and moving to no purpose. The engine can be plugged in to a power outlet, but it can't be harnessed. In short, Prism symbolizes the state of English letters since the nineteen-fifties.

"You ought to write your memoirs," Grippes said to Prism at Miss Pugh's funeral. Prism thought Grippes was hoping to be provided with grounds for a successful libel action. (He concedes that Grippes looked fine that day: dark tie, dark suit, well brushed—he hadn't begun collecting cats yet.)

Actually, Prism is pretty sure he could fill two volumes, four hundred pages each, dark-green covers, nice paper, nice to touch. A title he has in mind is *Bridge Building Between Cultures*.

Grippes started his own memoirs about a year ago, basing them on his diaries. He wouldn't turn down a Bibliothèque de la Pléiade edition, about a thousand pages of Bible-weight paper, fifty pages of pictures, full Grippes bibliography, appreciative introductory essay by someone he has not quarrelled with, frontispiece of Grippes at the window, back to the light, three-quarter profile, cat on his shoulder. He'd need pictures of Miss Pugh: there are none. She loathed sitting for portraits, photographs, snapshots. Old prints of her house exist, their negatives lost or chewed by mice. The Pugh Memorial Committee donated a few to the Museum of Popular Arts and Traditions, where they were immediately filed under "Puget, Pierre, French sculptor."

"Research might have better luck at the University of Zurich," writes Grippes, at Miss Pugh's Louis XVI period table. "A tireless Swiss team has been on the trail of Miss Pugh for some time now, and a cowed Swiss computer throws up only occasional anarchy, describing Pugh M. M., Pullman G. M., and Pulitzer J. as the same generous American."

Prism's quiet collaboration with Zurich, expected to culminate in a top-quality volume, *Hostess to Fame*, beige linen cover, ended when he understood that he was not going to be paid anything, and that it would be fifteen years before the first word was transferred from tape to paper.

Grippes says he heard one of the tapes:

"Mr. Prism, kindly listen to the name I shall now pronounce. François Mauriac. The thin, sardonic gentleman who put on a bowler hat every morning before proceeding to Mass was François Mauriac. Right?"

"I don't remember a François."

"Think. François. Mauriac."

"I don't remember a bowler hat."

At the centennial commemoration, Prism stood on a little dais, dressed in a great amount of tweed and flannel that seemed to have been cut for a much larger man. Grippes suspects that Prism's clothes are being selected by his widowed sister, who, after years of trying to marry him off to her closest friends, is now hoping to make him seem as unattractive as possible. Imagining Prism's future—a cottage in Devon, his sister saying, "There was a letter for you, but I can't remember what I did with it"—he heard Prism declare he was happy to be here, in a place obligingly provided; the firm's old boardroom, back in the days when Paris was still; the really fine walnut panelling on two of the; about the shortage of chairs, but the Committee had not expected such a large; some doubtless disturbed by an inexplicable smell of moth repellent, but the Committee was in no way; in honor of a great and charitable American, to whom the cultural life of; looking around, he was pleased to see one or two young faces.

With this, Prism stepped down, and had to be reminded he was chairman and principal speaker. He climbed back, and delivered from memory an old lecture of his on Gertrude Stein. He then found and read a letter Miss Pugh had received from the President of the Republic, in 1934, telling her that although she was a woman, and a foreigner, she was surely immortal. Folding the letter, Prism suddenly recalled and described a conversation with Miss Pugh.

"Those of us who believe in art," Prism had started to say.

Miss Pugh had coughed and said, "I don't."

She did not believe in art, only in artists. She had no interest in books, only in their authors. Reading an early poem of Prism's (it was years since he had written any poetry, he hastened to say), she had been stopped by the description of a certain kind of butterfly, "pale yellow, with a spot like the Eye of God." She had sent for her copy of the Larousse dictionary, which Rosalia was using in the kitchen as a weight on sliced cucumbers. Turning to a color plate, Miss Pugh had found the butterfly at once. It turned out to be orange rather than yellow, and heavily spotted with black. Moreover, it was not a European butterfly but an Asian moth. The Larousse must be mistaken. She had shut the dictionary with a slap, blaming its editors for carelessness. If only there had been more women like her, Prism concluded, there would be more people today who knew what they were doing.

Grippes says that, for once, he feels inclined to agree. All the same, he wishes Prism had suppressed the anecdote. Prism knows as well as Grippes does that some things are better left as legends.

LARRY

S ome men give their children sound advice about property
and investment. The elder Pugh had the nerve to give
advice about marriage—this to the son of a wife he had
deserted. He was in Paris on a visit and had come round to see
what Larry was up to. It was during the hot, quiet summer of
1954.

Larry was caretaking for July and August. He had the run of
sixteen dust-sheeted rooms, some overlooking the Parc de Mon-
ceau, some looking straight onto the shuttered windows of other
stone houses. Twice a week a woman arrived to clean and, Larry
supposed, to make sure he hadn't stolen anything.

He was not a thief—only a planner. His plans required the
knowledge of where things were kept and what they amounted
to. After a false start as a sculptor he was trying to find an open
road. He went through the drawers and closets left unlocked and
came across a number of towels and bathmats and blankets stolen
from hotels; pilfering of that sort was one of the perks of the rich.
A stack of hotel writing paper gave him a new idea for teasing

Maggie, his half sister, who also lived in Paris—near the Trocadéro, about eight Métro stops away.

The distance between Larry and Maggie was greater than any stretch of city blocks. He saw it as a treeless plain. It was she who kept the terrain bare, so that she could see Larry coming. He had to surmise, because it would be senseless to do anything else, that Maggie failed to trust him. He wondered why. Total strangers, with even more reason to feel suspicious, gave him the keys to their house. When he looked in a mirror, he felt he could trust himself. A French law obliges children to support indigent parents and, in one or two rare cases Larry had heard of, siblings—a sister or brother. Maggie probably lived with the fear of seeing Larry shuffling up to the front door, palm up. Or carrying a briefcase stuffed with claims and final warnings. Or ringing the bell, in a tearing hurry, with a lawyer waiting in a taxi. Or that she would be called to his bedside at the American Hospital in Neuilly, with an itemized statement for intensive care prepared at checkout. She might even be afraid she would have to bury him, in the unlikely event of his dying first. Maggie's mother, but not Larry's, had been crowningly rich. Larry's generation would have said that he and Maggie had different genes; Maggie's would have taken it for granted they had different prospects.

Fiddling around with the hotel stationery, he sent Maggie letters from Le Palais in Biarritz, the Hôtel de Paris in Monte Carlo, Le Royal at Évian-les-Bains, Le Golf at Deauville. Some carried the terrifying P.S. "See you soon!" From the Paris Ritz he counselled her not to mind the number of bills he was having referred to her from Biarritz and those other places: he had made a killing in Portuguese oysters and would settle up with her before long.

He wondered if the tease had worked, and if she had bothered to look at the postmarks. He had sent all the letters from the same post office, on Boulevard Malesherbes. The postmarks should have shown Maggie that it was just a prank, not an operation. But then she probably thought him too old for practical jokes and wholly unsuited for operations. A true trickster needed to have the elder Pugh's clear conscience—his perfect innocence.

Paris was hushed, eerie, Larry's father said. That was what he noticed after so many years. He'd gone back to America long before the war. For some time now Maggie had been paying him an allowance to keep away. She lived in Paris because she always had; it did not mean that she kept open house. Larry was here for a different reason: he had been at the Beaux Arts for as long as he could stretch the G.I. Bill. He was just wavering at present: stay or go.

He told his father why Paris was silent. There was a new law about traffic horns. His father said he didn't believe it.

Here, near the park, in midsummer, there was no traffic to speak of. In the still of the afternoon they heard the braking of a bus across the empty streets. Shutters were bolted, curtains drawn on the streets with art names: Murillo, Rembrandt, Van Dyck.

Larry's father said, "I suppose you found out there wasn't much to art in the long run." From anyone else it would have been wounding. His father meant only that there were better things in life, not that anyone had failed him.

Larry took the dust sheets off an inlaid table and two pink easy chairs. The liquor cabinet was easy to pry open; he managed with a fork and spoon. They pushed their chairs over to a window. It was curious, his father remarked, how the French never wanted to look *out*. Notice the way salon furniture is placed—those stiff little circles. People always sat as if they weren't sure what to do with their ankles and knees.

The drawing room was pale in color, and yet it soaked up the light. Larry was about to ask if his father had ever seen a total eclipse, when the old man said, "Who lives around here? It was a good address before the war."

Before the other war, he meant—before 1914. He was fine-looking—high-bridged nose, only slightly veined; tough, kindly blue eyes. He seemed brainless to Larry, like Maggie, but a stranger might not have noticed. His gaze was alert as a wren's, his expression one of narrow sincerity. If there were such a thing as artistic truth, his face would have been more ingratiating; about half his plots and schemes had always died on the branch. He must have seen the other half as enough. Unlike most con men, Larry's father acted on sudden inclinations. It was a wonder anything bloomed at all.

Larry did not think of himself as brainless. He did not even consider himself unlucky, which proved he was smart. He was not sure whether his face said anything useful. It was almost too late to decide. He had stopped being young.

His father had no real age; certainly none in his own mind. He sat, comfortable and alert, drinking Larry's patron's best Scotch, telling Larry about a wonderful young woman who was dying to marry him. But, he said, probably having quite correctly guessed that Maggie would cut his funds at the very glimmer of a new wedding, he thought he'd keep the dew on the rose; stick to untrammelled romance; maintain the constant delight and astonishment reserved for unattached lovers. She was attractive, warmhearted, and intelligent; made all her own clothes.

Larry refrained from asking questions, partly out of loyalty to his late, put-upon mother. Dead or alive, she had heard enough.

"Marriage is sex," said his father. "But money is not necessarily anything along that line." In spite of his wish not to be drawn, Larry could not help mulling this over. His father was always at his most dangerous, morally speaking, when he made no sense. "The richer she is, the lower the class of her lovers. If you marry a rich woman, keep an eye on the chauffeur. Watch out for unemployed actors, sailors, tailors. *Customs* officers," he said, as though suddenly remembering. He may have been recalling Maggie's mother. He sighed, though not out of discontent or sorrow, and lifted his firm blue gaze to an oil portrait of a woman wearing pearls Maggie's mother would have swum the Amazon for. "I was never really excited by rich women," he said calmly. "Actually, I think only homosexuals are. Well, it is all a part of God's good plan, laid out for our pleasure, like the flower beds down there in the park."

Larry's father was a pagan who regularly prayed for guidance. He thought nothing of summoning God to smile on His unenlightened creations. Maggie, another object of close celestial attention, believed something should be done about the nature of the universe—some tidying-up job. She was ready to take it on and was only waiting to be asked. Larry lived at about eye level. He tried the Catholics, who said, "What would you like? Jam for breakfast? Eternal life? They're yours, but there's a catch." The Protestants greeted his return with "Shut up. Sit down. Think it over." It was like swimming back and forth between two crowded rafts.

"I met *your* mother just before I lost most of my money," his father said, which was a whitewashed way of explaining he had been involved in a mining-stock scandal of great proportions. "Never make the mistake of imagining a dumb woman is going to be more restful than a smart one. Most men crack up on that. They think 'dumb' means 'silent.' They think it's going to be like the baaing of a lamb and the cooing of a dove, and they won't need to answer. But soon it's 'Do you still love me?,' and that can't be left in the air. Then it turns into 'Did you love me when we got married? Did you love me when I was pregnant? Did you love me last week? Do you love me now?'"

Larry said, "I saw Maggie about a year ago. She says she's leaving everything to an arts foundation."

"She can't," said his father.

"She thinks she can, and she's got lawyers. It's her way of wanting to be remembered. But it's the wrong way. The French never remember anything except their own wars. She won't even have her name on a birdbath."

"Now, that's where you're wrong," his father said. "There'll be a memorial birdbath and Maggie's name—which, incidentally is yours and mine; I'm leaving you both a good name—and in the bowl of the birdbath there'll be the Stars and Stripes in red-white-and-blue mosaic. That is exactly what they'll give Maggie's memory. Where they will choose to put the monument I can't predict. No sane man wants to survive his own children, so I won't say I'd like to see the inaugural ceremony. You'll be there, though—well dressed and smiling. Life has been good to me. I hope it's just as good to you."

It was true that life had treated the old man gently; it had kept him out of jail and in cheerful company.

"I haven't made a formal will yet," he said, quite as though he had anything to leave. "But there's one particular thing I want *you* to have. It's a painting of me. I sat for it here, in Paris, before the war. Around 1912. I don't remember the artist's name, but he was big in those days. If you ever have a son, I want him to have the picture. Promise me you'll come and get it no matter where you happen to be when I go."

He helped himself to a drink and, as though no answer from Larry were needed, began to talk about something else he owned—an ancient hookah, a museum piece. Maggie would appreciate having it, he thought.

Larry noticed that their drinks were leaving rings on the inlaid table. He rubbed them with a corner of a dust sheet, but it was too late.

The next day, while he was trying to sandpaper the stains, Larry remembered the portrait. It showed his father wearing a hat at a jaunty angle, his hands clasped on a walking stick. He appeared to be elegant and reliable, the way things and people are always said to have been when one looks back at them across a war.

When Larry's father left Larry and his mother, he took the portrait with him. It must have been hanging in a dining room, because Larry saw him taking it down, and then tossing a bundle of money, cash, on a polished table. His mother sat in profile, turned away, arms folded. She looked toward, but not at, the little glass shelves at the window, where she kept her collection of miniature cacti in pottery dishes. She wore the look of dark grieving no child can enter. When he saw that she was not going to turn back his way or say something to him, Larry's father secured the portrait under his arm and walked out. There was a blank place on the wall, and on the table, deeply reflected, a packet of bills that seemed a lot but that never was or could be enough.

Over the next few days and until the end of August, when it was time for Larry to move on, he continued to work on the inlaid table, repeating the operation of sandpaper and wax until the rings showed but palely, and only under direct, strong light. Except for those faint circles, and a few sheets of hotel stationery and a few ounces of whiskey gone, he left no other trace behind him of loss or mischief.

A FLYING START

The project for a three-volume dictionary of literary biography, *Living Authors of the Fourth Republic*, was set afloat in Paris in 1952, with an eleven-man editorial committee in the same lifeboat. The young and promising Henri Grippes, spokesman for a new and impertinent generation, waited on shore for news of mass drownings; so he says now. A few years later, when the working title had to be changed to *Living Authors of the Fifth Republic*, Grippes was invited aboard. In 1964, Grippes announced there were not enough living authors to fill three volumes, and was heaved over the side. Actually, he had just accepted a post as writer-in-residence at a women's college in California; from the Pacific shore he sent a number of open letters to Paris weeklies, denouncing the dictionary scheme as an attempt to establish a form of literary pecking order. Anti-élitism was in the air, and Grippes' views received great prominence. His return to Paris found a new conflict raging: *two* volumes were now to be produced, under the brusque and fashionable title *Contemporary Writers, Women and Others*. Grippes at once published a pamphlet revealing that it was a police dodge for feeding women and others into a multinational computer. In the event of invasion, the computer would cough up the names and the authors would be lined up and marched to forced labor in insurance companies. He carried the day, and for a time the idea of any contemporary literary directory was dropped.

Grippes had by then come into a little money, and had bought himself an apartment over a cinema in Montparnasse. He wore a wide felt hat and a velvet jacket in cool weather and a panama straw and a linen coat when it was fine. Instead of a shopping bag he carried a briefcase. He wrote to the mayor of Paris—who answered, calling him "Maître"—to protest a plan to remove the statue of Balzac from Boulevard Raspail, just north of the Boulevard du Montparnasse intersection. It was true that the statue was hemmed in by cars illegally parked and that it was defiled by pigeons, but Grippes was used to seeing it there. He also deplored that the clock on the corner near the Dôme no longer kept time; Grippes meant by this that it did not keep the same time as his watch, which he often forgot to wind.

In the meantime the old two-volume project, with its aging and dwindled editorial committee and its cargo of card-index files, had floated toward a reliable firm that published old-fashioned history manuals with plenty of color plates, and geography books that drew attention only to territories that were not under dispute. The Ministry of Culture was thought to be behind the venture. The files, no one quite knew how, were pried away from the committee and confided to a professor of English literature at a provincial university. The *Angliciste* would be unlikely to favor one school of French writing over another, for the simple reason that he did not know one from the other. The original committee had known a great deal, which was why for some thirty years its members had been in continual deadlock.

It seemed to the *Angliciste* that the work would have wider appeal if a section was included on British writers known for their slavish cultural allegiance to France. First on the list was, of

course, Victor Prism, lifelong and distinguished Francophile and
an old academic acquaintance. He recalled that Prism had once
lived in Paris as the protégé of Miss Mary Margaret Pugh, a
patroness of the arts; so, at about the same time, had the future
novelist and critic Henri Grippes. "Two golden lion cubs in the
golden cage of the great lioness," as the *Angliciste* wrote
Grippes, asking him to contribute a concise appreciation of his
comrade in early youth. "Just say what semed to you to be
prophetic of his achievement. We are in a great hurry. The work
is now called *French Authors, 1950–2000*, and we must go to
press by 1990 if it is to have any meaning for our time. Don't
trouble about Prism's career; the facts are on record. Payment
upon receipt of contribution, alas. The Ministry is being firm."

Grippes received the letter a week before Christmas. He
thought of sending Prism a sixteen-page questionnaire but
decided, reasonably, that it might dull the effect of surprise. He
set to work, and by dint of constant application completed his
memoir the following Easter. It was handwritten, of course; even
his sojourn in California had not reconciled Grippes to typewriters. "I feel certain this is what you are after," he wrote the
Angliciste. "A protrait of Prism as protégé. It was an experience
that changed his external image. Miss Pugh often said he had
arrived on her doorstep looking as if he had spent his life in the
rain waiting for a London bus. By the time he left, a few weeks
later, a wholehearted commitment to the popular Parisian idols
of the period—Sartre, Camus, and Charles Trenet—caused him
to wear a little gray hat with turned-up brim, a black shirt, an off-
white tie, and voluminous trousers. At his request, Miss Pugh
gave him a farewell present of crêpe-soled shoes. Perhaps, with
luck, you may find a picture of him so attired."

G rippes' memoir was untitled.
     "'The drawing room at the Duchess of B——'s over-
looked a leafy avenue and a rustic bandstand in the city of O——.

There, summer after summer, the Duchess had watched children rolling their hoops to the strains of a polka, or a waltz, or a mazurka, or a sparkling military march, remote indeed from the harsh sound of warfare that assailed her today.'

"Would anyone believe, now, that Victor Prism could have written this? That Prism could have poured out, even once, the old bourgeois caramel sauce?

"He did. The time was soon after the end of the Second World War. They were the first words of his first unfinished novel, and they so impressed Miss Mary Margaret Pugh, an American lady then living in a bosky, sunless, and costly corner of Paris, that she invited Prism to complete the novel in her house.

"His benefactress, if extant, would be well over a hundred. In his unpublished roman à clef, *Goldfinches Have Yellow Feathers*, Prism left a picture of Miss Pugh he may still consider fair: 'Miss Melbourne, from a distance, reminded Christopher of those statues of deposed monarchs one can see at seedy summer resorts along the Adriatic. Close up, she looked softer, middle-class, and wholly alarming. Often as Christopher sat across from Miss Melbourne, trying to eat his lunch and at the same time answer her unexpected questions, he would recall a portrait he had seen of a Renaissance merchant's shrewd, hardy wife. It had something to do with Miss Melbourne's plump shoulders and small pink nose, with her habit of fingering the lockets and laces she wore as though drawing the artist's attention to essentials.'

"Miss Pugh had spent most of her life abroad, which was not unusual for rich spinsters of her generation. She seldom mentioned her father, a common fortune hunter, soon shed by her mother—tactful hostess, careful parent, trusted friend to artists and writers. The ash tree whose shade contributed no little to the primeval twilight of the dining room had grown from a sapling presented by Edith Wharton. As a girl, Miss Pugh had been allowed to peer round the door and watch her renowned compatriot eating sole meunière. She had not been presented to Mrs. Wharton, who was divorced.

"What constituted the difference between Mrs. Pugh, also divorced, and the novelist? It is likely that Miss Pugh never asked herself this question. Most of her interesting anecdotes drifted off in this way, into the haze of ancient social mystery.

"The house that was to be Victor Prism's refuge for a summer had been built in the eighteen-fifties, in a quiet street straggling downhill from the Trocadéro. Miss Pugh had inherited, along with the house, a legend that Balzac wrote *Cousine Bette* in the upstairs sitting room, though the prolific author had been buried a good three years before the foundation was dug. *Madame mère* probably bought the house in the eighteen-eighties. Soon after that, the character of the street changed. A considerable amount of low-value property changed hands. Most of the small houses were destroyed or became surrounded by seven-story apartment buildings made of stone, sturdily Third Republic in style. The house we are speaking of was now actually at the heart of a block, connected to the world by a narrow carriage drive, the latter a subject of perennial litigation. Tenants of the apartments could look down upon a low red-brick dwelling with a slate roof, an ash tree that managed to flourish without sunlight, dense thickets of indeterminate urban shrubbery, a bronze Italian birdbath, and a Cupid on tiptoe. The path from gate to door was always wet underfoot, like the floor of a forest.

"Inside, the rooms were low and dim, the floors warped and uneven. Coal fires burned to no great effect except further to darken the walls. Half the rooms by the nineteen-forties were shut off. Miss Pugh was no stingier than any other rich woman, nor had there as yet been an appreciable decline in her income. She was taking it for granted there would soon be another war, followed this time by the definitive revolution. Her daydreams were populated by Bolsheviks, swarming up the Trocadéro hill, waving eviction notices. Why create more comfort than one could bear to lose?

" 'To enjoy it, even for a minute' would have been the answer of a Victor Prism, or, for that matter, of any other of the gifted drifters for whom Paris had become a catchall, and to whom Miss Pugh offered conversation and asylum. Some were political refugees of the first postwar wave, regarded everywhere with immense suspicion. It was thought they should go back to wherever they'd come from and help build just, Spartan societies. Not so Miss Pugh, who thought they should sit down in one of the upstairs rooms and write about their mothers. Some were young men on the run from the legend of a heroic father, whose jaunty wartime face, smiling from a mantelshelf, was enough to launch any son into a life of firm and steady goldbricking. Some, like Prism, were trying to climb on the right American springboard for a flying start.

"'What is your ideal?' Miss Pugh liked to ask. 'At your age, you can't live without one.'

"Thirty, forty years ago, 'ideal' opened the way to tumbledown houses like Miss Pugh's that were really fairy castles. The moat was flooded with American generosity and American contrition. Probably no moat in history was ever so easy to bridge. (Any young European thinking of making that crossing today should be warned that the contrition silted up in the early nineteen-seventies, after which the castle was abandoned.) Miss Pugh did not expect gratitude for material favors, and would have considered it a base emotion. But she had no qualms about showing a stern face to any protégé who revealed himself to be untalented, bereft of an ideal in working order, mentally idle, or coarsely materialistic. This our poor Victor Prism was to learn before the summer was out. Miss Pugh belonged to a small Christian congregation that took its substance from Buddhism. She treated most living creatures equally and made little distinction between man and worm.

"How did Prism turn into a protégé? Easily; he rang a doorbell. Rosalia answered to a young man who was carrying a manila envelope, manuscript-sized, and a letter. She reached for the letter of introduction but did not let Prism in, even though large drops of rain had started to fall.

"Miss Pugh, upstairs in the Balzac sitting room, addressed, from the window, a troubled-looking patch of sky. 'Hasn't this been going on long enough?' Rosalia heard her say. 'Why don't you do something?'

"The answer to Miss Pugh's cosmic despair, or impertinence, was Victor Prism. She had been acknowledged by the universe before now, but perhaps never so quickly. She sat down with her back to the window, read the letter Rosalia gave her, folded it, thought it over, and said, 'All right. Bring him up.'

"Prism came into her presence with a step that lost its assurance as he drew near. He asked permission to sit down. Having obtained a nod, he placed his manila envelope on a low table, where Miss Pugh could reach it easily, and repeated everything she had just read in the letter: He was promising but poor. He had been staying with Mrs. Hartley-Greene on Avenue Gabriel. Mrs. Hartley-Greene had been indescribably helpful and kind. However, she was interested in painters, not in writers—particularly writers of prose.

"Miss Pugh said, 'Then you aren't that poet.'

"'No, no,' said Prism. 'I am not that...that.'

"He was puzzled by the house, believing that it had deliberately been built at the heart of a hollow square, perhaps by a demented architect, for nonsensical people. Rain poured down on the ash tree and naked Cupid. In a flat across the way a kitchen light went on. Miss Pugh pressed the switch of a green-shaded lamp and considered Prism. He turned his head slightly and observed an oil painting of the martyrdom of St. Sebastian. He thought of mile upon mile of museum portraits—young men, young saints pierced with arrows, with nothing to protect them from the staring of women but a coat of varnish.

"The passage of the envelope from his hands to Miss Pugh's was crucial to his adventure. He wondered if he should speak. At the same time, he hated to let the envelope go. It held his entire capital—two chapters of a novel. He did not know if he would ever write anything better, or even if he could write anything else at all.

"Miss Pugh settled the matter by picking it up. 'It's for me to read, isn't it? I'll do so at once. Perhaps you could come back after dinner tonight.'

"*During* dinner would have suited Prism better: Mrs. Hartley-Greene was under the impression he had already moved out and would not be back except to pick up some luggage. *Goldfinches* gives a vivid account of his retreat: 'Christopher seemed to leave a trail of sawdust. There were arrow wounds everywhere. He did not know what other people thought and felt about anything, but he could sense to a fine degree how they thought and felt about him. He lived on the feelings he aroused, sought acquaintances among those in whom these feelings were not actively hostile, and did not know of any other way to be.'

"Eighty pages were in the envelope, thirty of them blank. Miss Pugh was not forced to spend every minute between tea and dinner reading, though she would have done so gladly. She read anything recommended to her, proceeding slowly, pausing often to wonder if the author was sure of his facts. She had a great fear of being hoodwinked, for she knew by now that in art deception is the rule.

"What Prism had described was an elderly duchess, a loyal old manservant named Norbert, a wounded pigeon, and a nation at war. His fifty completed pages were divided into two chapters.

"Chapter 1: In a city under siege, a duchess wonders how to save the priceless eighteenth-century china presented to her family by the Empress. Whatever food Norbert manages to forage she feeds to her cats. She and Norbert adopt and discard schemes for saving the china. They think about this and discuss it all day long.

"Chapter 2: A pigeon flutters in the window. A cat jumps at it, breaking its wing. The duchess and Norbert hear gunfire moving closer. They discuss a plan for saving the pigeon.

"That was as far as it went. Either Prism did not know what came next or did not want to say. It seemed to Miss Pugh that a good deal had been left in the air. The first thing she asked when he came back that night was if the china was really worth saving.

If it was priceless, as he claimed, then Norbert ought to pack it into cases lined with heavy silver paper. The cases could then be buried in the garden, if the ground was soft. That would depend on the season, which Prism had not described.

"She had begun a process that Prism had not foreseen and that was the most flattering success he might have imagined. Everything in the story was *hers*, from the duchess to the pigeon.

"Next, she gave her attention to the duchess's apartments, which seemed to be in the wing of a palace. Prism had not mentioned the style of architecture of the palace, or its condition. Most palaces nowadays were museums. Miss Pugh advised Prism to give the duchess an address more realistic and to eliminate from her life the threat of war.

"Then, at last, she said the only thing that mattered: she was ready to offer Prism the opportunity for creative endeavor Mrs. Hartley-Greene had been obliged to refuse because of her predilection for painters. Prism could return in the morning, by which time Rosalia would have his room ready. In the meantime, Miss Pugh would comb through the manuscript again.

"In *Goldfinches*, Prism skims over the next few hours. We have only the testimony of Rosalia, which is that he turned up in the morning looking as if he had spent the night curled up in a doorway.

"Miss Pugh was eating her breakfast in the sitting room with the green-shaded lamp and the portrait of St. Sebastian. Through a half-open door Prism caught a glimpse of her large, canopied bed. There was an extra place laid at the table.

" 'I was expecting my brother,' said Miss Pugh. 'But he has been delayed.'

"Instead of breakfast, Pugh was to have the manila envelope. In his account of the scene, Prism makes a curious mistake: 'The morning sun, kept from Christopher by the angle of the yellow awning, slid into view and hit him square in the face. His eyes watered, and as if a film of illusion had been removed. . .' and so on. There was no awning, no sun; the house was down a well.

"Miss Pugh asked Prism what he thought of Picasso. He understood the question as a test. Her rooms gave no clue to her own opinion; there were no Picassos in sight, but that was not to say there never could be. He drew a square in his mind, as a way of steadying his thoughts, and put Picasso in it.

"All at once, in a rush of blinding anger, he knew what he believed. His first words were inaudible, but as he regained hold on his feelings the sense of his wild protest became clear: 'All that money. All that *money*. Does he enjoy it? They say he lives in the kitchen, like a squatter. As if the house did not belong to him. He could travel. He could own things. He could have twenty-two servants. He does not deserve to have a fortune, because he doesn't know how to use one.'

"His hostess plucked at her table napkin. She was accustomed to hearing poor young men say what they could do with money. She had heard the hunger in the voice, the incoherence and the passion. She had often aroused this longing, putting out the bait and withdrawing it, which was the only form of wickedness she knew. She seemed to be reflecting on what Prism had just said. There was no denying it was original. Who ever had seen Picasso at an auction of rare furniture? At the races, straining after one of his own horses? Photographed at a gala evening in Monte Carlo? Boarding a yacht for a cruise in Greek waters?

" 'What do you think?' said Prism boldly.

" 'He is the most attractive man in the world. My brother would look good, too, if he could stop drinking and pull himself together. What's your opinion of his goats?' Prism shook his head. 'The sculpture. You can see Picasso doesn't care for animals. Those goats are half starved. I suppose you'll be wanting to get to work.'

"Prism in a very short time came to the conclusion he had climbed on the wrong springboard. He saw that the anxiety and frustration of patronage, the backer's terror of being duped, of having been taken in, was second only to the protégé's fear of being despoiled, stripped, robbed, and left bankrupt by the side of the road. Miss Pugh did not loosen her grip on his two chapters, and even Prism's decision that he wanted to have nothing more to do with them did not lessen the tension.

"He would not claim those two chapters today. If they followed him in the street, he would probably threaten them with an umbrella. And yet the story is his; it is *his* duchess, *his* rustic bandstand. It was also Miss Pugh's. 'Have you moved that poor woman out of that filthy old palace yet?' she would ask Prism at lunch. 'Have you found out any more about the china?' When the leaves of Mrs. Wharton's ash tree began to droop and turn yellow, patroness and protégé were at a stalemate that could be ended only by sincere admission of defeat. Miss Pugh was in her own house; Prism had to play the loser. One day he sat down at the Louis XVI period table in his room and considered the blank pages still in the manila envelope. He wondered if the time had not come to return to England, try for a good degree, and then teach.

" 'I can always branch out from there,' he said to himself. (How easy it must have sounded.)

"He saw in his mind the museum rooms full of portraits of St. Sebastian, with nothing for protection but a thin coat of varnish. There were two opinions about the conservation of art. One claimed it was a mistake to scour paintings in order to lay bare the original color. The other believed it was essential to do so, even if the artist had made allowances for the mellowing and darkening effect of the glaze, and even if the colors revealed turned out to be harsher than the artist had intended. Prism drew a blank sheet toward him and began to write, 'Are we to take it for granted that the artist thinks he knows what he is doing?' At that moment, Prism the critic was born.

"Miss Pugh was sorry when she heard he wanted to give up the duchess, but it was not her policy to engage the Muses in battle. Prism presented her with the manuscript; she gave him the crêpe-soled shoes. She was never heard to speak of him slightingly, and she read with generous pleasure all the newspaper cuttings concerning himself that he sent her over the years. Whenever he came to Paris Miss Pugh would ask him to tea and rejoiced in the rich texture of his career, which he unfolded by the hour, without tiring speaker or audience. Prism made Miss Pugh the subject of countless comic anecdotes and the central female character of *Goldfinches*. He was always evenhanded."

Another Easter went by before Grippes received an acknowledgment—a modest check in lieu of the promised fee, and an apology: His memoir had been mailed to Victor Prism to be checked for accuracy, and Prism had still not replied. During the year sweeping changes had been made. The *Angliciste* had published a paper on the Common Market as seen through English fiction. It was felt to contain a political bias, and the Ministry had withdrawn support. The publisher had no choice but to replace him as editor by the only responsible person who seemed to be free at the time, a famous *Irlandiste* on leave from a university in Belgium. The *Irlandiste* restored the project to its original three volumes, threw out the English section as irrelevant, and added a division with potted biographies of eight hundred Irish poets favorable to France and the Common Market.

Grippes has heard that it is to be published in 2010, at the very latest. He knows that in the meantime they are bound to call on him again—more and more as time goes on. He is the only person still alive with any sort of memory.

GRIPPES AND POCHE

At an early hour for the French man of letters Henri Grippes—it was a quarter to nine, on an April morning— he sat in a windowless, brown-painted cubicle, facing a slight, mop-headed young man with horn-rimmed glasses and dimples. The man wore a dark tie with a narrow knot and a buttoned-up blazer. His signature was "O. Poche"; his title, on the grubby, pulpy summons Grippes had read, sweating, was "Controller." He must be freshly out of his civil-service training school, Grippes guessed. Even his aspect, of a priest hearing a confession a few yards from the guillotine, seemed newly acquired. Before him lay open a dun-colored folder with not much in it—a letter from Grippes, full of delaying tactics, and copies of his correspondence with a bank in California. It was not true that American banks protected a depositor's secrets; anyway, this one hadn't. Another reason Grippes thought O. Poche must be recent was the way he kept blushing. He was not nearly as pale or as case-hardened as Grippes.

At this time, President de Gaulle had been in power five years, two of which Grippes had spent in blithe writer-in-residenceship in California. Returning to Paris, he had left a bank account behind. It was forbidden, under the Fifth Republic, for a French citizen to have a foreign account. The government might not have cared so much about drachmas or zlotys, but dollars were supposed to be scraped in, converted to francs at bottom rate, and, of course, counted as personal income. Grippes' unwise and furtive moves with trifling sums, his somewhat paranoid disagreements with California over exchange, had finally caught the eye of the Bank of France, as a glistening minnow might attract a dozing whale. The whale swallowed Grippes, found him too small to matter, and spat him out, straight into the path of a water ox called Public Treasury, Direct Taxation, Personal Income. That was Poche.

What Poche had to discuss—a translation of Grippes' novel, the one about the French teacher at the American university and his doomed love affair with his student, Karen-Sue—seemed to embarrass him. Observing Poche with some curiosity, Grippes saw, unreeling, scenes from the younger man's inhibited boyhood. He sensed, then discerned, the Catholic boarding school in bleakest Brittany: the unheated forty-bed dormitory, a nightly torment of unchaste dreams with astonishing partners, a daytime terror of real Hell with real fire.

"Human waywardness is hardly new," said Grippes, feeling more secure now that he had tested Poche and found him provincial. "It no longer shocks anyone."

It was not the moral content of the book he wished to talk over, said Poche, flaming. In any case, he was not qualified to do so: he had flubbed Philosophy and never taken Modern French Thought. (He must be new, Grippes decided. He was babbling.) Frankly, even though he had the figures in front of him, Poche found it hard to believe the American translation had earned its author so little. There must be another considerable sum, placed in some other bank. Perhaps M. Grippes could try to remember.

The figures were true. The translation had done poorly. Failure played to Grippes' advantage, reducing the hint of deliberate tax evasion to a simple oversight. Still, it hurt to have things put so plainly. He felt bound to tell Poche that American readers were no longer interested in the teacher-student imbroglio, though there had been some slight curiosity as to what a foreigner might wring out of the old sponge.

Poche gazed at Grippes. His eyes seemed to Grippes as helpless and eager as those of a gun dog waiting for a command in the right language. Encouraged, Grippes said more: in writing his novel, he had overlooked the essential development—the erring professor was supposed to come home at the end. He could be half dead, limping, on crutches, toothless, jobless, broke, impotent—it didn't matter. He had to be judged and shriven. As further mortification, his wife during his foolish affair would have gone on to be a world-class cellist, under her maiden name. "Wife" had not entered Grippes' cast of characters, probably because, like Poche, he did not have one. (He had noticed Poche did not wear a wedding ring.) Grippes had just left his professor driving off to an airport in blessed weather, whistling a jaunty air.

Poche shook his head. Obviously, it was not the language he was after. He began to write on a clean page of the file, taking no more notice of Grippes.

What a mistake it had been, Grippes reflected, still feeling pain beneath the scar, to have repeated the male teacher–female student pattern. He should have turned it around, identified himself with a brilliant and cynical woman teacher. Unfortunately, unlike Flaubert (his academic stalking-horse), he could not put himself in a woman's place, probably because he thought it an absolutely terrible place to be. The novel had not done well in France, either. (Poche had still to get round to that.) The critics had found Karen-Sue's sociological context obscure. She seemed at a remove from events of her time, unaware of improved literacy figures in North Korea, never once mentioned, or that since the advent of Gaullism it cost twenty-five centimes to mail a letter. The Pill was still unheard of in much of Europe; readers could not understand what it was Karen-Sue

kept forgetting to take, or why Grippes had devoted a contempla-
tive no-action chapter to the abstract essence of risk. The
professor had not given Karen-Sue the cultural and political
enlightenment one might expect from the graduate of a pre-
eminent Paris school. It was a banal story, really, about a pair of
complacently bourgeois lovers. The real victim was Grippes,
seduced and abandoned by the American middle class.

It was Grippes' first outstanding debacle and, for that reason,
the only one of his works he ever reread. He could still hear
Karen-Sue—the true, the original—making of every avowal a
poignant question: "I'm Cairn-Sioux? I know you're busy? It's
just that I don't understand what you said about Flaubert and his
own niece?" He recalled her with tolerance—the same tolerance
that had probably weakened the book.

Grippes was wise enough to realize that the California-bank
affair had been an act of folly, a con man's aberration. He had
thought he would get away with it, knowing all the while he
could not. There existed a deeper treasure for Poche to uncover,
well below Public Treasury sights. Computers had not yet come
into government use; even typewriters were rare—Poche had
summoned Grippes in a cramped, almost secretive hand. It took
time to strike an error, still longer to write a letter about it. In his
youth, Grippes had received from an American patroness of the
arts three rent-bearing apartments in Paris, which he still owned.
(The patroness had been the last of a generous species, Grippes
one of the last young men to benefit from her kind.) He collected
the rents by devious and untraceable means, stowing the cash
obtained in safe deposit. His visible way of life was stoic and plain;
not even the most vigilant Controller could fault his underfur-
nished apartment in Montparnasse, shared with some cats he had
already tried to claim as dependents. He showed none of the
signs of prosperity Public Treasury seemed to like, such as
membership in a golf club.

After a few minutes of speculative anguish in the airless
cubicle, Grippes saw that Poche had no inkling whatever about

the flats. He was chasing something different—the inexistent royalties from the Karen-Sue novel. By a sort of divine even-handedness, Grippes was going to have to pay for imaginary earnings. He put the safe deposit out of his mind, so that it would not show on his face, and said, "What will be left for me, when you've finished adding and subtracting?"

To his surprise, Poche replied in a bold tone, pitched for reciting quotations: "'What is left? What is left? Only what remains at low tide, when small islands are revealed, emerging...'" He stopped quoting and flushed. Obviously, he had committed the worst sort of blunder, had been intimate, had let his own personality show. He had crossed over to his opponent's ground.

"It sounds familiar," said Grippes, enticing him further. "Although, to tell the truth, I don't remember writing it."

"It is a translation," said Poche. "The Anglo-Saxon British author, Victor Prism." He pronounced it "Prissom."

"You've read Prism?" said Grippes, pronouncing correctly the name of an old acquaintance.

"I had to. Prissom was on the preparatory program. Anglo-Saxon Commercial English."

"They stuffed you with foreign writers?" said Grippes. "With so many of us having to go to foreign lands for a living?"

That was perilous: he had just challenged Poche's training, the very foundation of his right to sit there reading Grippes' private mail. But he had suddenly recalled his dismay when as a young man he had looked at a shelf in his room and realized he had to compete with the dead—Proust, Flaubert, Balzac, Stendhal, and on into the dark. The rivalry was infinite, a Milky Way of dead stars still daring to shine. He had invented a law, a moratorium on publication that would eliminate the dead, leaving the skies clear for the living. (All the living? Grippes still couldn't decide.) Foreign writers would be deported to a remote solar system, where they could circle one another.

For Prism, there was no system sufficiently remote. Not so

long ago, interviewed in *The Listener*, Prism had dragged in Grippes, saying that he used to cross the Channel to consult a seer in Half Moon Street, hurrying home to set down the prose revealed from a spirit universe. "Sometimes I actually envied him," Prism was quoted as saying. He sounded as though Grippes were dead. "I used to wish ghost voices would speak to me, too," suggesting ribbons of pure Prism running like ticker tape round the equator of a crystal ball. "Unfortunately, I had to depend on my own creative intelligence, modest though I am sure it was."

Poche did not know about this recent libel in Anglo-Saxon Commercial English. He had been trying to be nice. Grippes made a try of his own, jocular: "I only meant, you could have been reading *me*." The trouble was that he meant it, ferociously.

Poche must have heard the repressed shout. He shut the file and said, "This dossier is too complex for my level. I shall have to send it up to the Inspector." Grippes made a vow that he would never let natural pique get the better of him again.

" Vhat will be left for me?" Grippes asked the Inspector. "When you have finished adding and subtracting?"

Mme. de Pelle did not bother to look up. She said, "Somebody should have taken this file in hand a long time ago. Let us start at the beginning. How long, in all, were you out of the country?"

When Poche said "send up," he'd meant it literally. Grippes looked out on a church where Delacroix had worked and the slow summer rain. At the far end of the square, a few dark shops displayed joyfully trashy religious goods, like the cross set with tiny seashells Mme. de Pelle wore round her neck. Grippes had been raised in an anticlerical household, in a small town where opposing factions were grouped behind the schoolmaster— Grippes' father—and the parish priest. Women, lapsed agnostics, sometimes crossed enemy lines and started going to church. One glimpsed them, all in gray, creeping along a gray-walled street.

"You are free to lodge a protest against the fine," said Mme. de Pelle. "But if you lose the contestation, your fine will be tripled. That is the law."

Grippes decided to transform Mme. de Pelle into the manager of a brothel catering to the Foreign Legion, slovenly in her habits and addicted to chloroform, but he found the idea unpromising. In due course he paid a monstrous penalty, which he did not contest, for fear of drawing attention to the apartments. (It was still believed that he had stashed away millions from the Karen-Sue book, probably in Switzerland.) A summons addressed in O. Poche's shrunken hand, the following spring, showed Grippes he had been tossed back downstairs. After that he forgot about Mme. de Pelle, except now and then.

It was at about this time that a series of novels offered themselves to Grippes—shadowy outlines behind a frosted-glass pane. He knew he must not let them crowd in all together, or keep them waiting too long. His foot against the door, he admitted, one by one, a number of shadows that turned into young men, each bringing his own name and address, his native region of France portrayed on color postcards, and an index of information about his tastes in clothes, love, food, and philosophers, his bent of character, his tics of speech, his attitudes toward God and money, his political bias, and the intimation of a crisis about to explode underfoot. "Antoine" provided a Jesuit confessor, a homosexual affinity, and loss of faith. Spiritual shilly-shallying tends to run long; Antoine's covered more than six hundred pages, making it the thickest work in the Grippes canon. Then came "Thomas," with his Spartan mother on a Provençal fruit farm, rejected in favor of a civil-service career. "Bertrand" followed, adrift in frivolous Paris, tempted by neo-Fascism in the form of a woman wearing a bedjacket trimmed with marabou. "René" cycled round France, reading Chateaubriand when he stopped to rest. One morning he set fire to the barn he had been sleeping in, leaving his books to burn. This was the shortest of the novels, and the most popular with the young. One critic scolded Grippes for using crude symbolism. Another begged him to stop hiding behind "Antoine" and "René" and to take the metaphysical risk of revealing "Henri." But Grippes had tried that once with Karen-Sue, then with a roman à clef mercifully destroyed in the confusion of May, 1968. He took these contretemps for a sign that he was to leave the subjective Grippes alone. The fact that each novel appeared even to Grippes to be a slice of French writing about life as it had been carved up and served a generation before made it seem quietly insurrectional. Nobody was doing this now; no one but Grippes. Grippes, for a time uneasy, decided to go on letting the shadows in.

The announcement of a new publication would bring a summons from Poche. When Poche leaned over the file, now, Grippes saw amid the mop of curls a coin-sized tonsure. His diffident, steely questions tried to elicit from Grippes how many copies were likely to be sold and where Grippes had already put the money. Grippes would give him a copy of the book, inscribed. Poche would turn back the cover and glance at the signature, probably to make certain Grippes had not written something compromising and friendly. He kept the novels in a metal locker, fastened together with government-issue webbing tape and a military-looking buckle. It troubled Grippes to think of his work all in a bundle, in the dark. He thought of old-fashioned milestones, half hidden by weeds, along disused roads. The volumes marked time for Poche, too. He was still a Controller. Perhaps he had to wait for the woman upstairs to retire, so he could take over her title and office. The cubicle needed paint. There was a hole in the brown linoleum, just inside the door. Poche now wore a wedding ring. Grippes wondered if he should congratulate him, but decided to let Poche mention the matter first. He tried to imagine Mme. Poche.

Grippes could swear that in his string of novels nothing had been chipped out of his own past. Antoine, Thomas, Bertrand, and René (and, by now, Clément, Didier, Laurent, Hugues, and Yves) had arrived as strangers, almost like historical figures. At the same time, it seemed to Grippes that their wavering, ruffled reflection should deliver something he alone might recognize. What did he see, bending over the pond of his achievement? He saw a character close-mouthed, cautious, unimaginative, ill at ease, obsessed with particulars. Worse, he was closed against progress, afraid of reform, shut into a literary, reactionary France. How could this be? Grippes had always and sincerely voted left. He had proved he could be reckless, open-minded, indulgent. He was like a father gazing round the breakfast table and suddenly realizing that none of the children are his. His children, if he could call them that, did not even look like him. From Antoine to Yves, his reflected character was small and slight, with a mop of curly hair, horn-rimmed glasses, and dimples.

Grippes believed in the importance of errors. No political system, no love affair, no native inclination, no life itself would be tolerable without a wide mesh for mistakes to slip through. It pleased him that Public Treasury had never caught up with the three apartments—not just for the sake of the cash piling up in safe deposit but for the black hole of error revealed. He and Poche had been together for some years—another blunder. Usually Controller and taxpayer were torn apart after a meeting or two, so that the revenue service would not start taking into consideration the client's aged indigent aunt, his bill for dental surgery, his alimony payments, his perennial mortgage. But possibly no one except Poche could be bothered with Grippes, always making some time-wasting claim for minute professional expenses, backed by a messy-looking certified receipt. Some-times Grippes dared believe Poche admired him, that he hung on to the dossier out of devotion to his books. (This conceit was intensified when Poche began calling him "*Maître*.") Once, Grippes won some City of Paris award and was shown in *France-Soir* shaking hands with the mayor and simultaneously receiving a long, check-filled envelope. Immediately summoned by Poche, expecting a discreet compliment, Grippes found him interested only in the caption under the photo, which made much of the size of the check. Grippes later thought of sending a sneering letter—"Thank you for your warm congratulations"—but he decided in time it was wiser not to fool with Poche. Poche had recently given him a thirty-three-per-cent personal exemption, three per cent more than the outer limit for Grippes' category of unsalaried earners—according to Poche, a group that included, as well as authors, door-to-door salesmen and prostitutes.

The dun-colored Gaullist-era jacket on Grippes' file had worn out long ago and been replaced, in 1969, by a cover in cool banker's green. Green presently made way for a shiny black-and-white marbled effect, reflecting the mood of opulence of the early seventies. Called in for his annual springtime confession, Grippes remarked about the folder: "Culture seems to have taken a decisive turn."

Poche did not ask what culture. He continued bravely, "Food for the cats, *Maître*. We *can't*."

"They depend on me," said Grippes. But they had already settled the cats-as-dependents question once and for all. Poche drooped over Grippes' smudged and unreadable figures. Grippes tried to count the number of times he had examined the top of Poche's head. He still knew nothing about Poche, except for the wedding ring. Somewhere along the way, Poche had tied himself to a need for retirement pay and rich exemptions of his own. In the language of his generation, Poche was a fully structured individual. His vocabulary was sparse and to the point, centered on a single topic. His state training school, the machine that ground out Pelles and Poches all sounding alike, was in Clermont-Ferrand. Grippes was born in the same region. That might have given them something else to talk about, except that Grippes had never been back. Structured Poche probably attended class reunions, was godfather to classmates' children, jotted their birthdays in a leather-covered notebook he never mislaid. Unstructured Grippes could not even remember his own age.

Poche turned over a sheet of paper, read something Grippes could not see, and said, automatically, "We *can't*."

"Nothing is ever as it was," said Grippes, still going on about the marbled-effect folder. It was a remark that usually shut people up, leaving them nowhere to go but a change of subject. Besides, it was true. Nothing can be as it was. Poche and Grippes had just lost a terrifying number of brain cells. They were an instant closer to death. Death was of no interest to Poche. If he ever thought he might cease to exist, he would stop concentrating on other people's business and get down to reading Grippes while there was still time. Grippes wanted to ask, "Do you ever imagine your own funeral?," but it might have been taken as a threatening, gangsterish hint from taxpayer to Controller— worse, far worse, than an attempted bribe.

A folder of a pretty mottled-peach shade appeared. Poche's cubicle was painted soft beige, the torn linoleum repaired. Poche sat in a comfortable armchair resembling the wide leathery seats in smart furniture stores at the upper end of Boulevard Saint-Germain. Grippes had a new, straight metallic chair that shot him bolt upright and hurt his spine. It was the heyday of the Giscardian period, when it seemed more important to keep the buttons polished than to watch where the regiment was heading. Grippes and Poche had not advanced one inch toward each other. Except for the paint and the chairs and "*Maître*," it could have been 1963. No matter how many works were added to the bundle in the locker, no matter how often Grippes had his picture taken, no matter how many Grippes paperbacks blossomed on airport bookstalls, Grippes to Poche remained a button.

The mottled-peach jacket began to darken and fray. Poche said to Grippes, "I asked you to come here, *Maître*, because I find we have overlooked something concerning your income." Grippes' heart gave a lurch. "The other day I came across an old ruling about royalties. How much of your income do you kick back?"

"Excuse me?"

"To publishers, to bookstores," said Poche. "How much?"

"Kick back?"

"What percentage?" said Poche. "Publishers. Printers."

"You mean," said Grippes, after a time, "how much do I pay editors to edit, publishers to publish, printers to print, and booksellers to sell?" He supposed that to Poche such a scheme might sound plausible. It would fit his long view over Grippes' untidy life. Grippes knew most of the literary gossip that went round about himself; the circle was so small that it had to come back. In most stories there was a virus of possibility, but he had never heard anything as absurd as this, or as base.

Poche opened the file, concealing the moldering cover, apparently waiting for Grippes to mention a figure. The nausea Grippes felt he put down to his having come here without breakfast. One does not insult a Controller. He had shouted silently at Poche, years before, and had been sent upstairs to do penance with Mme. de Pelle. It is not good to kick over a chair and stalk out. "I have never been so insulted!" might have no meaning from Grippes, keelhauled month after month in one lumpy review or another. As his works increased from bundle to heap, so they drew intellectual abuse. He welcomed partisan ill-treatment, as warming to him as popular praise. Don't forget me, Grippes silently prayed, standing at the periodicals table in La Hune, the Left Bank bookstore, looking for his own name in those quarterlies no one ever takes home. Don't praise me. Praise is weak stuff. Praise me after I'm dead.

But even the most sour and despairing and close-printed essays were starting to mutter acclaim. The shoreline of the eighties, barely in sight, was ready to welcome Grippes, who had re-established the male as hero, whose left-wing heartbeat could be heard, loyally thumping, behind the armor of his right-wing traditional prose. His re-established hero had curly hair, soft eyes, horn-rimmed glasses, dimples, and a fully structured life. He was pleasing to both sexes and to every type of reader, except for a few thick-ribbed louts. Grippes looked back at Poche, who did not know how closely they were bound. What if he were to say, "This is a preposterous insinuation, a blot on a noble profession and on my reputation in particular," only to have Poche answer, "Too bad, *Maître*—I was trying to help"? He said, as one good-natured fellow to another, "Well, what if I own up to this crime?"

"It's no crime," said Poche. "I simply add the amount to your professional expenses."

"To my rebate?" said Grippes. "To my exemption?"

"It depends on how much."

"A third of my income?" said Grippes, insanely. "Half?"

"A reasonable figure might be twelve and a half per cent."

All this for Grippes. Poche wanted nothing. Grippes considered with awe the only uncorruptible element in a porous society. No secret message had passed between them. He could not even invite Poche to lunch. He wondered if this arrangement had ever actually existed—if there could possibly be a good dodge that he, Grippes, had never heard of. He thought of contemporary authors for whose success there could be no other explanation: it had to be celestial playfulness or twelve and a half per cent. The structure, as Grippes was already calling it, might also just be Poche's innocent, indecent idea about writers.

Poche was reading the file again, though he must have known everything in it by heart. He was as absorbed, as contented, and somehow as pure as a child with a box of paints. At any moment he would raise his tender, bewildered eyes and murmur, "Four dozen typewriter ribbons in a third of the fiscal year, *Maître*? We *can't*."

Grippes tried to compose a face for Poche to encounter, a face above reproach. But writers considered above reproach always looked moody and haggard, about to scream. "Be careful," he was telling himself. "Don't let Poche think he's doing you a favor. These people set traps." Was Poche angling for something? Was this bait? "Attempting to bribe a public servant" the accusation was called. "Bribe" wasn't the word: it was "corruption" the law mentioned—"an attempt to corrupt." All Grippes had ever offered Poche was his books, formally inscribed, as though Poche were an anonymous reader standing in line in a bookstore where Grippes, wedged behind a shaky table, sat signing away. "Your name?" "Whose name?" "How do you spell your name?" "Oh, the book isn't for me. It's for a friend of mine." His look changed to one of severity and impatience, until he remembered that Poche had never asked him to sign anything. He had never concealed his purpose, to pluck from Grippes' plumage every bright feather he could find.

"Careful," Grippes repeated. "Careful. Remember what happened to Prism."

Victor Prism, keeping pale under a parasol on the beach at Torremolinos, had made the acquaintance of a fellow-Englishman—pleasant, not well educated but eager to learn, blistered shoulders, shirt draped over his head, pages of the *Sunday Express* round his red thighs. Prism lent him something to read—his sunburn was keeping him awake. It was a creative essay on three émigré authors of the nineteen-thirties, in a review so obscure and ill-paying that Prism had not bothered to include the fee on his income-tax return. (Prism had got it wrong, of course, having Thomas Mann—whose plain name Prism could not spell—go to East Germany and with his wife start a theatre that presented his own plays, sending Stefan Zweig to be photographed with movie stars in California, and putting Bertolt Brecht to die a bitter man in self-imposed exile in Brazil. As it turned out, none of Prism's readers knew the difference. Chided by Grippes, Prism had been defensive, cold, said that no letters had come in. "One, surely?" said Grippes. "Yes, I thought that must be you," Prism said.)

Prism might have got off with the whole thing if his new friend had not fallen sound asleep after the first lines. Waking, refreshed, he had said to himself, "I must find out what they get paid for this stuff," a natural reflex—he was of the Inland Revenue. He'd found no trace, no record; for Inland Revenue purposes "Death and Exile" did not exist. The subsequent fine was so heavy and Prism's disgrace so acute that he fled England to spend a few days with Grippes and the cats in Montparnasse. He sat on a kitchen chair while Grippes, nose and mouth protected by a checked scarf, sprayed terror to cockroaches. Prism, weeping in the fumes and wiping his eyes, said, "I'm through with Queen and Country"—something like that—"and I'm taking out French citizenship tomorrow."

"You would have to marry a Frenchwoman and have at least five male children," said Grippes, through the scarf. He was feeling the patriotic hatred of a driver on a crowded road seeing foreign license plates in the way.

"Oh, well, then," said Prism, as if to say, "I won't bother."

"Oh, well, then," said Grippes, softly, not quite to Poche. Poche added one last thing to the file and closed it, as if something definite had taken place. He clasped his hands and placed them on the dossier; it seemed shut for all time now, like a grave. He said, "Maître, one never stays long in the same fiscal theatre. I have been in this one for an unusual length of time. We may not meet again. I want you to know I have enjoyed our conversations."

"So have I," said Grippes, with caution.

"Much of your autobiographical creation could apply to other lives of our time, believe me."

"So you have read them," said Grippes, an eye on the locker.

"I read those I bought," said Poche.

"But they are the same books."

"No. The books I bought belong to me. The others were gifts. I would never open a gift. I have no right to." His voice rose, and he spoke more slowly. "In one of them, when What's-His-Name struggles to prepare his civil-service tests, '...the desire for individual glory seemed so inapposite, suddenly, in a nature given to renunciation.'"

"I suppose it *is* a remarkable observation," said Grippes. "I was not referring to myself." He had no idea what that could be from, and he was certain he had not written it.

Poche did not send for Grippes again. Grippes became a commonplace taxpayer, filling out his forms without help. The frosted-glass door was reverting to dull white; there were fewer shadows for Grippes to let in. A fashion for having well-behaved Nazi officers shore up Western culture gave Grippes a chance to turn Poche into a tubercular poet, trapped in Paris by poverty and the Occupation. Grippes threw out the first draft, in which Poche joined a Christian-minded Resistance network and performed a few simple miracles, unaware of his own powers. He had the instinctive feeling that a new generation would not know what he was talking about. Instead, he placed Poche, sniffling and wheezing, in a squalid hotel room, cough pastilles spilled on the table, a stained blanket pinned round his shoulders. Up the fetid staircase came a handsome colonel, a Curt Jurgens type, smelling of shaving lotion, bent on saving liberal values, bringing Poche butter, cognac, and a thousand sheets of writing paper.

After that, Grippes no longer felt sure where to go. His earlier books, government tape and buckle binding them into an œuvre, had accompanied Poche to his new fiscal theatre. Perhaps, finding his career blocked by the woman upstairs, he had asked for early retirement. Poche was in a gangster-ridden Mediterranean city, occupying a shoddy boom-period apartment he'd spent twenty years paying for. He was working at black-market jobs, tax adviser to the local mayor, a small innocent cog in the regional Mafia. After lunch, Poche would sit on one of those southern balconies that hold just a deck chair, rereading in chronological order all Grippes' books. In the late afternoon, blinds drawn, Poche totted up Mafia accounts by a chink of light. Grippes was here, in Montparnasse, facing a flat-white glass door.

He continued to hand himself a forty-five-and-a-half-per-cent personal exemption—the astonishing thirty-three plus the unheard-of twelve and a half. No one seemed to mind. No shabby envelope holding an order for execution came in the mail. Sometimes in Grippes' mind a flicker of common sense flamed like revealed truth: the exemption was an error. Public Treasury was now tiptoeing toward computers. The computer brain was bound to wince at Grippes and stop functioning until the Grippes exemption was settled. Grippes rehearsed: "I was seriously misinformed."

He had to go farther and farther abroad to find offal for the cats. One tripe dealer had been turned into a driving school, another sold second-hand clothes. Returning on a winter evening after a long walk, carrying a parcel of sheep's lung wrapped in newspaper, he crossed Boulevard du Montparnasse just as the lights went on—the urban moonrise. The street was a dream street, faces flat white in the winter mist. It seemed to Grippes that he had crossed over to the nineteen-eighties, had only just noticed the new decade. In a recess between two glassed-in sidewalk cafés, four plainclothes cops were beating up a pair of pickpockets. Nobody had to explain the scene to Grippes; he knew what it was about. One prisoner already wore handcuffs. Customers on the far side of the glass gave no more than a glance. When they had got handcuffs on the second man, the cops pushed the two into the entrance of Grippes' apartment building to wait for the police van. Grippes shuffled into a café. He put his parcel of lights on the zinc-topped bar and started to read an article on the wrapping. Someone unknown to him, a new name, pursued an old grievance: Why don't they write about real life anymore?

Because to depict life is to attract its ill-fortune, Grippes replied.

He stood sipping coffee, staring at nothing. Four gun-bearing young men in jeans and leather jackets were not final authority; final authority was something written, the printed word, even when the word was mistaken. The simplest final authority in Grippes' life had been O. Poche and a book of rules. What must have happened was this: Poche, wishing to do honor to a category that included writers, prostitutes, and door-to-door salesmen, had read and misunderstood a note about royalties. It had been in italics, at the foot of the page. He had transformed his mistake into a regulation and had never looked at the page again.

Grippes in imagination climbed three flights of dirty wooden stairs to Mme. de Pelle's office. He observed the seashell crucifix and a brooch he had not noticed the first time, a silver fawn curled up as nature had never planned—a boneless fawn. Squinting, Mme. de Pelle peered at the old dun-colored Gaullist-era file. She put her hand over a page, as though Grippes were trying to read upside down. "It has all got to be paid back," she said.

"I was seriously misinformed," Grippes intended to answer, willing to see Poche disgraced, ruined, jailed. "I followed instructions. I am innocent."

But Poche had vanished, leaving Grippes with a lunatic exemption, three black-market income-bearing apartments he had recently, unsuccessfully, tried to sell, and a heavy reputation for male-oriented, left-feeling, right-thinking books. This reputation Grippes thought he could no longer sustain. A Socialist government was at last in place (hence his hurry about unloading the flats and his difficulty in finding takers). He wondered about the new file cover. Pink? Too fragile—look what had happened with the mottled peach. Strong denim blue, the shade standing for *giovinezza* and workers' overalls? It was no time for a joke, not even a private one. No one could guess what would be wanted, now, in the way of literary entertainment. The fitfulness of voters is such that, having got the government they wanted, they were now reading nothing but the right-wing press. Perhaps a steady right-wing heartbeat ought to set the cadence for a left-wing outlook, with a complex, bravely conservative heroine contained within the slippery but unyielding walls of left-wing style. He would have to come to terms with the rightist way of considering female characters. There seemed to be two methods, neither of which suited Grippes' temperament: treat her disgustingly, then cry all over the page, or admire and respect her—she is the equal at least of a horse. The only woman his imagination offered, with some insistence, was no use to him. She moved quietly on a winter evening to Saint-Nicolas-du-Chardonnet, the rebel church at the lower end of Boulevard Saint-Germain, where services were still conducted in Latin. She wore a hat ornamented with an ivory arrow, and a plain gray coat, tubular in shape, with a narrow fur collar. Kid gloves were tucked under the handle of her sturdy leather purse. She had never heard of video games, push-button telephones, dishwashers, frozen filleted sole, computer horoscopes. She entered the church and knelt down and brought out her rosary, oval pearls strung on thin gold. Nobody saw rosaries anymore. They were not even in the windows of their traditional venues, across the square from the tax bureau. Believers went in for different articles now: cherub candles, quick prayers on plastic cards. Her iron meekness resisted change. She prayed constantly into the past. Grippes knew that one's view of the past is just as misleading as speculation about the future. It was one of the few beliefs he would have gone to the stake for. She was praying to a mist, to mist-shrouded figures she persisted in seeing clear.

He could see the woman, but he could not approach her. Perhaps he could get away with dealing with her from a distance. All that was really needed for a sturdy right-wing novel was its pessimistic rhythm: and then, and then, and then, and death. Grippes had that rhythm. It was in his footsteps, coming up the stairs after the departure of the police van, turning the key in his triple-bolted front door. And then, and then, the cats padding and mewing, not giving Grippes time to take off his coat as they made for their empty dishes on the kitchen floor. Behind the gas stove, a beleaguered garrison of cockroaches got ready for the evening sortie. Grippes would be waiting, his face half veiled with a checked scarf.

In Saint-Nicolas-du-Chardonnet the woman shut her missal, got up off her knees, scorning to brush her coat; she went out to the street, proud of the dust marks, letting the world know she still prayed the old way. She escaped him. He had no idea what she had on, besides the hat and coat. Nobody else wore a hat with an ivory arrow or a tubular coat or a scarf that looked like a weasel biting its tail. He could not see what happened when she took the hat and coat off, what her hair was like, if she hung the coat in a hall closet that also contained umbrellas, a carpet sweeper, and a pile of old magazines, if she put the hat in a round box on a shelf. She moved off in a gray blur. There was a streaming window between them Grippes could not wipe clean. Probably she entered a dark dining room—fake Henri IV buffet, bottles of pills next to the oil and vinegar cruets, lace tablecloth folded over the back of a chair, just oilcloth spread for the family meal. What could he do with such a woman? He could not tell who was waiting for her or what she would eat for supper. He could not even guess at her name. She revealed nothing; would never help.

Grippes expelled the cats, shut the kitchen window, and dealt with the advance guard from behind the stove. What he needed now was despair and excitement, a new cat-and-mouse chase. What good was a computer that never caught anyone out?

After airing the kitchen and clearing it of poison, Grippes let the cats in. He swept up the bodies of his victims and sent them down the ancient cast-iron chute. He began to talk to himself, as he often did now. First he said a few sensible things, then he heard his voice with a new elderly quaver to it, virtuous and mean: "After all, it doesn't take much to keep me happy."

Now, that was untrue, and he had no reason to say it. Is that what I am going to be like, now, he wondered. Is this the new-era Grippes, pinch-mouthed? It was exactly the sort of thing that the woman in the dark dining room might say. The best thing that

could happen to him would be shock, a siege of terror, a knock at
the door and a registered letter with fearful news. It would
sharpen his humor, strengthen his own, private, eccentric heart.
It would keep him from making remarks in his solitude that were
meaningless and false. He could perhaps write an anonymous
letter saying that the famous author Henri Grippes was guilty of
evasion of a most repulsive kind. He was, moreover, a callous
landlord who had never been known to replace a doorknob.
Fortunately, he saw, he was not yet that mad, nor did he really
need to be scared and obsessed. He had got the woman from
church to dining room, and he would keep her there, trapped,
cornered, threatened, watched, until she yielded to Grippes and
told her name—as, in his several incarnations, good Poche had
always done.

A RECOLLECTION

I married Magdalena here, in Paris, more than forty years ago. It was at the time when anti-Jewish thoughts and feelings had suddenly hardened into laws, and she had to be protected. She was a devout, light-hearted, probably wayward Catholic convert, of the sort Dominicans like to have tea with, but she was also Jewish and foreign—to be precise, born in Budapest, in 1904. A Frenchman who had grown rich manufacturing and exporting fine china brought her to Paris—oh, a long time ago, even before the Popular Front. He gave her up for the daughter of a count, and for his new career in right-wing politics, preaching moral austerity and the restoration of Christian values. Whenever Magdalena opened *Le Temps* and saw his name, she would burst out laughing. (I never noticed Magdalena actually *reading* a newspaper. She subscribed to a great many, but I think it was just to see what her friends and former friends were up to.) He let her keep the apartment on Quai Voltaire and the van Dongen portraits he'd bought because they looked like her—the same pert face and slender throat.

I never lived with Magdalena. After our wedding we spent part of a week together (to calm my parents down, I went home to sleep) and a night sitting up in a train. I never imagined sharing an address, my name over the doorbell, friends calling me at Magdalena's number, myself any more than a guest in the black-red-and-white-lacquered apartment on Quai Voltaire. The whole place smelled of gardenias. Along the hall hung stills from films she had worked in, in Vienna, Berlin—silent, minor, forgotten pictures, probably all destroyed. (The apartment was looted during the Occupation. When Magdalena came back, she had to sleep on the floor.) Her two pug dogs yapped and wore little chimes. The constant jangling drove them crazy. She washed them with scented soap and fed them at table, sitting on her lap. They had rashes all over their bodies, and were always throwing up.

I was twenty-two, still a student. My parents, both teachers in the lower grades, had made great sacrifices so that I could sit reading books into early manhood. The only home I could have offered Magdalena was a corner of their flat, in the Rue des Solitaires, up in the Nineteenth Arrondissement. Arabs and Africans live there now. In those days, it was the kind of district Jean Renoir and René Clair liked to use for those films that show chimney pots, and people walking around with loaves of bread, and gentle young couples that find and lose a winning lottery ticket. Until she met me, Magdalena had never heard of the Rue des Solitaires, or of my Métro stop, Place des Fêtes. The names sounded so charming that she thought I'd made them up. I begged her to believe that I never invented anything.

She was fair and slight, like all the women in Paris. In my view of the past, the streets are filled with blond-haired women, wearing absurd little hats, walking miniature dogs. (Wait, my memory tells me; not all women—not my mother.) Why had she given up acting? "Because I wasn't much good," she told me once. "And I was so lazy. I could work, really work, for a man in love with me—to do him a favor. That was all." From her sitting room, everything in it white, you saw across the Seine to the

Place du Carrousel and part of the Tuileries. Between five and eight, men used to drop in, stand about with their backs to the view, lean down to scratch the ears of the pugs. Raymonde, the maid, knew everyone by name. They treated me kindly, though nobody ever went so far as to scratch my ears.

My parents were anticlerical and republican. In their conversation, Church and Republic locked horns like a couple of battling rams. I was never baptized. It broke their hearts that my marriage to Magdalena had to be blessed, at her insistence. The blessing was given in the church of Saint-Thomas-d'Aquin, in deep shadow, somewhere behind the altar. I had never been in a church before, except to admire windows or paintings; art belonged to the people, whatever the Vatican claimed. The ceremony was quick, almost furtive, but not because of Magdalena: *I* was the outsider, the pagan, unbaptized, unsaved.

My father and mother stayed home that day, eating the most solid lunch they could scrape together, to steady their nerves. They would have saved Magdalena, if only someone had asked— gladly, bravely, and without ruining my life. (That was how they saw it.) I suppose they could have locked her up in the broom closet. She could have stood in the dark, for years and years—as many as she needed. They could only hope, since they never prayed, that there would be no children.

I had already signed our children over to Rome a few days before the wedding, one afternoon just after lunch. Bargaining for their souls, uncreated, most certainly unwished for (I did not separate soul from body, since the first did not exist), went on in the white sitting room. Magdalena, as ever blithe and light-hearted, repeated whatever she'd been told to tell me, and I said yes, and signed. I can still hear the sound of her voice, though not the words she used; it was lower in pitch than a Frenchwoman's, alien to the ear because of its rhythm. It was a voice that sang a foreign song. Did she really expect to have children? She must have been thirty-six, and we were about to be separated for as long as the war might last. My signature was part of an elaborate ritual, in which she seemed to take immense delight. She had never been married before.

She had on a soft navy-blue dress, which had only that morning been brought to the door. This in war, in defeat. There were dressmakers and deliverymen. There was Chanel's Gardenia. There was coffee and sugar, there were polished silver trays and thin coffee cups. There was Raymonde, in black with white organdie, and Magdalena, with her sunny hair, her deep-red nails, to pour.

I looked over at the far side of the Place du Carrousel, to some of the windows of the Ministry of Finance. Until just a few months ago, Magdalena had been invited to private Ministry apartments to lunch. The tables were set with the beautiful glass and china that belonged to the people. Steadfast, uncomplaining men and women like my father and mother had paid their taxes so that Magdalena could lunch off plates they would never see— unless some further revolution took place, after which they might be able to view the plates in a museum.

I felt no anger thinking this. It was Magdalena I intended to save. As my wife, she would have an identity card with a French name. She would never have to baste a yellow star on her coat. She would line up for potatoes at a decent hour once France had run out of everything else.

Actually, Magdalena never lined up for anything. On the day when the Jews of Paris stood in long queues outside police stations, without pushing and shoving, and spelled their names and addresses clearly, so that the men coming to arrest them later on would not make a mistake, Magdalena went back to bed and read magazines. Nobody ever offered her a yellow star, but she found one for herself. It was lying on the ground, in front of the entrance to the Hôtel Meurice—so she said.

Walking the pugs in the rain, Magdalena had looked back to wave at Raymonde, polishing a window. (A publisher of comic books has the place now.) She crossed the Tuileries, then the

Rue de Rivoli, and, stepping under the arcades, furled her silk umbrella. Rain had driven in; she skirted puddles in her thin shoes. Just level with the Meurice, where there were so many German officers that some people were afraid to walk there, or scorned to, she stopped to examine a star—soiled, trodden on. She moved it like a wet leaf with the point of her umbrella, bent, picked it up, dropped it in her purse.

"Why?" I had good reason to ask, soon after.

"To keep as a souvenir, a curiosity. To show my friends in Cannes, so that they can see what things are like in Paris."

I didn't like that. I had wanted to pull her across to my side, not to be dragged over to hers.

A day later we set off by train for the South, which was still a free zone. The only Nazis she would be likely to encounter there would be French; I gave Magdalena a lecture on how to recognize and avoid them. We sat side by side in a second-class compartment, in the near dark. (Much greater suspicion attended passengers in first; besides that, I could not afford it.) Magdalena, unfortunately, was dressed for tea at the Ritz. She would have retorted that nothing could be plainer than a Molyneux suit and a diamond pin. The other passengers, three generations of a single family, seemed to be asleep. On the new, unnatural frontier dividing France North from South, the train came to a halt. We heard German soldiers coming on board, to examine our papers. Trying not to glance at Magdalena, I fixed my eyes on the small overnight case she had just got down from the rack and sat holding on her lap. When the train stopped, all the lights suddenly blazed—seemed to blaze; they were dull and brown. Magdalena at once stood up, got her case down without help, removed a novel (it was *Bella*, by Jean Giraudoux), and began to read.

I thought that she had done the very thing bound to make her

seem suspect. Her past, intricate and inscrutable, was summed
up by the rich leather of the case and the gold initials on the lid
and the tiny gold padlock and key, in itself a piece of jewelry.
That woman could not possibly be the wife of that young man,
with his rolled-up canvas holdall with the cracked leather straps.
The bag was not even mine; it had belonged to my mother, or an
aunt. I reached over and turned her case around, so that I could
open it, as if I were anxious to co-operate, to get things ready for
inspection. The truth was, I did not want the German peasants in
uniform to read her initials, to ask what her maiden name was, or
to have cause for envy; the shut case might have been offered for
sale in a window along the Rue du Faubourg-Saint-Honoré, at
extortionate cost. I thought that if those peasants, now approaching our compartment, had not been armed, booted, temporarily
privileged, they might have served a different apprenticeship—
learned to man mirror-walled elevators, carry trays at shoulder
level, show an underling's gratitude for Magdalena's escort's tip.
I flung the lid back, against her jacket of thin wool; and there,
inside, on top of some folded silk things the color of the palest
edge of sunrise, lay a harsh star. I smoothed the silken stuff and
palmed the star and got it up my sleeve.

In my terrible fright my mind caught on something incidental—that Magdalena had never owned anything else so coarse to
the touch. She had never been a child, had never played with
sand and mud. She had been set down in a large European city,
smart hat tilted, rings swivelled so that she could pull her gloves
on, knowing all there is about gold padlocks and keys. "Cosmopolitan," an incendiary word now, flared in my mind. In the
quiet train (no train is so still as one under search), its light
seemed to seek out crude editorials, offensive cartoons, repulsive
graffiti.

The peasants in uniform—they were two—slid open the
compartment door. They asked no more than any frontier
inspector, but the reply came under the heading of life and death.
"Cosmopolitan" had flared like a star; it dissolved into a dirty

little puddle. Its new, political meaning seeped into my brain and ran past my beliefs and convictions, and everything my parents stood for. I felt it inside my skull, and I wondered if it would ever evaporate.

One of the peasants spoke, and Magdalena smiled. She told me later that he had the accent said to have been Wagner's. Seeing the open case, he plunged his hand under the silks and struck a hairbrush. He shut the lid and stared dumbly at the initials. The other one in the meanwhile frowned at our papers. Then the pair of them stumbled out.

Our fellow-passengers looked away, as people do when someone with the wrong ticket is caught in first class. I put the case back on the rack and muttered an order. Magdalena obediently followed me out to the corridor. It may have looked as if we were just standing, smoking, but I was trying to find out how she, who had never owned anything ugly, had come into possession of this thing. She told me about the Rue de Rivoli, and that she had thought the star would interest her friends in Cannes: they would be able to see how things were now up in Paris. If she had buried it next to her hairbrush, it would have seemed as though she had something to hide. She said she had nothing to hide; absolutely nothing.

I had been running with sweat; now I felt cold. I asked her if she was crazy. She took this for the anxious inquiry of a young man deeply in love. Her nature was sunny, and as good as gold. She laughed and told me she had been called different things but never crazy. She started to repeat some of them, and I kissed her to shut her up. The corridor was jammed with people lying sprawled or sitting on their luggage, and she sounded demented and foreign.

I wondered what she meant by "friends in Cannes." To women of her sort, "friend" is often used as a vague substitute for "lover." (Notice how soon after thinking "cosmopolitan" I thought "of her sort.") She had mentioned the name of the people who were offering her shelter in Cannes; it was a French name but perhaps an alias. I had a right to know more. She was my wife. For the first and the last time I considered things in that particular way: After all, she *is* my wife. I was leaving the train at Marseilles, though my ticket read Cannes. From Marseilles, I would try to get to North Africa, then to England. Magdalena would sit the war out in an airy villa—the kind aliens can afford.

When I next said something—about getting back to our seats—my voice was too high. It still rises and thins when I feel under strain. (In the nineteen-fifties, when I was often heard over the radio, interviewing celebrated men about their early struggles and further ambitions, I would get about two letters a year from women saying they envied my mother.)

It was probably just as well that we were spending our last night among strangers. After our wedding we had almost ceased to be lovers. I had to keep the peace at home, and Magdalena to prepare to leave without showing haste. I thought she was tense and tired; but I appreciate now that Magdalena was never fatigued or wrought up, and I can only guess she had to say goodbye to someone else. She sent the dogs away to Raymonde's native town in Normandy, mentioning to the concierge that it was for the sake of their health and for a few days only. At the first sign of fright, of hurry, or of furniture removed to storage, the concierge might have been halfway to the police station to report on the tenant who had so many good friends, and whose voice sang a foreign tune.

In the compartment, I tried to finish the thoughts begun in the corridor. I had married her to do the right thing; that was established. Other men have behaved well in the past, and will continue to do so. It comforted me to know I was not the only one with a safe conscience. Thinking this in the darkened, swaying compartment meant that I was lucid and generous, and also something of a louse. I whispered to Magdalena, "What is bad behavior? What is the worst?" The question did not seem to astonish her. Our union was blessed, and she was my wife forevermore, and she could fall back on considerable jurispru-

dence from the ledgers of Heaven to prove it; but I was still the
student who had brought his books to Quai Voltaire, who had
looked up to make sure she was still in the room, and asked some
question from beyond his experience. She took my hand and said
the worst *she* remembered was the Viennese novelist who had
taken some of her jewelry (she meant "stolen") and pawned it
and kept all the money.

We said goodbye in Marseilles, on the station platform. In
the southern morning light her eyes were pale blue.
There were armed men in uniform everywhere. She wore a
white suit and a thin blouse and a white hat I had never seen
before. She had taken a suitcase into the filthy toilet and emerged
immaculate. I had the feeling that she could hardly wait to get
back on the train and roll on to new adventures.

"And now I am down here, away from all my friends in Paris,"
she had the gall to say, shading her eyes. It was a way of showing
spirit, but I had never known anyone remotely like her, and I
probably thought she should be tight-lipped. By "all my friends"
she must have meant men who had said, "If you ever need help,"
knowing she would never ask; who might have said, "Wasn't it
awful, tragic, about Magdalena?" if she had never been seen
again.

She had left her luggage and jewelry untended in the compartment. I was glad to see she wore just her wedding ring; otherwise,
she might have looked too actressy, and drawn attention. (I had
no idea how actresses were supposed to look.) Sometimes she
used an amber cigarette holder with a swirl of diamond dust like
the tail of a comet. She must have sold it during the war; or
perhaps lost it, or given it away.

"You look like a youth leader," she said. I was Paris-pale, but
healthy. My hair was clipped short. I might have been about to
lead police and passengers in patriotic singsong. I was patriotic,
but not as the new regime expected its young to be; I was on my

way to be useful to General de Gaulle, if he would have me. I saw myself floating over the map of France, harnessed to a dazzling parachute, with a gun under my arm.

We had agreed not to stare at each other once we'd said goodbye. Magdalena kissed me and turned and pulled herself up the high steps of the train. I got a soft, bent book out of my canvas holdall and began to read something that spoke only to me. So the young think, and I was still that young: poetry is meant for one reader only. Magdalena, gazing tenderly down from the compartment window, must have seen just the shape of the poem on the page. I turned away from the slant of morning sunlight— not away from her. When the train started to move, she reached down to me, but I was too far to touch. A small crucifix on a chain slipped free of her blouse. I stuck to our promise and never once raised my eyes. At the same time, I saw everything—the shade of her white hatbrim aslant on her face, her hand with the wedding ring.

I put the star in my book, to mark the place: I figured that if I was caught I was done for anyway. When my adventures were over, I would show it to my children; I did not for a second see Magdalena as their mother. They were real children, not souls to be bargained. So it seems to me now. It shows how far into the future I thought you could safely carry a piece of the past. Long after the war, I found the star, still in the same book, and I offered to give it back to Magdalena, but she said she knew what it was like.

RUE DE LILLE

My second wife, Juliette, died in the apartment on Rue de Lille, where she had lived—at first alone, more or less, then with me—since the end of the war. All the rooms gave onto the ivy-hung well of a court, and were for that reason dark. We often talked about looking for a brighter flat, on a top floor with southern exposure and a wide terrace, but Parisians seldom move until they're driven to. "We know the worst of what we've got," we told each other. "It's better than a bad surprise."

"And what about your books?" Juliette would add. "It would take you months to get them packed, and in the new place you'd never get them sorted." I would see myself as Juliette saw me, crouched over a slanting, shaking stack of volumes piled on a strange floor, cursing and swearing as I tried to pry out a dictionary. "Just the same, I don't intend to die here," she also said.

I once knew someone who believed drowning might be easy, even pleasant, until he almost drowned by accident. Juliette's father was a colonel who expected to die in battle or to be shot by a German firing squad, but he died of typhus in a concentration camp. I had once, long ago, imagined for myself a clandestine burial with full honors after some Resistance feat, but all I got out of the war was a few fractures and a broken nose in a motorcycle accident.

Juliette had thirty-seven years of blacked-out winter mornings in Rue de Lille. She was a few days short of her sixtieth birthday when I found her stretched out on the floor of our bedroom, a hand slackened on a flashlight. She had been trying to see under a chest of drawers, and her heart stopped. (Later, I pulled the chest away from the wall and discovered a five-franc coin.) Her gray-and-dark hair, which had grown soft and wayward with age, was tied back with a narrow satin ribbon. She looked more girlish than at any time since I'd first met her. (She fell in love with me young.) She wore a pleated flannel skirt, a tailored blouse, and one of the thick cardigans with gilt buttons she used to knit while watching television. She had been trained to believe that to look or to listen quietly is to do nothing; she would hum along with music, to show she wasn't idle. She was discreet, she was generous to a sensible degree, she was anything but contentious. I often heard her remark, a trifle worriedly, that she was never bored. She was faithful, if "faithful" means avoiding the acknowledged forms of trouble. She was patient. I know she was good. Any devoted male friend, any lover, any husband would have shown up beside her as selfish, irritable, even cruel. She displayed so little of the ordinary kinds of jealousy, the plain marital do-you-often-have-lunch-with-her? sort, that I once asked her if she had a piece missing.

"Whoever takes this place over," she said, when we spoke of moving, "will be staggered by the size of the electricity bills." (Juliette paid them; I looked after a number of other things.) We had to keep the lights turned on all day in winter. The apartment was L-shaped, bent round two sides of a court, like a train making a sharp turn. From our studies, at opposite ends of the train, we could look out and see the comforting glow of each other's working life, a lamp behind a window. Juliette would be giving some American novel a staunch, steady translation; I might be getting into shape my five-hour television series, "Stendhal and the Italian Experience," which was to win an award in Japan.

We were together for a duration of time I daren't measure against the expanse of Juliette's life; it would give me the feeling that I had decamped to a height of land, a survivor's eminence, so as to survey the point at which our lives crossed and mingled and began to move in the same direction: a long, narrow reach of time in the Rue de Lille. It must be the washy, indefinite colorations of blue that carpeted, papered, and covered floors, walls, and furniture and shaded our lamps which cast over that reach the tone of a short season. I am thinking of the patches of distant, neutral blue that appear over Paris in late spring, when it is still wet and cold in the street and tourists have come too early. The tourists shelter in doorways, trying to read their soaked maps, perennially unprepared in their jeans and thin jackets. Overhead, there are scrapings of a color that carries no threat and promises all.

That choice, Juliette's preference, I sometimes put down to her Calvinist sobriety—call it a temperament—and sometimes to a refinement of her Huguenot taste. When I was feeling tired or impatient, I complained that I had been consigned to a Protestant Heaven by an arbitrary traffic cop, and that I was better suited to a pagan Hell. Again, as I looked round our dining-room table at the calm, clever faces of old friends of Juliette's family, at their competent and unassuming wives, I saw what folly it might be to set such people against a background of buttercup yellow or apple green. The soft clicking of their upper-class Protestant consonants made conversation distant and neutral, too. It was a voice that had puzzled me the first time I'd heard it from Juliette. I had supposed, mistakenly, that she was trying it on for effect; but she was wholly natural.

The sixteenth-century map of Paris I bought for her birthday is still at the framer's; I sent a check but never picked it up. I destroyed her private correspondence without reading it, and gave armfuls of clothes away to a Protestant charity. To the personal notice of her death in *Le Monde* was attached a brief mention of her father, a hero of the Resistance for whom suburban streets are named; and of her career as a respected translator, responsible for having introduced postwar American literature to French readers; and of her husband, the well-known radio and television interviewer and writer, who survived her.

Another person to survive her was my first wife. One night when Juliette and I were drinking coffee in the little sitting room where she received her women friends, and where we watched television, Juliette said, again, "But how much of what she says does she believe? About her Catholicism, and all those fantasies running round in her head—that she is your true and only wife, that your marriage is registered in Heaven, that you and she will be together in another world?"

"Those are things people put in letters," I said. "They sit down alone and pour it out. It's sincere at that moment. I don't know why she would suddenly be *in*sincere."

"After all the trouble she's made," said Juliette. She meant that for many years my wife would not let me divorce.

"She couldn't help that," I said.

"How do you know?"

"I don't know. It's what I think. I hardly knew her."

"You must have known *something*."

"I haven't seen her more than three or four times in the last thirty-odd years, since I started living with you."

"What do you mean?" said Juliette. "You saw her just once, with me. We had lunch. You backed off asking for the divorce."

"You can't ask for a divorce at lunch. It had to be done by mail."

"And since then she hasn't stopped writing," said Juliette. "Do you mean three or four times, or do you mean once?"

I said, "Once, probably. Probably just that once."

Viewing me at close range, as if I were a novel she had to translate, Juliette replied that one ought to be spared unexpected visions. Just now, it was as if three walls of the court outside had been bombed flat. Through a bright new gap she saw straight through to my first marriage. We—my first wife and I—postured in the distance, like characters in fiction.

I had recently taken part in a panel discussion, taped for television, on the theme "What Literature, for Which Readers, at Whose Price?" I turned away from Juliette and switched on the set, about ten minutes too early. Juliette put the empty cups and the coffeepot on a tray she had picked up in Milan, the summer I was researching the Stendhal, and carried the tray down the dim passage to the kitchen. I watched the tag end of the late news. It must have been during the spring of 1976. Because of the energy crisis, daylight saving had been established. Like any novelty, it was deeply upsetting. People said they could no longer digest their food or be nice to their children, and that they needed sedation to help them through the altered day. A doctor was interviewed; he advised a light diet and early bed until mind and body adjusted to the change.

I turned, smiling, to where Juliette should have been. My program came on then, and I watched myself making a few points before I got up and went to find her. She was in the kitchen, standing in the dark, clutching the edge of the sink. She did not move when I turned the light on. I put my arms around her, and we came back to her sitting room and watched the rest of the program together. She was knitting squares of wool to be sewn together to make a blanket; there was always, somewhere, a flood or an earthquake or a flow of refugees, and those who outlasted jeopardy had to be covered.

THE COLONEL'S CHILD

I got to London by way of Marseilles and North Africa, having
left Paris more than a year before. My aim was to join the
Free French and General de Gaulle. I believed the weight of
my presence could tip the scales of war, like one vote in a close
election. There was no vanity in this. London was the peak of my
hopes and desires. I could look back and see a tamed landscape.
My past life dwindled and vanished in that long perspective. I was
twenty-three.

In my canvas hold-all I carried a tobacco pouch someone had
given me, filled with thin reddish soil from Algeria. In those days
earth from France and earth from Algeria meant the same thing.
Only years later was I able to think, I must have been crazy.
When you are young, your patriotism is like metaphysical frenzy.
Later, it becomes one more aspect of personal crankiness.

Instead of a hero's welcome I was given forms to fill out. These
questionnaires left no room for postscripts, and so only a skeleton
of myself could be drawn. I was Édouard B., born in Paris, father
a schoolteacher (so was my mother, but I wasn't asked), student
of literature and philosophy, single, no dependents.

Some definitions seemed incomplete. For instance, I was not

entirely single: before leaving Paris I had married a Jewish-born
actress, so as to give her the security of my name. As far as I knew,
she was now safe and in Cannes. At the same time, I was not a
married man. The marriage was an incident, gradually being
rubbed out in the long perspective I've described. So I saw it; so I
would insist. You have to remember the period, and France
occupied, to imagine how one could think and behave. We
always say this—"Think of the times we had to live in"—when
the past is dragged forward, all the life gone out of it, and left
unbreathing at our feet.

Instead of sending me off to freeze on a parade ground, the
Free French kept me in London. I took it to mean they wanted to
school me in sabotage work and drop me into France. I did not
know special parachute training might be needed. I thought you
held your breath and jumped.

Two months later I lay in a hospital ward with a broken nose,
broken left arm, and fractures in both legs. They had been trying
to teach me to ride a motorbike, and on my first time out I
skidded into a wall. The instructor came and sat by my bedside.
He was about twice my age, a former policeman from Rouen. He
said the Free French weren't quite casting me off, but some of
them wondered if I was meant for a fighting force in exile. I was a
cerebral type, who needed the peace of an office job, with no
equipment to smash—not even a typewriter. I asked if General
de Gaulle had been informed about my accident.

"Is he a friend of yours?" said the instructor.

"I've seen him," I said. "I saw him in Carlton Gardens. He
came out the door and down some steps, and got into his car. I
was carrying a lot of parcels, so I couldn't salute. I don't think he
noticed. I hope not."

There was a silence, during which the instructor stared at his
watch. Presently, he inquired what I wanted to do with my life.

"I think I am a poet," I said. "I can't be sure."

After that they sent me a regular hospital visitor, a volunteer.
Juliette was her name. She was seventeen, from Bordeaux, the
daughter of a colonel who had followed de Gaulle to London.

She had a precise, particular way of speaking, with every syllable given full value and the consonants treated like little stones. It was not the native accent of Bordeaux, which anyone can imitate, or the everyday French of Paris I'd grown up with, but the tone, almost undefinable, of the French Protestant upper class. I had not heard it before, not consciously, and for the moment had no means of placing it. I thought she had picked up an affectation of some sort while learning English and had carried it over to French. She had, besides, the habit of thrusting into French conversation brief, joyous, and usually irrelevant remarks in English: "You don't say!" "Oh, what a shame!" "How glad I am for you!" "How gorgeous!"

From behind a mask of splints and bandages I appraised her face, which was still childlike, rounded as if over a layer of cream. A beret kept slipping and sliding off her dark hair. "Oh, what a pity!" she remarked, pulling it back on. She was dressed in the least becoming clothes I had ever seen on a young woman—a worn and drooping tunic, thick black stockings, and a navy sweater frayed at the cuffs. She had spent five months in an English girls' school, she told me, and this was the remains of a uniform. She had nothing else to wear, nothing that fitted. Her mother was too busy to shop.

"Can't you shop for yourself?"

"It's not done," she said. "I mean, we don't do things that way."

"Who is we?"—for she still puzzled me.

"Besides, I've got no money." This seemed a sensible explanation. I wondered why she had bothered to make another. "My mother teaches English to French recruits. Actually, she doesn't know much, but she can make them read traffic signs."

"You mean, 'Stop'?"

"Well, there are other things—'No Entry.'" She looked troubled, as if she were not succeeding in the tranquil, sleepy conversation that is supposed to keep a victim's mind off his wounds.

I had lost six front teeth in the accident. Through the gap, Juliette fed me the mess the English call custard. My right arm was fine, but I let her do it. She was grave, intent—a little girl playing. She might have been poking a spoon into a doll's porcelain face. When I refused to swallow any more, she got a bottle of eau de cologne and a facecloth out of a satchel and carefully wiped my hands and wrists and around my neck— whatever was bare and visible. I wondered if she would offer to comb my hair and cut my nails, but the nursing part of the game was over. She sat with her ankles crossed and her hands clasped, a good girl on a visit, and told me that her father, the colonel, was an outcast with a price on his head. From the care she took not to say where he was, I understood they had sent him to France, on a mission. Forgetting about secrets, she suddenly said she yearned to be smuggled into France, too, so that she could join him and they might blow up bridges together.

"I wanted to do that," I said. "That's why I came here. But I'm useless. I may come out of this with a scarred face, or a limp. I'd be at risk."

"Oh, I know," said Juliette. "The Germans would catch you and shoot you. They'd look for a secret agent all covered with scars. Oh, what a nuisance!"

Sweet Juliette. Her dark eyes held all the astonished eagerness of a child of twelve. I often think I should want to be back there, with a Juliette still virginal, untouched, saying encouraging things such as "all covered with scars," but at the age I am now it would bore me.

She came to the hospital twice a week, then every day. Her mother was at work, and I felt the girl had time on her hands and was often lonely. She was with me when they took the last of the mask off. "Well?" I said. "Tell me the worst."

"I can't," she said. "I don't know how you were before." She held up a pocket mirror. My nose was broken, all right, and I had thick, bruised cheekbones, like a Cossack. For someone who had never been to war, I was amazingly the image of an old soldier.

I left the hospital on crutches. There was no such thing as therapy—you got going or you did not. The organization found me a room on Baker Street, not far from where Juliette lived with her mother, as it turned out, and they gave me low-grade and harmless work to do. As my instructor had predicted, I was let nowhere near a typewriter, and once, I remember, someone even snatched a pencil sharpener away. Juliette used to come to the office, though she wasn't supposed to, and sit by my desk as if it were a bed. She had got rid of the uniform, but her new clothes, chosen by her mother, were English and baggy, in the grays and mustards Englishwomen favored. They seemed picked deliberately to make her creamy skin sallow, her slenderness gaunt. The mother was keeping her plain, I thought, perhaps to keep her out of trouble. Why didn't Juliette rebel? She was eighteen by now, but forty years ago eighteen was young. I wondered why she hung around me, what she wanted. I thought I guessed, but I decided not to know. I didn't want it said I had destroyed two items of French property—a motorcycle and a colonel's child. It was here, in London, that I was starting to get the hang of French society. In our reduced world, everyone in it a symbol of native, inborn rank, Juliette stood higher than some random young man who had merely laid his life on the line. She had connections, simply by the nature of how things were ordered.

I asked her once if there was a way of getting a message to my mother, in Paris—just a word to say I was safe. She pretended not to hear but about a month later said, "No, it's too dangerous. Besides, they don't trust you."

"Don't trust me? Why not?"

"I'm not sure."

"Do you?" I said.

"That's different."

Her mother was out most evenings. When Juliette was alone, I brought my rations around, and she cooked our supper. We drank—only because everybody did—replacing the whiskey in her mother's precious Haig bottle with London tap water. Once, Juliette tried restoring the color with cold tea, and there was hell to pay. When the news came from France that her father had been arrested and identified, she came straight to me.

"I'll never see him again," she said. "I haven't even got a decent snapshot of him. My mother has them all. She's got them in a suitcase. I feel sick. Feel my forehead. Feel my cheeks." She took my hand. "Feel the back of my neck. Feel my throat," she said, dragging my hand. We left the office and went to her flat and pulled the blackout curtain. The sun was shining on the other side of the street, where everything was bombed, but she didn't want to see it.

"How do you know your mother's not going to walk in?" I said. "She may want to be alone with you. She may want a quiet place to cry."

Juliette shook her head. "We're not like that. We don't do those things."

I think of the love and despair she sent out to me, the young shoots wild and blind, trusting me for support. She asked me to tell my most important secret, so that we would be bound. The most intimate thing I could say was that I was writing less poetry and had started a merciless novel about the French in London.

"I could tell you a lot," said Juliette. "Heroes' wives sleeping with other men."

"It's not that sort of novel," I said. "In my novel, they're all dead, but they don't know it. Every character is in a special Hell, made to measure."

"That's not how it is," she said. "We're not dead or in Hell. We're just here, waiting. We don't know what Hell will be like. Nobody knows. And some of us are going to be together in Heaven." She put her face against mine, saying this. It never occurred to me that she meant it, literally. I thought her Calvinism was just an organized form of disbelief. "Haven't you got some better secret?" she said. I supposed that schoolgirls talked this way, pledging friendship, and I wondered what she was taking me for. "Well," she said presently, "will you marry me anyway, even without a secret?"

Nobody coerced me into a life with Juliette. There were no tears, no threats, and I was not afraid of her mother. All I had to say was "I don't know yet" or "We'll see." I think I wanted to get her out of her loneliness. When for all her shyness she asked if I loved her, I said I would never leave her, and I am sure we both thought it meant the same thing. A few days later she told her mother that we were engaged and that nothing would keep her from marrying me after the war, and, for the first time since she could remember, she saw her mother cry.

Instead of a ring I gave Juliette some of the Algerian soil. She thanked me but confessed she had no idea what to do with it. Should it be displayed in a saucer, on a low table? Should she seal it up in a labelled, dated envelope? Tactful from infancy, she offered the gift to her mother, her rival in grief.

Now that we were "engaged," I began to see what the word covered for Juliette, and I had no qualms about smuggling her into my room—though never, of course, late at night. We took the mattress off the sagging daybed and put it on the floor, in front of the gas fire. Juliette would take her clothes off and tell me about her early years, though I didn't always listen. Sometimes she talked about the life waiting for us in Paris, and the number of children we would have, and the names we would give them. I remember a Thomas and a Claire.

"How many children should we have?" she said. "I'd say about ten. Well, seven. At least five."

Her clothes were scattered all over the floor, and the room was cold, in spite of the fire, but she didn't seem to feel it. "I hate children," I said. I was amazed that I could say something so definite and so cruel, and that sounded so true. When had I stopped liking them? Perhaps when I adopted the colonel's child, believing she would never grow up. I could have said, "I don't like *other* children," but nothing about this conversation was thought out.

"You will love them," she said happily. "You'll see." She held her spread fingers against the gas flame, counting off their names. Each finger stood for a greedy, willful personality, as tough as a fist. An only child, she invented playmates and named them, and I was supposed to bring them to life.

"I know it sounds stupid," she said, "but I kept my dolls until I was fifteen. My mother finally gave them away."

"Brothers and sisters," I said.

"No, just dolls. But they did have names."

"Is that one of your secrets?" "Secrets" had become charged with erotic meaning, when we were alone.

"You've got a special secret," she said.

"Yes. I've torn up my novel."

"Oh, how lovely for you! Or is that sad?"

"I'm just giving it up. I'll never start another."

"You've got another secret," she said. "You're married to someone." As she said this, she seemed to become aware that the room was cold. She shivered and reached for her dress, and drew it around her like a shawl. "A person went to see your mother. She—your mother—said to tell you your wife was all right. Your *wife*," said Juliette, trying to control her voice, "is in the South of France. She has managed to send your mother a pound of onions. To eat," said Juliette, as I went on staring. "Onions, to eat."

"I did get married," I said. "But she's not my wife. I did it to save her. I've got her yellow star somewhere."

"I'd like to see it," said Juliette, politely.

"It is made of cheap, ugly material," I said, as if that were the only thing wrong.

"I think you should put some clothes on," said Juliette. "If you're going to tell about your wife."

"She isn't my wife," I said. "The marriage was just something legal. Apart from being legal, it doesn't count."

"She may not be your wife," said Juliette, "but she is your mother's daughter-in-law." She drew up her knees and bent her head on them, as if it were disgraceful to watch me dressing. "You mean," she said, after a time, "that it doesn't count as a secret?" I gathered up the rest of her clothes and put them beside her on the mattress. "Does it count as anything?"

"I'll walk you home," I said.

"You don't need to."

"It's late. I can't have you wandering around in the blackout."

She dressed, slowly, sitting and kneeling. "I am glad she is safe and well," she said. "It would be too bad if you had done all that for nothing. She must be very grateful to you."

I had never thought about gratitude. It seemed to me that, yes, she was probably grateful. I suddenly felt impatient for the war to end, so that I could approach her, hand in hand with Juliette, and ask for a divorce and a blessing.

Juliette, kneeling, fastened the buttons of the latest flour sack her mother had chosen. "Why did you tear up your novel?" she said.

Because I can't wrench life around to make it fit some fantasy. Because I don't know how to make life sound worse or better, or how to make it sound true. Instead of saying this, I said, "How do you expect me to support ten children?" The colonel's wife didn't like me much, but she had said that after the war there were a few people she could introduce me to. She had mentioned something about radio broadcasting, and I liked the idea. Juliette was still kneeling, with only part of the hideous dress buttoned up. I looked down at her bent head. She must have been thinking that she had tied herself to a man with no money, no prospects, and no connections. Who wasn't entirely single. Who might be put on a charge for making a false declaration. Who had a broken nose and a permanent limp. Who, so far, had never finished anything he'd started. Perhaps she was forgetting one thing: I had got to London.

"I could stay all night," she said. "If you want me to."

"Your mother would have the police out," I said.

"She'd never dare," said Juliette. "I've never called the police because *she* didn't come home."

"It would be..." I tried to think of what it could be for us. "It would be radical."

Her hands began to move again, the other way, unbuttoning. She was the colonel's child, she had already held her breath and jumped, and that was the start and the end of it.

"We may be in big trouble over this," I said.

"Oh, what a pity," she said. "We'll always be together. We will always be happy. How lovely! What a shame!"

I think she still trusted me at that moment; I hope so.

LENA

In her prime, by which I mean in her beauty, my first wife, Magdalena, had no use for other women. She did not depend upon women for anything that mattered, such as charm and enjoyment and getting her bills paid; and as for exchanging Paris gossip and intimate chitchat, since she never confided anything personal and never complained, a man's ear was good enough. Magdalena saw women as accessories, to be treated kindly—maids, seamstresses, manicurists—or as comic minor figures, the wives and official fiancées of her admirers. It was not in her nature to care what anyone said, and she never could see the shape of a threat even when it rolled over her, but I suspect that she was called some of the senseless things she was called, such as "Central European whore" and "Jewish adventuress," by women.

Now that she is nearly eighty and bedridden, she receives visits from women—the residue of an early wave of Hungarian emigration. They have small pink noses, wear knitted caps pulled down to their eyebrows, and can see on dark street corners the terrible ghost of Béla Kun. They have forgotten that Magdalena once seemed, perhaps, disreputable. She is a devout Catholic, and she says cultivated, moral-sounding things, sweet to the ears of half a dozen widows of generals and bereft sisters of bachelor diplomats. They crowd her bedside table with bottles of cough mixture, lemons, embroidered table napkins, jars of honey, and covered bowls of stewed plums, the juice from which always spills. They call Magdalena "Lena."

She occupies a bed in the only place that would have her—a hospital on the northern rim of Paris, the color of jails, daubed with graffiti. The glass-and-marble lobby commemorates the flashy prosperity of the nineteen-sixties. It contains, as well as a vandalized coffee machine and a plaque bearing the name of a forgotten Minister of Health, a monumental example of the art of twenty years ago: a white foot with each toenail painted a different color. In order to admire this marvel, and to bring Magdalena the small comforts I think she requires, I need to travel a tiring distance by the underground suburban train. On these expeditions I carry a furled umbrella: the flat, shadeless light of this line is said to attract violent crime. In my wallet I have a card attesting to my right to sit down, because of an accident suffered in wartime. I never dare show the card. I prefer to stand. Anything to do with the Second World War, particularly its elderly survivors, arouses derision and ribaldry and even hostility in the young.

Magdalena is on the fourth floor (no elevator) of a wing reserved for elderly patients too frail to be diverted to nursing homes—assuming that a room for her in any such place could be found. The old people have had it drummed into them that they are lucky to have a bed, that the waiting list for their mattress and pillow lengthens by the hour. They must not seem too capricious, or dissatisfied, or quarrelsome, or give the nurses extra trouble. If they persist in doing so, their belongings are packed and their relatives sent for. A law obliges close relatives to take them in. Law isn't love, and Magdalena has seen enough distress and confusion to make her feel thoughtful.

"Families are worse than total war," she says. I am not sure what her own war amounted to. As far as I can tell, she endured all its rigors in Cannes, taking a daily walk to a black-market restaurant, her legs greatly admired by famous collaborators and German officers along the way. Her memory, when she wants to be bothered with it, is like a brief, blurry, self-centered dream.

"But what were you *doing* during those years?" I have asked her. (My mother chalked Gaullist slogans on walls in Paris. The father of my second wife died deported. I joined the Free French in London.)

"I was holding my breath," she answers, smiling.

She shares a room with a woman who suffers from a burning rash across her shoulders. Medicine that relieves the burning seems to affect her mind, and she will wander the corridors, wondering where she is, weeping. The hospital then threatens to send her home, and her children, in a panic, beg that the treatment be stopped. After a few days the rash returns, and the woman keeps Magdalena awake describing the pain she feels—it is like being flogged with blazing nettles, she says. Magdalena pilfers tranquillizers and gets her to take them, but once she hit the woman with a pillow. The hospital became nasty, and I had to step in. Fortunately, the supervisor of the aged-and-chronic department had seen me on television, taking part in a literary game ("Which saint might Jean-Paul Sartre have wanted most to meet?"), and that helped our case.

Actually, Magdalena cannot be evicted—not just like that. She has no family, and nowhere to go. Her continued existence is seen by the hospital as a bit of a swindle. They accepted her in the first place only because she was expected to die quite soon, releasing the bed.

"Your broken nose is a mistake," she said to me the other day. My face was damaged in the same wartime accident that is supposed to give me priority seating rights in public transport. "It lends you an air of desperate nerve, as if a Malraux hero had wandered into a modern novel and been tossed out on his face."

Now, this was hard on a man who had got up earlier than usual and bought a selection of magazines for Magdalena before descending to the suburban line, with its flat, worrying light. A man who had just turned sixty-five. Whose new bridge made him lisp. She talks the way she talked in the old days, in her apartment with the big windows and the sweeping view across the Seine. She used to wear white, and sit on a white sofa. There were patches of red in the room—her long fingernails and her lipstick, and the Legion of Honor on some admirer's lapel. She had two small, funny dogs whose eyes glowed red in the dusk.

"I heard you speaking just the other day," she went on. "You were most interesting about the way Gide always made the rounds of the bookstores to see how his work was selling. Actually, I think I told you that story."

"It couldn't have been just the other day," I said. "It sounds like a radio program I had in the nineteen-fifties."

"It couldn't have been you, come to think of it," she said. "The man lisped. I said to myself, 'It *might* be Édouard.'"

Her foreign way of speaking enchanted me when I was young. Now it sharpens my temper. Fifty years in France and she still cannot pronounce my name, "Édouard," without putting the stress on the wrong syllable and rolling the "r." "When you come to an 'r,'" I have told her, "keep your tongue behind your lower front teeth."

"It won't stay," she says. "It curls up. I am sorry." As if she cared. She will accept any amount of petulance shown by me, because she thinks she owes me tolerance: she sees me as youthful, boyish, to be teased and humored. She believes we have a long, unhampered life before us, and she expects to occupy it as my wife and widow-to-be. To that end, she has managed to outlive my second wife, and she may well survive me, even though I am fourteen years younger than she is and still on my feet.

Magdalena's Catholic legend is that she was converted after hearing Jacques Maritain explain Neo-Thomism at a tea party. Since then, she has never stopped heaping metaphysical rules about virtue on top of atavistic arguments concerning right and wrong. The result is a moral rock pile, ready to slide. Only God himself could stand up to the avalanche, but in her private arrangements he is behind her, egging her on. I had to wait until a law was passed that allowed divorce on the ground of separation before I was free to marry again. I waited a long time. In the meantime, Magdalena was writing letters to the Pope, cheering his stand on marriage and urging him to hold firm. She can choose among three or four different languages, her choice depending on where her dreams may have taken her during the night. She used to travel by train to Budapest and Prague wearing white linen. She had sleek, fair hair, and wore a diamond hair clip behind one ear. Now no one goes to those places, and the slim linen suits are crumpled in trunks. Her mind is clear, but she says absurd things. "I never saw her," she said about Juliette, my second wife. "Was she anything like me?"

"You did see her. We had lunch, the three of us."

"Show me her picture. It might bring back the occasion."

"No."

They met, once, on the first Sunday of September, 1954—a hot day of quivering horizons and wasps hitting the windshield. I had a new Renault—a model with a reputation for rolling over and lying with its wheels in the air. I drove, I think, grimly. Magdalena was beside me, in a nimbus of some scent—jasmine, or gardenia—that made me think of the opulent, profiteering side of wars. Juliette sat behind, a road map on her knee, her finger on the western outskirts of Fontainebleau. Her dark hair was pulled back tight and tied at the nape of her neck with a dark-blue grosgrain ribbon. It is safe to say that she smelled of soap and lemons.

We were taking Magdalena out to lunch. It was Juliette's idea. Somewhere between raspberries-and-cream and coffee, I was supposed to ask for a divorce—worse, to coax from Magdalena the promise of collusion in obtaining one. So far, she had resisted any mention of the subject and for ten years had refused to see me. Juliette and I had been living together since the end of the war. She was thirty now, and tired of waiting. We were turning into one of those uneasy, shadowy couples, perpetually waiting for a third person to die or divorce. I was afraid of losing her. That summer, she had travelled without me to America (so much farther from Europe then than it is today), and she had come back with a different coloration to her manner, a glaze of independence, as though she had been exposed to a new kind of sun.

I remember how she stared at Magdalena with gentle astonishment, as if Magdalena were a glossy illustration that could not look back. Magdalena had on a pale dress of some soft, floating stuff, and a pillbox hat tied on with a white veil, and long white gloves. I saw her through Juliette's eyes, and I thought what Juliette must be thinking: Where does Magdalena think we're taking her? To a wedding? Handing her into the front seat, I had shut the door on her skirt. I wondered if she had turned into one of the limp, pliant women whose clothes forever catch.

It was Juliette's custom to furnish social emptiness with some rattling anecdote about her own activities. Guests were often grateful. Without having to cast far, they could bring up a narrative of their own, and the result was close to real conversation. Juliette spoke of her recent trip. She said she was wearing an American dress made of a material called cotton seersucker. It washed like a duster and needed next to no ironing.

For answer, she received a side view of Magdalena's hat and a blue eye shadowed with paler blue. Magdalena was not looking but listening, savoring at close quarters the inflections of the French Protestant gentry. She knew she was privileged. As a rule, they speak only to one another. Clamped to gearshift and wheel, I was absolved of the need to comment. My broken profile had foxed Magdalena at first. She had even taken me for

an impostor. But then the remembered face of a younger man
slid over the fraud and possessed him.

Juliette had combed through the *Guide Michelin* and selected
a restaurant with a wide terrace and white umbrellas, set among
trees. At some of the tables there were American officers, in
uniform, with their families—this is to show how long ago it was.
Juliette adjusted our umbrella so that every inch of Magdalena
was in shade. She took it for granted that my wife belonged to a
generation sworn to paleness. From where I was sitting, I could
see the interior of the restaurant. It looked cool and dim, I
thought, and might have been better suited to the soft-footed
conversation to come.

I adjusted my reading glasses, which Magdalena had never
seen, and stared at a long handwritten menu. Magdalena made
no move to examine hers. She had all her life let men decide.
Finally, Juliette wondered if our guest might not like to start with
asparagus. I was afraid the asparagus would be canned. Well,
then, said Juliette, what about melon. On a hot day, something
cool followed by cold salmon. She broke off. I started to remove
my glasses, but Juliette reminded me about wine.

Magdalena was engaged in a ritual that Juliette may not have
seen before and that I had forgotten: pulling off her tight, long
gloves finger by finger and turning her rings right side up.
Squeezed against a great sparkler of some kind was a wedding
ring. Rallying, Juliette gave a little twitch to the collar of the
washable seersucker and went on about America. In Philadel-
phia, a celebrated Pentecostal preacher had persuaded the Holy
Spirit to settle upon a member of the congregation, a woman
whose hearing had been damaged when she was brained by a
flying shoe at a stock-car race. The deaf woman rose and said she
could hear sparrows chirping in High German, on which the
congregation prayed jubilant thanks.

Juliette did not stoop to explain that she was no Pentecostalist.
She mentioned the Holy Spirit as an old acquaintance of her own
class and background, a cultivated European with an open mind.

We were no longer young lovers, and I had heard this story

several times. I said that the Holy Spirit might find something more useful to attend to than a ruptured eardrum. We were barely ten years out of a disastrous war. All over the world, there were people sick, afraid, despairing. Only a few days before, the President of Brazil had shot himself to death.

Juliette replied that there were needs beyond our understanding. "God knows what he wants," she said. I am sure she believed it.

"God wanted Auschwitz?" I said.

I felt a touch on my arm, and I looked down and saw a middle-aged hand and a wedding ring.

With her trained inclination to move back from rising waters, Juliette made the excuse of a telephone call. I knew that her brief departure was meant to be an intermission. When she came back, we would speak about other things. Magdalena and I sat quietly, she with her hand still on my arm, as if she had finally completed a gesture begun a long time before. Juliette, returning, her eyes splashed with cold water, her dark hair freshly combed, saw that I was missing a good chance to bring up the divorce. She sat down, smiled, picked up her melon spoon. She was working hard these days, she said. She was translating an American novel that should never have been written. (Juliette revealed nothing more about this novel.) From there, she slid along to the subject of drastic separations—not so much mine from Magdalena as divorcement in general. Surely, she said, a clean parting was a way of keeping life pleasant and neat? This time, it was Magdalena's hearing that seemed impaired, and the Holy Spirit was nowhere. The two women must have been thinking the same thing at that moment, though for entirely different reasons: that I had forfeited any chance of divine aid by questioning God's intentions.

It was shortly before her removal to the hospital that Magdalena learned about Juliette's death. One of her doddering friends may have seen the notice in a newspaper. She at once resumed her place as my only spouse and widow-to-be. In fact, she had never relinquished it, but now the way back to me shone clear. The divorce, that wall of pagan darkness, had been torn down and dispersed with the concubine's ashes. She saw me delivered from an adulterous and heretical alliance. It takes a convert to think "heretical" with a straight face. She could have seen Juliette burned at the stake without losing any sleep. It is another fact about converts that they make casual executioners.

She imagined that I would come to her at once, but I went nowhere. Juliette had asked to be cremated, thinking of the purification of the flame, but the rite was accomplished by clanking, hidden, high-powered machinery that kept starting and stopping, on cycle. At its loudest, it covered the voice of the clergyman, who affirmed that Juliette was eying us with great good will from above, and it prevailed over Juliette's favorite recordings of Mozart and Bach. Her ashes were placed in a numbered niche that I never saw, for at some point in the funeral service I lost consciousness and had to be carried out. This nightmare was dreamed in the crematorium chapel of Père Lachaise cemetery. I have not been back. It is far from where I live, and I think Juliette is not there, or anywhere. From the moment when her heart stopped, there has been nothing but silence.

L ast winter, I had bronchitis and seldom went out. I managed to send Magdalena a clock, a radio, an azalea, and enough stamps and stationery to furnish a nineteenth-century literary correspondence. Nevertheless, the letters that reached my sick-bed from hers were scrawled in the margins of newspapers, torn off crookedly. Sometimes she said her roommate had lent her the money for a stamp. The message was always the same: I must not allow my wife to die in a public institution. Her pink-nosed woman friends wrote me, too, signing their alien names, announcing their titles—there was a princess.

It was no good replying that everybody dies in hospital now. The very idea made them sick, of a sickness beyond any wasting last-ditch illusion. Then came from Magdalena "On Saturday at nine o'clock, I shall be dressed and packed, and waiting for you to come and take me away."

Away from the hospital bed? It took weeks of wangling and soft-soaping and even some mild bribery to obtain it. Public funds, to which she is not entitled, and a voluntary contribution from me keep her in it. She has not once asked where the money comes from. When she was young, she decided never to worry, and she has kept the habit.

I let several Saturdays go by, until the folly had quit her mind. Late in April I turned up carrying a bottle of Krug I had kept on ice until the last minute and some glasses in a paper bag. The woman who shares her room gave a great groan when she saw me, and showed the whites of her eyes. I took this to mean that Magdalena had died. The other bed was clean and empty. The clock and the radio on the table had the look of objects left behind. I felt shock, guilt, remorse, and relief, and I wondered what to do with the wine. I turned, and there in the doorway stood Magdalena, in dressing gown and slippers, with short white hair. She shuffled past me and lay on the bed with her mouth open, struggling for breath.

"Shouldn't I ring for a nurse?" I said, unwrapping the bottle.

"No one will come. Open the champagne."

"I'd better fetch a nurse." Instead, I made room on the table for the glasses. I'd brought three, because of the roommate.

Magdalena gasped, "Today is my birthday." She sat up, apparently recovered, and got her spectacles out from under the pillow. Leaning toward me, she said, "What's that red speck on your lapel? It looks like the Legion of Honor."

"I imagine that's what it is."

"Why?" she said. "Was there a reason?"

"They probably had a lot to give away. Somebody did say something about 'cultural enrichment of the media.'"

"I am glad about the enrichment," she said. "I am also very happy for you. Will you wear it all the time, change it from suit to suit?"

"It's new," I said. "There was a ceremony this morning." I sat down on the shaky chair kept for visitors, and with a steadiness that silenced us both I poured the wine. "What about your neighbor?" I said, the bottle poised.

"Let her sleep. This is a good birthday surprise."

I felt as if warm ashes were banked round my heart, like a residue of good intentions. I remembered that when Magdalena came back to Paris after the war, she found her apartment looted, laid waste. One of the first letters to arrive in the mail was from me, to say that I was in love with a much younger woman. "If it means anything at all to you," I said, the coals glowing brighter, "if it can help you to understand me in any way—well, no one ever fascinated me as much as you." This after only one glass.

"But, perhaps, you never loved me," she said.

"Probably not," I said. "Although I must have."

"You mean, in a way?" she said.

"I suppose so."

The room became so quiet that I could hear the afternoon movie on television in the next room. I recognized the voice of the actor who dubs Robert Redford.

Magdalena said, "Even a few months ago this would have been my death sentence. Now I am simply thankful I have so little time left to wander between 'perhaps' and 'probably not' and 'in a way.' A crazy old woman, wringing my hands."

I remembered Juliette's face when she learned that her menopause was irreversible. I remember her shock, her fright, her gradual understanding, her storm of grief. She had hoped for children, then finally a child, a son she would have called "Thomas." "Your death sentence," I said. "Your death sentence. What about Juliette's life sentence? She never had children. By the time I was able to marry her, it was too late."

"She could have had fifteen children without being married," said Magdalena.

I wanted to roar at her, but my voice went high and thin. "Women like Juliette, people like Juliette, don't do that sort of thing. It was a wonder she consented to live with me for all those years. What about her son, her Thomas? I couldn't even have claimed him—not legally, as long as I was married to you. Imagine him, think of him, applying for a passport, finding out he had no father. Nothing on his birth certificate. Only a mother."

"You could have adopted Thomas," said Magdalena. "That way, he'd have been called by your name."

"I couldn't—not without your consent. *You* were my wife. Besides, why should I have to adopt my own son?" I think this was a shout; that is how it comes back to me. "And the inheritance laws, as they were in those days. Have you ever thought about that? I couldn't even make a will in his favor."

Cheek on hand, blue eyes shadowed, my poor, mad, true, and only wife said, "Ah, Édouard, you shouldn't have worried. You know I'd have left him all that I had."

It wasn't the last time I saw Magdalena, but after that day she sent no more urgent messages, made no more awkward demands. Twice since then, she has died and come round. Each time, just when the doctor said, "I think that's it," she has squeezed the nurse's hand. She loves rituals, and she probably wants the last Sacraments, but hospitals hate that. Word that there is a priest in the place gets about, and it frightens the other patients. There are afternoons when she can't speak and lies with her eyes shut, the lids quivering. I hold her hand, and feel the wedding ring. Like the staunch little widows, I call her "Lena," and she turns her head and opens her eyes.

I glance away then, anywhere—at the clock, out the window. I have put up with everything, but I intend to refuse her last imposition, the encounter with her blue, enduring look of pure love.

THE ASSEMBLY

M. Alexandre Caisse, civil servant, employed at the Ministry of Agriculture, bachelor, thanked the seven persons sitting in his living room for having responded to his mimeographed invitation. Actually, he had set chairs out for fifteen.

General Portoret, ret., widower, said half the tenants of the building had already left for their summer holiday.

Mme. Berthe Fourneau, widow, no profession, said Parisians spent more time on vacation than at work. She could remember when two weeks in Brittany seemed quite enough.

M. Louis Labarrière, author and historian, wife taking the cure at Vichy, said that during the Middle Ages Paris had celebrated 230 religious holidays a year.

M. Alberto Minazzoli, industrialist, wife thought to be living in Rome with an actor, said that in his factories strikes had replaced religious feasts. (All smiled.)

Dr. Edmond Volle, dental surgeon, married, said he had not taken a day off in seven years.

Mme. Volle said she believed a wife should never forsake her husband. As a result, she never had a holiday either.

Mlle. de Renard's aunt said it depended on the husband. Some could be left alone for months on end. Others could not. (No one knew Mlle. de Renard's aunt's name.)

M. Alexandre Caisse said they had all been sorry to hear Mlle. de Renard was not feeling well enough to join them.

Mlle. de Renard's aunt said her niece was at this moment under sedation, in a shuttered room, with cotton stuffed in her ears. The slightest sound made her jump and scream with fright.

General Portoret said he was sure a brave woman like Mlle. de Renard would soon be on her feet again.

Mme. Berthe Fourneau said it was probably not easy to forget after one had been intimately molested by a stranger.

Mlle. de Renard's aunt said her niece had been molested, but not raped. There was an unpleasant story going around.

M. Labarrière had heard screaming, but had supposed it was someone's radio.

M. Minazzoli had heard the man running down five flights of stairs. He thought it was a child playing tag.

Mme. Volle had been the first to arrive on the scene; she had found Mlle. de Renard, collapsed, on the fifth-floor landing, her purse lying beside her. The man had not been after money. The stranger, described by his victim as French, fair, and blue-eyed, had obviously crept in from the street and waited for Mlle. de Renard to come home from vesper service.

General Portoret wondered why Mlle. de Renard had not run away the minute she saw him.

Mlle. de Renard's aunt said her niece had been taken by surprise. The man looked respectable. His expression was sympathetic. She thought he had come to the wrong floor.

Mme. Berthe Fourneau said the man must have known his victim's habits.

Dr. Volle said it was simply the cunning of the insane.

M. Labarrière reminded them that the assault of Mlle. de

Renard had been the third in a series: there had been the pots of ivy pilfered from the courtyard, the tramp found asleep in the basement behind the hot-water boiler, and now this.

Mme. Berthe Fourneau said no one was safe.

Mme. Volle had a chain-bolt on her door. She kept a can of insect spray conveniently placed for counteraggression.

M. Alexandre Caisse had a bronze reproduction of "The Dying Gaul" on a table behind the door. He never answered the door without first getting a good grip around the statue's waist.

Mlle. de Renard's aunt said her niece had been too trusting, even as a child.

M. Minazzoli said his door was fully armored. However, the time had come to do something about the door at the entrance to the building. He hoped they would decide, now, once and for all, about putting in an electronic code-lock system.

M. Alexandre Caisse said they were here to discuss, not to decide. The law of July 10, 1965, regulating the administration of cooperatively owned multiple dwellings, was especially strict on the subject of meetings. This was an assembly.

M. Minazzoli said one could arrive at a decision at an assembly as well as at a meeting.

M. Alexandre Caisse said anyone could get the full text of the law from the building manager, now enjoying a photo safari in Kenya. (Having said this, M. Caisse closed his eyes.)

Mlle. de Renard's aunt said she wanted one matter cleared up, and only one: her niece had been molested. She had not been raped.

Mme. Berthe Fourneau wondered how much Mlle. de Renard could actually recall.

Mlle. de Renard's aunt said her niece had given a coherent account from the beginning, an account from which she had never wavered. The man had thrown her against the wall and perpetrated something she called "an embrace." Her handbag had fallen during the struggle. He had run away without stopping to pick it up.

Dr. Volle said it proved the building was open to madmen.

M. Alexandre Caisse asked if anyone would like refreshments. He could offer the ladies a choice of tonic water or bottled lemon soda. The gentlemen might like something stronger. (All thanked him, but refused.)

M. Minazzoli supposed everyone knew how the electronic code system worked and what it would cost.

Mme. Berthe Fourneau asked if it would keep peddlers out. The place was infested with them. Some offered exotic soaps, others ivory trinkets. The peddlers had one thing in common— curly black hair.

M. Labarrière said the tide of color was rising in Paris. He wondered if anyone had noticed it in the Métro. Even in the first-class section you could count the white faces on one hand.

Mme. Volle said it showed the kind of money being made, and by whom.

Black, brown, and yellow, said M. Labarrière. He felt like a stranger in his own country.

Dr. Volle said France was now a doormat for the riffraff of five continents.

M. Alexandre Caisse said the first thing foreigners did was find out how much they could get for free. Then they sent for their families.

General Portoret had been told by a nurse that the hospitals were crammed with Africans and Arabs getting free operations. If you had the bad luck to be white and French you could sit in the waiting room while your appendix burst.

M. Minazzoli said he had flown his mother to Paris for a serious operation. He had paid every centime himself. His mother had needed to have all her adrenalin taken out.

Mme. Volle said when something like that happened there was no such thing as French or foreign—there was just grief and expense.

M. Alexandre Caisse said it was unlikely that a relative of M. Minazzoli would burden the taxpaying community. M. Minazzoli probably knew something about paying taxes, when it came to that. (All laughed gently.)

Mlle. de Renard's aunt said all foreigners were not alike.

General Portoret had commanded a regiment of Montagnards forty years before. They had been spunky little chaps, loyal to France.

M. Labarrière could not understand why Mlle. de Renard had said her attacker was blue-eyed and fair. Most molested women spoke of "the Mediterranean type."

General Portoret wondered if his Montagnards had kept up their French culture. They had enjoyed the marching songs, swinging along happily to "Sambre et Meuse."

M. Minazzoli said in case anyone did not understand the code-lock system, it was something like a small oblong keyboard. This keyboard, affixed to the entrance of the building just below the buzzer one pressed in order to release the door catch, contained the house code.

Mme. Berthe Fourneau asked how the postman was supposed to get in.

M. Labarrière knew it was old-fashioned of him, but he thought a house phone would be better. It was somehow more dignified than all these codes and keyboards.

M. Minazzoli said the code system was cheaper and very safe. The door could not be opened unless the caller knew what the code was, say, J-8264.

Mme. Berthe Fourneau hoped for something easier to remember—something like A-1111.

M. Labarrière said the Montagnards had undoubtedly lost all trace of French culture. French culture was dying everywhere. By 2500 it would be extinct.

M. Minazzoli said the Lycée Chateaubriand was still flourishing in Rome, attended by sons and daughters of the nobility.

Mme. Volle had been told that the Lycée Français in London accepted just anyone now.

Mme. Berthe Fourneau's daughter had spent an anxious au pair season with an English family in the 1950s. They had the curious habit of taking showers together to save hot water.

M. Alexandre Caisse said the hot-water meters in the building needed to be checked. His share of costs last year had been enough to cover all the laundry in Paris.

Mme. Berthe Fourneau said a washing machine just above her living room made a rocking sound.

Mme. Volle never ran the machine before nine or after five.

Mme. Berthe Fourneau had been prevented at nine o'clock at night from hearing the President of the Republic's television interview about the domestic fuel shortage.

M. Minazzoli said he hoped all understood that the security code was not to be mislaid or left around or shared except with a trusted person. No one knew nowadays who might turn out to be a thief. Not one's friends, certainly, but one knew so little about their children.

Mlle. de Renard's aunt wondered if anyone recalled the old days, when the concierge stayed in her quarters night and day like a watchdog. It had been better than a code.

M. Labarrière could remember how when one came in late at night one would call out one's name.

General Portoret, as a young man—a young lieutenant, actually—had given his name as "Jack the Ripper." The concierge had made a droll reply.

M. Alexandre Caisse believed people laughed more easily then.

General Portoret said that the next day the concierge had complained to his mother.

Dr. Volle envied General Portoret's generation. Their pleasures had been of a simple nature. They had not required today's thrills and animation.

M. Labarrière knew he was being old-fashioned, but he did object to the modern inaccurate use of *animation*. Publications from the mayor's office spoke of "animating" the city.

M. Minazzoli could not help asking himself who was paying for these glossy full-color handouts.

Dr. Volle thought the mayor was doing a good job. He

particularly enjoyed the fireworks. As he never took a holiday the fireworks were about all he had by way of entertainment.

M. Labarrière could recall when the statue of the lion in the middle of Place Denfert-Rochereau had been painted the wrong shade. Everyone had protested.

Mlle. de Renard's aunt had seen it—brilliant iridescent coppery paint.

M. Labarrière said no, a dull brown.

Dr. Volle said that had been under a different administration.

General Portoret's mother had cried when she was told that he had said "Jack the Ripper."

Mlle. de Renard's aunt did not understand why the cost of the electronic code system was to be shared out equally. Large families were more likely to wear out the buttons than a lady living alone.

M. Alexandre Caisse said this was an assembly, not a meeting. They were all waiting for the building manager to return from Kenya. The first thing M. Caisse intended to have taken up was the cost of hot water.

Mlle. de Renard's aunt reminded M. Caisse that it was her grandfather, founder of a large Right Bank department store, who had built this house in 1899.

M. Labarrière said there had been a seventeenth-century convent on the site. Tearing it down in 1899 had been an act of vandalism that would not be tolerated today.

General Portoret's parents had been among the first tenants. When he was a boy there had been a great flood of water in the basement. When the waters abated the graves of nuns were revealed.

Mlle. de Renard's aunt said she often wished she were a nun. Peace was all she wanted. (She looked around threateningly as she said this.)

General Portoret said the bones had been put in large canvas bags and stored in the concierge's kitchen until a hallowed resting place could be found.

M. Labarrière said it was hard not to yearn for the past they were describing. That was because he had no feeling for the future. The final French catastrophe would be about 2080.

General Portoret said he hoped that the last Frenchman to die would not die in vain.

M. Alexandre Caisse looked at his watch and said he imagined no one wanted to miss the film on the Third Channel, an early Fernandel.

General Portoret asked if it was the one where Fernandel was a private who kept doing all the wrong things.

Mme. Volle wondered if her husband's patients would let him get away for a few days this year. There was always someone to break a front tooth at the last moment.

General Portoret was going to Montreux. He had been going to the same pension for twelve years, ever since his wife died.

M. Alexandre Caisse said the film would be starting in six minutes. It was not the one about the army; it was the one where Fernandel played a ladies' hairdresser.

Mlle. de Renard's aunt planned to take her niece on a cruise to Egypt when she felt strong enough.

Mme. Berthe Fourneau and her daughter were travelling to Poland in the footsteps of the Pope.

M. Labarrière knew it was dull and old-fashioned of him, but he loved his country and refused to spend any money outside France.

M. Minazzoli was taking a close friend to Greece and Yugoslavia. He believed in Europe.

M. Alexandre Caisse said sometimes it was hard to get a clear image on the Third Channel. He hoped there would be no interference with the Fernandel, which must be just about starting.

Dr. Volle said he was not likely to see that or any other film. He went to bed every night before ten. He rose every morning before six.

M. Alexandre Caisse said he thought they would all be quite safe if they left, now, together, in a group. (He held the door open.)

Mlle. de Renard's aunt said she thought the assembly had been useful. Her niece would feel reassured.

Mme. Berthe Fourneau said perhaps she would no longer feel impelled to open and close her bedroom shutters the whole time.

Mlle. de Renard's aunt said her niece slept all day.

Mme. Berthe Fourneau said yes, but not all night.

General Portoret said, After you.

M. Labarrière said, Ladies first.

(All said goodbye.)

HOME TRUTHS

THANK YOU FOR THE
LOVELY TEA

That year, it began to rain on the twenty-fourth of May —
a holiday still called, some thirty years after her death,
Queen Victoria's Birthday. It rained — this was
Canada — until the middle of June. The girls, kept indoors,
exercising listlessly in the gym, quarrelled over nothing, and
complained of headache. Between showers they walked along
spongy gravel paths, knocking against spiraea bushes that suddenly spattered them with water and white. It was the last lap of
term, the dead period between the end of exams and the start of
freedom. Handicrafts and extra art classes were improvised to
keep them busy, but it was hopeless; glooming over their desks,
they quarrelled, dreamed of summer, wrote plaintive letters
home. Their raincoats were suddenly hot and heavy, their long
black stockings scratchy and damp.

"Life is Hell," Ruth Cook wrote on the lid of a desk, hoping
that someone would see it and that there would be a row. It
was the slow time of day — four o'clock. Yawning over a
drawing of flowerpots during art class, she looked despairingly
out the streaked window and saw Mrs. Holland coming up the
walk. Mrs. Holland looked smart, from that distance. Her

umbrella was furled. On her head was a small hat, tilted to
one side, circled with a feather. She looked smart but
smudged, as if paint had spilled over the outline of a drawing.
Ruth took her in coldly, leaning on a plump, grubby hand.
Mrs. Holland was untidy — she had heard people say so. She
was emotional. This, too, Ruth had overheard, always said
with disapproval. Emotion meant "being American"; it meant
placing yourself unarmed in the hands of the enemy. Emotion
meant not getting one's lipstick on straight, a marcel wave
coming apart in wild strands. It accounted for Mrs. Holland's
anxious blue eyes, for the button missing on a blouse, the odds
and ends forever falling out of purse or pocket. Emotion was
worse than bad taste; it was calamitous. Ruth had only to look
at Mrs. Holland to see what it led to. Mrs. Holland passed up
the front steps and out of sight. Ruth went back to her bold
lettering: "Life is Hell." Any other girl in the room, she
thought with satisfaction, would have gone importantly up to
the desk and whispered that a lady had come to take her to tea,
and could she please go and get ready now? But Ruth knew
that things happened in their own good time. She looked at
her drawing, admired it, and added more flowerpots, dimin-
ishing to a fixed point at the center of the page.

"Well done," said Miss Fischer, the art teacher, falsely,
strolling between the ranks of desks. If she saw "Life is Hell,"
she failed to comment. They were all cowards; there was no
one to fight. "Your horizon line is too low," said Miss Fischer.
"Look at the blackboard; see how I have shown Proportion."

Indicating patience and self-control, Ruth looked at the
blackboard, over it, around it. The blackboard was filled with
receding lines, the lesson having dealt with Perspective as well
as Proportion. Over it hung a photograph of the King — the
late King, that is. He had died that year, and so had Kipling
(although far less fuss was made about him), and the girls had
to get used to calling Kipling "our late beloved poet" and the
Prince of Wales "King Edward." It was hopeless where the
Prince was concerned, for there hung the real King still, with

his stiff, elegant Queen by his side. He had died on a cold January day. They had prayed for him in chapel. His picture was in their prayer books because he was head of the Church — something like that. "It is a year of change," the head-mistress had said, announcing his death.

"It's a year of change, all right," Ruth said softly, imitating the headmistress's English accent. Even the term "head-mistress" was new; the old girl, who had retired to a cottage and a faithful spinster friend, had been content with "princi-pal." But the new one, blonde, breathless, pink-cheeked, was fresh from England, full of notions, and felt that the place wanted stirring up. "I'm afraid I am progress-minded," she told the stone-faced, wary girls. "We must learn never to fear change, provided it is for the best." But they did fear it; they were shocked when the tinted image of George V was taken down from the dining-room wall and the famous picture of the Prince of Wales inspecting the front during the Great War put in its place. The Prince in the photo was a handsome boy, blond, fresh, pink-cheeked — much like the new head-mistress, in fact. "A year of change," the headmistress repeated, as if to impress it forever on their minds.

Scrubbing at her flowerpots with artgum, Ruth thought it over and decided there had been no real change. She had never met the King and didn't care for poetry. She was still in school. Her mother had gone to live abroad, but then she had never been around much. The only difference was that her father had met unfortunate Mrs. Holland.

Coming into the flagged entrance hall, Mrs. Holland was daunted by the chilly gloom. She stared at the row of raincoats hanging from pegs, the sombre portraits of business-men and clergymen on the walls. Governess-trained, she considered herself hopelessly untutored, and attached to the smell of drying coats an atmosphere of learning. Someone came, and went off to fetch the headmistress. Mrs. Holland sat down on a carved bench that looked like a pew. Irreligious but fond of saying she would believe in something if only she could, she gazed with respectful interest at the oil portrait of the school's chief financial rock, a fruit importer who had abandoned Presbyterianism for the Church of England when a sudden rise in wealth and status demanded the change. Although he wore a gay checked suit and looked every inch himself, a small-town Presbyterian go-getter, Mrs. Holland felt he must, surely, be some sort of Anglican dignitary; his portrait was so much larger than the rest; besides, the hall was so hushed and damp that religion had to come into it somewhere. She recalled a story she had been told — that the school had been a Bernardine abbey, transported from England to Canada stone by stone. The lightless corridors, the smell of damp rot emanating from the linen cupboards, the drafts, the cunning Gothic windows with Tudor panes, the dark classrooms and sweating walls, the chill, the cold, the damp, the discomfort, wistfully British, staunchly religious, all suggested this might indeed have been the case. How nice for the girls, Mrs. Holland thought, vaguely but sincerely.

In point of fact, the school had never been an abbey. Each of its clammy stones had been quarried in North America, and the architectural ragout was deliberate; it was intended to provide the pupils with character and background otherwise lacking in a new continent. As for the fruit importer, the size of his portrait had to do only with the size of his endowment. The endowment had been enormous; the school was so superlatively uncomfortable that it cost a fortune to run. The fruit importer's family had been — still were — exceedingly annoyed. They wished he would take up golf and quit meddling in church affairs. He could not help meddling. Presbyterianism had left its scar. Still, he felt uneasy, he was bound to admit, if there were nuns about, or too much incense. Hence his only injunction, most difficult to follow: The school should be neither too High nor too Low. Every regime had interpreted this differently. The retiring principal, to avoid the vulgarity of being Low, had brought in candles and Evensong. The new headmistress, for her part, found things disturbingly High, almost Romish. The white veils the girls wore to chapel distressed her. They were so long that they made the girls look like Carmelite nuns, at least from the waist up. From the waist down, they looked like circus riders, with their black-stockinged legs exposed to garter level. The pleated serge tunics were worn so short, in fact, that the older girls, plump with adolescence, could not sit down without baring a pink inch between tunic and stocking top. The modernism she had threatened took form. She issued an order: lengthen the tunics, shorten the veils. Modernism met with a mulish and unaccountable resistance. Who would have believed that young girls, children of a New World, would so obstinately defend tradition? Modernism, broadmindedness foundered. The headmistress gave up the fight, though not her claim to the qualities in which she took greatest pride.

It was broadmindedness now that compelled her to welcome Mrs. Holland briskly and cordially, ignoring Mrs. Holland's slightly clouded glance and the cigarette stain on the hand she extended. Ruth's father had rung up about tea, so it was quite in order to let Ruth go; still, Mrs. Holland was a family friend, not a parent — a distinction that carried its own procedure. It meant that she need not be received in the private sitting room and given cake but must wait in the office. It meant that Ruth was not to go alone but must be accompanied by a classmate. Waved into the office, Mrs. Holland sat down once more. She propped her umbrella against her chair, offered the headmistress a cigarette. The umbrella slid and fell with a clatter. The cigarette was refused. Reaching for her umbrella, Mrs. Holland tipped her case upside down, and cigarettes rolled everywhere. The headmistress, smiling, helped collect them, marvelling at the variety of experience inherent in teaching, at the personal tolerance that permitted her contact with a woman of Mrs. Holland's sort.

"My hair's all undone, too," said Mrs. Holland, wretchedly, clutching her properties. And, really, watching her, one felt she had too much for any one woman to handle — purse, umbrella, and gloves.

The headmistress retrieved the last cigarette and furtively dropped it in the wastebasket. "With all this rain, one can hardly cope with one's hair," she said, almost as cordially as if Mrs. Holland were a parent. Resolved to be lenient, she remembered that Ruth's father's money did, after all, lend the situation a certain amount of social decency. The headmistress had heard, soon after her arrival, this wayward story of divorce and confusion — Ruth's parents divorced; Ruth's mother, who had behaved badly, gone abroad; the sudden emergence of Mrs. Holland — and she had decided that Ruth ought to be watched. There might be tendencies — what someone less broadminded might have called bad blood. But Ruth was a placid girl, to all appearances — plump, lazy, rather Latin in looks, with glossy blue-black hair, which she brushed into drooping ringlets. In spite of the laziness, one could detect a nascent sense of leadership; she was quite bossy, in fact. The headmistress was satisfied; like the school, the imitation abbey, Ruth was almost the real thing.

Summoned, Ruth came in her own good time. Conversation between the two women had frozen, and they turned to the door with relief. Ruth was trailing not one friend but two, May Watson and Helen McDonnell. The three girls stood, berets on their heads, carrying raincoats. Their long black legs looked more absurd than ever. They shook hands with Mrs. Holland, mumbling courteously. For some reason, they gave the appearance of glowering, rather like the portraits in the hall.

"What time do we have to be back, please?" said Ruth.

"I expect Mrs. Holland will want to bring you back soon after tea," said the headmistress. She made a nervous movement toward Mrs. Holland, who, however, was collecting her belongings without difficulty. The girls were being taken to the tearoom of a department store, Mrs. Holland said. "I *am* pleased," said the headmistress, too enthusiastically. The girls glanced at her with suspicion. But her pleasure was authentic; she had feared that they might be going to Ruth's house, where Mrs. Holland, the family friend, might seem too much at home. Mrs. Holland pressed on the headmistress a warm, frantic farewell and followed the girls out. It had begun to rain again, the slow warm rain of June. Mrs. Holland, distracted, stopped to admire the Tudor-Gothic façade of the school, feeling that this was expected, and was recalled by the fidgeting of her charges. There was more fumbling, this time for car keys, and, at last, they were settled — Ruth in front, as a matter of course (the car was her father's), and Helen and May in back.

"Out of jail," said Ruth, pulling off her beret and shaking out her hair.

"Is it jail, dear? Do you hate it?" said Mrs. Holland. She drove carefully away from the curb, mindful of her responsibilities. "Would you rather —"

"Oh, Ruth," Helen protested, from the back. "You don't mean it."

"Jail," said Ruth, but without much interest. She groped in the side pocket on the door and said, "I left a chocolate bar here last time I was out. Who ate it?"

"Perhaps your father," said Mrs. Holland, wishing Helen had not interrupted that most promising lead about hating school.

"He hates chocolate. You know that. He'd be the last person to eat it. But honestly," she said, placid again, "just listen to me. As if it even mattered."

Situations like this were Mrs. Holland's undoing. The absence of the chocolate bar, Ruth's young, averted profile, made her feel anxious and guilty. The young, to her, were exigent, full of mystery, to be wooed and placated. 'Shall we stop somewhere and get another chocolate bar?" she said. "Would you like that?"

It was terrible to see a grown woman so on the defensive,

made uneasy by someone like Ruth. Helen McDonnell, taller than the others, blond, ill at ease, repeated her eternal prayer that she might never grow up and be made unhappy. As far as she knew, there were no happy adults, other than teachers. She looked at May, to see if she had noticed and if she minded, but May had turned away and was staring at her pale, freckled reflection in the window, thrown back from the dark of the rainy streets. She knew that May was grieving for an identical face, that of her twin, who this year had been sent to another school, across the continent. Driving through thicket suburbs and into town now, they passed May's house, a white house set back on a lawn.

"There's your house, May," Ruth said, twisting around on the front seat. "How come you're a boarder when you are right near?"

"How about you?" said May, angrily.

Ruth twisted a curl and said, "Haven't got a mother at home, that's why."

"Would you like to live at home?" said Mrs. Holland eagerly, and Ruth stiffened. Oh, if only she could teach herself not to be so spontaneous! Instead of drawing the child toward her, she drove her away.

"It's much better to board," said Helen, before Ruth could reply. "I mean, you learn more, and they make you a lady."

"Don't be so stupid," said Ruth, and May said, "Who cares about that?"

Helen, reminded that these two would grow up ladies in any case, colored. But then, she thought, seeing the three of us together, no one could tell. They wore the same uniform, and who was to guess that Ruth's father was rich and May's clever? As long as she had the uniform, everything was all right. Pious, Helen repeated another prayer — that God might miraculously give her different parents.

Furious with Helen for having again interrupted, Mrs. Holland clamped and relaxed her gloved hands on the wheel. Traffic lights came at her through a blur of rain. If only she

and Ruth were alone. If only Ruth, with the candor Ruth's
father was so proud of, would turn to her and say, "Are you
and Daddy getting married?" Then Mrs. Holland might say,
"That depends on you, dear. You see, your father feels, and I
quite agree . . ." Or if Ruth were hostile, openly hating her, if
it were a question of winning her confidence, of replacing the
mother, of being a sister, a companion, a friend . . . But the
girl was closed, indifferent. She seemed unable to grasp the
importance of Mrs. Holland in her father's life. There was an
innocence, a lack of prudence, in her references to the
situation; she said things that made shame and caution fill
Mrs. Holland's heart. She was able to remark, casually, to
Helen and May, "My father and Mrs. Holland drove all the
way to California in this car," reducing the trip (undertaken
with many doubts, with fear, with a feeling that hotel clerks
were looking through and through her) to a simple, unimpor-
tant outing involving two elderly people, long past love.

They crawled into the center of town, in the wake of
streetcars. Mrs. Holland, afraid for her charges, drove so
slowly that she was a traffic hazard. An irritated policeman
waved them by.

"Is the store all right?" Mrs. Holland said to Ruth. "Would
you rather go somewhere else?" She had circled the block
twice, looking for a parking space.

Ruth, annoyed by all this caution, said, "Don't ask me. It's
up to the girls. They're the guests."

But neither of the girls could choose. Helen was shy, May
absorbed. Mrs. Holland found a parking place at last, and they
filed into the store.

"I used to come here all the time with my sister," May said,
suddenly coming to as they stood, jammed, in the elevator.
"We came for birthdays and for treats. We had our birthdays
two days in a row, because we're twins and otherwise it
wouldn't be fair. We wore the same clothes and hardly
anybody could tell us apart. But now," she said, echoing a
parental phrase, "we have different clothes and we go to

different schools, because we have to develop separate personalities."

"Well," said Mrs. Holland, unable to take this in. "Have you a sister?" she said to Helen.

There was a silence; then Helen blurted out, "We're seven at home."

"How nice," said Mrs. Holland. But Helen knew that people said this just to be polite, and that being seven at home was just about the most shameful thing imaginable.

"Are your sisters at school with you?" Mrs. Holland asked.

Everyone in the elevator was listening. Helen hung her head. She had been sent to school by an uncle who was also her godfather and who had taken his duties seriously. Having promised to renounce Satan and all his works in Helen's name, he uprooted her, aged six, from her warm, rowdy, half-literate family and packed her off to school. In school, Helen had been told, she would learn to renounce Satan for herself and, more important, learn to be a lady. Some of the teachers still remembered her arriving, mute and frightened, quite as frightened as if the advantages of superior schooling had never been pointed out. There were only three boarders Helen's age. They were put in the care of an elderly housekeeper, who filled a middle role, neither staff nor servant. After lessons they were sent to sit with her, in her red-papered, motto-spangled room. She taught them hymns; the caterwauling got on her nerves, but at least they sat still while singing. She supervised their rushed baths and murderously washed their hair. Sometimes some of the staff wondered if more should not be done for the little creatures, for although they were clean and good and no trouble, the hand that dressed them was thorough but unaffectionate, and they never lost the wild-eyed hopelessly untidy look of unloved children. Helen now remembered very little of this, nor could she imagine life away from school. Her uncle-godfather conscientiously sent her home each summer, to what seemed to her a common, clamorous, poverty-stricken family. "They're so loud," she would confide to the now quite elderly person who had once taught her hymns. "Their voices are so loud. And they drink, and everything." She had grown up to be a tall, quiet girl, much taller than most girls her own age. In spite of her height she wore her short, ridiculous tunic unselfconsciously. Her dearest wish was to wear this uniform as long as she could, to stay on at the school forever, to melt, with no intervening gap, from the students' dining hall to the staff sitting room. Change disturbed her; she was hostile to new girls, could scarcely bear it when old girls came back to be married from the school chapel. Hanging over the stairs with the rest of the girls, watching the exit of the wedding party from chapel to street, she would wonder how the bride could bear to go off this way, with a man no one knew, having seen school again, having glimpsed the girls on the stairs. When the headmistress said, in chapel, confusing two esteemed poets, "The old order changeth, girls. The Captains and Kings depart. Our King has gone, and now our beloved Kipling has left us," Helen burst into tears. She did not wish the picture of George V to leave the walls; she did not want Kipling to be "the late." For a few days afterward, the girls amused themselves by saying, "Helen, listen. The Captains and Kings depart," so that they could be rewarded, and slightly horrified, by her astonishing grief. But then they stopped, for her shame and silence after such outbursts were disconcerting. It never became a joke, and so had to be abandoned.

Mrs. Holland and her guests settled into an oval tearoom newly done up with chrome and onyx, stuffed with shoppers, smelling of tea, wet coats, and steam heating. Helen looked covertly at Mrs. Holland, fearing another question. None came. The waitress had handed them each a giant, tasselled menu. "I'll have whatever the rest of them have," Helen said, not looking at hers.

"Well," said Ruth, "I'll have chocolate ice cream with marshmallow. No, wait. Strawberry with pineapple."

May forgot her sister. The choice before her was insupport-
able. "The same as Ruth," she said, at last, agonized and
uncertain.

Mrs. Holland, who loathed sweets, ordered a sundae, as a
friendly gesture, unaware that in the eyes of the girls she had
erred. Mothers and their substitutes were expected to drink tea
and nibble at flabby pâté sandwiches.

As soon as their ice cream was before them, Ruth began
again about the chocolate bar. "My father never eats chocolate," she said, quite suddenly. "And he knew it was mine.
He'd never touch anything that wasn't his. It would be
stealing."

"Maybe it got thrown away," said May.

"That'd be the same as stealing." said Ruth.

Mrs. Holland said, "Ruth, I do not know what became of
your bit of chocolate."

Ruth turned to Mrs. Holland her calm brown eyes. "Goodness!" she said. "I never meant to say you took it. Anyway,
even if you did make a mistake and eat it up sometime when
you were driving around — Well, I mean, who cares? It was
only a little piece, half a Cadbury bar in blue paper."

"I seldom eat chocolate," said Mrs. Holland. "If I had seen
it, let alone eaten it, I should certainly have remembered."

"Then he must have had somebody else with him," said
Ruth. The matter appeared to be settled. She went on eating,
savoring every mouthful.

Mrs. Holland put down her spoon. The trend of this outing,
she realized now, could lead only to tears. It was one of the
situations in her life — and they were frequent — climaxed by
a breakdown. The breakdown would certainly be her own: she
wept easily. Ruth, whose character so belied her stormy Latin
looks, had rarely wept since babyhood. May, the thin, freckled
one, appeared quite strung up about something, but held in by
training, by discipline. I lack both, Mrs. Holland thought. As
for the big girl, Helen, Mrs. Holland had already dismissed
her as cold and stupid. Mrs. Holland said softly, "*Les larmes*

d'un adolescent." But it doesn't apply to cold little Canadians, she thought.

"I know what that means," said Ruth. She licked her spoon on both sides.

Mrs. Holland's phrase, the image it evoked, came from the outer circle of experience. Disturbed, the girls moved uneasily in their chairs, feeling that nothing more should be said.

"Don't you girls *ever* cry?" said Mrs. Holland, almost with hostility.

"Never," said Ruth, settling that.

"My sister cried," said May. She turned her light-lashed gaze to Helen and said, "And Helen cries."

"I don't," said Helen. She drew in, physically, with the first apprehension of being baited. "I do not."

"Oh, Helen, you do," said May. She turned to Ruth for confirmation, but Ruth, indifferent, having spoken for herself, was scooping up the liquid dregs of her ice cream. "Do you want to see Helen cry?" said May. Like Mrs. Holland, she seemed to have accepted the idea that one of them was going to break down and disgrace them; it might as well be Helen. Or perhaps the remark went deeper than that. Mrs. Holland, who could barely follow Ruth's mental and emotional spirals, felt unable, and disinclined, to cope with this one. May leaned forward, facing Helen. Mrs. Holland suddenly answered "No," too late, for May was saying, in a pretty, piping voice, "Hey, Helen, listen. The King has left us, and Kipling is dead."

Helen failed to reward her. She stared, stolid, as if the words had been in a foreign language. But there remained about the table the knowledge that an attempt had been made, and Mrs. Holland and Helen, both natural victims, could not look away from May, or at each other. Ruth had finished eating. She sighed, stretched, began to tug on her coat. She said to Mrs. Holland. "Thankyouverymuchforalovelytea. I mean, if our darling new headmistress asks did we thank you, well, we did. I was afraid I might forget to say it later on."

"Thanks for a lovely tea," said May. She had been afraid to speak, in case the effort of forming words should release the tight little knot of tears she felt in her throat. It was so much more difficult to be cruel than to be hurt.

"Thank you," said Helen, as if asleep.

"I can only hope they thanked you," the headmistress said when Mrs. Holland delivered them, safe, half an hour later. "Girls are apt to forget."

"They thanked me," said Mrs. Holland. The three girls had curtsied, muttering some final ritual phrase, and vanished into an area of dim, shrill sound.

"Study hall," said the headmistress. "Their studies are over for the term, but they respect the discipline."

"Yes, I suppose they do."

"It was kind of you to take them out," said the headmistress. She laid her cold pink hand on Mrs. Holland's for a moment, then withdrew it, perplexed by the wince, the recoil. "One forgets how much it can mean at that age, a treat on a rainy day."

"Perhaps that's the answer," Mrs. Holland said.

The headmistress sensed that things were out of hand, but she had no desire to be involved; perhaps the three had been noisy, had overeaten. She smiled with such vague good manners that Mrs. Holland was released and could go.

From an upstairs window, Ruth watched Mrs. Holland make her way to the car. May and Helen were not speaking. Helen was ready to forgive, but to May, who had been unkind, the victim was odious, and she avoided her with a kind of prudishness impossible to explain to anyone, let alone herself. They had all made mistakes, Ruth thought. She wondered if she would ever care enough about anyone to make all the mistakes those around her had made during the rainy-day tea with Mrs. Holland. She breathed on the window, idly drew a heart, smiled placidly, let it fade.

JORINDA
AND JORINDEL

A summer night: all night someone has been learning the Charleston.

"I've got it!" the dancer cries. "I've got it, everybody. Watch me, now!" But no one is watching. The dancer is alone in the dining room, clinging to the handle of the door; the rest of the party is in the living room, across the hall. "Watch me!" travels unheard over the quiet lawn and the silent lake, and then dissolves.

The walls of the summer house are thin. The doors have been thrown back and the windows pushed as high as they will go. Young Irmgard wakes up with her braids undone and her thumb in her mouth. She has been dreaming about her cousin Bradley; about an old sidewalk with ribbon grass growing in the cracks. "I've got it," cried the witch who had captured Jorinda, and she reached out so as to catch Jorindel and change him into a bird.

Poor Mrs. Bloodworth is learning to dance. She holds the handle of the dining-room door and swivels her feet in satin shoes, but when she lets go the handle, she falls down flat on her behind and stays that way, sitting, her hair all over her face, her feet pointing upward in her new shoes. Earlier, Mrs. Bloodworth was sitting that way, alone, when, squinting through her hair, she saw Irmgard sitting in her nightgown on the stairs. "Are you watching the fun?" she said in a tragic voice. "Is it really you, my sweet pet?" And she got to her feet and crawled up the stairs on her hands and knees to kiss Irmgard with ginny breath.

There is prohibition where Mrs. Bloodworth comes from. She has come up to Canada for a party; she came up for just one weekend and never went away. The party began as a wedding in Montreal, but it has been days since anyone mentioned the bride and groom. The party began in Montreal, came down to the lake, and now has dwindled to five: Irmgard's mother and father, Mrs. Bloodworth, Mrs. Bloodworth's friend Bill, and the best man, who came up for the wedding from Buffalo. "Darling pet, may I always stay?" said Mrs. Bloodworth, sobbing, her arms around Irmgard's mother's neck. Why she was sobbing this way nobody knows; she is always crying, dancing, embracing her friends.

In the morning Mrs. Bloodworth will be found in the hammock outside. The hammock smells of fish, the pillow is stuffed with straw; but Mrs. Bloodworth can never be made to go to bed. Irmgard inspects her up and down, from left to right. It isn't every morning of the year that you find a large person helplessly asleep. She is still wearing her satin shoes. Her eyeballs are covered with red nets. When she wakes up she seems still asleep, until she says stickily, "I'm having a rotten time, I don't care what anybody says." Irmgard backs off and then turns and runs along the gallery — the veranda, Mrs. Bloodworth would say — and up the side of the house and into the big kitchen, where behind screen doors Mrs. Queen and Germaine are drinking tea. They are drinking it in silence, for Germaine does not understand one word of English and Mrs. Queen is certainly not going to learn any French.

Germaine is Irmgard's *bonne d'enfant*. They have been together about a century, and have a history stuffed with pageants, dangers, near escapes. Germaine has been saving Irmgard for years and years; but now Irmgard is nearly eight, and there isn't much Germaine can do except iron her summer dresses and braid her hair. They know a separation is near; and Irmgard is cheeky now, as she never was in the past; and Germaine pretends there have been other children she has liked just as well. She sips her tea. Irmgard drops heavily on her lap, joggling the cup. She will never be given anything even approaching Germaine's unmeasured love again. She leans heavily on her and makes her spill her tea. Germaine is mild and simple, a little dull. You can be rude and impertinent if necessary, but she must never be teased.

Germaine remembers the day Irmgard was kidnapped. When she sees a warm August morning like this one, she remembers that thrilling day. There was a man in a motorcar who wanted to buy Irmgard ice cream. She got in the car and it started moving, and suddenly there came Germaine running behind, with her mouth open and her arms wide, and Molly, the collie they had in those days, running with her ears back and her eyes slits. "Stop for Molly!" Irmgard suddenly screamed, and she turned and threw up all over the man's coat. "*Le matin du kidnap.*" Germaine begins softly. It is a good thing she is here to recall the event, because the truth is that Irmgard remembers nothing about that morning at all.

Mrs. Queen is standing up beside the stove. She never sits down to eat, because she wants them to see how she hasn't a minute to waste; she is on the alert every second. Mrs. Queen is not happy down at the lake. It is not what she expected by "a country place." When she worked for Lady Partridge things were otherwise, you knew what to expect by "a country place." Mrs. Queen came out to Canada with Lady Partridge. The wages were low, and she had no stomach for travel, but she was devoted to Lady P. and to Ty-Ty and Buffy, the two cairns. The cairns died, because of the change of air, and after Lady P. had buried them, she went out to her daughter in California, leaving Mrs. Queen to look after the graves. But

Mrs. Queen has never taken to Canada. She can't get used to it. She cannot get used to a place where the railway engines are that size and make that kind of noise, and where the working people are as tall as anyone else. When Mrs. Queen was interviewing Irmgard's mother, to see if Irmgard's mother would do, she said she had never taken to the place and couldn't promise a thing. The fancy might take her any minute to turn straight around and go back to England. She had told Lady Partridge the same thing. "When was that, Mrs. Queen?" "In nineteen ten, in the spring." She has never felt at home, and never wants to, and never will. If you ask her why she is unhappy, she says it is because of Ty-Ty and Buffy, the cairns; and because this is a paltry rented house and a paltry kitchen; and she is glad that Ty-Ty and Buffy are peacefully in their graves.

The party last night kept Mrs. Queen awake. She had to get up out of her uncomfortable bed and let the collies out of the garage. They knew there was a party somewhere, and were barking like fools. She let them out, she says, and then spent some time on the gallery, looking in the living-room window. It was a hot, airless night. (She happens to have the only stuffy room in the house.) The party was singing "Little Joe." Apparently, she did not see Mrs. Bloodworth dancing and falling down; at least she doesn't mention it.

Mrs. Queen is not going to clean up the mess in the living room. It is not her line of country. She is sick, sore, and weary. Germaine will, if asked, but just now she is braiding Irmgard's hair. Eating toast, Irmgard leans comfortably against Germaine. They are perfectly comfortable with each other, but Mrs. Queen is crying over by the stove.

Irmgard's cousin Bradley went back to Boston yesterday. She should be missing him, but he has vanished, fallen out of summer like a stone. He got on the train covered with bits of tape and lotion, and with a patch on one eye. Bradley had a terrible summer. He got poison ivy, in July, before coming here. In August, he grew a sty, which became infected, and then he strained his right arm. "I don't know what your mother will say," Irmgard's mother said. At this, after a whole summer of being without them, Bradley suddenly remembered he had a father and mother, and started to cry. Bradley is ten, but tall as eleven. He and Irmgard have the same look — healthy and stubborn, like well-fed, intelligent mice. They often stare in the mirror, side by side, positively blown up with admiration. But Bradley is superior to Irmgard in every way. When you ask him what he wants to be, he says straight off, "A mechanical and electrical engineer," whereas Irmgard is still hesitating between a veterinary and a nun.

"Have you dropped Freddy now that Bradley is here?" It seems that she was asked that a number of times.

"Oh, I still like Freddy, but Bradley's my cousin and everything." This is a good answer. She has others, such as, "I'm English-Canadian only I can talk French and I'm German descent on one side." (Bradley is not required to think of answers; he is American, and that does. But in Canada you have to keep saying what you are.) Irmgard's answer — about Freddy — lies on the lawn like an old skipping rope, waiting to catch her up. "Watch me," poor Mrs. Bloodworth said, but nobody cared, and the cry dissolved. "I like Freddy," Irmgard said, and was heard, and the statement is there, underfoot. For if she still likes Freddy, why isn't he here?

Freddy's real name is Alfred Marcel Dufresne. He has nine sisters and brothers, but doesn't know where they are. In winter he lives in an orphanage in Montreal. He used to live there all the year round, but now that he is over seven, old enough to work, he spends the summer with his uncle, who has a farm about two miles back from the lake. Freddy is nearly Irmgard's age, but smaller, lighter on his feet. He looks a tiny six. When he comes to lunch with Irmgard, which they have out in the kitchen with Germaine, everything has to be cut on his plate. He has never eaten with anything but a spoon. His chin rests on the edge of the table. When he is eating, you see nothing except his blue eyes, his curly dirty hair, and his hand around the bowl of the spoon. Once, Germaine said calmly, uncritically, "You eat just like a pig," and Freddy repeated in the tone she had used, "*comme un cochon*," as if it were astonishing that someone had, at last, discovered the right words.

Freddy cannot eat, or read, or write, or sing, or swim. He has never seen paints and books, except Irmgard's; he has never been an imaginary person, never played. It was Irmgard who taught him how to swim. He crosses himself before he goes in the water, and looks down at his wet feet, frowning — a worried mosquito — but he does everything she says. The point of their friendship is that she doesn't have to say much. They can read each other's thoughts. When Freddy wants to speak, Irmgard tells him what he wants to say, and Freddy stands there, mute as an animal, grave, nodding, at ease. He does not know the names of flowers, and does not distinguish between the colors green and blue. The apparitions of the Virgin, which are commonplace, take place against a heaven he says is "*vert*."

Now, Bradley has never had a vision, and if he did he wouldn't know what it was. He has no trouble explaining anything. He says, "Well, this is the way it is," and then says. He counts eight beats when he swims, and once saved Irmgard's life — at least he says he did. He says he held on to her braids until someone came by in a boat. No one remembers it but Bradley; it is a myth now, like the *matin du kidnap*. This year, Bradley arrived at the beginning of August. He had spent July in Vermont, where he took tennis lessons and got poison ivy. He was even taller than the year before, and he got down from the train with pink lotion all over his sores and, under his arm, a tennis racket in a press. "What a little stockbroker Bradley is," Irmgard heard her mother say later on; but Mrs. Queen declared that his manners left nothing wanting.

Bradley put all his own things away and set out his toothbrush in a Mickey Mouse glass he travelled with. Then he came down, ready to swim, with his hair water-combed. Irmgard was there, on the gallery, and so was Freddy, hanging on the outside of the railings, his face poked into the morning-glory vines. He thrusts his face between the leaves, and grins, and shows the gaps in his teeth. "How small he is! Do you play with him?" says Bradley, neutrally. Bradley is after information. He needs to know the rules. But if he had been sure about Freddy, if he had seen right away that they could play with Freddy, he would never have asked. And Irmgard replies, "No, I don't," and turns her back. Just so, on her bicycle, coasting downhill, she has lost control and closed her eyes to avoid seeing her own disaster. Dizzily, she says, "No, I don't," and hopes Freddy will disappear. But Freddy continues to hang on, his face thrust among the leaves, until Bradley, quite puzzled now, says, "Well, is he a friend of yours, or what?" and Irmgard again says, "No."

Eventually, that day or the next day, or one day of August, she notices Freddy has gone. Freddy has vanished; but Bradley gives her a poor return. He has the tennis racket, and does nothing except practice against the house. Irmgard has to chase the balls. He practices until his arm is sore, and then he is pleased and says he has tennis arm. Everybody bothers him. The dogs go after the balls and have to be shut up in the garage. "Call the dogs!" he implores. This is Bradley's voice, over the lake, across the shrinking afternoons. "Please, some-body, call the dogs!"

Freddy is forgotten, but Irmgard thinks she has left some-thing in Montreal. She goes over the things in her personal suitcase. Once, she got up in the night to see if her paintbox was there — if that hadn't been left in Montreal. But the paintbox was there. Something else must be missing. She goes over the list again.

"The fact is," Bradley said, a few days ago, dabbing pink lotion on his poison ivy, "I don't really play with any girls now.

So unless you get a brother or something, I probably won't come again." Even with lotion all over his legs he looks splendid. He and Irmgard stand side by side in front of the bathroom looking glass, and admire. She sucks in her cheeks. He peers at his sty. "My mother said you were a stockbroker," Irmgard confides. But Bradley is raised in a different political climate down there in Boston and does not recognize "stockbroker" as a term of abuse. He smiles fatly, and moves his sore tennis arm in a new movement he has now.

During August Freddy no longer existed; she had got in the habit of not seeing him there. But after Bradley's train pulled out, as she sat alone on the dock, kicking the lake, she thought, What'll I do now?, and remembered Freddy. She knows what took place the day she said "No" and, even more, what it meant when she said "Oh, I still like Freddy." But she has forgotten. All she knows now is that when she finds Freddy — in his uncle's muddy farmyard — she understands she hadn't left a paintbox or anything else in Montreal; Freddy was missing, that was all. But Freddy looks old and serious. He hangs his head. He has been forbidden to play with her now, he says. His uncle never wanted him to go there in the first place; it was a waste of time. He only allowed it because they were summer people from Montreal. Wondering where to look, both look at their shoes. Their meeting is made up of Freddy's feet in torn shoes, her sandals, the trampled mud of the yard. Irmgard sees blackberries, not quite ripe. Dumb as Freddy, having lost the power to read his thoughts, she picks blackberries, hard and greenish, and puts them in her mouth.

Freddy's uncle comes out of the foul stable and says something so obscene that the two stand frozen, ashamed — Irmgard, who does not know what the words mean, and Freddy, who does. Then Freddy says he will come with her for just one swim, and not to Irmgard's dock but to a public beach below the village, where Irmgard is forbidden to go: the water is said to be polluted there.

Germaine has her own way of doing braids. She holds the middle strand of hair in her teeth until she has a good grip on the other two. Then she pulls until Irmgard can feel her scalp lifted from her head. Germaine crosses hands, lets go the middle strand, and is away, breathing heavily. The plaits she makes are glossy and fat, and stay woven in water. She works steadily, breathing on Irmgard's neck.

Mrs. Queen says, "I'll wager you went to see poor Freddy the instant that Bradley was out of sight."

"Mmm."

"Don't 'Mmm' me. I hope he sent you packing."

"We went for a swim."

"I never saw a thing like it. That wretched boy was nothing but a slave to you all summer until Bradley came. It was Freddy do this, come here, go there. That charming English Mrs. Bustard who was here in July remarked the same thing. 'Irmgard is her mother all over again,' Mrs. Bustard said. 'All over again, Mrs. Queen.'"

"*Mrs. Bustard est une espèce de vache*," says Germaine gently, who cannot understand a word of English.

"Irmgard requires someone with an iron hand. 'A hand of iron,' Mrs. Bustard said."

Irmgard was afraid to tell Freddy, "But we haven't got our bathing suits or any towels." He was silent, and she could no longer read his mind. The sun had gone in. She was uneasy, because she was swimming in a forbidden place, and frightened by the water spiders. There had been other bathers; they had left their candy wrappers behind and a single canvas shoe. The lake was ruffled, brown. She suggested, "It's awfully cold," but Freddy began undressing, and Irmgard, not sure of her ground, began to unbuckle her sandals. They turned their backs, in the usual manner. Irmgard had never seen anybody undressed, and no one had ever seen her, except Germaine.

Her back to Freddy, she pulled off her cotton dress, but kept on her bloomers. When she turned again, Freddy was naked. It was not a mistake; she had not turned around too soon. He stood composedly, with one hand on his skinny ribs. She said only, "The water's dirty here," and again, "It's cold." There were tin cans in the lake, half sunk in mud, and the water spiders. When they came out, Irmgard stood goosefleshed, blue-lipped. Freddy had not said a word. Trembling, wet, they put on their clothes. Irmgard felt water running into her shoes. She said miserably, "I think my mother wants me now," and edged one foot behind the other, and turned, and went away. There was nothing they could say, and nothing they could play any longer. He had discovered that he could live without her. None of the old games would do.

G ermaine knows. This is what Germaine said yesterday afternoon; she was simple and calm, and said, "*Oui, c'est comme ça. C'est bien malheureux. Tu sais, ma p'tite fille, je crois qu'un homme, c'est une déformation.*"

Irmgard leans against Germaine. They seem to be consoling each other, because of what they both know. Mrs. Queen says, "Freddy goes back to an orphan asylum. I knew from the beginning the way it would end. It was not a kindness, allowing him to come here. It was no kindness at all." She would say more, but they have come down and want their breakfast. After keeping her up all night with noise, they want their breakfast now.

Mrs. Bloodworth looks distressed and unwashed. Her friend has asked for beer instead of coffee. Pleasure followed by gloom is a regular pattern here. But no matter how they feel, Irmgard's parents get up and come down for breakfast, and they judge their guests by the way they behave not in pleasure but in remorse. The man who has asked for beer as medicine and not for enjoyment, and who described the condition of his stomach and the roots of his hair, will never be invited again.

Irmgard stands by her mother's chair; for the mother is the mirror, and everything is reflected or darkened, given life or dismissed, in the picture her mother returns. The lake, the house, the summer, the reason for doing one thing instead of another are reflected here, explained, clarified. If the mirror breaks, everything will break too.

They are talking quietly at the breakfast table. The day began in fine shape, but now it is going to be cloudy again. They think they will all go to Montreal. It is nearly Labor Day. The pity of parties is that they end.

"Are you sad, too, now that your little boy friend has left you?" says Mrs. Bloodworth, fixing Irmgard with her still-sleeping eyes. She means Bradley; she thought he and Irmgard were perfectly sweet.

Now, this is just the way they don't like Irmgard spoken to, and Irmgard knows they will not invite Mrs. Bloodworth again, either. They weigh and measure and sift everything people say, and Irmgard's father looks cold and bored, and her mother gives a waking tiger's look his way, smiles. They act together, and read each other's thoughts – just as Freddy and Irmgard did. But, large, and old, and powerful, they have greater powers: they see through walls, and hear whispered conversations miles away. Irmgard's father looks cold, and Irmgard, without knowing it, imitates his look.

"Bradley is Irmgard's cousin," her mother says.

Now Irmgard, who cannot remember anything, who looked for a paintbox when Freddy had gone, who doesn't remember that she was kidnapped and that Bradley once saved her life – now Irmgard remembers something. It seems that Freddy was sent on an errand. He went off down the sidewalk, which was heaving, cracked, edged with ribbon grass; and when he came to a certain place he was no longer there. Something was waiting for him there, and when they came looking for him, only Irmgard knew that whatever had been waiting for Freddy was the disaster, the worst thing. Irmgard's mother said, "Imagine sending a child near the woods at this time of day!" Sure enough, there were trees nearby. And only Irmgard knew that whatever had been waiting for Freddy had come out of the woods. It was the worst thing; and it could not be helped. But she does not know exactly what it was. And then, was it Freddy? It might have been Bradley, or even herself.

Naturally, no child should go near a strange forest. There are chances of getting lost. There is the witch who changes children into birds.

Irmgard grows red in the face and says loudly, "I remember my dream. Freddy went on a message and got lost."

"Oh, no dreams at breakfast, please," her father says.

"Nothing is as dreary as a dream," her mother says, agreeing. "I think we might make a rule on that; no dreams at breakfast. Otherwise it gets to be a habit."

Her father cheers up. Nothing cheers them up so fast as a new rule, for when it comes to making rules, they are as bad as children. You should see them at croquet.

SATURDAY

1

After the girl across the aisle had glanced at Gérard a few times (although he was not talking to her, not even trying to), she went down to sit at the front of the bus, near the driver. She left behind a bunch of dark, wet, purple lilac wrapped in wet newspaper. When Gérard followed to tell her, she did not even turn her head. Feeling foolish, he suddenly got down anywhere, in a part of Montreal he had never seen before, and in no time at all he was lost. He stood on the curb of a gloomy little street recently swept by a spring tempest of snow. A few people, bundled as Russians, scuffled by. A winter haze like a winter evening sifted down through a lattice of iron and steel. The sudden lowering of day, he saw, was caused by an overhead railway. This railway was smart and new, as if it had been unpacked out of sawdust quite recently and snapped into place.

What was it for? "Of all the unnecessary . . ." Gérard muttered, just as his father might. Talking aloud to oneself was a family habit. You could grumble away for minutes at

home without anyone's taking the least notice. "Yes, they have
to spend our money somehow," he went on, just as if he were
old enough to vote and pay taxes. Luckily no one heard him.
Everyone's attention had been fixed by a funeral procession of
limousines grinding along in inches of slush. The Russian
bundles crossed themselves, but Gérard kept his hands in his
pockets. "Clogging up the streets," he offered, as an opinion
about dying and being taken somewhere for burial. At that
moment the last cars broke away, climbed the curb, and
continued along the sidewalk. Gérard pressed back to the wall
behind him, as he saw the others doing. No one appeared
astonished, and he supposed that down here, in the east end,
where there was a funeral a minute, this was the custom.
"Otherwise you'd never have any normal traffic," he said.
"Only all these hearses."

He thought, all at once, Why is everybody looking at me?

He was smiling. That was why. He could not help smiling.
It was like a cinématèque comedy — the black cars in the
whitish fog, the solemn bystanders wiping their noses on their
gloves and crossing themselves, and everyone in winter
cocoon clothes, with a white bubble of breath. But it was not
black and gray, like an old film: it was the color of winter and
cities, brown and brick and sand. What was more, the friends
and relations of the dead were now descending from their
stopped cars, and he feared that his smile might have offended
them, or made him seem gross and unfeeling; and so, in a
propitiatory gesture he at once regretted, he touched his
forehead, his chest, and a point on each shoulder.

He had never done this for himself. Until now, he had
never craved approval. From the look of the mourners, they
were all Protestants anyway. He wanted to tell them he had
crossed himself by mistake; that he was an atheist, from a
singular and perhaps a unique family of anti-clerics. But the
mourners were too grieved to pay attention. Even the men
were sobbing. They held their hands against their mouths,
they blinked and choked, they all but doubled over with pain

— they were laughing at something. Perhaps at Gérard? Well, they were terrible people. He had always known. He was relieved to see one well-behaved person among them. She had been carried from her car and placed, with gentle care, in a collapsible aluminum wheelchair. Loving friends attended her, one to hold her purse, another to tie her scarf, a third to tuck a fur robe around her knees. Gérard had often been ill, and he recognized on her face the look of someone who knows about separateness and nightmares and all the vile tricks that the body can play. Her hair was careless, soft, and long, but the face seemed thirty, which was, to him, rather old. She turned her dark head and he heard her say gravely, "Not since the liberation of Elizabeth Barrett . . ."

The coffin lay in the road. It had been let down from a truck, parked there as if workmen were about to jump out and begin shovelling snow or mending the pavement. The dead man must have left eccentric instructions, Gérard thought, for his coffin was nothing more than pieces of brown carton stapled together in a rough shape. The staples were slipping out; that was how carelessly and above all how cheaply the thing had been done. Gérard had a glimpse of a dark suit and a watch chain before he looked away. The hands, he saw, rested upon a long white envelope. He was to be buried with a packet of securities, as all Protestants probably were. The crippled woman touched Gérard on the arm and said, "Just reach over and get it, will you?" — that way, casually, used to service. No one stopped Gérard or asked him what he thought he was doing. As he slipped the envelope away he knew that this impertinence, this violation, would turn the dead man into a fury where he was concerned. By his desire to be agreeable, Gérard had deliberately and foolishly given himself some bad nights.

Jazz from an all-night program invaded the house until Gérard's mother, discovering its source in the kitchen, turned the radio off. She supposed Gérard had walked in his sleep. What else could she think when she found him kneeling, in the dark, with his head against the refrigerator door? Beside him was a smashed plate and the leftover ham that had been on it, and an overturned stool. She knelt too, and drew his head on her shoulder. His father stood in the doorway. The long underwear he wore at all times and in every season showed at his wrists and ankles, where the pajamas stopped. Without his teeth and without his glasses he seemed younger and clearer about the eyes, but frighteningly helpless and almost female. His head and his hands were splashed with large, soft-looking freckles.

"He looks so peaceful," the old man said. "This is how he always looks when we aren't around."

She did not answer, for once, "Oh, nobody cares," but her expression cried for her, "What useless, pointless remark will you think of next?" She clasped her son and tried to rock him. As Gérard resisted, she held still. Of all her children, he was the one with whom she blundered most. His uneven health, his moods, his temper, his choked breathing, were signs of starvation, she had been told, but not of the body. The mother was to blame. How to blame? How? Why not the father? They hadn't said. Her daughters were married; Léopold was still small; in between came this strange boy. One of Queen Victoria's children had been flogged for having asthma. Why should she think of this now? She had never punished her children. The very word had been banned.

Gérard heard his father open the refrigerator and then heard him pouring beer in a glass.

"He's been out with his girl," his father said. "She's no Cleopatra, but it's better than having him queer."

All Gérard felt then was how her grip slackened. She said softly, "Get rid of that girl. Just until you've passed your exams. Look at what she's doing to you. One day you'll meet her in the street and you'll wonder why you fought with your mother over her. Get rid of her and I'll believe everything you ever say. You've never walked in your sleep. You came in late. You were hungry . . ."

"What about the funeral?" the old man said. "Whose funeral?"

"Leave him," said his mother. "He's been dreaming."

Gérard, no longer refusing, let his mother rock him. If it had been a dream, then why in English? Dreaming in English made him feel powerless, as if his mind were dying, ill-fed from the soil. They spoke English at home, but he, Gérard, tried to dream in French. He read French; he went to French movies; he tried to speak it with his little brother; and yet his mind made fun of him and sent up to the surface "Elizabeth Barrett." The family had not deserted French for social betterment, or for business reasons, but on the matter of belief that set them apart. His mother wanted English to be freedom, at least from the Church. There were no public secular schools, but that was only part of it. Church and language were inextricably enmeshed, and you had to leave the language if you wanted your children brought up some other way. That was how it was. It was as simple, and as complex, as that. But (still pressed to his mother) he thought that here in the house there had never been freedom, only tension and conversation (oh, such a lot of conversation!) and a few corrupted qualities disguised as "speaking your mind," "taking a stand," and "drawing the line somewhere." Caressed by his mother, he seemed privileged. Being privileged, he weakened, and that meant even his rage was fouled. He had so much to hate that he seemed to carry in his brain a miniature Gérard, sneering and dark.

"If you would just do something about your children instead of all the time thinking about yourself," he heard his mother say, "Oh, anything. Do anything. Who cares what you do now? Nobody cares."

There had been a shortage of bedrooms until Gérard's five sisters married. His mother kept for her private use a sitting room with periwinkle paper on the walls. It could have done as a bedroom for the two boys, but her need for this extra space was never questioned. She had talks with her daughters there, and she kept the household accounts. Believing it her duty, she read her children's personal letters and their diaries as long as they lived under her roof. She carried the letters to the bright room and sat, leaning her head on her hand, reading. If someone came in she never tried to hide what she read, or slip it under a book, but let her hand fall, indifferently. In this room Gérard had lived the most hideous adventure of his life. Sometimes he thought it was a dream and he willed it to be a dream, even if it meant reversing sleeping and waking forever and accepting as friends and neighbors the strangers he saw in his sleep. He would remember it sometimes and say, "I must have dreamed it." His collection of pornography was heaped in plain sight on his mother's desk. There were the pictures, the books carefully dissimulated under fake covers, and the post-cards from France and India turned face down. His mother sat with these at her elbow, and, of course, he could see them, and she said, "Gérard, I won't always be here. I'm not immortal. Your father is thirty years older than I am but he didn't have to bear his own children and he's as sound as this house. He might very well outlive me. I want you to see that he is always looked after and that he always uses saccharine to sweeten his tea. There is a little box I slip in his pajama pocket and another in the kitchen. Promise me. Now, the sweater you had on yesterday. I want to throw it out. It's past mending. I don't want you to sulk for a week, and that's why I'm asking you first." He wanted to say, "Those things aren't mine, I've got to give them back." He saw through her eyes and all at once understood that the cards from India were the worst of all, for they were all about people scarcely older than Léopold, and the reason they looked so funny was that they were starving to death. All Gérard had seen until now was what they were doing, not who they were, or could be. Meanwhile the room rocked around him, and his mother stood up to show that was all she had to say.

She did not sleep in the pretty room, but in a Spartan cell where there were closets full of linen and soap, and a shelf of preserves behind a curtain, and two painters' stepladders, and two large speckled mirrors in gilt frames. One wall was covered with photographs of a country house the children had never seen, and of her old convent school. The maid, when there was one, went freely in without knocking if she needed a jar of fruit or clean bedsheets. Even when her daughters married and liberated their rooms one by one, she stayed where she was. The bed was hard and narrow and the old man could not comfortably spend the night. For years Gérard had slept in a basement room that contained a Ping-Pong table, and from which he could hear, at odd hours, the furnace coming to life with a growl. A lighted tank of tropical fish separated two divans, one of which was used now by his father, now by his little brother. He had never understood why his father would suddenly appear in the middle of the night, and why the little brother, aged three and four and five, was led, stumbling and protesting, to finish the night in his mother's bed. Gérard was used to someone's presence at night, the warm light of the tank had comforted him. Now that he had a room of his own and slept alone in it, he discovered he was afraid of the dark.

His mother sat by his bed, holding his hand, until he pretended to be asleep. His door was open and a ray from the passage bent over the bed and along the wall. "I'm sure I must be pale," she said, though her cheeks and brow were rosy. She believed her children had taken her blood to make their own and that hers was diminished. Having had seven babies, she could not have left much over a pint. Bitterly anti-clerical, she sometimes hinted that nuns had the best of it after all. Gérard had been wrong to wake her; he had no business walking in his sleep. Tomorrow was what she called "a hell day." It was Léopold's ninth birthday, she was without help, and twenty-two people were going to sit down to lunch. Directly after the meal, she was to take all the uneaten cake to an aged religious who had once been a teacher of hers and was now ending her life bedridden in a convent for the old. The home was seventy miles north of the city, but might have been seven hundred. One son-in-law had undertaken to drive her. Instead of coming back with him, she proposed to spend the night. This meant that another son-in-law would have to fetch her the next day. The interlocked planning this required surpassed tunnelling under the Alps. "Hell day," she said, but she said it so often that Gérard supposed most days were some kind of hell.

The first thing he did when he wakened was light a cigarette, the second turn on his radio. He felt oddly drunk, as if he might miss his footing stumbling down to breakfast. She was already prepared for the last errand of the day. She wore a tweed suit and her overnight case stood in the hall. She moved back and forth between the kitchen and the dining room. His father, still in underwear and pajamas, sat breakfasting at the counter in the kitchen. She paused and watched him stir too much sugar into his coffee, but did not, this time, remark on it. The old man, excited, tapped his spoon on his saucer.

"It was a movie," he said. "Your dream. I saw it, I think, in a movie about an old man. You've dreamed an old man's dream. I've looked through the paper," he said, pushing it toward his son. "There's nothing about that funeral. It couldn't have been a funeral. Anyway, not anyone important."

"Leave him," said the mother, patiently. "He dreamed it. There is something you can do today. Take over the dog. *Completely*. Léopold has him now." Gérard knew it was his father thus addressed. He held his cup in both hands. "As for you, Gérard, I want a word with you."

"Another thing I thought," continued the old man. "Maybe they were making a movie around there and you got mixed up with the crowd. What you took for a railway was some kind of scaffolding, cameras. Eh?"

"Gérard, I want you to . . ." She turned to her husband: "Back me up! He's your son, too! Gérard, I want you to tell that girl you're too young to be tied to one person." Her face was blazing, her eyes brilliant and clear. "What will you do when she starts a baby? Marry her? I want you to tell that girl there's no money to inherit in this family, and that after Léopold's education is finished there won't be a cent for anybody. Not even us."

"She's not really a dancer," said the old man, forestalling the next bit. "She gives dancing *lessons*. It's not the same thing."

"I don't care what she gives. What about your son?"

Gérard was about to say, "I did tell her," but he remembered, "I never got there. I only started out."

He stopped hearing them. He had set his cup down as his mother spoke his name, and pushed it to the back of the counter. As his father handed him the paper, he remembered, he had taken it with his left hand, and opened it wide instead of carefully folding it, as he usually did. This was so important that he did not hear what was said after a minute or two. He had always given importance to his gestures, noticing whether he put his watch or his glasses to the left or the right of a bedlamp. He always left his coffee cup about four inches from the edge of the counter. When he studied, he piled his books on the right, and whatever text he was immediately using was at his left hand. His radio had to be dead center. He saw, and had been noticing for some time, that his mind was not keeping quiet order for him anymore and that his gestures were not automatic. He felt that if he did not pay close attention to everything now, something literally fantastic could happen. Gestures had kept things controlled, as they ought to be. Whatever could happen now was in the domain of magic.

2

The conviction that she was married against her will never leaves her. If she had been born royal it could not have been worse. She has led the life of a crown princess, sapped by boredom and pregnancies. She told each of her five daughters as they grew up that they were conceived in horror; that she could have left them in their hospital cots and not looked back, so sickened was she by their limp spines and the autumn smell of their hair, by their froglike movements and their animal wails. She liked them when they could reason, and talk, and answer back — when they became what she called "people."

She makes the girls laugh. She is French-Canadian, whether she likes it or not. They see at the heart of her a sacrificial mother; her education has removed her in degree only from the ignorant, tiresome, moralizing mother, given to mysterious female surgery, subjugated by miracles, a source of infinite love. They have heard her saying, "Why did I get married? Why did I have all these large dull children?" They have heard, "If any of my children had been brilliant or unusual, it would have justified my decision. Yes, they might have been narrow and warped in French, but oh how commonplace they became in English!" "We are considered traitors and renegades," she says. "And I can't point to even one of my children and say, "Yes but it was worth it — look at Pauline — or Lucia — or Gérard.'" The girls ought to be wounded at this, but in fact they are impermeable. They laugh and call it "Mother putting on an act." Her passionate ambition for them is her own affair. They have chosen exactly the life she tried to renounce for them: they married young, they are frequently pregnant, and sometimes bored.

This Saturday she has reunited them, the entire family and one guest, for Léopold's ninth birthday. There are fourteen adults at the dining-room table and eight at the children's, which is in the living room, through the arch. Léopold, so small he seems two years younger than nine, so clever and quick that other children are slightly afraid of him, keeps an eye on his presents. He has inherited his brother's electric train. It is altogether old-fashioned; Gérard has had it nine years. Still, Léopold will not let anyone near it. It is his now, and therefore charmed. If any of these other children, these round-eyed brats with English names, lays a hand on the train, he disconnects it; if the outrage is repeated, he goes in the kitchen and stands on a stool and turns off the electricity for the whole house. No one reprimands him. He is not like other children. He is more intelligent, for one thing, and so much uglier. Unlike Gérard, who speaks French as if through a muslin curtain, or as if translating from another language, who wears himself out struggling for one complete dream, Léopold can, if he likes, say anything in a French more limpid and accurate than anything they are used to hearing. He goes to a private, secular school, the only French one in the province; he has had a summer in Montreux. Either his parents have more money than when the others were small, or they have chosen to invest in their last chance. French is Léopold's private language; he keeps it as he does his toys, to himself, polished, personal, a lump of crystalline rock he takes out, examines, looks through, and conceals for another day.

Léopold's five sisters think his intelligence is a disease, and one they hope their own children will not contract. Their mother is *bright*, their father is *thoughtful* (*deep* is another explanation for him), but Léopold's intelligence will always show him the limit of a situation and the last point of possibility where people are concerned; and so, of course, he is bound to be unhappy forever. How will he be able to love? To his elder brother, he seems like a small illegitimate creature raised in secret, in the wrong house. One day Léopold will show them extraordinary credentials. But this is a fancy, for Léopold is where he belongs, in the right family; he has simply been planted — little stunted, ugly thing — in the wrong generation. The children at his table are his nieces and nephews, and the old gentleman at the head of the adult table, the old man bowed over a dish of sieved, cooked fruit, is his father. Léopold is evidence of an old man's foolishness. His existence is an embarrassment. The girls wish he had never been born, and so they are especially kind, and they load him with presents. Even Gérard, who would have found the family quite complete, quite satisfactory, without any Léopold, ever, has given the train (which he was keeping for his own future children) and his camera.

When Léopold is given something, he walks round it and decides what the gift is worth in terms of the giver. If it seems cheap, he mutters without raising his eyes. If it seems important, he flashes a brief, shrewd look that any adult, but no child, mistakes for a glance of complicity. The camera, though second-hand, has been well received. It is round his neck; he puts down his fork and holds the camera and makes all the children uneasy by staring at each in turn and deciding none of them worth an inch of film.

"Poor little lad," says his mother, who flings out whatever she feels, no matter who is in the way. "He has never had a father — only a grandfather."

The old man may not have heard. He is playing his private game of trying to tell his five English-Canadian sons-in-law apart. The two Bobs, the Don, the Ian, and the Ken are interchangeable, like postage stamps of the Queen's profile. Two are Anglicans, two United Church, and the most lackluster is a Lutheran, but which is he? The old man lifts his head and smiles a great slow smile. His smile acquits his daughters; he forgives them for having ever thought him a shameless old person; but the five sons-in-law are made uneasy. They wonder if they are meant to smile back, or something *weird* like that. Well, they may not have much in common with each other, but here they are five together, not isolated, not alone. Their children, with round little noses, and round little blue eyes, are at the next table, and two or three babies are sleeping in portable cots upstairs.

It is a windy spring day, with a high clean sky, and black branches hitting on the windows. The family's guest that day is Father Zinkin, who is dressed just like anyone, without even a clerical collar to make him seem holy. This, to the five men,

is another reason for discomposure; for they might be respectful of a robe but *what* is this man, with his polo-necked
sweater and his nose in the wine and his rough little jokes? Is
he really the Lord's eunuch? I mean, they silently ask each
other, would you trust him? You know what I mean . . .
Father Zinkin has just come back from Rome. He says that the
trees are in leaf, and he got his pale jaundiced sunburn sitting
at a sidewalk café. This is Montreal, it is still cold, and the
daughters' five fur coats are piled upstairs on their mother's
bed. They accept the news about Rome without grace. If he
thinks it is so sunny in Rome, why didn't he stay there? Who
asked him to come back? That is how every person at that table
feels about news from abroad, and it is the only sentiment that
can ever unite them. When you say it is sunny elsewhere, you
are suggesting it is never sunny here. When you describe the
trees of Rome, what you are *really* saying is there are no trees
in Montreal.

Why is he at the table, then, since he brings them nothing
but unwelcome news? The passionately anti-clerical family
cannot keep away from priests. They will make an excuse: they
will say they admire his mind, or his gifts with language — he
speaks seven. He eats and drinks just like anyone, he has
travelled, and been psychoanalyzed, and is not frightened by
women. At least, he does not seem to be. Look at the way he
pours wine for Lucia, and then for Pauline, and how his tone
is just right, not a scrap superior. And then, he is not
Canadian. He does not remind them of anything. None of the
children, from Lucia, who is twenty-nine, to Léopold, nine
today, has been baptized. Father Zinkin sits down and eats
with them as if they were. Until the girls grew up and married
they never went to church. Now that they are Protestants they
go because their husbands want to; so, their mother thinks,
this is what all the fighting and the courage came to, finally; all
the struggling and being condemned and cut off from one's
kind: the five girls simply joined another kind, just as stupid.

No, thinks the old father at the head of the table: more

stupid. At any rate, less interesting. Less interesting because
too abstract. You would have to be a genius to be a true
Protestant, and those he has met . . . At night, when he is
trying to get to sleep, he thinks of his sons-in-law. He
remembers their names without trouble: the two Bobs, the
Don, the Ian, and the last one — Keith, or Ken? Ken.
Monique married Ken. Alone, in the dark, he tries to match
names and faces. Are both Bobs thin? Pink in the face? Yes,
and around the neck. They lose their hair young — something
to do with English hairbrushes, he invents. The old man
droops now, for the sight of his sons-in-law can send him off to
sleep. His five daughters — he knows their names, and he
knows his own sons. His grandchildren seem to belong to a
new national type, with round heads, and quite large front
teeth. You would think some Swede or other had been around
Montreal on a bicycle so as to create this new national type.
Sharon, and Marilyn and Cary and Gary and Gail. Cary and
Gary.

"Nobody cares," his wife says, very sharply.

He has been mumbling, talking to himself, saying the
names of children aloud. She minds because of Father
Zinkin. When she and her husband are alone, and he talks too
much, repeats the same thing over and over, she squeezes her
eyes until only a pinpoint of amber glows between the lids,
and she squeezes out through a tight throat, "All right, all
right," and even, "Shut UP" in a rising crescendo of three. Not
even her children know she says "Shut up" to the old man;
"nobody cares" is just a family phrase. When it is used on Don
Carlos, the basset, now under the children's table, it makes
him look as if he might cry real tears.

She speaks lightly, quickly now, in English. She sits, very
straight, powdered and pretty, and says, in a musical English
all her own, not the speech of the city at all, "They say Jews
look after their own people but it's not true. I was told about
some people who had a very old sick father. They had to tie
him to a chair sometimes, because he would go downtown

and steal things or start to cry in the street. As they couldn't afford a home for him, and he wouldn't have gone anyway, they decided to leave him. They moved half the furniture away and the old man sat crying on a chair and saw his family go. He sat weeping, not protesting, and his children slouched out without saying goodbye. Yes, he sat weeping, a respectable old man. Now, this man's wife gave Russian lessons to earn her living, and one day, when she was giving a lesson to a woman I know, she said, 'Come to the window.' My friend looked out and saw an old-fashioned Jew going by. The woman said, 'That was my husband.' She seemed pleased with herself, as though she had done what was right for her children."

"Was he dead?" asks Gérard. He is always waiting for some simple, casual confirmation about the existence of ghosts.

"No, of course not. He was just an old man, and someone had taken him in. Some Russian. So," she concedes, "he was looked after." But, as she likes her stories cruel, so that her children will know more about life than she once did, unhappy endings are her habit. She feels obliged to add, "Someone took him in, but probably gave him a miserable time. He must be dead now. This was long ago, during the last war, when people were learning Russian. It was the thing to do then."

Her children are worried by this story, but perhaps the father has not heard it. He is still eating his fruit, taking a mouthful and then forgetting to swallow. Suddenly something he has been thinking silently must have excited him, for he taps his spoon on the edge of the glass dish.

"As you get old you lose everything," he says. "You lose your God, if you ever had one. When you know they want you to die, you want to live. You want to be loved. Even that."

His children are so embarrassed, so humiliated, they feel as if ashes and sand were being ground in their skins. The sons-in-law are revolted. They look at their plates. Honestly, they can never come to this house without something being said about religion or something personal.

"You lose your parents," the old man continues. "You have

to outlive them. Everything is loss." Before they can say
"nobody cares" he is off once more: "No need for priests,"
he mutters. "If there is no sin, then no need for redemption. Dead words. Tell me, Father whoever you are," (he
asks the glass dish of fruit) "will you explain why these
words should be used?" Muttering — he has been muttering
all his life.

"Oh, shut *up*," they are thinking. A chorus of silent
English: "Shut *up*!" If only the old man could hear the
words, he would see a great black wall; he would hear a sigh,
a rattle, like the black trees outside the windows, hitting the
panes.

The old man shakes his head over his plate: No, no, he
never wanted to marry. He wanted to become a priest. Either
God is, or He is not. If He is, I shall live for Him. If He is not,
I shall fight His ghost. At forty-nine he was married off by a
Jesuit, who was an old school friend. He and the shy, soft,
orphaned girl who had been placed in a convent at six, and
had left it, now, at eighteen, exchanged letters about comparative religion. She seemed intelligent — he has forgotten now
what he imagined their life could ever be like. Presently what
they had in common was her physical horror of him and his
knowledge of it, and then they had in common all their
children.

3

When the old man had finished his long thoughts,
everyone except Gérard and Father Zinkin had disappeared. The small children were made to kiss him — moist
reluctant mouths on his cheek — "Before Granpa takes his
nap." Léopold, who never touched anyone, looked at him
briefly through his new camera and said softly to him, and
only to him, "*Il n'y a pas assez de lumière*." Their dark
identical eyes reflected each other. Then everyone vanished,

the women to rattle plates in the kitchen, Léopold to his room, the five fathers to play some game with the children at the back of the house. He sat in his leather armchair, sometimes he slept, and he heard Gérard protesting. "I know the difference between seeing and dreaming."

"Well, it was a waking dream," said the priest. "There is no snow on the streets, but you say there had been a storm."

The old man looked. The white light in the room surely was the reflection of a snowy day? The room seemed filled with white furniture, white flowers. The priest, because he was dressed like Gérard, tried to sound like a young man and an old friend. Only when the priest turned his head, seeking an ashtray, did the old man see what Father Zinkin knew. His interest in Gérard was intellectual. His mind was occupied with its own power. The old man imagined him, narrow, suspicious, in a small parish, lording it over a flock of old maids. They were thin, their eyebrows met over their noses.

Gérard said, "All right, what if I was analyzed? What difference would it make?"

"You would be yourself. You would be yourself *without effort*."

The old man had been waiting for him to say, "it would break the mirror;" for what is the good of being yourself, if you are Gérard?

"What I mean is, you can't understand about this girl. So there's no use talking about her."

"I know about girls," said the other. "I went out. I even danced."

It struck the old man how often he had been told by priests they knew about life because they had, once, danced with girls. He was willing to let them keep that as a memory of life, but what about Gérard, as entangled with a woman as a man of thirty? But then Gérard lost interest and said, "I'd want to be analyzed in French," so it didn't matter.

"It wouldn't work. Your French isn't spontaneous enough.

Now, begin again. You were on the street, it was daylight, then you were in the kitchen in the dark."

How the old man despised this self-indulgence! He felt it was not his business to put a stop to it. His wife stopped it simply by coming in and beginning to talk about herself. When she talked about her children she seemed to be talking about herself, and when the priest said, to console some complaint she was making, "The little one will be brilliant," meaning Léopold, he seemed to be prophesying a future in which she would shine. Outside, the others were breaking up into groups, carrying cots, ushering children into cars. It would take a good ten minutes, and so she sat perched on the arm of a sofa with her hat on her head and her coat on her arm, and said, "Léopold will be brilliant, but I never wanted him. I'd had six children, five close together. French Canadians of our background, for I daren't say class, it sounds so . . . Well, we, people like ourselves, do *not* usually have these monstrous families, regardless of what you may have been told, Father. My mother had no one but me, and when she tried having a second child, it killed her. When I knew I was having Léopold I took ergot. I lay here, on this very sofa, in the middle of the afternoon. Nothing happened, and nothing showed. He was born without even a strawberry mark to condemn me."

She likes to shock, the old man remembered. How much you can take is measure of your intelligence. So she thinks. Oddly enough, she can be shocked.

She stopped speaking and sighed and smoothed the collar of her coat. When she thought, "My son Gérard is sleeping with a common girl," it shocked her. She thought, now, seeing him slouch past the doorway, scarcely able to wait for the house to empty so that he could go off and find that girl and spend a disgusting Saturday night with her, "Gérard knows. He looks at his father, and me, and now he knows. Before, he only thought he knew. He knows now why the old man follows me up the stairs."

She said very lightly, "My son has sex on the brain. It's all he thinks about now. I suppose all boys are the same. You must have been that way once, Father." Really, that was farther than she had ever gone. The priest looked like a statue resembling the person he had been a moment before.

Once she had departed the house seemed to relax, like an animal that feels safe and can sleep. The old man was to walk the dog and do something about his children. Those had been his instructions for the day. Oh, yes, and he was to stop thinking about himself. He put on his hat and coat and walked down the street with Don Carlos. Don Carlos dug the wet spring lawns with tortoiseshell nails. Let off the leash, he at once rolled in something horrible. The old man wanted to scold, but the wind made all conversation between himself and the dog impossible. The wind suddenly dropped; it was to the old man like a sudden absence of fear. He could dream as well as Gérard. He invented: he and Don Carlos went through the gap of a fence and were in a large sloping pasture. He trod on wildflowers. From the spongy spring soil grew crab apple trees and choke cherries, and a hedge of something he no longer remembered, that was sweet and white. Presently they — he and the dog — looked down on a village and the two silvery spires of a church. He saw the date over the door: 1885. The hills on the other side of the water were green and black with shadows. He had never seen such a blue and green day. But he was still here, on the street, and had not forgotten it for a second. Imagination was as good as sleepwalking any day.

Léopold stood on the porch, watching him through his camera. He seemed to be walking straight into Léopold's camera, magically reduced in size.

"Why, Léo," he said. "You're not supposed to be here," not caring to show how happy it made him that Léopold was here. They were bound so soon to lose each other — why start?

"Wouldn't."

"Wouldn't what?"

"Wouldn't go to Pauline's. She's coming back to get us for supper."

"I don't want anything more to eat today."

"Neither do I. And I'm not going."

Who would dare argue with Léopold? He put his camera down. One day he would have the assurance of a real street, a real father, a real afternoon.

"Well, well," his father said. "So they're all gone." He felt shy. He would never have enough of Léo — he would never know what became of him. He edged past and held the door open for the dog.

"All gone. *Il n'y a que moi.*" Léopold, who never touched anyone, pressed his lips to his father's hand.

UP NORTH

When they woke up in the train, their bed was black with soot and there was soot in his Mum's blondie hair. They were miles north of Montreal, which had, already, sunk beneath his remembrance. "Do'you know what I sor in the night?" said Dennis. He had to keep his back turned while she dressed. They were both in the same berth, to save money. He was small, and didn't take up much room, but when he woke up in that sooty autumn dawn, he found he was squashed flat against the side of the train. His Mum was afraid of falling out and into the aisle; they had a lower berth, but she didn't trust the strength of the curtain. Now she was dressing, and sobbing; really sobbing. For this was worse than anything she had ever been through, she told him. She had been right through the worst of the air raids, yet this was the worst, this waking in the cold, this dark, dirty dawn, everything dirty she touched, her clothes — oh, her clothes! — and now having to dress as she lay flat on her back. She daren't sit up. She might knock her head.

"You know what I sor?" said the child patiently. "Well, the train must of stopped, see, and some little men with bundles on their backs got on. Other men was holding lanterns. They were all little. They were all talking French."

"Shut up," said Mum. "Do you hear me?"

"Sor them," said the boy.

"You and your bloody elves."

"They was people."

"Little men with bundles," said Mum, trying to dress again. "You start your fairy tales with your Dad and I don't know what *he'll* give you."

It was this mythical, towering, half-remembered figure they were now travelling to join up north.

Roy McLaughlin, travelling on the same train, saw the pair, presently, out of his small red-lidded eyes. Den and his Mum were dressed and as clean as they could make themselves, and sitting at the end of the car. McLaughlin was the last person to get up, and he climbed down from his solitary green-curtained cubicle conspicuous and alone. He had to pad the length of the car in a trench coat and city shoes — he had never owned slippers, bathrobe, or pajamas — past the passengers, who were drawn with fatigue, pale under the lights. They were men, mostly; some soldiers. The Second World War had been finished, in Europe, a year and five months. It was a dirty, rickety train going up to Abitibi. McLaughlin was returning to a construction camp after three weeks in Montreal. He saw the girl, riding with her back to the engine, doing her nails, and his faculties absently registered "Limey bride" as he went by. The kid, looking out the window, turned and stared. McLaughlin thought "Pest," but only because children and other men's wives made him nervous and sour when they were brought around camp on a job.

After McLaughlin had dressed and had swallowed a drink in the washroom — for he was sick and trembling after his holiday — he came and sat down opposite the blond girl. He did not bother to explain that he had to sit somewhere while his berth was being dismantled. His arms were covered with coarse red hair; he had rolled up the sleeves of his khaki shirt.

He spread his pale, heavy hands on his knees. The child stood between them, fingertips on the sooty window sill, looking out at the breaking day. Once, the train stopped for a long time; the engine was being changed, McLaughlin said. They had been rolling north but were now turning west. At six o'clock, in about an hour, Dennis and his mother would have to get down, and onto another train, and go north once more. Dennis could not see any station where they were now. There was a swamp with bristling black rushes, red as ink. It was the autumn sunrise; cold, red. It was so strange to him, so singular, that he could not have said an hour later which feature of the scene was in the foreground or to the left or right. Two women wearing army battle jackets over their dresses, with their hair piled up in front, like his mother's, called and giggled to someone they had put on the train. They were fat and dark — grinny. His mother looked at them with detestation, recognizing what they were; for she hated whores. She had always acted on the desire of the moment, without thought of gain, and she had taken the consequences (Dennis) without complaint. Dennis saw that she was hating the women, and so he looked elsewhere. On a wooden fence sat four or five men in open shirts and patched trousers. They had dull, dark hair, and let their mouths sag as though they were too tired or too sleepy to keep them closed. Something about them was displeasing to the child, and he thought that this was an ugly place with ugly people. It was also a dirty place; every time Dennis put his hands on the window sill they came off black.

"Come down any time to see a train go by." said McLaughlin, meaning those men. "Get up in the *night* to see a train."

The train moved. It was still dark enough outside for Dennis to see his face in the window and for the light from the windows to fall in pale squares on the upturned vanishing faces and on the little trees. Dennis heard his mother's new friend say, "Well, there's different possibilities." They passed into an unchanging landscape of swamp and bracken and stunted trees. Then the lights inside the train were put out and he saw that the sky was blue and bright. His mother and McLaughlin, seen in the window, had been remote and bodiless; through their transparent profiles he had seen the yellowed trees going by. Now he could not see their faces at all.

"He's been back in Canada since the end of the war. He was wounded. Den hardly knows him," he heard his mother say. "I couldn't come. I had to wait my turn. We were over a thousand war brides on that ship. He was with Aluminium when he first came back." She pronounced the five vowels in the word.

"You'll be all right there," said McLaughlin. "It's a big place. Schools. All company."

"Pardon me?"

"I mean it all belongs to Aluminum. Only if that's where you're going you happen to be on the wrong train."

"He isn't there now. He hates towns. He seems to move about a great deal. He drives a bulldozer, you see."

"Owns it?" said McLaughlin.

"Why, I shouldn't *think* so. Drives for another man, I think he said."

The boy's father fell into the vast pool of casual labor, drifters; there was a social hierarchy in the north, just as in Heaven. McLaughlin was an engineer. He took another look at the boy: black hair, blue eyes. The hair was coarse, straight, rather dull; Indian hair. The mother was a blonde; touched up a bit, but still blonde.

"What name?" said McLaughlin on the upward note of someone who has asked the same question twice.

"Cameron. Donald Cameron."

That meant nothing, still; McLaughlin had worked in a place on James Bay where the Indians were named Mac-Donald and Ogilvie and had an unconquered genetic strain of blue eyes.

"D'you know about any ghosts?" said the boy, turning to

McLaughlin. McLaughlin's eyes were paler than his own, which were a deep slate blue, like the eyes of a newly born child. McLaughlin saw the way he held his footing on the rocking train, putting out a few fingers to the window sill only for the form of the thing. He looked all at once ridiculous and dishonored in his cheap English clothes — the little jacket, the Tweedledum cap on his head. He outdistanced his clothes; he was better than they were. But he was rushing on this train into an existence where his clothes would be too good for him.

"D'you know about any ghosts?" said the boy again.

"Oh, sure," said McLaughlin, and shivered, for he still felt sick, even though he was sharing a bottle with the Limey bride. He said, "Indians see them," which was as close as he could come to being crafty. But there was no reaction out of the mother; she was not English for nothing.

"You seen any?"

"*I'm* not an Indian," McLaughlin started to say; instead he said, "Well, yes, I saw the ghost, or something like the ghost, of a dog I had."

They looked at each other, and the boy's mother said, "Stop that, you two. Stop that this minute."

"I'll tell you a strange thing about Dennis," said his mother. "It's this. There's times he gives me the creeps."

Dennis was lying on the seat beside her with his head on her lap.

She said, "If I don't like it I can clear out. I was a waitress. There's always work."

"Or find another man," McLaughlin said. "Only it won't be me, girlie. I'll be far away."

"Den says that when the train stopped he saw a lot of elves," she said, complaining.

"Not elves — men," said Dennis. "Some of them had mattresses rolled up on their backs. They were little and bent over. They were talking French. They were going up north."

McLaughlin coughed and said, "He means settlers. They were sent up on this same train during the depression. But that's nine, ten years ago. It was supposed to clear the unemployed out of the towns, get them off relief. But there wasn't anything up here then. The winters were terrible. A lot of them died."

"He couldn't know that," said Mum edgily. "For that matter, how can he tell what is French? He's never heard any."

"No, he couldn't know. It was around ten years ago, when times were bad."

"Are they good now?"

"Jeez, after a *war*?" He shoved his hand in the pocket of his shirt, where he kept a roll, and he let her see the edge of it.

She made no comment, but put her hand on Den's head and said to him, "You didn't see anyone. Now shut up."

"Sor 'em," the boy said in a voice as low as he could descend without falling into a whisper.

"You'll see what your Dad'll give you when you tell lies." But she was halfhearted about the threat and did not quite believe in it. She had been attracted to the scenery, whose persistent sameness she could no longer ignore. "It's not proper country," she said. "It's bare."

"Not enough for me," said McLaughlin. "Too many people. I keep on moving north."

"I want to see some Indians," said Dennis, sitting up.

"There aren't any," his mother said. "Only in films."

"I don't like Canada." He held her arm. "Let's go home now."

"It's the train whistle. It's so sad. It gets him down."

The train slowed, jerked, flung them against each other, and came to a stop. It was quite day now; their faces were plain and clear, as if drawn without shading on white paper. McLaughlin felt responsible for them, even compassionate; the change in him made the boy afraid.

"We're getting down, Den," said his Mum, with great, wide eyes. "We take another train. See? It'll be grand. Do you hear what Mum's telling you?"

He was determined not to leave the train, and clung to the

window sill, which was too smooth and narrow to provide a grip; McLaughlin had no difficulty getting him away. "I'll give you a present," he said hurriedly. But he slapped all his pockets and found nothing to give. He did not think of the money, and his watch had been stolen in Montreal. The woman and the boy struggled out with their baggage, and McLaughlin, who had descended first so as to help them down, reached up and swung the boy in his arms.

"The Indians!" the boy cried, clinging to the train, to air; to anything. His face was momentarily muffled by McLaughlin's shirt. His cap fell to the ground. He screamed. "Where's Mum? I never say *any*thing!"

"You saw Indians," said McLaughlin. "On the rail fence, at that long stop. Look, don't worry your mother. Don't keep telling her what you haven't seen. You'll be seeing plenty of everything now."

ORPHANS' PROGRESS

When the Collier girls were six and ten they were taken away from their mother, whom they loved without knowing what the word implied, or even that it existed, and sent to their father's mother. Their grandmother was scrupulous about food, particularly for these underfed children, and made them drink goat's milk. Two goats bought specially to supply the orphans were taken by station wagon to a buck fifty miles away, the girls accompanying them for reasons of enlightenment. A man in a filling station was frightened by the goats, because of their oblong eyes. The girls were not reflected in the goats' eyes, as they were in each other's. What they remembered afterwards of their grandmother was goat's milk, goat eyes, and the frightened man.

They went to school in Ontario now, with children who did not have the same accent as children in Montreal. When their new friends liked something they said it was smart. A basketball game was smart, so was a movie: it did not mean elegant, it just meant all right. Ice cream made out of goat's milk was not smart: it tasted of hair.

Their grandmother died when the girls were seven and eleven and beginning to speak in the Ontario way. Their mother had been French-Canadian — they were now told — but had spoken French and English to them. They had called her Mummy, a habit started when their father was still alive, for he had not learned French. They understood, from their grandmother, and their grandmother's maid, and the social worker who came to see their grandmother but had little to say to them, that French was an inferior kind of speech. At first, when they were taken away from their mother, Cathie, the elder girl, would wake up at night holding her head, her elbows on her knees, saying in French, "My head hurts," but a few minutes later, the grandmother having applied cold wrung-out towels, she would say in English, "It's better."

Mildred had pushed out two front teeth by sucking her thumb. She had been doing that forever, even before they were taken away from their mother. Ontario could not be blamed. Nevertheless, their grandmother told the social worker about it, who wrote it down.

They did not know, and never once asked, why they had been taken away. When the new social worker said to Cathie, "Were you disturbed because your mother was unhappy?" Cathie said, "She wasn't." When the girls were living with their mother, they knew that sometimes she listened and sometimes could not hear; nevertheless, she was there. They slept in the same bed, all three. Even when she sat on the side of the bed with her head hanging and her undone jagged-cut hair hiding her eyes, mumbling complaints that were not their concern, the children were close to her and did not know they were living under what would be called later "unsheltered conditions." They never knew, until told, that they were uneducated and dirty and in danger. Now they learned that their mother never washed her own neck and that she dressed in layers of woollen stuff, covered with grease, and wore men's shoes because some man had left them behind and she liked the shape or the comfort of them. They did not know, until they were told, that they had never been properly fed.

"We ate chicken," said Cathie Collier, the elder girl.

"They say she served it up half raw," said their grandmother's maid. "Survet" said the maid for "served," and that was not the way their mother had spoken. "The sheets was so dirty, the dirt was like clay. All of yez slept in the one bed," said the maid.

"Yes, we slept together." The apartment — a loft, they were told, over a garage; not an apartment at all — must still exist, it must be somewhere, with the piano that Mildred, the little one, had banged on with her palms flat. What about the two cats who were always fighting or playing, depending on their disposition? There were pictures on the wall, their mother's, and the children's own drawings.

"When one of the pictures was moved there was a square mass of bugs," said the grandmother's maid. "The same shape as the pitcher."

"To the day I die," said the social worker from Montreal to her colleague in Ontario, "I won't forget the screams of Mildred when she was dragged out of that pigsty." This was said in the grandmother's parlor, where the three women — the two social workers, and the grandmother — sat with their feet freezing on the linoleum floor. The maid heard, and told. She had been in and out, serving coffee, coconut biscuits, and damson preserves in custard made of goat's milk. The room was heated once or twice a year; even the maid said her feet were cold. But "To the day I die" was a phrase worth hearing. She liked the sound of that, and said it to the children. The maid was from a place called Waterloo, where, to hear her tell it, no one behaved strangely and all the rooms were warm.

Thumb-sucker Mildred did not remember having screamed, or anything at all except the trip from Montreal by train. "Boy, is your grandmother ever a rich old lady!" said the maid from Waterloo. "If she wasn't, where'd you be? In an orphung asylum. She's a Christian, I can tell you." But another day, when she was angry with the grandmother over something, she said, "She's a damned old sow. It's in the mattress and she's lying on it. You can hear the bills crackle when you turn the mattress Saturdays. I hope they find it when she dies, is all I can say."

The girls saw their grandmother dead, in the bed, on that mattress. The person crying hardest in the room was the maid. She had suddenly dyed her hair dark red, and the girls did not know her, because of her tears, and her new clothes, and because of the way she fondled and kissed them. "We'll never see each other again," said the maid.

Now that their grandmother had died, the girls went to live with their mother's brother and his wife and their many children. It was a suburb of Montreal called Ahuntsic. They did not see anything that reminded them of Montreal, and did not recall their mother. There was a parlor here full of cut glass, which was daily rubbed and polished, and two television sets, one for the use of the children. The girls slept on a pull-out divan and wrangled about bedclothes. Cathie wanted them pushed down between them in a sort of trough, because she felt a draft, but Mildred complained that the blankets thus arranged were tugged away from her side. She was not properly covered and afraid of falling on the floor. One of their relations (they had any number here on their mother's side) made them a present of a box of chocolate almonds, but the cousins they lived with bought exactly the same box, so as to tease them. When Cathie and Mildred rushed to see if their own box was still where they had hidden it, they were bitterly mocked. Their Ontario grandmother's will was not probated and every scrap of food they put in their mouths was taken from the mouths of cousins: so they were told. Their cousins made them afraid of ghosts. They put out the lights and said, "Look out, she is coming to get you, all in black," and when Mildred began to whimper, Cathie said, "Our mother wouldn't try to frighten us." She had not spoken of her until now. One of the cousins said, "I'm talking about your old grandmother. Your mother isn't dead." They were shown their father's grave, and made to kneel and pray. Their lives were in the dark now, in the dark of ghosts, whose transparent shadows stood round their bed; soon they lived in the black of nuns. Language was black, until they forgot their English. Until they spoke French, nothing but French, the family pretended not to understand them, and stared as if they were peering in the dark. They very soon forgot their English.

They could not stay here with these cousins forever, for the flat was too small. When they were eight and twelve, their grandmother's will was probated and they were sent to school. For the first time in their lives, now, the girls did not sleep in the same bed. Mildred slept in a dormitory with the little girls, where a green light burned overhead, and a nun rustled and prayed or read beside a green lamp all night long. Mildred was bathed once every fortnight, wearing a rubber apron so that she would not see her own body. Like the other little girls, she dressed, in the morning, sitting on the floor, so that they would not see one another. Her thumb, sucked white, was taped to the palm of her hand. She caught glimpses of Cathie sometimes during recreation periods, but Cathie was one of the big girls, and important. She did not play, as the little ones still did, but walked up and down with the supervisor, walking backwards as the nun walked forward.

One day, looking out of a dormitory window, Mildred saw a rooftop and an open skylight. She said to a girl standing nearby, "That's our house." "What house?" "Where Mummy lives." She said that sentence, three words, in English. She had not thought or spoken "Mummy" since she was six and a half. It turned out that she was lying about the house. Lying was serious; she was made to promenade through the class-rooms carrying a large pair of shears and the sign "I am a liar." She did not know the significance of the shears, nor, it seemed, did the nun who organized the punishment. It had always been associated with lying, and (the nun suddenly remembered) had to do with cutting out the liar's tongue. The tattling girl, who had told about "Where Mummy lives," was punished too, and made to carry a wastebasket from room to room with "I am a basket-carrier" hung round her neck. This meant a tale-bearer. Everyone was in the wrong.

Cathie was not obliged to wear a rubber apron in her bath, but a muslin shift. She learned the big girls' trick, which was to take it off and dip it in water, and then bathe properly. When Mildred came round carrying her scissors and her sign Cathie had had her twice-monthly bath and felt damp and new. She said to someone, "That's my sister," but "sister" was a dark scowling little thing. "Sister" got into still more trouble: a nun, a stray from Belgium, perhaps as one refugee to another, said to Mildred, swiftly drawing her into a broom-cupboard, "Call me Maman." "Maman" said the child, to whom "Mummy" had meaning until the day of the scissors. Who was there to hear what was said in the broom-cupboard? What basket-carrier repeated that? It was forbidden for nuns to have favorites, forbidden to have pet names for nuns, and the Belgian stray was sent to the damp wet room behind the chapel and given flower-arranging to attend to. There Mildred found her, by chance, and the nun said, "Get away, haven't you made enough trouble for me?"

Cathie was told to pray for Mildred, the trouble-maker, but forgot. The omission weighed on her. She prayed for mother, grandmother, father, herself (with a glimpse in the prayer of her own future coffin, white) and the uncles and aunts and cousins she knew and those she had never met. Her worry about forgetting Mildred in her prayers caused her to invent a formula; "Everyone I have ever known who is dead or alive, anyone I know now who is alive but might die, and anyone I shall ever know in the future." She prayed for her best friend, who wanted like Cathie to become a teacher, and for a nun with a mustache who was jolly, and for her confessor, who liked to hear her playing the Radetzky March on the piano. Her hair grew lighter and was brushed and combed by her best friend.

Mildred was suddenly taken out of school and adopted. Their mother's sister, one of the aunts they had seldom seen, had lost a daughter by drowning. She said she would treat Mildred as she did her own small son, and Mildred, who wished to leave the convent school, but did not know if she cared to go and live in a place called Chicoutimi, did not decide. She made them decide, and made them take her away. When the girls were fifteen and nineteen, and Mildred was called Desaulniers and not Collier, the sisters were made to meet. Cathie had left school and was studying nursing, but she came back to the convent when she had time off, not because she did not have anywhere else to go, but because she did not want to go to any other place. The nuns had said of Cathie, laughing. "She doesn't want to leave — we shall have to push her out." When Cathie's sister, Mildred Desaulniers, came to call on her, the girls did not know what to say. Mildred wore a round straw hat with a clump of plastic cherries hanging over the brim; her adoptive brother, in long trousers and bow tie, did not get out of the car. He was seven, and had slick wet-looking hair, as if he had been swimming. "Kiss your sister," said Mildred's mother, to Cathie, admonishingly. Cathie did as she was told, and Mildred immediately got back in the car with her brother and snatched a comic book out of his hands. "Look, Mildred," said her father, and let the car slow down on a particular street. The parents craned at a garage, and at dirty-legged children with torn sneakers on their feet. Mildred glanced up and then back at her book. She had no reason to believe she had seen it before, or would ever again.

THE PRODIGAL
PARENT

W e sat on the screened porch of Rhoda's new house,
which was close to the beach on the ocean side of
Vancouver Island. I had come here in a straight
line, from the East, and now that I could not go any farther
without running my car into the sea, any consideration of
wreckage and loss, or elegance of behavior, or debts owed (not
of money, of my person) came to a halt. A conqueror in a
worn blazer and a regimental tie, I sat facing my daughter,
listening to her voice — now describing, now complaining —
as if I had all the time in the world. Her glance drifted round
the porch, which still contained packing cases. She could not
do, or take in, a great deal at once. I have light eyes, like
Rhoda's, but mine have been used for summing up.

Rhoda had bought this house and the cabins round it and a
strip of maimed landscape with her divorce settlement. She
hoped to make something out of the cabins, renting them
weekends to respectable people who wanted a quiet place to
drink. "Dune Vista" said a sign, waiting for someone to nail it
to a tree. I wondered how I would fit in here — what she
expected me to do. She still hadn't said. After the first formal

Martinis she had made to mark my arrival, she began drinking rye, which she preferred. It was sweeter, less biting than the whiskey I remembered in my youth, and I wondered if my palate or its composition had changed. I started to say so, and my daughter said. "Oh, God, your accent again! You know what I thought you said now? 'Oxbow was a Cheswick charmer.'"

"No, no. Nothing like that."

"Try not sounding so British," she said.

"I don't, you know."

"Well, you don't sound Canadian."

The day ended suddenly, as if there had been a partial eclipse. In the new light I could see my daughter's face and hands.

"I guess I'm different from all my female relatives," she said. She had been comparing herself with her mother, and with half sisters she hardly knew. "I don't despise men, like Joanne does. There's always somebody. There's one now, in fact. I'll tell you about him. I'll tell you the whole thing, and you say what you think. It's a real mess. He's Irish, he's married, and he's got no money. Four children. He doesn't sleep with his wife."

"Surely there's an age limit for this?" I said. "By my count, you must be twenty-eight or -nine now."

"Don't I know it." She looked into the dark trees, darkened still more by the screens, and said without rancor, "It's not my fault. I wouldn't keep on falling for lushes and phonies if you hadn't been that way."

I put my glass down on the packing case she had pushed before me, and said, "I am not, I never was, and I never could be an alcoholic."

Rhoda seemed genuinely shocked. "I never said *that*. I never heard you had to be put in a hospital or anything, like my stepdaddy. But you used to stand me on a table when you had parties, Mother told me, and I used to dance to 'Piccolo Pete.' What happened to that record, I wonder? One of your wives most likely got it in lieu of alimony. But may God strike us both dead here and now if I ever said you were alcoholic." It must have been to her a harsh, clinical word, associated with straitjackets. "I'd like you to meet him," she said. "But I never know when he'll turn up. He's Harry Pay. The writer," she said, rather primly. "Somebody said he was a new-type Renaissance Man — I mean, he doesn't just sit around, he's a judo expert. He could throw *you* down in a second."

"Is he Japanese?"

"God, no. What makes you say that? I already told you what he is. He's white. Quite white, *entirely* white I mean."

"Well — I could hardly have guessed."

"You shouldn't have to guess," she said. "That name should be enough. He's famous. Round here, anyway."

"I'm sorry," I said. "I've been away so many years. Would you write the name down for me? So I can see how it's spelled?"

"I'll do better than that." It touched me to see the large girl she was suddenly moving so lightly. I heard her slamming doors in the living room behind me. She had been clumsy as a child, in every gesture like a wild creature caught. She came back to me with a dun folder out of which spilled loose pages, yellow and smudged. She thrust it at me and, as I groped for my spectacles, turned on an overhead light. "You read this," she said, "and I'll go make us some sandwiches, while I still can. Otherwise we'll break into another bottle and never eat anything. This is something he never shows *anyone*."

"It is my own life exactly," I said when she returned with the sandwiches, which she set awkwardly down. "At least, so far as school in England is concerned. Cold beds, cold food, cold lavatories. Odd that anyone still finds it interesting. There must be twenty written like it every year. The revolting school, the homosexual master, then a girl — saved!"

"Homo *what*?" said Rhoda, clawing the pages. "It's possible. He has a dirty mind, actually."

"Really? Has he ever asked you to do anything unpleasant, such as type his manuscripts?"

"Certainly not. He's got a perfectly good wife for that."

When I laughed, she looked indignant. She had given a serious answer to what she thought was a serious question. Our conversations were always like this — collisions.

"Well?" she said.

"Get rid of him."

She looked at me and sank down on the arm of my chair. I felt her breath on my face, light as a child's. She said, "I was waiting for something. I was waiting all day for you to say something personal, but I didn't think it would be that. Get rid of him? He's all I've got."

"All the more reason. You can do better."

"Who, for instance?" she said. "You? You're no use to me."

She had sent for me. I had come to Rhoda from her half sister Joanne, in Montreal. Joanne had repatriated me from Europe, with an air passage to back the claim. In a new bare apartment, she played severe sad music that was like herself. We ate at a scrubbed table the sort of food that can be picked up in the hand. She was the richest of my children, through her mother, but I recognized in her guarded, slanting looks the sort of avarice and fear I think of as a specific of women. One look seemed meant to tell me, "You waltzed off, old boy, but look at me now," though I could not believe she had wanted me only for that. "I'll never get married" was a remark that might have given me a lead. "I won't have anyone to lie to me, or make a fool of me, or spend my money for me." She waited to see what I would say. She had just come into this money.

"Feeling as you do, you probably shouldn't marry," I said. She looked at me as Rhoda was looking now. "Don't expect too much from men," I said.

"Oh, I don't!" she cried, so eagerly I knew she always would. The cheap sweet Ontario wine she favored and the smell of paint in her new rooms and the raw meals and incessant music combined to give me a violent attack of claustrophobia. It was probably the most important conversation we had.

"We can't have any more conversation now," said Rhoda. "Not after that. It's the end. You've queered it. I should have known. Well, eat your sandwiches now that I've made them."

"Would it seem petulant if, at this point, I did not eat a tomato sandwich?" I said.

"Don't be funny. I can't understand what you're saying anyway."

"If you don't mind, my dear," I said. "I'd rather be on my way."

"What do you mean, on your way? For one thing, you're in no condition to drive. Where d'you think you're going?"

"I can't very well go that way," I said, indicating the ocean I could not see. "I can't go back as I've come."

"It was a nutty thing, to come by car," she said. "It's not even all that cheap."

"As I can't go any farther," I said, "I shall stay. Not here, but perhaps not far."

"Doing what? What *can* you do? We've never been sure."

"I can get a white cane and walk the streets of towns. I can ask people to help me over busy intersections and then beg for money."

"You're kidding."

"I'm not. I shall say — let me think — I shall say I've had a mishap, lost my wallet, pension check not due for another week, postal strike delaying it even more —"

"That won't work. They'll send you to the welfare. You should see how we hand out welfare around here."

"I'm counting on seeing it," I said.

"You can't. It would look —" She narrowed her eyes and said, "If you're trying to shame me, forget it. Someone comes and says, 'That poor old blind bum says he's your father,' I'll just answer, 'Yes, what about it?'"

"My sight *is* failing, actually."

"There's welfare for that, too."

"We're at cross-purposes," I said. "I'm not looking for money."

"Then waja come here for?"

"Because Regan sent me on to Goneril, I suppose."

"That's a lie. Don't try to make yourself big. Nothing's ever happened to you."

"Well, in my uneventful life," I began, but my mind answered for me, "No, nothing." There are substitutes for incest but none whatever for love. What I needed now was someone who knew nothing about me and would never measure me against a promise or a past. I blamed myself, not for anything I had said but for having remembered too late what Rhoda was like. She was positively savage as an infant, though her school tamed her later on. I remember sitting opposite her when she was nine — she in an unbecoming tartan coat — while she slowly and seriously ate a large plate of ice cream. She was in London on a holiday with her mother, and as I happened to be there with my new family I gave her a day.

"Every Monday we have Thinking Day," she had said, of her school. "We think about the Brownies and the Baden-Powells and sometimes Jesus and all."

"Do you, really?"

"I can't *really*," Rhoda had said. "I never met any of them."

"Are you happy, at least?" I said, to justify my belief that no one was ever needed. But the savage little girl had become an extremely careful one.

That afternoon, at a matinée performance of *Peter Pan*, I went to sleep. The slaughter of the pirates woke me, and as I turned, confident, expecting her to be rapt, I encountered a face of refusal. She tucked her lips in, folded her hands, and shrugged away when I helped her into a taxi.

"I'm sorry, I should not have slept in your company," I said. "It was impolite."

"It wasn't that," she burst out. "It was *Peter Pan*. I hated it. It wasn't what I expected. You could see the wires. Mrs. Darling didn't look right. She didn't have a lovely dress on — only an old pink thing like a nightgown. Nana wasn't a real dog, it was a lady. I couldn't understand anything they said. Peter Pan wasn't a boy, he had bosoms."

"I noticed that, too," I said. "There must be a sound traditional reason for it. Perhaps Peter is really a mother figure."

"No, he's a *boy*."

I intercepted, again, a glance of stony denial — of me? We had scarcely met.

"I couldn't understand. They all had English accents," she complained.

For some reason that irritated me. "What the hell did you expect them to have?" I said.

"When I was little," said the nine-year-old, close to tears now, "I thought they were all Canadian."

The old car Joanne had given me was down on the beach, on the hard sand, with ribbons of tire tracks behind it as a sign of life, and my luggage locked inside. It had been there a few hours and already it looked abandoned — an old heap someone had left to rust among the lava rock. The sky was lighter than it had seemed from the porch. I picked up a sand dollar, chalky and white, with the tree of life on its underside, and as I slid it in my pocket, for luck, I felt between my fingers a rush of sand. I had spoken the truth, in part; the landscape through which I had recently travelled still shuddered before my eyes and I would not go back. I heard, then saw, Rhoda running down to where I stood. Her hair, which she wore gathered up in a bun, was half down, and she breathed, running, with her lips apart. For the first time I remembered something of the way she had seemed as a child, something more than an anecdote. She clutched my arm and said, "Why did you say I should ditch him? *Why?*"

I disengaged my arm, because she was hurting me, and said, "He can only give you bad habits."

"At my age?"

"Any age. Dissimulation. Voluntary barrenness — someone else has had his children. Playing house, a Peter-and-Wendy game, a life he would never dare try at home. There's the real meaning of Peter, by the way." But she had forgotten.

She clutched me again, to steady herself, and said, "I'm old enough to know everything. I'll soon be in my thirties. That's all I care to say."

It seemed to me I had only recently begun making grave mistakes. I had until now accepted all my children, regardless of who their mothers were. The immortality I had imagined had not been in them but on the faces of women in love. I saw, on the dark beach, Rhoda's mother, the soft hysterical girl whose fatal "I am pregnant" might have enmeshed me for life.

I said, "I wish they would find a substitute for immortality."

"I'm working on it," said Rhoda, grimly, seeming herself again. She let go my arm and watched me unlock the car door. "You'd have hated it here," she said, then, pleading, "You wouldn't want to live here like some charity case — have me support you?"

"I'd be enchanted," I said.

"No, no, you'd hate it," she said. "I couldn't look after you. I haven't got time. And you'd keep thinking I should do better than *him*, and the truth is I can't. You wouldn't want to end up like some old relation, fed in the kitchen and all."

"I don't know," I said. "It would be new."

"Oh," she cried, with what seemed unnecessary despair, "what did you come for? All right," she said. "I give up. You asked for it. You can stay. I mean, I'm inviting you. You can sit around and say, 'Oxbow was a Cheswick charmer,' all day and when someone says to me, 'Where jer father get his accent?' I'll say, 'It was a whole way of life.' But remember, you're not a prisoner or anything, around here. You can go whenever you don't like the food. I mean, if you don't like it, don't come to me and say, 'I don't like the food.' You're not my prisoner," she yelled, though her face was only a few inches from mine. "You're only my father. That's all you are."

IN
THE TUNNEL

Sarah's father was a born widower. As she had no memory of a mother, it was as though Mr. Holmes had none of a wife and had been created perpetually bereaved and knowing best. His conviction that he must act for two gave him a jocular heaviness that made the girl react for a dozen, but his jokes rode a limitless tide of concern. He thought Sarah was subjective and passionate, as small children are. She knew she was detached and could prove it. A certain kind of conversation between them was bound to run down, wind up, run down again: you are, I'm not, yes, no, you should, I won't, you'll be sorry. Between eighteen and twenty, Sarah kept meaning to become a psychosociologist. Life would then be a tribal village through which she would stalk soft-footed and disguised: that would show him who was subjective. But she was also a natural *amoureuse*, as some girls were natural actresses, and she soon discovered that love refused all forms of fancy dress. In love she had to show her own face, and speak in a true voice, and she was visible from all directions.

One summer, after a particularly stormy spring, her father sent her to Grenoble to learn about French civilization

— actually, to get her away from a man he always pretended to think was called Professor Downcast. Sarah raged mostly over the harm her father had brought to Professor Downcast's career, for she had been helping with his "Urban and Regional Studies of the Less Privileged in British Columbia," and she knew he could not manage without her. She did not stay long in Grenoble; she had never intended to. She had decided beforehand that the Alps were shabby, the cultural atmosphere in France was morbid and stifling, and that every girl she met would be taking the civilization course for the wrong reason. She packed and caught a bus down the Napoleon Route to the Mediterranean.

Professor Downcast had been forced to promise he would not write, and so, of course, Sarah would not write her father. She wanted to have new friends and a life that was none of his business. The word "Riviera" had predicted yellow mornings and snowy boats, and crowds filling the streets in the way dancers fill a stage. Her mind's eye had kept them at a distance so that they shimmered and might have been plumed, like peacocks. Up close, her moralist's eye selected whatever was bound to disappoint: a stone beach skirted with sewage, a promenade that was really a through speedway, an eerie bar. For the first time she recognized prostitutes; they clustered outside her hotel, gossiping, with faces like dead letters. For friends she had a pair of middle-aged tourists who took her sightseeing and warned her not to go out at night by herself. Grenoble had been better after all. Who was to blame? She sent her father a letter of reproach, of abuse, of cold reason, and also of apology — the postmark was bound to be a shock. She then began waiting round American Express for an answer. She was hoping it would be a cable saying "Come on home."

His feelings, when he got round to describing them, filled no more than one flimsy typewritten page. She thought she was worth more than that. What now? She walked out of American Express, still reading her letter. A shadow fell over the page. At the same time a man's soft voice said, "Don't be frightened."

She looked up, not frightened — appraising. The man was about twice her age, and not very tall. He was dressed in clean, not too new summer whites, perhaps the remains of a naval officer's uniform. His accent was English. His eyes were light brown. Once he had Sarah's attention, and had given her time to decide what her attention would be, he said his name was Roy Cooper and asked if she wouldn't like to have lunch with him somewhere along the port.

Of course, she answered: it was broad daylight and there were policemen everywhere — polite, old-fashioned, and wearing white, just like Roy Cooper. She was always hungry, and out of laziness had been living on pizzas and ice cream. Her father had never told her to keep experience at bay. For mystery and horror he had tried to substitute common sense, which may have been why Sarah did not always understand him. She and Roy Cooper crossed the promenade together. He held her arm to guide her through traffic, but let go the minute they reached the curb. "I've been trying to talk to you for days now," he said. "I was hoping you might know someone I knew, who could introduce us."

"Oh, I don't know anyone *here*," said Sarah. "I met a couple of Americans in my hotel. We went to see this sort of abandoned chapel. It has frescoes of Jesus and Judas and . . ." He was silent. "Their name was Hayes?"

He answered that his car was parked over near the port in the shade. It was faster to walk than drive, down here. He was staying outside Nice; otherwise he wouldn't bother driving at all.

They moved slowly along to the port, dragging this shapeless conversation between them, and Sarah was just beginning to wonder if he wasn't a friend of her father's, and if this might be one of her father's large concrete jokes, when he took her bare arm in a way no family friend would have dared and said look here, what about this restaurant? Again he quickly dropped her arm before she could tug away. They sat down under an awning with a blue tablecloth between them. Sarah frowned, lowered her eyes, and muttered something. It might have been a grace before eating had she not seemed so determined; but her words were completely muffled by the traffic grinding by. She leaned forward and repeated, "I'd like to know what your motives are, exactly." She did not mean anything like "What do you want?" but "What is it? Why Roy Cooper? Why me?" At the back of her mind was the idea that he deserved a lesson: she would eat her lunch, get up, coolly stroll away.

His answer, again miles away from Sarah's question, was that he knew where Sarah was staying and had twice followed her to the door of the hotel. He hadn't dared to speak up.

"Well, it's a good thing you finally did," she said. "I was only waiting for a letter, and now I'm going back to Grenoble. I don't like it here."

"Don't do that, don't leave." He had a quiet voice for a man, and he knew how to slide it under another level of sound and make himself plain. He broke off to order their meal. He seemed so at ease, so certain of other people and their reactions — at any moment he would say he was the ambassador of a place where nothing mattered but charm and freedom. Sarah was not used to cold wine at noon. She touched the misty decanter with her fingertips· and wet her forehead with the drops. She wanted to ask his motives again but found he was questioning hers — laughing at Sarah, in fact. Who was she to frown and cross-examine, she who wandered around eating pizzas alone? She told him about Professor Downcast and her father — she had to, to explain what she was doing here — and even let him look at her father's letter. Part of it said, "My poor Sarah, no one ever seems to interest you unless he is

no good at his job

small in stature, I wonder why?

'Marxist-Leninist' (since you sneer at 'Communist' and will not allow its use around the house)

married or just about to be

in debt to God and humanity.

I am not saying you should look for the opposite in every case, only for some person who doesn't combine all these qualities at one time."

"I'm your father's man," said Roy Cooper, and he might well have been, except for the problem of height. He was a bachelor, and certainly the opposite of a Marxist-Leninist: he was a former prison inspector whose career had been spent in an Asian colony. He had been retired early when the Empire faded out and the New Democracy that followed no longer required inspection. As for "debt to God and humanity," he said he had his own religion, which made Sarah stare sharply at him, wondering if his idea of being funny was the same as her father's. Their conversation suddenly became locked; an effort would be needed to pull it in two, almost a tug-of-war. I could stay a couple of days or so, she said to herself. She saw the south that day as she would see it finally, as if she had picked up an old dress and first wondered, then knew, how it could be changed to suit her.

They spent that night talking on a stony beach. Sarah half lay, propped on an elbow. He sat with his arms around his knees. Behind him, a party of boys had made a bonfire. By its light Sarah told him all her life, every season of it, and he listened with the silent attention that honored her newness. She had scarcely reached the end when a fresh day opened, streaky and white. She could see him clearly: even unshaven and dying for sleep he was the ambassador from that easy place. She tossed a stone, a puppy asking for a game. He smiled, but still kept space between them, about the distance of the blue tablecloth.

They began meeting every day. They seemed to Sarah to be moving toward each other without ever quite touching; then she thought they were travelling in the same direction, but still apart. They could not turn back, for there was nothing to go back to. She felt a pause, a hesitation. The conversation began to unlock; once Sarah had told all her life she could not think of anything to say. One afternoon he came to the beach nearly two hours late. She sensed he had something to tell her, and waited to hear that he had a wife, or was engaged, or on drugs, or had no money. In the most casual voice imaginable he asked Sarah if she would spend the rest of her holiday with him. He had rented a place up behind Nice. She would know all his friends, quite openly; he did not want to let her in for anything squalid or mean. She could come for a weekend. If she hated it, no hard feelings. It was up to her.

This was new, for of course she had never *lived* with anyone. Well, why not? In her mind she told her father. After all, it was a bachelor you wanted for me. She abandoned her textbooks and packed instead four wooden bowls she had bought for her father's sister and an out-of-print Matisse poster intended for Professor Downcast. Now it would be Roy's. He came to fetch her that day in the car that was always parked somewhere in shade — it was a small open thing, a bachelor's car. They rolled out of Nice with an escort of trucks and buses. She thought there should have been carnival floats spilling yellow roses. Until now, this was her most important decision, for it supposed a way of living, a style. She reflected on how no girl she knew had ever done quite this, and on what her father would say. He might not hear of it; at least not right away. Meanwhile, they made a triumphant passage through blank white suburbs. Their witnesses were souvenir shops, a village or two, a bright solitary supermarket, the walls and hedges of villas. Along one of these flowering barriers they came to a stop and got out of the car. The fence wire looked tense and new; the plumbago it supported leaned every way, as if its life had been spared but only barely. It was late evening. She heard the squeaky barking of small dogs, and glimpsed, through an iron gate, one of those stucco bungalows that seem to beget their own palm trees. They went straight past it, down four shallow garden steps, and came upon a low building that Sarah thought looked like an Indian lodge. It was half under a plane tree. Perhaps it was the tree, whose leaves were like

plates, that made the house and its terrace seem microscopic.
One table and four thin chairs was all the terrace would hold.
A lavender hedge surrounded it.

"They call this place The Tunnel," Roy said. She wondered
if he was already regretting their adventure; if so, all he had to
do was drive her back at once, or even let her down at a bus
stop. But then he lit a candle on the table, which at once made
everything dark, and she could see he was smiling as if in
wonder at himself. The Tunnel was a long windowless room
with an arched whitewashed ceiling. In daytime the light must
have come in from the door, which was protected by a soft
white curtain of mosquito netting. He groped for a switch on
the wall, and she saw there was next to no furniture. "It used to
be a storage place for wine and olives," he said. "The Reeves
fixed it up. They let it to friends."

"What are Reeves?"

"People — nice people. They live in the bungalow."

She was now in this man's house. She wondered about
procedure: whether to unpack or wait until she was asked, and
whether she had any domestic duties and was expected to
cook. Concealed by a screen was a shower bath; the stove was
in a cupboard. The lavatory, he told her, was behind the
house in a garden shed. She would find it full of pictures of
Labour leaders. The only Socialist the Reeves could bear was
Hugh Dalton (Sarah had never heard of him, or most of the
others, either), because Dalton had paid for the Queen's
wedding out of his own pocket when she was a slip of a girl
without a bean of her own. Sarah said, "What did he want to
do that for?" She saw, too late, that he meant to be funny.

He sat down on the bed and looked at her. "The Reeves
versus Labour," he said. "Why should you care? You weren't
even born." She was used to hearing that every interesting
thing had taken place before her birth. She had a deadly
serious question waiting: "What shall I do if you feel
remorseful?"

"If I am," he said, "you'll never know. That's a promise."

It was not remorse that overcame him but respectability: first thing next day, Sarah was taken to meet his friends, landlords, and neighbors, Tim and Meg Reeve. "I want them to like you," he said. Wishing to be liked by total strangers was outside anything that mattered to Sarah: all the same, quickened by the new situation and its demands, she dressed and brushed her hair and took the path between the two cottages. The garden seemed a dry, cracked sort of place. The remains of daffodils lay in brown ribbons on the soil. She looked all round her, at an olive tree, and yesterday's iron gate, and at the sky, which was fiercely azure. She was not as innocent as her father still hoped she might turn out to be, but not as experienced as Roy thought, either. There was a world of knowledge between last night and what had gone before. She wondered, already, if violent feelings were going to define the rest of her life, or simply limit it. Roy gathered her long hair in his hand and turned her head around. They'd had other nights, or attempts at nights, but this was their first morning. Whatever he read on her face made him say, "You know, it won't always be as lovely as this." She nodded. Professor Downcast had a wife and children, and she was used to fair warnings. Roy could not guess how sturdy her emotions were. Her only antagonist had been her father, who had not touched her self-confidence. She accepted Roy's caution as a tribute: *he*, at least, could see that Sarah was objective.

Roy rang the doorbell, which set off a gunburst of barking. The Reeves' hall smelled of toast, carpets, and insect spray. She wanted southern houses to smell of jasmine. "Here, Roy," someone called, and Roy led her by the hand into a small sitting room where two people, an old man and an old woman, sat in armchairs eating breakfast. The man removed a tray from his knees and stood up. He was gaunt and tall, and looked oddly starched, like a nurse coming on duty. "Jack Sprat could eat no fat" came to Sarah's mind. Mrs. Reeve was

— she supposed — obese. Sarah stared at her; she did not know how to be furtive. Was the poor woman ill? *No*, answered the judge who was part of Sarah too. *Mrs. Reeve is just greedy. Look at the jam she's shovelled on her plate.*

"Well, this is Sarah Holmes," said Roy, stroking her hair, as if he was proving at the outset there was to be no hypocrisy. "We'd adore coffee."

"You'd better do something about it, then," said the fat woman. "We've got tea here. You know where the kitchen is, Roy." She had a deep voice, like a moo. "You, Sarah Holmes, sit down. Find a pew with no dog hair, if you can. Of course, if you're going to be fussy, you won't last long around *here* — eh, boys? You can make toast if you like. No, never mind. I'll make it for you."

It seemed to Sarah a pretty casual way for people their age to behave. Roy was older by a long start, but the Reeves were *old*. They seemed to find it natural to have Roy and Sarah drift over for breakfast after a night in the guesthouse. Mr. Reeve even asked quite kindly, "Did you sleep well? The plane tree draws mosquitoes, I'm afraid."

"I'll have that tree down yet," said Mrs. Reeve. "Oh, I'll have it down one of these days. I can promise you that." She was dressed in a bathrobe that looked like a dark parachute. "We decided not to have eggs," she said, as though Sarah had asked. "Have 'em later. You and Roy must come back for lunch. We'll have a good old fry-up." Here she attended to toast, which meant shaking and tapping an antique wire toaster set on the table before her. "When Tim's gone — bless him — I shall never cook a meal again," she said. "Just bits and pieces on a tray for the boys and me." The boys were dogs, Sarah guessed — two little yappers up on the sofa, the color of Teddy-bear stuffing.

"I make a lot of work for Meg," Mr. Reeve said to Sarah. "The breakfasts — breakfast every day, you know — and she is the one who looks after the Christmas cards. Marriage has been a bind for her. She did a marvellous job with evacuees in the war. And poor old Meg loathed kids, still does. You'll never hear her say so. I've never known Meg to complain."

Mrs. Reeve had not waited for her husband to die before starting her widow's diet of tea and toast and jam and gin (the bottle was there, by the toaster, along with a can of orange juice). Sarah knew about this, for not only was her father a widower but they had often spent summers with a widowed aunt. The Reeves seemed like her father and her aunt grown elderly and distorted. Mrs. Reeve now unwrapped a chocolate bar, which caused a fit of snorting and jostling on the sofa. "No chockie bits for boys with bad manners," she said, feeding them just the same. Yes, there she sat, a widow with two dogs for company. Mr. Reeve, delicately buttering and eating the toast meant for Sarah, murmured that when he *did* go he did not want poor Meg to have any fuss. He seemed to be planning his own modest gravestone; in a heightened moment of telepathy Sarah was sure she could see it too. To Sarah, the tall old man had already ceased to be. He was not Mr. Reeve, Roy's friend and landlord, but an ectoplasmic impression of somebody like him, leaning forward, lips slightly parted, lifting a piece of toast that was caving in like a hammock with a weight of strawberry jam. Panic was in the room, but only Sarah felt it. She had been better off, safer, perhaps happier even, up in Grenoble, trying not to yawn over *"Tout m'afflige, et me nuit, et conspire à me nuire."* What was she doing here, indoors, on this glowing day, with these two snivelly dogs and these gluttonous old persons? She turned swiftly, hearing Roy, and in her heart she said, in a quavering spoiled child's voice, "I want to go home." (How many outings had she ruined for her father. How many picnics, circuses, puppet shows, boat rides. From how many attempted holidays had he been fetched back with a telegram from whichever relation had been trying to hold Sarah down for a week. The strong brass chords of "I want my own life" had always been followed by this dismal piping.)

Roy poured their coffee into pottery mugs and his eyes met

Sarah's. His said, Yes, these are the Reeves. They don't matter. I only want one thing, and that's to get back to where we were a few hours ago.

So they were to be conspirators: she liked that.

The Reeves had now done with chewing, feeding, swallowing, and brushing crumbs, and began placing Sarah. Who was she? Sarah Holmes, a little transatlantic pickup, a student slumming round for a summer? What had she studied? Sociology, psychology, and some economics, she told them.

"Sounds Labour," was Mr. Reeve's comment.

She simplified her story and mentioned the thesis. "Urban and Regional Studies of the Less Privileged in British Columbia," as far as Mr. Reeve was concerned, contained only one reassuring word, and that was "British." Being the youngest in the room, Sarah felt like the daughter of the house. She piled cups and plates on one of the trays and took them out to the kitchen. The Reeves were not the sort of people who would even bother to whisper; she heard that she was "a little on the tall side" and that her proportions made Roy seem slight and small, "like a bloody dago." Her hair was too long; the fringe on her forehead looked sparse and pasted down with soap. She also heard that she had a cast in one eye, which she did not believe.

"One can't accuse her of oversmartness," said Mrs. Reeve.

Roy, whose low voice had carrying qualities, said, "No, Meg. Sarah's jeans are as faded, as baggy, as those brown corduroys of yours. However, owing to Sarah's splendid and enviable shape, hers are not nearly so large across the beam end." This provoked two laughs — a cackle from Jack Sprat and a long three-note moo from his wife.

"Well, Roy," said Tim Reeve, "all I can say is, you amaze me. How do you bring it off?"

"What about me?" said Sarah to herself. "How do I bring it off?"

"At least she's had sense enough not to come tramping around in high-heeled shoes, like some of our visitors," said Mrs. Reeve — her last word for the moment.

Roy warned Sarah what lunch — the good old fry-up — would be. A large black pan the Reeves had brought to France from England when they emigrated because of taxes and Labour would be dragged out of the oven; its partner, a jam jar of bacon fat, stratified in a wide extent of suety whites, had its permanent place on top of the stove. The lowest, or Ur, line of fat marked the very first fry-up in France. A few spoonfuls of this grease, releasing blue smoke, received tomatoes, more bacon, eggs, sausages, cold boiled potatoes. To get the proper sausages they had to go to a shop that imported them, in Monte Carlo. This was no distance, but the Reeves' car had been paid for by Tim, and he was mean about it. He belonged to a generation that had been in awe of batteries: each time the ignition was turned on, he thought the car's lifeblood was seeping away. When he became too stingy with the car, then Meg would not let him look at television: the set was hers. She would push it on its wheeled table over bumpy rugs into their bedroom and put a chair against the door.

Roy was a sharp mimic and he took a slightly feminine pleasure in mocking his closest friends. Sarah lay on her elbow on the bed as she had lain on the beach and thought that if he was disloyal to the Reeves then he was all the more loyal to her. They had been told to come back for lunch around three; this long day was in itself like a whole summer. She said, "It sounds like a movie. Are they happy?"

"Oh, blissful," he answered, surprised, and perhaps with a trace of reproval. It was as if he were very young and she had asked an intimate question about his father and mother.

The lunch Roy had described was exactly the meal they were given. She watched him stolidly eating eggs fried to a kind of plastic lace, and covering everything with mustard to damp out the taste of grease. When Meg opened the door to the kitchen she was followed by a blue haze. Tim noticed

Sarah's look — she had wondered if something was burning —
and said, "Next time you're here that's where we'll eat. It's
what we like. We like our kitchen."

"Today we are honoring Sarah," said Meg Reeve, as though
baiting Roy.

"So you should," he said. It was the only attempt at
sparring; they were all much too fed and comfortable. Tim,
who had been to Monte Carlo, had brought back another
symbol of their roots, the Hovis loaf. They talked about his
shopping, and the things they liked doing — gambling a little,
smuggling from Italy for sport. One thing they never did was
look at the Mediterranean. It was not an interesting sea. It had
no tides. "I do hope you aren't going to bother with it," said
Tim to Sarah. It seemed to be their private measure for a guest
— that and coming round in the wrong clothes.

The temperature in full sun outside the sitting-room
window was thirty-three degrees centigrade. "What does it
mean?" said Sarah. Nobody knew. Tim said that 16°C. was
the same thing as 61°F. but that nothing else corresponded.
For instance, 33°C. could not possibly be 33°F. — No, it felt
like a lot more.

After the trial weekend Sarah wrote to her father, "I am in
this interesting old one-room guesthouse that belongs to
an elderly couple here. It is in their garden. They only let
reliable people stay in it." She added, "Don't worry, I'm
working." If she concealed information she did not exactly lie:
she thought she *was* working. Instead of French civilization
taught in airless classrooms she would study expatriates at first
hand. She decided to record the trivia first — how visitors of
any sort were a catastrophe, how a message from old friends
staying at Nice brought Tim back from the telephone wearing
the look of someone whose deepest feelings have been raked
over.

"Come on, Tim, what was it?" his wife would call. "The

who? What did they want? An invitation to their hotel? Damned cheek. More likely a lot of free drinks here, that's what they want." They lived next to gas fires with all the windows shut, yelling from room to room. Their kitchen was comfortable providing one imagined it was the depth of January in England and that sleet was battering at the garden. She wanted to record that Mr. Reeve said "heith" and "strenth" and that they used a baby language with each other — walkies, tummy, spend-a-penny. When Sarah said "cookie" it made them laugh: a minute later, feeding the dogs a chocolate cookie, Meg said, "Here, have a chockie bicky." If Tim tried to explain anything, his wife interrupted with, "Come on, get to Friday." Nobody could remember the origin of the phrase; it served merely to rattle him.

Sarah meant to record this, but Professor Downcast's useful language had left her. The only words in her head were so homespun and plain she was ashamed to set them down. The heat must have flattened her brain, she thought. The Reeves, who never lowered their voices for anyone, bawled one night that "old Roy was doting and indulgent" and "the wretched girl is in love." That was the answer. She had already discovered that she could live twenty-four hours on end just with the idea that she was in love; she also knew that a man could think about love for a while but then he would start to think about something else. What if Roy never did? Sarah Cooper didn't sound bad; Mrs. R. Cooper was better. But Sarah was not that foolish. She was looking ahead only because she and Roy had no past. She did say to him, "What do you do when you aren't having a vacation?"

"You mean in winter? I go to Marbella. Sometimes Kenya. Where my friends are."

"Don't you work?"

"I did work. They retired me."

"You're too young to be retired. My father isn't even retired. You should write your memoirs — all that colonial stuff."

He laughed at her. She was never more endearing to him

than when she was most serious; that was not her fault. She abandoned the future and rearranged their short history to suit herself. Every word was recollected later in primrose light. Did it rain every Sunday? Was there an invasion of red ants? She refused the memory. The Reeves' garden incinerator, which was never cleaned out, set oily smoke to sit at their table like a third person. She drank her coffee unaware of this guest, seeing nothing but butterflies dancing over the lavender hedge. Sarah, who would not make her own bed at home, insisted now on washing everything by hand, though there was a laundry in the village. Love compelled her to buy enough food for a family of seven. The refrigerator was a wheezy old thing, and sometimes Roy got up and turned it off in the night because he could not sleep for its sighing. In the morning Sarah piled the incinerator with spoiled meat, cheese, and peaches, and went out at six o'clock to buy more and more. She was never so bathed in love as when she stood among a little crowd of villagers at a bus stop — the point of creation, it seemed — with her empty baskets; she desperately hoped to be taken for what the Reeves called "part of the local populace." The market she liked was two villages over; the buses were tumbrils. She could easily have driven Roy's car or had everything sent from shops, but she was inventing fidelities. Once, she saw Meg Reeve, wearing a floral cotton that compressed her figure and gave her a stylized dolphin shape, like an ornament on a fountain. On her head was a straw hat with a polka-dot ribbon. She found a place one down and across the aisle from Sarah, who shrank from her notice for fear of that deep voice letting the world know Sarah was not a peasant. Meg unfolded a paper that looked like a prescription; slid her glasses along her nose; held them with one finger. She always sat with her knees spread largely. In order not to have Meg's thigh crushing his, her neighbor, a priest in a dirty cassock, had to squeeze against the window.

"She doesn't care," Sarah said to herself. "She hasn't even looked to see who is there." When she got down at the next village Meg was still rereading the scrap of paper, and the bus rattled on to Nice.

Sarah never mentioned having seen her; Meg was such a cranky, unpredictable old lady. One night she remarked, "Sarah's going to have trouble landing Roy," there in front of him, on his own terrace. "He'll never marry." Roy was a bachelor owing to the fact he had too many rich friends, and because men were selfish . . . Here Meg paused, conceding that this might sound wrong. No, it sounded right; Roy was a bachelor because of the selfishness of men, and the looseness and availability of young women.

"True enough, they'll do it for a ham sandwich," said Tim, as if a supply of sandwiches had given him the pick of a beach any day.

His wife stared at him but changed her mind. She plucked at her fork and said, "When Tim's gone — bless him — I shall have all my meals out. Why bother cooking?" She then looked at her plate as if she had seen a mouse on it.

"It's all right, Meg," said Roy, "Sarah favors the cooking of the underdeveloped countries. All our meals are raw and drowned in yogurt." He said it so kindly Sarah had to laugh. For a time she had tried to make them all eat out of her aunt's bowls, but the untreated wood became stained and Roy found it disgusting. The sight of Sarah scouring them out with ashes did not make him less squeamish. He was, in fact, surprisingly finicky for someone who had spent a lifetime around colonial prisons. A dead mosquito made him sick — even the mention of one.

"It is true that Roy has never lacked for pretty girls," said Tim. "We should know, eh, Roy?" Roy and the Reeves talked quite a lot about his personal affairs, as if a barrier of discretion had long ago been breached. They were uncomfortable stories, a little harsh sometimes for Sarah's taste. Roy now suddenly chose to tell about how he had met his own future brother-in-law in a brothel in Hong Kong — by accident, of course. They became the best of friends and remained so, even after Roy's engagement was broken off.

"Why'd she dump you?" Sarah said. "She found out?"

Her way of asking plain questions froze the others. They looked as if winter had swept over the little terrace and caught them. Then Roy took Sarah's hand and said, "I'm ashamed to say I wasn't gallant — I dumped the lady."

"Old Roy probably thought, um, matrimony," said Tim. "Eh, Meg?" This was because marriage was supposed to be splendid for Tim but somehow confining for his wife.

"She said I was venomous," said Roy, looking at Sarah, who knew he was not.

"She surely didn't mean venomous," said Tim. "She meant something more like, moody." Here he lapsed into a mood of his own, staring at the candles on the table, and Sarah remembered her shared vision of his unassuming gravestone; she said to Roy in an undertone, "Is anything wrong with him?"

"Wrong with him? Wrong with old Tim? Tim!" Roy called, as if he were out of sight instead of across the table. "When was the last time you ever had a day's illness?"

"I was sick on a Channel crossing — I might have been ten," said Tim.

"Nothing's the matter with Tim, I can promise you that," said his wife. "Never a headache, never a cold, no flu, no rheumatism, no gout, nothing."

"Doesn't feel the amount he drinks," said Roy.

"Are you ever sick, Mrs. Reeve?" Sarah asked.

"Oh, poor Meg," said Tim immediately. "You won't get a word out of her. Never speaks of herself."

"The ailments of old parties can't possibly interest Sarah," said Meg. "Here, Roy, give Sarah something to drink," meaning that her own glass was empty. "My niece Lisbet will be here for a weekend. Now, *that*'s an interesting girl. She interviews people for jobs. She can see straight through them, mentally speaking. She had stiff training — had to see a trick cyclist for a year."

"I abhor that subject," said Roy. "No sensible prison governor ever allowed a trick cyclist anywhere near. The good were good and the bad were bad and everyone knew it."

"Psycho-whatnot does no harm if the person is sound," said Meg. "Lisbet just went week after week and had a jolly old giggle with the chap. The firm was paying."

"A didactic analysis is a waste of time," said Sarah, chilling them all once more.

"I didn't say that or anything like it," said Meg. "I said the firm was paying. But you're a bit out of it, Roy," turning to him and heaving her vast garments so Sarah was cut out. "Lisbet said it did help her. You wouldn't believe the number of people she turns away, whatever their education. She can tell if they are likely to have asthma. She saves the firm thousands of pounds every year."

"Lisbet can see when they're queer," said Tim.

"What the hell do you mean?" said Roy.

"What did she tell you?" said Meg, now extremely annoyed. "Come on, Tim, get to Friday."

But Tim had gone back to contemplating his life on the Other Side, and they could obtain nothing further.

Sarah forgot all about Mrs. Reeve's niece until Lisbet turned up, wearing a poncho, black pants, and bracelets. She was about Roy's age. All over her head was a froth of kinky yellow hair — a sort of Little Orphan Annie wig. She stared with small blue eyes and gave Sarah a boy's handshake. She said, "So you're the famous one!"

Sarah had come back from the market to find them all drinking beer in The Tunnel. Her shirt stuck to her back. She pulled it away and said, "Famous one what?" From the way Lisbet laughed she guessed she had been described as a famous comic turn. Roy handed Sarah a glass without looking at her. Roy and Tim were talking about how to keep Lisbet amused for the weekend. Everything was displayed — the night racing at Cagnes, the gambling, the smuggling from Italy, which bored Sarah but which even Roy did for amusement. "A picnic," Sarah said, getting in something she liked. Also, it sounded cool. The Hayeses, those anxious tourists at her hotel in Nice, suddenly rose up in her mind offering advice. "There's this chapel," she said, feeling a spiky nostalgia, as if she were describing something from home. "Remember, Roy, I mentioned it? Nobody goes there . . . you have to get the keys from a café in the village. You can picnic in the churchyard; it has a gate and a wall. There's a river where we washed our hands. The book said it used to be a pagan place. It has these paintings now, of the Last Judgment, and Jesus, naturally, and one of Judas after he hung himself."

"Hanged," said Roy and Lisbet together.

"Hanged. Well somebody had really seen a hanging — the one who painted it, I mean."

"Have you?" said Roy, smiling.

"No, but I can imagine."

"No," he said, still smiling. "You can't. All right, I'm for the picnic. Sunday, then. We'll do Italy tomorrow."

His guests got up to leave. Tim suddenly said, for no reason Sarah could see, "I'm glad I'm not young."

As soon as the others were out of earshot Roy said, "God, what a cow! Planeloads of Lisbets used to come out to Asia looking for Civil Service husbands. Now they fly to Majorca and sleep with the waiters."

"Why do we have to be nice to her, if you feel like that?" said Sarah.

"Why don't you know about these things without asking?" said Roy.

My father didn't bring me up well, Sarah thought, and resolved to write and tell him so. Mr. Holmes would not have been nice to Lisbet and then called her a cow. He might have done one or the other, or neither. His dilemma as a widower was insoluble; he could never be too nice for fear of someone's taking it into her head that Sarah wanted a mother. Also, he was not violent about people, even those he had to eliminate. That was why he gave them comic names. "Perhaps you are right," she said to Roy, without being any more specific. He cared for praise, however ambiguous; and so they had a perfect day, and a perfect night, but those were the last: in the morning, as Sarah stood on the table to tie one end of the clothesline to the plane tree, she slipped, had to jump, landed badly, and sprained her ankle. By noon the skin was purple and she had to cut off her canvas shoe. The foot needed to be bandaged, but not by Roy: the very sight of it made him sick. He could not bear a speck of dust anywhere, or a chipped cup. She remembered the wooden bowls, and how he'd had to leave the table once because they looked a little doubtful, not too clean. Lisbet was summoned. Kneeling, she wrapped Sarah's foot and ankle in strips of a torn towel and fixed the strips with safety pins.

"It'll do till I see a doctor," Sarah said.

Lisbet looked up. How small her eyes were! "You don't want a doctor for that, surely?"

"Yes, I do. I think it should be X-rayed," Sarah said. "It hurts like anything."

"Of course she doesn't," said Roy.

Getting well with the greatest possible amount of suffering, and with your bones left crooked, was part of their code. It seemed to Sarah an unreasonable code, but she did not want to seem like someone making a fuss. All the same, she said, "I feel sick."

"Drink some brandy," said Lisbet.

"Lie down," said Roy. "We shan't be long." It would have been rude not to have taken Lisbet on the smuggling expedition just because Sarah couldn't go.

In the late afternoon Meg Reeve strolled down to see how Sarah was managing. She found her standing on one foot hanging washing on a line. The sight of Sarah's plaid slacks, bought on sale at Nice, caused Meg to remark, "My dear, are you a Scot? I've often wondered, seeing you wearing those." Sarah let a beach towel of Roy's fall to the ground.

"Damn, it'll have to be washed again," she said.

Meg had brought Roy's mail. She put the letters on the table, face down, as if Sarah were likely to go over the postmarks with a magnifying glass. The dogs snuffled and snapped at the ghosts of animal-haters. "What clan?" said Meg.

"Clan? Oh, you're still talking about my slacks. Clan *salade niçoise*, I guess."

"Well, you must not wear tartan," said Meg. "It is an insult to the family, d'you see? I'm surprised Roy hasn't . . Ticky! Blue! Naughty boys!"

"Oh, the dogs come down here and pee all over the terrace every day," said Sarah.

"Roy used to give them chockie bits. They miss being spoiled. But now he hasn't time for them, has he?"

"I don't know. I can't answer for him. He has time for what interests him."

"Why do you hang your washing where you can see it?" said Meg. "Are you Italian?" Sarah made new plans; next time the Reeves were invited she would boil Ticky and Blue with a little sugar and suet and serve them up as pudding. I must look angelic at this moment, she thought.

She said, "No, I'm not Italian. I don't think so."

"There are things I could never bring myself to do," said Meg. "Not in my walk of life."

The sociologist snapped to attention. Easing her sore ankle, Sarah said, "Please, what is your walk of life, exactly?"

It was so dazzling, so magical, that Meg could not name it, but merely mouthed a word or two that Sarah was unable to lip-read. A gust of incinerator smoke stole between them and made them choke. "As for Tim," said Meg, getting her breath again, "you, with all your transatlantic money, couldn't buy what Tim has in his veins."

Sarah limped indoors and somehow found the forgotten language. "Necessity for imparting status information," she recorded, and added "erroneous" between "imparting" and "status." She was still, in a way, half in love with Professor Downcast.

She discovered this was a conversation neither Roy nor Lisbet could credit. They unpacked their loot from Italy on the wobbly terrace table — plastic table mats, plastic roses, a mermaid paperweight, a bottle of aperitif that smelled like medicine, a Florentine stamp box . . . "Rubbish, garbage," Sarah said in her mind. "But Roy is happy." Also, he was drunk. So was Lisbet.

"Meg could not have said those things," said Roy, large-eyed.

"Meg doesn't always understand Sarah," said Lisbet. "The accent."

"Mrs. Reeve was doing the talking," said Sarah.

"She wouldn't have talked that way to an Englishwoman," said Roy, swinging round to Sarah's side.

"Wouldn't have dared," said Lisbet. She shouted, "Wouldn't have dared to me!"

"As for Tim, well, Tim really is the real thing," said Roy. "I mean to say that Tim really *is*."

"So is my aunt," said Lisbet, but Roy had disappeared behind the white net curtain, and they heard him fall on the bed. "He's had rather a lot," said Lisbet. Sarah felt anxiety for Roy, who had obviously had a lot of everything — perhaps of Lisbet too. And there was still the picnic next day, and no one had bought any food for it. Lisbet looked glowing and superb, as if she had been tramping in a clean wind instead of sitting crouched in a twilit bar somewhere on the Italian side. She should have been haggard and gray.

"Who was driving?" Sarah asked her.

"Took turns."

"What did you talk about?" She was remembering his "God, what a cow!"

"Capital punishment, apartheid, miscegenation, and my personal problems with men. That I seem cold, but I'm not really."

"Boys, boys, boys!" That was Meg Reeve calling her dogs. They rolled out of the lavender hedge like a pair of chewed tennis balls. They might well have been eavesdropping. Sarah gave a shiver, and Lisbet laughed and said, "Someone's walking on your grave."

The sunlight on the terrace next morning hurt Roy's eyes; he made little flapping gestures, meaning Sarah was not to speak. "What were you drinking in Italy?" she said. He shook his head. Mutely, he took the dried laundry down and folded it. Probably, like Meg, he did not much care for the look of it. "I've made the picnic," Sarah next offered. "No reason why I can't come — we won't be doing much walking." She stood on one leg, like a stork. The picnic consisted of anything Sarah happened to find in the refrigerator. She included plums in brandy because she noticed a jar of them, and iced white wine in a thermos. At the last minute she packed olives, salted peanuts, and several pots of yogurt.

"Put those back," said Roy.

"Why? Do you think they'll melt?"

"Just do as I say, for once. Put them back."

"Do you know what I think?" said Sarah after a moment. "I think we're starting out on something my father would call The Ill-Fated Excursion."

For the first time ever, she saw Roy looking angry. The vitality of the look made him younger, but not in a nice way. He became a young man, an ugly one. "Liz will have to drive," he said. "I've got a blinding headache, and you can't, not with *that*." He could not bring himself to name her affliction. "How do you know about this place?" he said. "Who took you there?"

"I told you. Some Americans in my hotel. Haynes — no, Hayes."

"Yes, I can imagine." He looked at her sidelong and said, "Just who were you sleeping with when I collected you?"

She felt what it was like to blush — like a rash of needles and pins. He knew every second of her life, because she had told it to him that night on the beach. What made her blush was that she sensed he was only pretending to be jealous. It offended her. She said, "Let's call the picnic off."

"I don't want to."

She was not used to quarrels, only to tidal waves. She did not understand that they were quarrelling now. She wondered again what he had been drinking over in Italy. Her ankle felt in a vice, but that was the least of it. They set off, all three together, and Lisbet drove straight up into the hills as if pursuing escaped prisoners. They shot past towns Sarah had visited with the Americans, who had been conscientious about churches; she saw, open-and-shut, views they had stopped to photograph. When she said, "Look," nobody heard. She sat crumpled in the narrow back seat, with the picnic sliding all over as they rounded the mountain curves, quite often on the wrong side.

"That was the café, back there, where you get the key," Sarah had to say twice — once very loudly. Lisbet braked so they were thrown forward and then reversed like a bullet ricocheting. "Sarah knows about this," said Roy, as if it were a good thing to know about. That was encouraging. She gripped her ankle between her hands and set her foot down. She tested her weight and managed to walk and hop to the cool café, past the beaded curtain. She leaned on the marble counter; she had lost something. Was it her confidence? She wanted someone to come and take her home, but was too old to want that; she knew too many things. She said to the man standing behind the counter, *"J'ai mal,"* to explain why she did not take the keys from him and at once go out. His reaction was to a confession of sorrow and grief; he poured out something to drink. It was clear as water, terribly strong, and smelled of warm fruit. When she gestured to show him she had no money, he said, *"Ça va."* He was kind; the Hayeses, such an inadequate substitute for peacocks, had been kind too. She said to herself, "How awful if I should cry."

The slight inclination of Roy's head when she handed the

keys to him meant he might be interested. She felt embold-
ened: "One's for the chapel, the other's the gate. There isn't a
watchman or anything. It's too bad, because people write on
the walls."

"Which way?" Lisbet interrupted. She chased her prisoners
another mile or so.

Sarah had told them no one ever came here, but they were
forced to park behind a car with Swiss license plates. Next to
the gate sat a large party of picnickers squeezed round a card
table. There was only one man among them, and Sarah
thought it must be a harem and the man had been allowed
several wives for having been reasonable and Swiss until he
was fifty. She started to tell this to Roy, but he had gone blank
as a monument; she felt overtaken by her father's humor, not
her own. Roy gave the harem an empty look that reminded
her of the prostitutes down in Nice, and now she knew what
their faces had been saying. It was "I despise you." The chapel
was an icebox; and she saw Roy and Lisbet glance with some
consternation at the life of Jesus spread around for anyone to
see. They would certainly have described themselves as
Christians, but they were embarrassed by Christ. They went
straight to Judas, who was more reassuring. Hanged, disem-
bowelled, his stomach and liver exposed to ravens, Judas gave
up his soul. His soul was a small naked creature. Perceiving
Satan, the creature held out its arms.

"Now, *that* man must have eaten Sarah's cooking," said
Roy, and such were their difficulties that she was grateful to
hear him say anything. But he added, "A risk many have
taken, I imagine." This was to Lisbet. Only Sarah knew what
he meant. She fell back and pretended to be interested in a
rack of postcards. The same person who trusted visitors not to
write their names on paintings had left a coin box. Sarah had
no money and did not want to ask Roy for any. She stole a
reproduction of the Judas fresco and put it inside her shirt.

Roy and Lisbet ate some of the picnic. They sat where
Sarah had sat with the Americans, but it was in no way the

same. Of course, the season was later, the river lower, the grass drooping and dry. The shadows of clouds made them stare and comment, as if looking for something to say. Sarah was relieved when the two decided to climb up in the maquis, leaving her "to rest a bit" — this was Lisbet. "Watch out for snakes," Sarah said, and got from Roy one blurred, anxious, puzzled look, the last straight look he ever gave her. She sat down and drank all the brandy out of the jar of plums. Roy had an attitude to people she had never heard of: nothing must ever go wrong. An accident is degrading for the victim. She undid the towelling strips and looked at her bloated ankle and foot. Of course, it was ugly; but it was part of a living body, not a corpse, and it hurt Sarah, not Roy. She tipped out the plums so the ants could have a party, drank some of the white wine, and, falling asleep, thought she was engaged in an endless and heated discussion with some person who was in the wrong.

She woke up cramped and thirsty on the back seat of the car. They were stopped in front of the café and must have been parked for some time, for they were in an oblique shadow of late afternoon. Roy was telling Lisbet a lie: he said he had been a magistrate and was writing his memoirs. Next he told her of hangings he'd seen. He said in his soft voice. "Don't you think some people are better out of the way?" Sarah knew by heart the amber eyes and the pupils so small they seemed a mistake sometimes. She was not Sarah now but a prisoner impaled on a foreign language, seeing bright, light, foreign eyes offering something nobody wanted — death. "Flawed people, born rotten," Roy went on.

"Oh, everyone thinks that now," said Lisbet.

They were alike, with fortunes established in piracy. He liked executions; she broke people before they had a chance to break themselves. Lisbet stroked the back of her own neck. Sarah had noticed before that when Lisbet was feeling sure of herself she made certain her neck was in place. *Neurotic habit*, Sarah's memory asked her to believe; but no, it was only the gesture of someone at ease in a situation she recognized.

Tranquil as to her neck, Lisbet now made sure of her hair. She patted the bright steel wool that must have been a comfort to her mother some thirty-five — no, forty — years before.

I am jealous, Sarah said to herself. How unwelcome. Jealousy is only . . . the jealous person is the one keeping something back and so . . .

"Oh, keys, always keys," said Roy, shaking them. He slammed out in a way that was surely rude to Lisbet. She rested her arm over the back of the seat and looked at Sarah. "You drank enough to stun a rhinoceros, little girl," she said. "We had to take you out behind the chapel and make you be sick before we could let you in the car." Sarah began to remember. She saw Roy's face, a gray flash in a cracked old film about a catastrophe. Lisbet said, "Look, Sarah, how old are you? Aren't you a bit out of your depth with Roy?" She might have said more, but a native spitefulness, or a native prudence, prevented her. She flew to Majorca the next day, as Roy had predicted, leaving everyone out of step.

Now Roy began hating; he hated the sea, the Reeves, the dogs, the blue of plumbago, the mention of Lisbet, and most of all he hated Sarah. The Reeves laughed and called it "old Roy being bloody-minded again," but Sarah was frightened. She had never known anyone who would simply refuse to speak, who would take no notice of a question. Meg said to her, "He misses that job of his. It came to nothing. He tried to give a lot of natives a sense of right and wrong, and then some Socialist let them vote."

"Yes, he liked that job," Sarah said slowly. "One day he'd watch a hanging, and the next he'd measure the exercise yard to see if it was up to standard." She said suddenly and for no reason she knew, "I've disappointed him."

Their meals were so silent that they could hear the swelling love songs from the Reeves' television, and the Reeves' voices bawling away at each other. Sarah's throat would go tight. In daytime the terrace was like an oven now, and her ankle kept her from sleeping at night. Then Roy gave up eating and lay on the bed looking up at the ceiling. She still went on shopping, but now it took hours. Mornings, before leaving, she would place a bowl of coffee for him, like an offering; it was still there, at the bedside, cold and oily-looking now, when she came back. She covered a tray with leaves from the plane tree — enormous powdery leaves, the size of her two hands — and she put cheese on the leaves, and white cheese covered with pepper, a Camembert, a salty goat cheese he had liked. He did not touch any. Out of a sort of desperate sentiment, she kept the tray for days, picking chalky pieces off as the goat cheese grew harder and harder and became a fossil. He must have eaten sometimes; she thought of him gobbling scraps straight from the refrigerator when her back was turned. She wrote a letter to her father that of course she did not send. It said, "I've been having headaches lately. I wind a thread around a finger until the blood can't get past and that starts a new pain. The headache is all down the back of my neck. I'm not sure what to do next. It will be terrible for you if I turn out to have a brain tumor. It will cost you a lot of money and you may lose your only child."

One dawn she knew by Roy's breathing that he was awake. Every muscle was taut as he pulled away, as if to touch her was defilement. No use saying what they had been like not long before, because he could not remember. She was a disgusting object because of a cracked ankle, because she had drunk too much and been sick behind a chapel, and because she had led an expedition to look at Jesus. She lay thinking it over until the dawn birds stopped and then she sat up on the edge of the bed, feeling absolutely out of place because she was undressed. She pulled clothes on as fast as she could and packed whatever seemed important. After she had pushed her suitcase out the door, she remembered the wooden bowls and the poster. These she took along the path and threw in the Reeves' foul incinerator, as if to get rid of all traces of witchery, goodness, and love. She realized she was leaving, a decision as final and stunning as her having crossed the promenade in Nice with Roy's hand on her arm.

She said through the white netting over the door, "I'm sorry, Roy." It was not enough; she added, "I'm sorry I don't understand you more." The stillness worried her. She limped near and bent over him. He was holding his breath, like a child in temper. She said softly, "I could stay a bit longer." No answer. She said, "Of course, my foot will get better, but then you might find something else the matter with me." Still no answer, except that he began breathing. Nothing was wrong except that he was cruel, lunatic, Fascist — No, not even that. Nothing was wrong except that he did not love her. That was all.

She lugged her suitcase as far as the road and sat down beside it. Overnight a pocket of liquid the size of a lemon had formed near the anklebone. Her father would say it was all her own fault again. Why? Was it Sarah's fault that she had all this loving capital to invest? What was she supposed to do with it? Even if she always ended up sitting outside a gate somewhere, was she any the worse for it? The only thing wrong now was the pain she felt, not of her ankle but in her stomach. Her stomach felt as if it was filled up with old oyster shells. Yes, a load of old, ugly, used-up shells was what she had for stuffing. She had to take care not to breathe too deeply, because the shells scratched. In her research for Professor Downcast she had learned that one could be alcoholic, crippled, afraid of dying and of being poor, and she knew these things waited for everyone, even Sarah; but nothing had warned her that one day she would not be loved. That was the meaning of "less privileged." There was no other.

Now that she had vanished, Roy would probably get up, and shave, and stroll across to the Reeves, and share a good old fry-up. Then, his assurance regained, he would start prowling the bars and beaches, wearing worn immaculate whites, looking for a new, unblemished story. He would repeat the first soft words, "Don't be frightened," the charm, the gestures, the rituals, and the warning "It won't always be lovely." She saw him out in the open, in her remembered primrose light, before he was trapped in the tunnel again and had to play at death. "Roy's new pickup," the Reeves would bawl at each other. "I said, Roy's new one . . . he hardly knows how to get rid of her."

At that, Sarah opened her mouth and gave a great sobbing cry; only one, but it must have carried, for next thing she heard was the Reeves' door, and, turning, she saw Tim in a dressing gown, followed by Meg in her parachute of a robe. Sarah stood up to face them. The sun was on her back. She clutched the iron bars of the gate because she had to stand like a stork again. From their side of it, Tim looked down at her suitcase. He said. "Do you want — are you waiting to be driven somewhere?"

"To the airport, if you feel like taking me. Otherwise I'll hitch."

"Oh, please don't do that!" He seemed afraid of another outburst from her — something low-pitched and insulting this time.

"Come in this minute," said Meg. "I don't know what you are up to, but we do have neighbors, you know."

"Why should I care?" said Sarah. "They aren't my neighbors."

"You *are* a little coward," said Meg. "Running away only because . . ." There were so many reasons that of course she hesitated.

Without unkind intention Sarah said the worst thing: "It's just that I'm too young for all of you."

Meg's hand crept between the bars and around her wrist. "Somebody had to be born before you, Sarah," she said, and unlocked her hand and turned back to the house. "Yes, boys, dear boys, here I am," she called.

Tim said, "Would you like — let me see — something to eat or drink?" It seemed natural for him to talk through bars.

"I can't stay in the same bed with someone who doesn't care," said Sarah, beginning to cry. "It isn't right."

"It is what most people do," said Tim. "Meg has the dogs,

and her television. She has everything. We haven't often lived together. We gradually stopped. When did we last live together? When we went home once for the motor show." She finally grasped what he meant by "live together." Tim said kindly, "Look, I don't mean to pry, but you didn't take old Roy too much to heart, did you? He wasn't what you might call the love of your life?"

"I don't know yet."

"Dear, dear," said Tim, as if someone had been spreading bad news. He seemed so much more feminine than his wife; his hands were powdery — they seemed dipped in talcum. His eyes were embedded in a little volcano of wrinkles that gave him in full sunlight the look of a lizard. A white lizard, Sarah decided. "This has affected Meg," he said. "The violence of it. We shall talk it over for a long time. Well. You have so much more time. You will bury all of us." His last words were loud and sudden, almost a squawk, because Meg, light of tread and silent on her feet, had come up behind him. She wore her straw hat and carried her morning glass of gin and orange juice.

"Sarah? She'll bury *you*," said Meg. "Fetch the car, Tim, and take Sarah somewhere. Come along. Get to Friday. *Tim*." He turned. "Dress first," she said.

The sun which had turned Tim into a white lizard now revealed a glassy stain on Meg's cheek, half under her hair. Sarah's attention jumped like a child's. She said, "Something's bitten you. Look. Something poisonous."

Meg moved her head and the poisoned bite vanished under the shade of her hat. "Observant. Tim has never noticed. Neither has Roy. It is only a small malignant thing," she said indifferently. "I've been going to the hospital in Nice twice a week for treatment. They burned it — that's the reason for the scar."

"Oh, Meg," said Sarah, drawn round the gate. "Nobody knew. That was why you went to Nice. I saw you on the bus."

"I saw you," said Meg, "but why talk when you needn't? I get plenty of talk at home. May I ask where you are going?"

"I'm going to the airport, and I'll sit there till they get me on a plane."

"Well, Sarah, you may be sitting for some time, but I know you know what you are doing," said Meg. "I am minding the summer heat this year. I feel that soon I won't be able to stand it anymore. When Tim's gone I won't ever marry again. I'll look for some woman to share expenses. If you ever want to come back for a holiday, Sarah, you have only to let me know."

And so Tim, the battery of his car leaking its lifeblood all over French roads, drove Sarah down to Nice and along to the airport. Loyal to the Reeve standards, he did not once glance at the sea. As for Sarah, she sat beside him crying quietly, first over Meg, then over herself, because she thought she had spent all her capital on Roy and would never love anyone again. She looked for the restaurant with the blue tablecloths, and for the beach where they had sat talking for a night, but she could not find them; there were dozens of tables and awnings and beaches, all more or less alike.

"You'll be all right?" said Tim. He wanted her to say yes, of course.

She said, "Tim, Roy needs help."

He did not know her euphemisms any more than she understood his. He said. "Help to do what?"

"Roy is unhappy and he doesn't know what he wants. If you're over forty and you don't know what you want, well, I guess someone should tell you."

"My dear Sarah," said the old man, "that is an unkind thing to say about a friend we have confidence in."

She said quickly, "Don't you see, before he had a life that suited him, inspecting people in jails. They didn't seem like people *or* jails. It kept him happy, it balanced . . ." Suddenly she gave a great shiver in the heat of the morning and heard Lisbet laugh and say, "Someone's walking on your grave." She went on, "For example, he won't eat."

"Don't you worry about that," cried Tim, understanding something at last. "Meg will see that he eats." Right to the end, everyone was at cross-purposes. "Think of it this way," said Tim. "You had to go home sometime."

"Not till September."

"Well, look on the happy side. Old Roy . . . matrimony. You might not enjoy it, you know, unless you met someone like Meg." He obviously had no idea what he was saying anymore, and so she gave up talking until he set her down at the departures gate. Then he said, "Good luck to you, child," and drove away looking indescribably happy.

S arah kept for a long time the picture of Judas with his guts spilling and with his soul (a shrimp of a man, a lesser Judas) reaching out for the Devil. It should have signified Roy, or even Lisbet, but oddly enough it was she, the victim, who felt guilty and maimed. Still, she was out of the tunnel. Unlike Judas she was alive, and that was something. She was so much younger than all those other people: as Tim had said, she would bury them all. She tacked the Judas card over a map of the world on a wall of her room. Plucked from its origins it began to flower from Sarah's; here was an image that might have followed her from the nursery. It was someone's photo, a family likeness, that could bear no taint of pain or disaster. One day she took the card down, turned it over, and addressed it to a man she was after. He was too poor to invite her anywhere and seemed too shy to make a move. He was also in terrible trouble — back taxes, ex-wife seizing his salary. He had been hounded from California to Canada for his political beliefs. She was in love with his mystery, his hardships, and the death of Trotsky. She wrote, "This person must have eaten my cooking. Others have risked it so please come to dinner on Friday, Sarah." She looked at the words for seconds before hearing another voice. Then she remembered where the card was from, and she understood what the entire message was about. She could have changed it, but it was too late to change anything much. She was more of an *amoreuse* than a psycho-anything, she would never use up her capital, and some summer or other would always be walking on her grave.

THE ICE WAGON GOING
DOWN THE STREET

Now that they are out of world affairs and back where they started, Peter Frazier's wife says, "Everybody else did well in the international thing except us."

"You have to be crooked," he tells her.

"Or smart. Pity we weren't."

It is Sunday morning. They sit in the kitchen, drinking their coffee, slowly, remembering the past. They say the names of people as if they were magic. Peter thinks, *Agnes Brusen*, but there are hundreds of other names. As a private married joke, Peter and Sheilah wear the silk dressing gowns they bought in Hong Kong. Each thinks the other a peacock, rather splendid, but they pretend the dressing gowns are silly and worn in fun.

Peter and Sheilah and their two daughters, Sandra and Jennifer, are visiting Peter's unmarried sister, Lucille. They have been Lucille's guests seventeen weeks, ever since they returned to Toronto from the Far East. Their big old steamer trunk blocks a corner of the kitchen, making a problem of the refrigerator door; but even Lucille says the trunk may as well stay where it is, for the present. The Fraziers' future is so unsettled; everything is still in the air.

Lucille has given her bedroom to her two nieces, and sleeps on a camp cot in the hall. The parents have the living-room divan. They have no privileges here; they sleep after Lucille has seen the last television show that interests her. In the hall closet their clothes are crushed by winter overcoats. They know they are being judged for the first time. Sandra and Jennifer are waiting for Sheilah and Peter to decide. They are waiting to learn where these exotic parents will fly to next. What sort of climate will Sheilah consider? What job will Peter consent to accept? When the parents are ready, the children will make a decision of their own. It is just possible that Sandra and Jennifer will choose to stay with their aunt.

The peacock parents are watched by wrens. Lucille and her nieces are much the same — sandy-colored, proudly plain. Neither of the girls has the father's insouciance or the mother's appearance — her height, her carriage, her thick hair, and sky-blue eyes. The children are more cautious than their parents; more Canadian. When they saw their aunt's apartment they had been away from Canada nine years, ever since they were two and four; and Jennifer, the elder, said, "Well, now we're home." Her voice is nasal and flat. Where did she learn that voice? And why should this be home? Peter's answer to anything about his mystifying children is, "It must be in the blood."

On Sunday morning Lucille takes her nieces to church. It seems to be the only condition she imposes on her relations: the children must be decent. The girls go willingly, with their new hats and purses and gloves and coral bracelets and strings of pearls. The parents, ramshackle, sleepy, dim in the brain because it is Sunday, sit down to their coffee and privacy and talk of the past.

"We weren't crooked," says Peter. "We weren't even smart."

Sheilah's head bobs up; she is no drowner. It is wrong to say they have nothing to show for time. Sheilah has the Balenciaga. It is a black afternoon dress, stiff and boned at the waist; long for the fashions of now, but neither Sheilah nor Peter would change a thread. The Balenciaga is their talisman, their treasure; and after they remember it they touch hands and think that the years are not behind them but hazy and marvellous and still to be lived.

The first place they went to was Paris. In the early fifties the pick of the international jobs was there. Peter had inherited the last scrap of money he knew he was ever likely to see, and it was enough to get them over: Sheilah and Peter and the babies and the steamer trunk. To their joy and astonishment they had money in the bank. They said to each other, "It should last a year." Peter was fastidious about the new job; he hadn't come all this distance to accept just anything. In Paris he met Hugh Taylor, who was earning enough smuggling gasoline to keep his wife in Paris and a girl in Rome. That impressed Peter, because he remembered Taylor as a sour scholarship student without the slightest talent for life. Taylor had a job, of course. He hadn't said to himself, I'll go over to Europe and smuggle gasoline. It gave Peter an idea; he saw the shape of things. First you catch your fish. Later, at an international party, he met Johnny Hertzberg, who told him Germany was the place. Hertzberg said that anyone who came out of Germany broke now was too stupid to be here, and deserved to be back home at a desk. Peter nodded, as if he had already thought of that. He began to think about Germany. Paris was fine for a holiday, but it had been picked clean. Yes, Germany. His money was running low. He thought about Germany quite a lot.

That winter was moist and delicate; so fragile that they daren't speak of it now. There seemed to be plenty of everything and plenty of time. They were living the dream of a marriage, the fabric uncut, nothing slashed or spoiled. All winter they spend their money, and went to parties, and talked about Peter's future job. It lasted four months. They spent their money, lived in the future, and were never as happy again.

After four months they were suddenly moved away from

Paris, but not to Germany — to Geneva. Peter thinks it was because of the incident at the Trudeau wedding at the Ritz. Paul Trudeau was a French Canadian Peter had known at school and in the Navy. Trudeau had turned into a snob, proud of his career and his Paris connections. He tried to make the difference felt, but Peter thought the difference was only for strangers. At the wedding reception Peter lay down on the floor and said he was dead. He held a white azalea in a brass pot on his chest, and sang, "Oh, hear us when we cry to Thee for those in peril on the sea." Sheilah bent over him and said, "Pete, darling, get up. Pete, listen, every single person who can do something for you is in this room. If you love me, you'll get up."

"I do love you," he said, ready to engage in a serious conversation. "She's so beautiful," he told a second face. "She's nearly as tall as I am. She was a model in London. I met her over in London in the war. I met her there in the war." He lay on his back with the azalea on his chest, explaining their history. A waiter took the brass pot away, and after Peter had been hauled to his feet he knocked the waiter down. Trudeau's bride, who was freshly out of an Ursuline convent, became hysterical; and even though Paul Trudeau and Peter were old acquaintances, Trudeau never spoke to him again. Peter says now that French Canadians always have that bit of spite. He says Trudeau asked the Embassy to interfere. Luckily, back home there were still a few people to whom the name "Frazier" meant something, and it was to these people that Peter appealed. He wrote letters saying that a French-Canadian combine was preventing his getting a decent job, and could anything be done? No one answered directly, but it was clear that what they settled for was exile to Geneva: a season of meditation and remorse, as he explained to Sheilah, and it was managed tactfully, through Lucille. Lucille wrote that a friend of hers, May Fergus, now a secretary in Geneva, had heard about a job. The job was filing pictures in the information service of an international agency in the Palais des

Nations. The pay was so-so, but Lucille thought Peter must be getting fed up doing nothing.

Peter often asks his sister now who put her up to it — what important person told her to write that letter suggesting Peter go to Geneva?

"Nobody," says Lucille. "I mean, nobody in the way *you* mean. I really did have this girl friend working there, and I knew you must be running through your money pretty fast in Paris."

"It must have been somebody pretty high up," Peter says. He looks at his sister admiringly, as he has often looked at his wife.

Peter's wife had loved him in Paris. Whatever she wanted in marriage she found that winter, there. In Geneva, where Peter was a file clerk and they lived in a furnished flat, she pretended they were in Paris and life was still the same. Often, when the children were at supper, she changed as though she and Peter were dining out. She wore the Balenciaga, and put candles on the card table where she and Peter ate their meal. The neckline of the dress was soiled with make-up. Peter remembers her dabbing on the make-up with a wet sponge. He remembers her in the kitchen, in the soiled Balenciaga, putting on the make-up with a filthy sponge. Behind her, at the kitchen table, Sandra and Jennifer, in buttonless pajamas and bunny slippers, ate their supper of marmalade sandwiches and milk. When the children were asleep, the parents dined solemnly, ritually, Sheilah sitting straight as a queen.

It was a mysterious period of exile, and he had to wait for signs, or signals, to know when he was free to leave. He never saw the job any other way. He forgot he had applied for it. He thought he had been sent to Geneva because of a misdemeanor and had to wait to be released. Nobody pressed him at work. His immediate boss had resigned, and he was alone for months in a room with two desks. He read the *Herald-Tribune*, and tried to discover how things were here — how the others ran their lives on the pay they were officially getting. But it was a closed conspiracy. He was not dealing with adventurers now but civil servants waiting for pension day. No one ever answered his questions. They pretended to think his questions were a form of wit. His only solace in exile was the few happy weekends he had in the late spring and early summer. He had met another old acquaintance, Mike Burleigh. Mike was a serious liberal who had married a serious heiress. The Burleighs had two guest lists. The first was composed of stuffy people they felt obliged to entertain, while the second was made up of their real friends, the friends they wanted. The real friends strove hard to become stuffy and dull and thus achieve the first guest list, but few succeeded. Peter went on the first list straight away. Possibly Mike didn't understand, at the beginning, why Peter was pretending to be a file clerk. Peter had such an air — he might have been sent by a universal inspector to see how things in Geneva were being run.

Every Friday in May and June and part of July, the Fraziers rented a sky-blue Fiat and drove forty miles east of Geneva to the Burleighs' summer house. They brought the children, a suitcase, the children's tattered picture books, and a token bottle of gin. This, in memory, is a period of water and water birds, swans, roses, and singing birds. The children were small and still belonged to them. If they remember too much, their mouths water, their stomachs hurt. Peter says, "It was fine while it lasted." Enough. While it lasted Sheilah and Madge Burleigh were close. They abandoned their husbands and spent long summer afternoons comparing their mothers and praising each other's skin and hair. To Madge, and not to Peter, Sheilah opened her Liverpool childhood with the words "rat poor." Peter heard about it later, from Mike. The women's friendship seemed to Peter a bad beginning. He trusted women but not with each other. It lasted ten weeks. One Sunday, Madge said she needed the two bedrooms the Fraziers usually occupied for a party of sociologists from Pakistan, and that was the end. In November, the Fraziers heard that the summer house had been closed, and that the

Burleighs were in Geneva, in their winter flat; they gave no sign. There was no help for it, and no appeal.

Now Peter began firing letters to anyone who had ever known his late father. He was living in a mild yellow autumn. Why does he remember the streets of the city dark, and the windows everywhere black with rain? He remembers being with Sheilah and the children as if they clung together while just outside their small shelter it rained and rained. The children slept in the bedroom of the flat because the window gave on the street and they could breathe air. Peter and Sheilah had the living-room couch. Their window was not a real window but a square on a well of cement. The flat seemed damp as a cave. Peter remembers steam in the kitchen, pools under the sink, sweat on the pipes. Water streamed on him from the children's clothes, washed and dripping overhead. The trunk, upended in the children's room, was not quite unpacked. Sheilah had not signed her name to this life; she had not given in. Once Peter heard her drop her aitches. "You kids are lucky," she said to the girls. "I never 'ad so much as a sit-down meal. I ate chips out of a paper or I 'ad a butty out on the stairs." He never asked her what a butty was. He thinks it means bread and cheese.

The day he heard "You kids are lucky" he understood they were becoming in fact something they had only *appeared* to be until now — the shabby civil servant and his brood. If he had been European he would have ridden to work on a bicycle, in the uniform of his class and condition. He would have worn a tight coat, a turned collar, and a dirty tie. He wondered then if coming here had been a mistake, and if he should not, after all, still be in a place where his name meant something. Surely Peter Frazier should live where "Frazier" counts? In Ontario even now when he says "Frazier" an absent look comes over his hearer's face, as if its owner were consulting an interior guide. What is Frazier? What does it mean? Oil? Power? Politics? Wheat? Real estate? The creditors had the house sealed when Peter's father died. His aunt collapsed with a heart attack in somebody's bachelor apartment, leaving three sons and a widower to surmise they had never known her. Her will was a disappointment. None of that generation left enough. One made it: the granite Presbyterian immigrants from Scotland. Their children, a generation of daunted women and maiden men, held still. Peter's father's crowd spent: they were not afraid of their fathers, and their grandfathers were old. Peter and his sister and his cousins lived on the remains. They were left the rinds of income, of notions, and the memories of ideas rather than ideas intact. If Peter can choose his reincarnation, let him be the oppressed son of a Scottish parson. Let Peter grow up on cuffs and iron principles. Let him make the fortune! Let him flee the manse! When he was small his patrimony was squandered under his nose. He remembers people dancing at his father's house. He remembers seeing and nearly understanding adultery in a guest room, among a pile of wraps. He thought he had seen a murder; he never told. He remembers licking glasses wherever he found them — on window sills, on stairs, in the pantry. In his room he listened while Lucille read Beatrix Potter. The bad rabbit stole the carrot from the good rabbit without saying please, and downstairs was the noise of the party — the roar of the crouched lion. When his father died he saw the chairs upside down and the bailiff's chalk marks. Then the doors were sealed.

He has often tried to tell Sheilah why he cannot be defeated. He remembers his father saying, "Nothing can touch us," and Peter believed it and still does. It has prevented his taking his troubles too seriously. "Nothing can be as bad as this," he will tell himself. "It is happening to me." Even in Geneva, where his status was file clerk, where he sank and stopped on the level of the men who never emigrated, the men on the bicycles — even there he had a manner of strolling to work as if his office were a pastime, and his real life a secret so splendid he could share it with no one except himself.

In Geneva Peter worked for a woman — a girl. She was a
Norwegian from a small town in Saskatchewan. He supposed they had been put together because they were Canadians; but they were as strange to each other as if "Canadian"
meant any number of things, or had no real meaning. Soon
after Agnes Brusen came to the office she hung her framed
university degree on the wall. It was one of the gritty, prideful
gestures that stand for push, toil, and family sacrifice. He
thought, then, that she must be one of a family of immigrants
for whom education is everything. Hugh Taylor had told him
that in some families the older children never marry until the
youngest have finished school. Sometimes every second child
is sacrificed and made to work for the education of the next
born. Those who finish college spend years paying back. They
are white-hot Protestants, and they live with a load of work and
debt and obligation. Peter placed his new colleague on scraps
of information. He had never been in the West.

She came to the office on a Monday morning in October.
The office was overheated and painted cream. It contained
two desks, the filing cabinets, a map of the world as it had been
in 1945, and the Charter of the United Nations left behind by
Agnes Brusen's predecessor. (She took down the Charter
without asking Peter if he minded, with the impudence of
gesture you find in women who wouldn't say boo to a goose;
and then she hung her college degree on the nail where the
Charter had been.) Three people brought her in — a whole
committee. One of them said, "Agnes, this Pete Frazier. Pete,
Agnes Brusen. Pete's Canadian, too, Agnes. He knows all
about the office, so ask him anything."

Of course he knew all about the office: he knew the exact
spot where the cord of the venetian blind was frayed, obliging
one to give an extra tug to the right.

The girl might have been twenty-three: no more. She wore
a brown tweed suit with bone buttons, and a new silk scarf and

new shoes. She clutched an unscratched brown purse. She seemed dressed in going-away presents. She said, "Oh, I never smoke," with a convulsive movement of her hand, when Peter offered his case. He was courteous, hiding his disappointment. The people he worked with had told him a Scandinavian girl was arriving, and he had expected a stunner. Agnes was a mole: she was small and brown, and round-shouldered as if she had always carried parcels or younger children in her arms. A mole's profile was turned when she said goodbye to her committee. If she had been foreign, ill-favored though she was, he might have flirted a little, just to show that he was friendly; but their being Canadian, and suddenly left together, was a sexual damper. He sat down and lit his own cigarette. She smiled at him, questioningly, he thought and sat as if she had never seen a chair before. He wondered if his smoking was annoying her. He wondered if she was fidgety about drafts, or allergic to anything, and whether she would want the blind up or down. His social compass was out of order because the others couldn't tell Peter and Agnes apart. There was a world of difference between them, yet it was she who had been brought in to sit at the larger of the two desks.

While he was thinking this she got up and walked around the office, almost on tiptoe, opening the doors of closets and pulling out the filing trays. She looked inside everything except the drawers of Peter's desk. (In any case, Peter's desk was locked. His desk is locked wherever he works. In Geneva he went into Personnel one morning, early, and pinched his application form. He had stated on the form that he had seven years' experience in public relations and could speak French, German, Spanish, and Italian. He has always collected anything important about himself — anything useful. But he can never get on with the final act, which is getting rid of the information. He has kept papers about for years, a constant source of worry.)

"I know this looks funny, Mr. Ferris," said the girl. "I'm not really snooping or anything. I just can't feel easy in a new place unless I know where everything is. In a new place everything seems so hidden."

If she had called him "Ferris" and pretended not to know he was Frazier, it could only be because they had sent her here to spy on him and see if he had repented and was fit for a better place in life. "You'll be all right here," he said. "Nothing's hidden. Most of us haven't got brains enough to have secrets. This is Rainbow Valley." Depressed by the thought that they were having him watched now, he passed his hand over his hair and looked outside to the lawn and the parking lot and the peacocks someone gave the Palais des Nations years ago. The peacocks love no one. They wander about the parked cars looking elderly, bad-tempered, mournful, and lost.

Agnes had settled down again. She folded her silk scarf and placed it just so, with her gloves beside it. She opened her new purse and took out a notebook and a shiny gold pencil. She may have written

Duster for desk

Kleenex

Glass jar for flowers

Air-Wick because he smokes

Paper for lining drawers

because the next day she brought each of these articles to work. She also brought a large black Bible, which she unwrapped lovingly and placed on the left-hand corner of her desk. The flower vase — empty — stood in the middle, and the Kleenex made a counterpoise for the Bible on the right.

When he saw the Bible he knew she had not been sent to spy on his work. The conspiracy was deeper. She might have been dispatched by ghosts. He knew everything about her, all in a moment: he saw the ambition, the terror, the dry pride. She was the true heir of the men from Scotland; she was at the start. She had been sent to tell him, "You can begin, but not begin again." She never opened the Bible, but she dusted it as she dusted her desk, her chair, and any surface the cleaning staff had overlooked. And Peter, the first days, watching her timid movements, her insignificant little face, felt, as you feel the approach of a storm, the charge of moral certainty round her, the belief in work, the faith in undertakings, the bread of the Black Sunday. He recognized and tasted all of it: ashes in the mouth.

After five days their working relations were settled. Of course, there was the Bible and all that went with it, but his tongue had never held the taste of ashes long. She was an inferior girl of poor quality. She had nothing in her favor except the degree on the wall. In the real world, he would not have invited her to his house except to mind the children. That was what he said to Sheilah. He said that Agnes was a mole, and a virgin, and that her tics and mannerisms were sending him round the bend. She had an infuriating habit of covering her mouth when she talked. Even at the telephone she put up her hand as if afraid of losing anything, even a word. Her voice was nasal and flat. She had two working costumes, both dull as the wall. One was the brown suit, the other a navy-blue dress with changeable collars. She dressed for no one; she dressed for her desk, her jar of flowers, her Bible, and her box of Kleenex. One day she crossed the space between the two desks and stood over Peter, who was reading a newspaper. She could have spoken to him from her desk, but she may have felt that being on her feet gave her authority. She had plenty of courage, but authority was something else.

"I thought — I mean, they told me you were the person . . ." She got on with it bravely: "If you don't want to do the filing or any work, all right, Mr. Frazier. I'm not saying anything about that. You might have poor health or your personal reasons. But it's got to be done, so if you'll kindly show me about the filing I'll do it. I've worked in Information before, but it was a different office, and every office is different."

"My dear girl," said Peter. He pushed back his chair and looked at her, astonished. "You've been sitting there fretting, worrying. How insensitive of me. How trying for you. Usually I file on the last Wednesday of the month, so you see, you just haven't been around long enough to see a last Wednesday. Not another word, please. And let us not waste another minute." He emptied the heaped baskets of photographs so swiftly, pushing "Iran — Smallpox Control" into "Irish Red Cross" (close enough), that the girl looked frightened, as if she had raised a whirlwind. She said slowly, "If you'll only show me, Mr. Frazier, instead of doing it so fast, I'll gladly look after it, because you might want to be doing other things, and I feel the filing should be done every day." But Peter was too busy to answer, and so she sat down, holding the edge of her desk.

"There," he said, beaming. "All done." His smile, his sunburst, was wasted, for the girl was staring round the room as if she feared she had not inspected everything the first day after all; some drawer, some cupboard, hid a monster. That evening Peter unlocked one of the drawers of his desk and took away the application form he had stolen from Personnel. The girl had not finished her search.

"How could you *not* know?" wailed Sheilah. "You sit looking at her every day. You must talk about *something*. She must have told you."

"She did tell me," said Peter, "and I've just told you."

It was this: Agnes Brusen was on the Burleighs' guest list. How had the Burleighs met her? What did they see in her? Peter could not reply. He knew that Agnes lived in a bed-sitting room with a Swiss family and had her meals with them. She had been in Geneva three months, but no one had ever seen her outside the office. "You *should* know," said Sheilah. "She must have something, more than you can see. Is she pretty? Is she brilliant? What is it?"

"We don't really talk," Peter said. They talked in a way: Peter teased her and she took no notice. Agnes was not a sulker. She had taken her defeat like a sport. She did her work and a good deal of his. She sat behind her Bible, her flowers, and her Kleenex, and answered when Peter spoke. That was how he learned about the Burleighs — just by teasing and being bored. It was a January afternoon. He said, "Miss Brusen. Talk to me. Tell me everything. Pretend we have perfect rapport. Do you like Geneva?"

"It's a nice clean town," she said. He can see to this day the red and blue anemones in the glass jar, and her bent head, and her small untended hands.

"Are you learning beautiful French with your Swiss family?"

"They speak English."

"Why don't you take an apartment of your own?" he said. Peter was not usually impertinent. He was bored. "You'd be independent then."

"I am independent," she said. "I earn my living. I don't think it proves anything if you live by yourself. Mrs. Burleigh wants me to live alone, too. She's looking for something for me. It mustn't be dear. I send money home."

Here was the extraordinary thing about Agnes Brusen: she refused the use of Christian names and never spoke to Peter unless he spoke first, but she would tell anything, as if to say, "Don't waste time fishing. Here it is."

He learned all in one minute that she sent her salary home, and that she was a friend of the Burleighs. The first he had expected; the second knocked him flat.

"She's got to come to dinner," Sheilah said. "We should have had her right from the beginning. If only I'd known! But *you* were the one. You said she looked like — oh, I don't even remember. A Norwegian mole."

She came to dinner one Saturday night in January, in her navy-blue dress, to which she had pinned an organdy gardenia. She sat upright on the edge of the sofa. Sheilah had ordered the meal from a restaurant. There was lobster, good wine, and a *pièce-montée* full of kirsch and cream. Agnes refused the lobster; she had never eaten anything from the sea unless it had been sterilized and tinned, and said so. She was afraid of skin poisoning. Someone in her family had skin poisoning after having eaten oysters. She touched her cheeks and neck to show where the poisoning had erupted. She sniffed her wine and put the glass down without tasting it. She could not eat the cake because of the alcohol it contained. She ate an egg, bread and butter, a sliced tomato, and drank a glass of ginger ale. She seemed unaware she was creating disaster and pain. She did not help clear away the dinner plates. She sat, adequately nourished, decently dressed, and waited to learn why she had been invited here — that was the feeling Peter had. He folded the card table on which they had dined, and opened the window to air the room.

"It's not the same cold as Canada, but you feel it more," he said, for something to say.

"Your blood has gotten thin," said Agnes.

Sheilah returned from the kitchen and let herself fall into an armchair. With her eyes closed she held out her hand for a cigarette. She was performing the haughty-lady act that was a family joke. She flung her head back and looked at Agnes through half-closed lids; then she suddenly brought her head forward, widening her eyes.

"Are you skiing madly?" she said.

"Well, in the first place there hasn't been any snow," said Agnes. "So nobody's doing any skiing so far as I know. All I hear is people complaining because there's no snow. Personally, I don't ski. There isn't much skiing in the part of Canada I come from. Besides, my family never had that kind of leisure."

"Heavens," said Sheilah, as if her family had every kind.

I'll bet they had, thought Peter. On the dole.

Sheilah was wasting her act. He had a suspicion that Agnes knew it was an act but did not know it was also a joke. If so, it made Sheilah seem a fool, and he loved Sheilah too much to enjoy it.

"The Burleighs have been wonderful to me," said Agnes.

She seemed to have divined why she was here, and decided to give them all the information they wanted, so that she could put on her coat and go home to bed. "They had me out to their place on the lake every weekend until the weather got cold and they moved back to town. They've rented a chalet for the winter, and they want me to come there, too. But I don't know if I will or not. I don't ski, and, oh, I don't know — I don't drink, either, and I don't always see the point. Their friends are too rich and I'm too Canadian."

She had delivered everything Sheilah wanted and more: Agnes was on the first guest list and didn't care. No, Peter corrected; doesn't know. Doesn't care and doesn't know.

"I thought with you Norwegians it was in the blood, skiing. And drinking," Sheilah murmured.

"Drinking, maybe," said Agnes. She covered her mouth and said behind her spread fingers, "In our family we were religious. We didn't drink or smoke. My brother was in Normandy in the war. He saw some cousins. Oh," she said, unexpectedly loud, "Harry said it was just terrible. They were so poor. They had flies in their kitchen. They gave him something to eat a fly had been on. They didn't have a real toilet, and they'd been in the same house for two hundred years. We've only recently built our own home, and we have a bathroom and two toilets. I'm from Saskatchewan," she said. "I'm not from any other place."

Surely one winter here had been punishment enough? In the spring they would remember him and free him. He wrote Lucille, who said he was lucky to have a job at all. The Burleighs had sent the Fraziers a second-guest-list Christmas card. It showed a Moslem refugee child weeping outside a tent. They treasured the card and left it standing long after the others had been given the children to cut up. Peter had discovered by now what had gone wrong in the friendship — Sheilah had charged a skirt at a dressmaker to Madge's account. Madge had told her she might, and then changed her mind. Poor Sheilah! She was new to this part of it — to the changing humors of independent friends. Paris was already a year in the past. At Mardi Gras, the Burleighs gave their annual party. They invited everyone, the damned and the dropped, with the prodigality of a child at prayers. The invitation said "in costume," but the Fraziers were too happy to wear a disguise. They might not be recognized. Like many of the guests they expected to meet at the party, they had been disgraced, forgotten, and rehabilitated. They would be anxious to see one another as they were.

On the night of the party, the Fraziers rented a car they had never seen before and drove through the first snowstorm of the year. Peter had not driven since last summer's blissful trips in the Fiat. He could not find the switch for the windshield wiper in this car. He leaned over the wheel. "Can you see on your side?" he asked. "Can I make a left turn here? Does it look like a one-way?"

"I can't imagine why you took a car with a right-hand drive," said Sheilah.

He had trouble finding a place to park; they crawled up and down unknown streets whose curbs were packed with snow-covered cars. When they stood at last on the pavement, safe and sound, Peter said, "This is the first snow."

"I can see that," said Sheilah. "Hurry, darling. My hair."

"It's the first snow."

"You're repeating yourself," she said. "Please hurry, dar-ling. Think of my poor shoes. My *hair*."

She was born in an ugly city, and so was Peter, but they have this difference: she does not know the importance of the first snow — the first clean thing in a dirty year. He would have told her then that this storm, which was wetting her feet and destroying her hair, was like the first day of the English spring, but she made a frightened gesture, trying to shield her head. The gesture told him he did not understand her beauty.

"Let me," she said. He was fumbling with the key, trying to

lock the car. She took the key without impatience and locked the door on the driver's side; and then, to show Peter she treasured him and was not afraid of wasting her life or her beauty, she took his arm and they walked in the snow down a street and around a corner to the apartment house where the Burleighs lived. They were, and are, a united couple. They were afraid of the party, and each of them knew it. When they walk together, holding arms, they give each other whatever each can spare.

Only six people had arrived in costume. Madge Burleigh was disguised as Manet's "Lola de Valence," which everyone mistook for Carmen. Mike was an Impressionist painter, with a straw hat and a glued-on beard. "I am all of them," he said. He would rather have dressed as a dentist, he said, welcoming the Fraziers as if he had parted from them the day before, but Madge wanted him to look as if he had created her. "You know?" he said.

"Perfectly," said Sheilah. Her shoes were stained and the snow had softened her lacquered hair. She was not wasted; she was the most beautiful woman here.

About an hour after their arrival, Peter found himself with no one to talk to. He had told about the Trudeau wedding in Paris and the pot of azaleas, and after he mislaid his audience he began to look round for Sheilah. She was on a window seat, partly concealed by a green velvet curtain. Facing her, so that their profiles were neat and perfect against the night, was a man. Their conversation was private and enclosed, as if they had in minutes covered leagues of time and arrived at the place where everything was implied, understood. Peter began working his way across the room, toward his wife, when he saw Agnes. He was granted the sight of her drowning face. She had dressed with comic intention, obviously with care, and now she was a ragged hobo, half tramp, half clown. Her hair was tucked up under a bowler hat. The six costumed guests who had made the same mistake — the ghost, the gypsy, the Athenian maiden, the geisha, the Martian, and the apache — were delighted to find a seventh; but Agnes was not amused; she was gasping for life. When a waiter passed with a crowded tray, she took a glass without seeing it; then a wave of the party took her away.

Sheilah's new friend was named Simpson. After Simpson said he thought perhaps he'd better circulate, Peter sat down where he had been. "Now look, Sheilah," he began. Their most intimate conversations have taken place at parties. Once at a party she told him she was leaving him; she didn't, of course. Smiling, blue-eyed, she gazed lovingly at Peter and said rapidly, "Pete, shut up and listen. That man. The man you scared away. He's a big wheel in a company out in India or someplace like that. It's gorgeous out there. Pete, the *servants*. And it's warm. It never never snows. He says there's heaps of jobs. You pick them off the trees like . . . orchids. He says it's even easier now than when we owned all those places, because now the poor pets can't run anything and they'll pay *fortunes*. Pete, he says it's warm, it's heaven, and Pete, they pay."

A few minutes later, Peter was alone again and Sheilah part of a closed, laughing group. Holding her elbow was the man from the place where jobs grew like orchids. Peter edged into the group and laughed at a story he hadn't heard. He heard only the last line, which was, "Here comes another tunnel." Looking out from the tight laughing ring, he saw Agnes again, and he thought, I'd be like Agnes if I didn't have Sheilah. Agnes put her glass down on a table and lurched toward the doorway, head forward. Madge Burleigh, who never stopped moving around the room and smiling, was still smiling when she paused and said in Peter's ear, "Go with Agnes, Pete. See that she gets home. People will notice if Mike leaves."

"She probably just wants to walk around the block," said Peter. "She'll be back."

"Oh, stop thinking about yourself, for once, and see that

that poor girl gets home," said Madge. "You've still got your Fiat, haven't you?"

He turned away as if he had been pushed. Any command is a release, in a way. He may not want to go in that particular direction, but at least he is going somewhere. And now Sheilah, who had moved inches nearer to hear what Madge and Peter were murmuring, said, "Yes, go, darling," as if he were leaving the gates of Troy.

Peter was to find Agnes and see that she reached home: this he repeated to himself as he stood on the landing, outside the Burleighs' flat, ringing for the elevator. Bored with waiting for it, he ran down the stairs, four flights, and saw that Agnes had stalled the lift by leaving the door open. She was crouched on the floor, propped on her fingertips. Her eyes were closed.

"Agnes," said Peter. "*Miss* Brusen, I mean. That's no way to leave a party. Don't you know you're supposed to curtsey and say thanks? My God, Agnes, anybody going by here just now might have seen you! Come on, be a good girl. Time to go home."

She got up without his help and, moving between invisible crevasses, shut the elevator door. Then she left the building and Peter followed, remembering he was to see that she got home. They walked along the snowy pavement, Peter a few steps behind her. When she turned right for no reason, he turned, too. He had no clear idea where they were going. Perhaps she lived close by. He had forgotten where the hired car was parked, or what it looked like; he could not remember its make or its color. In any case, Sheilah had the key. Agnes walked on steadily, as if she knew their destination, and he thought, Agnes Brusen is drunk in the street in Geneva and dressed like a tramp. He wanted to say, "This is the best thing that ever happened to you, Agnes; it will help you understand how things are for some of the rest of us." But she stopped and turned, and, leaning over a low hedge, retched on a frozen lawn. He held her clammy forehead and rested his hand on her arched back, on muscles as tight as a fist. She straightened up and drew a breath but the cold air made her cough. "Don't breathe too deeply," he said. "It's the worst thing you can do. Have you got a handkerchief?" He passed his own handkerchief over her wet weeping face, upturned like the face of one of his little girls. "I'm out without a coat," he said, noticing it. "We're a pair."

"I never drink," said Agnes. "I'm just not used to it." Her voice was sweet and quiet. He had never seen her so peaceful, so composed. He thought she must surely be all right, now, and perhaps he might leave her here. The trust in her tilted face had perplexed him. He wanted to get back to Sheilah and have her explain something. He had forgotten what it was, but Sheilah would know. "Do you live around here?" he said. As he spoke, she let herself fall. He had wiped her face and now she trusted him to pick her up, set her on her feet, take her wherever she ought to be. He pulled her up and she stood, wordless, humble, as he brushed the snow from her tramp's clothes. Snow horizontally crossed the lamplight. The street was silent. Agnes had lost her hat. Snow, which he tasted, melted on her hands. His gesture of licking snow from her hands was formal as a handshake. He tasted snow on her hands and then they walked on.

"I never drink," she said. They stood on the edge of a broad avenue. The wrong turning now could lead them anywhere; it was the changeable avenue at the edge of towns that loses its houses and becomes a highway. She held his arm and spoke in a gentle voice. She said, "In our house we didn't smoke or drink. My mother was ambitious for me, more than for Harry and the others." She said, "I've never been alone before. When I was a kid I would get up in the summer before the others, and I'd see the ice wagon going down the street. I'm alone now. Mrs. Burleigh's found me an apartment. It's only one room. She likes it because it's in the old part of town. I don't like old houses. Old houses are dirty. You don't know who was there before."

"I should have a car somewhere," Peter said. "I'm not sure where we are."

He remembers that on this avenue they climbed into a taxi, but nothing about the drive. Perhaps he fell asleep. He does remember that when he paid the driver Agnes clutched his arm, trying to stop him. She pressed extra coins into the driver's palm. The driver was paid twice.

"I'll tell you one thing about us," said Peter. "We pay everything twice." This was part of a much longer theory concerning North American behavior, and it was not Peter's own. Mike Burleigh had held forth about it on summer afternoons.

Agnes pushed open a door between a stationer's shop and a grocery, and led the way up a narrow inside stair. They climbed one flight, frightening beetles. She had to search every pocket for the latchkey. She was shaking with cold. Her apartment seemed little warmer than the street. Without speaking to Peter she turned on all the lights. She looked inside the kitchen and the bathroom and then got down on her hands and knees and looked under the sofa. The room was neat and belonged to no one. She left him standing in this unclaimed room — she had forgotten him — and closed a door behind her. He looked for something to do — some useful action he could repeat to Madge. He turned on the electric radiator in the fireplace. Perhaps Agnes wouldn't thank him for it; perhaps she would rather undress in the cold. "I'll be on my way," he called to the bathroom door.

She had taken off the tramp's clothes and put on a dressing gown of orphanage wool. She came out of the bathroom and straight toward him. She pressed her face and rubbed her cheek on his shoulder as hoping the contact would leave a scar. He saw her back and her profile and his own face in the mirror over the fireplace. He thought, this is how disasters happen. He saw floods of sea water moving with perfect punitive justice over reclaimed land; he saw lava covering vineyards and overtaking dogs and stragglers. A bridge over an abyss snapped in two and the long express train, suddenly V-shaped, floated like snow. He thought amiably of every kind of disaster and thought, This is how they occur.

Her eyes were closed. She said, "I shouldn't be over here. In my family we didn't drink or smoke. My mother wanted a lot from me, more than from Harry and the others." But he knew all that; he had known from the day of the Bible, and because once, at the beginning, she had made him afraid. He was not afraid of her now.

She said, "It's no use staying here, is it?"

"If you mean what I think, no."

"It wouldn't be better anywhere."

She let him see full on her blotched face. He was not expected to do anything. He was not required to pick her up when she fell or wipe her tears. She was poor quality, really — he remembered having thought that once. She left him and went quietly into the bathroom and locked the door. He heard taps running and supposed it was a hot bath. He was pretty certain there would be no more tears. He looked at his watch: Sheilah must be home, now, wondering what had become of him. He descended the beetles' staircase and for forty minutes crossed the city under a windless fall of snow.

The neighbor's child who had stayed with Peter's children was asleep on the living-room sofa. Peter woke her and sent her, sleepwalking, to her own door. He sat down, wet to the bone, thinking, I'll call the Burleighs. In half an hour I'll call the police. He heard a car stop and the engine running and a confusion of two voices laughing and calling goodnight. Presently Sheilah let herself in, rosy-faced, smiling. She carried his trenchcoat over her arm. She said. "How's Agnes?"

"Where were you?" he said. "Whose car was that?"

Sheilah had gone into the children's room. He heard her shutting their window. She returned, undoing her dress, and said, "Was Agnes all right?"

"Agnes is all right. Sheilah, this is about the worst . . ."

She stepped out of the Balenciaga and threw it over a chair. She stopped and looked at him and said, "Poor old Pete, are you in love with Agnes?" And then, as if the answer were of so little importance she hadn't time for it, she locked her arms around him and said, "My love, we're going to Ceylon."

Two days later, when Peter strolled into his office, Agnes was at her desk. She wore the blue dress, with a spotless collar. White and yellow freesias were symmetrically arranged in the glass jar. The room was hot, and the spring snow, glued for a second when it touched the window, blurred the view of parked cars.

"Quite a party," Peter said.

She did not look up. He sighed, sat down, and thought if the snow held he would be skiing at the Burleighs' very soon. Impressed by his kindness to Agnes, Madge had invited the family for the first possible weekend.

Presently Agnes said, "I'll never drink again or go to a house where people are drinking. And I'll never bother anyone the way I bothered you."

"You didn't bother me," he said. "I took you home. You were alone and it was late. It's normal."

"Normal for you, maybe, but I'm used to getting home by myself. Please never tell what happened."

He stared at her. He can still remember the freesias and the Bible and the heat in the room. She looked as if the elements had no power. She felt neither heat nor cold. "Nothing happened," he said.

"I behaved in a silly way. I had no right to. I led you to think I might do something wrong."

"I might have tried something," he said gallantly. "But that would be my fault and not yours."

She put her knuckle to her mouth and he could scarcely hear. "It was because of you. I was afraid you might be blamed, or else you'd blame yourself."

"There's no question of any blame," he said. "Nothing happened. We'd both had a lot to drink. Forget about it. Nothing *happened*. You'd remember if it had."

She put down her hand. There was an expression on her face. Now she sees me, he thought. She had never looked at him after the first day. (He has since tried to put a name to the look on her face; but how can he, now, after so many voyages, after Ceylon, and Hong Kong, and Sheilah's nearly leaving him, and all their difficulties — the money owed, the rows with hotel managers, the lost and found steamer trunk, the children throwing up the foreign food?) She sees me now, he thought. What does she see?

She said, "I'm from a big family. I'm not used to being alone. I'm not a suicidal person, but I could have done something after that party, just not to see any more, or think or listen or expect anything. What can I think when I see these people? All my life I heard, educated people don't do this, educated people don't do that. And now I'm here, and you're all educated people, and you're nothing but pigs. You're educated and you drink and do everything wrong and you know what you're doing, and that makes you worse than pigs. My family worked to make me an educated person, but they didn't know you. But what if I didn't see and hear and expect anything any more? It wouldn't change anything. You'd all be still the same. Only *you* might have thought it was your fault. You might have thought you were to blame. It could worry you all your life. It would have been wrong for me to worry you."

He remembered that the rented car was still along a snowy curb somewhere in Geneva. He wondered if Sheilah had the key in her purse and if she remembered where they'd parked.

"I told you about the ice wagon," Agnes said. "I don't remember everything, so you're wrong about remembering. But I remember telling you that. That was the best. It's the best you can hope to have. In a big family, if you want to be alone, you have to get up before the rest of them. You get up early in the morning in the summer and it's you, you, once in your life alone in the universe. You think you know every-thing that can happen . . . Nothing is ever like that again."

He looked at the smeared window and wondered if this day could end without disaster. In his mind he saw her falling in the snow wearing a tramp's costume, and he saw her coming to him in the orphanage dressing gown. He saw her drowning face at the party. He was afraid for himself. The story was still unfinished. It had to come to a climax, something threatening to him. But there was no climax. They talked that day, and afterward nothing else was said. They went on in the same office for a short time, until Peter left for Ceylon; until somebody read the right letter, passed it on for the right initials, and the Fraziers began the Oriental tour that should have made their fortune. Agnes and Peter were too tired to speak after that morning. They were like a married couple in danger, taking care.

But what were they talking about that day, so quietly, such old friends? They talked about dying, about being ambitious, about being religious, about different kinds of love. What did she see when she looked at him — taking her knuckle slowly away from her mouth, bringing her hand down to the desk, letting it rest there? They were both Canadians, so they had this much together — the knowledge of the little you dare admit. Death, near-death, the best thing, the wrong thing — God knows what they were telling each other. Anyway, nothing happened.

When, on Sunday mornings, Sheilah and Peter talk about those times, they take on the glamor of something still to come. It is then he remembers Agnes Brusen. He never says her name. Sheilah wouldn't remember Agnes. Agnes is the only secret Peter has from his wife, the only puzzle he pieces together without her help. He thinks about families in the West as they were fifteen, twenty years ago — the iron-cold ambition, and every member pushing the next one on. He thinks of his father's parties. When he thinks of his father he imagines him with Sheilah, in a crowd. Actually, Sheilah and

Peter's father never met, but they might have liked each other. His father admired good-looking women. Peter wonders what they were doing over there in Geneva — not Sheilah and Peter, *Agnes* and Peter. It is almost as if they had once run away together, silly as children, irresponsible as lovers. Peter and Sheilah are back where they started. While they were out in world affairs picking up microbes and debts, always on the fringe of disaster, the fringe of a fortune, Agnes went on and did — what? They lost each other. He thinks of the ice wagon doing down the street. He sees something he has never seen in his life — a Western town that belongs to Agnes. Here is Agnes — small, mole-faced, round-shouldered because she has always carried a younger child. She watches the ice wagon and the trail of ice water in a morning invented for her: hers. He sees the weak prairie trees and the shadows on the sidewalk. Nothing moves except the shadows and the ice wagon and the changing amber of the child's eyes. The child is Peter. He has seen the grain of the cement sidewalk and the grass in the cracks, and the dust, and the dandelions at the edge of the road. He is there. He has taken the morning that belongs to Agnes, he is up before the others, and he knows everything. There is nothing he doesn't know. He could keep the morning, if he wanted to, but what can Peter do with the start of a summer day? Sheilah is here, it is a true Sunday morning, with its dimness and headache and remorse and regrets, and this is life. He says, "We have the Balenciaga." He touches Sheilah's hand. The children have their aunt now, and he and Sheilah have each other. Everything works out, somehow or other. Let Agnes have the start of the day. Let Agnes think it was invented for her. Who wants to be alone in the universe? No, begin at the beginning: Peter lost Agnes. Agnes says to herself somewhere, Peter is lost.

BONAVENTURE

He was besieged, he was invaded, by his mother's account of the day he was conceived; and his father confirmed her version of history, telling him *why*. He had never been able to fling in their faces "Why did you have me?" for they told him before he could reason, before he was ready to think. He was their marvel. Not only had he kept them together, he was a musical genius, the most gifted child any two people ever had, the most deserving of love. He began to doubt their legend when he discovered the casualness of sex, and understood that anyone who was not detached (which he believed his own talent would oblige him to be) could easily turn into parent and slave. He was not like his own father, who, as a parent, seemed a man who had been dying and all at once found himself in possession of a total life. His father never said this or anything like it, though he once committed himself dangerously in a letter. The father was more reticent than the mother; perhaps more Canadian. He could say what he thought, but not always what he felt. His memories, like the mother's, were silent, flickering areas of light, surrounded by buildings that no longer exist.

The son could not place himself in their epic story. They talked, but until the son became an eyewitness their lives were imaginary. Before he *was* — Douglas Ramsay — the world was covered with mist, palm fronds, and vegetarian reptiles. He said to his father, "The trouble is there are still too many people alive who remember all that." "All what?" "Oh, everything. The last war." He was trying to show the distance between them, yet he would have died for either one — perhaps the father first. That made him more violent toward them, and sometimes more indifferent. A year ago, when he was nineteen, he was awarded a fellowship that permitted him to study in Europe. He seldom wrote. Sometimes he forgot all about them. Their existence was pale, their adventure niggling, compared to his own. Family feeling had never dominated his actions; never would. Nevertheless, he discovered this: when he was confused, misunderstood, or insufficiently appreciated, a picture of his father stood upright in his mind. His father's face, stoic and watchful, transferred from a wartime photograph taken before true history began, appeared when Ramsay's emotions were dispersed, and his intellect, on which he depended, reduced to water.

He was in Switzerland, it was a June day, he was recently twenty, and he had to get rid of chocolate wrappers. He had spent the morning in Montreux, and in the short train journey between Montreux and the stop nearest the chalet where he was a guest for the summer, Ramsay had eaten three quarter-pound bars of the sweet, mild chocolate only women are said to like. He could not abandon the wrappers on the impeccable train; he was suddenly daunted by Swiss neatness and the eyes of strangers. Hobbling up the path from the station, he concealed the papers under ferns and stones.

The chalet, set up on its shelf of lawn, seemed to be watching. It was like an animal, a bison, or a bear, hairy with vines and dark because of its balconies. Once he had got rid of the evidence, he stared boldly back. Parts of his body were unhinged; he was clamped together by invisible hooks that tore the fabric. His knees, his shoulders, his neck were wrenched loose, like the punishment of Judas in an engraving Katharine Moser had put in his room. He had been in a car accident two years before, and would never mend entirely. "Neither will my father," he said to himself. Their suffering — his own and his father's — burned the day black. The shrieking of birds, which Katharine Moser thought he ought to be like because he was a musician, sank and lodged in every bone. He shut his eyes and stood still, and waited for the seizure to pass, for the muscles to unlock; then he opened his eyes and looked at the lawn. It had not been wrecked by a war or by a woman in temper but by something ordinary — a country storm. The grass was bestrewn with branches, bark, leaves, peony petals, chairs knocked sideways, a child's watercolors, a strand of dripping vine. A branch shivered and the drops that fell were colder than any water he had ever touched. He imagined Katharine Moser standing here and saying to Heaven, "How dare you do this to my lawn?" As he thought this, the sun came on in a burst of fire, and his face and hands were riddled by stinging light. He saw the mountains, whose names he was daily told and at once forgot, and he saw the burning color of houses that were miles away. This was the landscape that had belonged to Adrien Moser, the great conductor; it had no other reason to command his gaze.

The prospects Ramsay had known until this summer were of cities — Montreal, and then Berlin. They were the same to him, whether their ruins were dark and soft, abandoned to pigeons and wavy pieces of sky, or created and destroyed by one process, like the machine that consumes itself. The air he had breathed was filled with particles of brick dust. He accepted faces, not one of which he would put a name to, and knew the smell and touch of wet raincoats worn by people he would never meet. In the streets of one place, Berlin, he walked on the dead, but both cities were built over annihilated walls scarcely anyone could remember. He knew that a lake is a lake — that is, a place to swim — and that parks and trees are good for children, but he had never known the name of a leaf or a tree until Moser's widow began telling him, comparing one wild grass with another, picking a flower, showing its picture in a book. In the morning, standing beside him in the ravine on the far side of the house, she pointed to fields of white anemones that seemed covered with frost, and the gathered forget-me-nots, wild geranium, mauve and violet and pink, and valerian like lace, and mare's-tails with fronds of green string. "The first plant life on earth," said Katharine, bending down. For a reason he could not immediately interpret, the words, and the sight of the plant in Katharine's hand, rushed him back to his mother screaming, and the wartime photograph of his father, which, of course, was mute.

Wishing for life without its past, for immeasurable distance from the first life on earth, he groped to Sabine and Berlin instead of Katharine and now. In the short daydream, Sabine frowned and turned her head sharply, then felt among the clothes on the floor for a cigarette. She told Ramsay she had had one abortion and would probably never marry. Later, she said she would travel and try a different husband in every country. She was not the doting German girl his father's crowd talked about in their anecdotes of the war. Her flat was shut up tight except when the janitor's wife came to clean and flung the windows wide. The janitor's wife was not concerned about Ramsay (who had not spent an entire night with a girl before) or Sabine dressed in two towels. "I saw a wild beast in the courtyard with black eyes, like an Italian," she said, scrubbing the sink. This was the only house on the street older than Ramsay, and the courtyard was full of rats and secrets. When it rained the courtyard smelled of ashes. Laughing about the janitor's wife and the Italian rat, Sabine stood naked before her mirror and said, "Look at how brown I am." One of her admirers had given her a sunlamp.

The first plant of life on earth was spongy and weak; and the sun, in and out of clouds, sucked up every trace of color from Katharine Moser's hair and hand and eyes. He had seen color paler than Katharine's hand on angles of brick — was it paint splashed? Car lights washing by? There were no fissures in the brick, no space for fronds and stems, no room for leftovers. Why is brick ugly? Who says it is? Ramsay's father knows how much gravel per cubic centimeter is needed for several different sorts of concrete; he wrote his thesis on this twenty years ago, when he came back from the war.

"In Berlin," Ramsay started to say — something about bright weeds growing — but Katharine saw a magpie. "This is their season," she said. "They prey on fledglings." She told of the shrike, the jay, but he was thinking about the black, red-brown, smoke-marked courtyard in Berlin, and Sabine, shivering because she was suddenly cold, tender when it was too late, when there was no need for tenderness, asking what she considered serious questions in her version of English: "Was that all? Worth it? All that important?" She was not looking into space but at a clock she could not bother winding that was stopped forever at six minutes to three.

He and Katharine walked back to the lawn and the breakfast table, and she tipped her head like Sabine's, though not in remembrance of pleasure, only because the sun was strong again. She spoke to the cook's little boy, in straw hat and red shorts, pretending to garden; he was at their feet. Then behind and above them a branch rocked. It was Katharine's cat attacking a nest. The fury of the battle could be measured by the leaves rustling and thrashing in the windless day. A cat face the size of the moon must be over the nest; the eyes and the paws — there was no help for it — came through sunny leaves. The sky was behind the head. "Stop him, stop him!" Ramsay screamed like a girl or like a child.

"Pip! Naughty Pip!" She clapped her hands. "He's got one, I'm afraid." She was not disturbed. Neither was the cook's little boy, though he sucked his lip and stared up at the tree a moment more. "It is the cat's nature," she said. "Some things die — look at the spruce." (To encourage him.) "We think it is dying, but those fresh bits are new." The trees were devoured by something he did not understand — a web, a tent of gray, a hideous veil. The shadows netted on the breakfast table, on cups and milk and crumpled napkins, seemed a web to catch anything — lovers, stretched fingers, claws. He tried to see through Katharine's eyes: the cat had its nature, and every living thing carried a name.

"Do you notice that scent, Douglas? Does it bother you? It is the acacia flowering down the valley. Some people mind it. It gives them headaches. Poor Moser," she said, of her late husband, the conductor, who had died at Christmas and would have been seventy-four this summer. "When he began having headaches he thought all trees were poisonous. he breathed through a scarf. That was the form his fears took."

"It's only natural to be scared if you're dying," said Ramsay. He supposed this; until this moment he had not given it a thought.

"Old people are afraid," she said, as if she and Douglas were alike, without a time gap. (He had reckoned the difference in their ages to be twenty-five years.) "Although we'll know one day," she said, as if they would arrive at old age together. Lowering her voice, in case her adolescent daughter was spying and listening, she told how Moser had made her stop smoking. He did not want her to make a widower of him. He had chosen to marry Katharine because she was young, and he wished to be outlived. He was afraid of being alone. She, a mere child then, a little American girl nearly thirty but simple for her age, untalented, could not even play the piano, had been chosen by the great old man. But he forgot about being alone in eternity. "I told him," she said, putting the wild flowers in a glass of water on the breakfast table. "Unless two people die at exactly the same moment, they can never meet again." With such considerations had she entertained the ill old man. He had clasped her hands, weeping. His headache marched from the roots of his hair to his eyebrows, down the temples, around the eyes.

Ramsay was careful how he picked his way through this. For all his early dash and promise he was as Canadian as his father, which is to say cautious and single-minded. He had a mother younger than Katharine, who began all her conversations on a deep and intimate level, as if coming up for air was a waste of time. That made him more prudent still. He said, "Those the acacias?"

"The plum trees? They can't be what you mean, surely. That's the cuckoo you're hearing, by the way. If you count the calls, you can tell how many years before you get married. Peggy and Anne count the whole day." He considered the lunatic cuckoo, but having before him infinite time, he let the count trail off. The cook's small boy, squatting over one mauled, exhausted, eternally transplanted geranium, heard Ramsay and Katharine, but they might have been cuckoos too for all he cared. The only English words he knew were "What's that for?" "Shut up," and "Idiot." This child, who was a pet of Katharine's, lunched with the family. Until Ramsay had come, a few days ago, the boy had been the only man in the house. He sat on a cushion, an atlas, and a history of nineteenth-century painting, so as to reach the table, and he bullied and had his way; he had been obeyed and cherished by Katharine Moser and by her daughter Anne; by fat Peggy Boon, who was Anne's friend; and by Nanette Stein, who was Katharine's. Now Ramsay was here, tall as a tree to the stooping child. When Ramsay said something to him, in French, he did not look, he went deaf, he muttered and sang to himself; and Ramsay, who had offered dominoes, and would have let the boy win the game, limped on up to the house, feeling wasted.

Peggy Boon, fourteen, too plump and too boring to be a friend for Anne — unless Anne, already, chose her friends for contrast — had been mooning about the lawn ever since the storm ended, watching for Ramsay to come up the path. She let him look at the Mosers' view a full minute, and then stepped round from behind a tree. She had been making up a poem, she said flutily. No one made up poetry; Ramsay had never seen anyone making up poems. He glared over her head. She stood there, straight of hair, small of eye, fat arms across new breasts she was flattening at night with a silk scarf—this information from Katharine, by way of Anne. She was an English rose, she feared silence, and pronounced her own name "Piggy."

"Everyone's out," she said, coloring deeply for no reason he cared to know. "Anne is playing tennis. I'm not keen . . . so . . . Nanette, well, I don't know *where* she is. She didn't say. Mrs. Moser went to visit the bees in case the thunder frightened them. She tells them everything. When Mr. Moser died she told the bees. She told them you were coming, and she's told them she is moving your things out of the house and into Mr. Moser's garden pavilion, and that you are his . . . his . . ." Unfolding her arms, stooping, she clutched at grass, as though weeding; she straightened up, she took courage, and announced, "*You* are Mr. Moser's spiritual heir." He was not listening to her. "If you don't tell the bees everything, Mrs. Moser says, they go away. But my mother," she added urgently, "says this is nonsense."

Like all English voices, hers sounded to him under-developed. He stared down at the cardigan, drooping and empty-armed, at the tight belt and bulging seat of what he supposed was a dainty frock. He had avoided one sort of Canadian girl all his life, and here was the pure, the original mold. He asked, "Did you know Adrien Moser?" It seemed impossible.

"Oh goodness, yes. This is the fourth time I've been here." She was gasping, as if he had splashed her with seawater. "I've been here a summer, and a Christmas, and an Easter, and *this* summer. Of course, he's not here now, is he?" If only Ramsay would say, "He must have been charming" — something like that. She pretended he had: "Oh he *was* charming! He used to do so many kind things. Once he offered to buy me a bicycle. I refused, of course. But imagine! He'd hardly known me five minutes then." Chewing on grass, airy and worldly now, she said. "I've been wondering . . . No one's told me. Are you a composer?"

"I'm studying with Jekel in Berlin." And I am his best and strongest pupil, and if you knew anything you would know that, his mind continued. He had heard, for years, "Are you really only twelve? . . . only sixteen?" The voices had stopped; no one is ever likely to say, "Are you really only twenty?"

"Don't you want a chair?" said Peggy, wiping the seat of one with her cardigan sleeve. "You're not supposed to stand too long. I've heard . . . there's something wrong."

"Nothing's *wrong*. I was in a smash-up about two years ago, that's all. This girl was driving," he said. "It wasn't even her own car. There was all hell with the insurance. No one was killed."

"Oh, *good*." Having offered Moser's kindness, and had news of Ramsay's health, Peggy said. "Do you like Switzerland?" But she had lost him. Katharine Moser, with her cat in attendance, came toward them, smiling. The shadows that bent over her hair were cast by trees whose bark was like the skin of a snake. He had imagined another face for her; until a few days ago, he had known her only in letters. He had given her soft hair streaked with white, and humorous, intelligent eyes. His idea of a great man's wife was very near a good hospital nurse. Even now, when he thought, I am in Moser's house, he was grateful to the intelligent hospital nurse, who did not exist; at least she was not Katharine. Her eyes were green, uptilted. The straight parting in her hair was coquetry, to show how perfectly proportioned was her face. The only flaws he had seen were the shape of her nose, slightly bulbous at the tip, and the too straight body, which was a column for the fine head. The bees' scent, which clung to her hands and dress, was like incense. She was impressive, beautiful, fragrant, and until she lifted her arm to point to the pavilion where he would now sleep, and saw the skin of the arm, palely freckled, spotted, slack, he almost accepted her own idea of herself, which was that she was guileless, a child bride, touchingly young.

"I wanted to know you before I put you in the pavilion. You do understand why? It mustn't be a museum, but I want it kept alive just by people he liked, or might have loved. It's furnished with — What is it, Peggy?" The smitten girl was following them across the grass. Katharine watched Peggy Boon skip off (pretending joy) and become excluded. "That girl is having a rotten time. My daughter is so rude," she said, and sighed, and forgot all about it. "Now, Moser's bed and his tiled stove came from the curé's room in a château. I bought them at an auction."

He ducked his head to enter the pavilion. The first thing he saw was the piano, small and gaily colored, looking like the piano sometimes given a little girl for her first lessons. He could not see the name of the maker, which had been covered over with paint.

"Those engravings belonged to a fervent German monarchist who collected caricatures of the new rich, unaware that he was mocking himself. Moser liked objects that came from rich houses, providing they looked poor. He always thought he might die of hunger any day. He saved screws and tacks and elastic bands — you'll find boxes full of rubbish, all labelled. Moser told me that the walls of his family's house were covered with rugs they would not put on the floor, and that there were sheets over the rugs to protect them from light. I hope you will like your bed."

The bed was carved and bore a coat of arms and an angel's head. The angel had a squint; Ramsay could not tell if it was looking reproachfully to Heaven or out of the window. The pavilion had been prepared in secret, while Ramsay was down in Montreux at a movie. He saw roses, a reading lamp, and then he saw the last photograph of the old man. The old man sat on a bench, in sunlight, holding a scarf. Katharine stood with one hand on his shoulder. Moser's eyes were wild and fixed.

"This is a great picture," he said, taking it up. "It was in the papers when he died. Someone in Berlin said it looked like a famous picture of Freud going into exile."

"I don't know what you mean by that. Moser was never in exile. He died in his native country." She shifted ornaments on the washstand. A shell porcelain soap dish was moved from the extreme left to the far right. The vase of roses took its place. "Now, there are things you can look at, if you want to. Testimonials. All the obituaries. Boxes of caramels — I found them after his last stroke. He loved them, but wasn't allowed to have any. When we found the empty boxes I knew he'd been eating on the quiet. I've kept them — I don't know why. This one wasn't opened." When she spoke of something she touched it. When she finished speaking she touched Ramsay's arm.

"Here's what they'll find after me," he said, and tumbled out of his pockets the marbles, the Yo-yo, and the sponge ball that were part of the re-education of his injured hands. He was arrogant, he never doubted; it was a joke only in part. When Douglas Ramsay died, his Yo-yo and the plastic marbles would be placed on a shelf and labelled and dated, and dusted every day. He had never had parents; there was nothing behind him, nothing to come; the first plant life on earth had never existed; the cities would be reduced to mossy boulders; he would never have children; he would be mourned nevertheless. The curé's bed, Moser's bed, was Ramsay's bed. "How did he sleep in it?" they would say. "He was so big, and the bed is so small!"

The first night Ramsay spent in the pavilion a large moth brushed against his face. He knew it would not bite or sting, but its touch was pure horror, and his reaction uncontrolled. The moth was paper-white until it blundered against the pillow, and then he saw it was cream. Indigo eyes were painted upon its wings. He shot XEX out of the blue can Katharine had left for mosquito-killing. The battle the moth put up for its life now frightened him witless. It flapped its way under the bed. The frantic wings were louder than his heart. During the fight, scores of incidental casualties — gnats, midges, spiders, flies — dropped from the ceiling. He was afraid to open the window or the glass doors in case any more creatures came in, and he lay in the poisoned room blowing his nose all night long. He was on a mattress of straw that was just slightly too short. He was covered with tons of eiderdown. In his mind he had an image of his mended bones beginning to slip. If he got up now, he would not be able to stand. He could see, in moonlight, the paved terrace and the chair that had been the old man's. The pavilion was like another beehive, and the old man had been sent here, with a curé's bed and a doll's piano, and told something: "You will be alone in eternity." "Don't eat sweets." "If you think you are dying, ring that bell."

At a quarter to six the sunlight on the wall made a stately shadow of the roses. The sun was smaller than a marble. Hills and trees received its light at an angle that made them a single spongy substance. Birds were shrieking. Ramsay pulled the eiderdown up to his eyes, which left his feet bare. When he woke up two hours after this, he took inventory of the roses; there were four yellow, two pale pink, and two garnet, which were dying. These were probably sensitive — like him — to XEX. He had nothing better to do than count by color; he was in the grip of believing that he would fail, that he was ungifted, that his crushed body would betray him, and that the years of his life — fifteen out of twenty — involved with music were a waste. He had a premonition that he would be the victim of an inherited fault. His father should help him now. His father had willed his existence: he existed in his father's mind from the moment his father knew he had survived the Dieppe raid in the last war. This extra time, when Ramsay existed in desire, gave him a margin of safety. He felt as if he had been given a present of time; no one else had this. He would outlive everyone. Moser had wanted to be outlived. His

father was better than Moser. His father would never have
whimpered and breathed through a scarf. His father had a
calm, closed, gentle disposition. Patience and endurance
distinguished his face, which otherwise might have seemed
boyish. If only his father had not depended on love, or on an
ideal of what a woman must mean in his life; if only he had
not been implicitly certain he could expect only good of
women, that love was the constant survivor; if only he had let
his wife leave him when she wanted to — but then, what
about Ramsay? After his accident, his father had put something in a letter that he was too reserved to say when he came
to see Ramsay in the hospital. (Where had he written the
letter, and how had he slipped it out to the mail? From his
office, probably. Ramsay's mother, having once tried to cast
his father away, was now devoutly jealous — a wastebasket
hunter, letter filcher, telephone spy. She thought his father's
pocket diary was written in code.) His father wrote, "I suppose
two things have bedevilled our life. First, that I am hideously
shy and totally lacking inwardly in any confidence. Second
(and this is fact, not fiction), that I've puzzled and puzzled
over what happened in 1942, over the hundred-million-to-one
shot that landed me back among living people when I had
joined the dead. The greatest denial of death is to love as I
always shall love you and your mother." Ramsay was too weak
and too ill when he read it. He began to cry. They kept feeding
him answers when he hadn't asked for anything. He would
never say (though he thought it), "You both make me sick."
There was still the early admiration for his father — not only
for his unfaltering conduct but because of a childhood illusion
that his father could, for example, look at the engine of a car
and see what was wrong with it. And there was more — the
conspiracy of two quiet men living in the same house with an
intolerant woman.

As the sun above the dying spruce expanded, rose, became
too brilliant to see, Ramsay surveyed his father's life and found
it simple. "I love you" or "I don't love you" seemed puerile.

His father had never had to cope — as Ramsay was doing — with doubts and terror and the possibility of lapsed genius. He had not even had to cope with a lot of women — only that one.

Owing to an exchange concluded with the enemy, Ramsay's father came back to Montreal about a year before the end of the war. He was part of a contingent of sick, wounded, and tubercular prisoners taken at Dieppe. Bonaventure Station received him. This was a dusty building with, on both the front and the back, a wooden porch that is called, in Montreal, a gallery. The paint on the gallery was scrofulous and diseased, and the station itself was the dark dry red that deflates the soul. It was at the foot of a steep hill; streetcars stopped before it after an awkward turn. For a long time the station had been used only for freight traffic, and then the Army took it over entirely. The Army put up cardboard squares with the letters of the alphabet so the next of kin would know where to wait, and assigned dozens of men to make sure the next of kin did not trample one another to death. Ramsay's mother was twenty-one. She sat under R for Ramsay the better part of a day, with her hands in the pockets of her camel-hair coat and her bare brown-painted legs stuck out straight before her. Ramsay knew, because she had told him, that there were no nylon stockings in those days, and that she wore her coat on a blazing hot day because of a guilty and confused desire to cover up. The men came through a door at the far end of the station, one by one. His father appeared; swung his kit down from his shoulder; stared into the dark. It was like a monkey house by then, with the dirt of the place, and the stopped-up toilets, and the children frightened, and the women screaming. She pushed her way up to him and with her fists in her pockets said, "I don't want to live with you. I don't want to be married at all. I couldn't tell you while you were a prisoner. Anyway the censor might not have let it through." Some women took their husbands home and lay like corpses so the husbands could see for themselves the marriage was over, but Ramsay's mother wouldn't have that. She was fiercely honest and saw nothing the matter with manslaughter. In the slow-motion film of someone else's memory, Ramsay saw his father there, home, alive, yes, but in a sense never seen or heard of again. His father was Canadian-silent, Canadian-trained, and had to make an intellectual effort not to be proud. He struggled out of the station and walked up the hill beside his wife and sat down with her on a bench in Dominion Square. A Salvation Army band played "Lamb of God, Sheep of God," which was taken up by a drunk woman sharing their bench. His father was so stunned, so exhausted, he forgot his name. He forgot what he was doing here — forgot the name of his native city. His wife said he would be an invalid all his life. He heard her say she hated sick people, and had married too young. Yet at the end of the afternoon she led him home and turned out the girl whose apartment she shared. Why? Pity, she told Ramsay. No, said his father; it was justice, the power of love. Bonaventure Station was destroyed before Ramsay could see it. Most of the buildings his father and mother looked at when they were deciding his existence or nonexistence stand only on old postcards and in their account of that day. The bed belonged to the girl turned temporarily out of the flat, and no one knows what became of her. She married some man, said Ramsay's mother, and they left Montreal.

Katharine Moser, companion of genius, generator of talent, dispenser of comfort, and mind reader as well, said, without leading up to it, "I suppose you were close to your mother?" They were in the car, and she was driving him he did not know quite where — to fetch drinking water from a spring, she said.

"I was closer to my father, actually" — this reluctantly. He pinched his lips together, for he had in his pocket one of his mother's long, self-justifying letters, jumpy with dates: "In January 1946," "Just after the Korean War," "When we met at Bonaventure" — that was the important date, when he was not conceived, was not present, was not even deaf, blind, and upside down. She defeated him by making him present on that occasion. He was still her witness, as if she had wanted nothing more than a witness. He saw her belted coat, her curly hair brushing the collar, her straight bare legs. He was afraid of contamination; his father's sweetness, his gentleness were in the blood. He knew — because many times told — how she had been persuaded. Victory for the man! Yet it was she who stood up abruptly, slung her handbag over her shoulder, and took him home to bed.

"You are so quiet — you live in music, I can see that," said Katharine, driving. "Do you have" — she sounded eighty-five and senile to him now — "time for girls?"

He had slept badly, and his legs were too long for the Mini-Minor. He edged slowly around so that he was facing her profile and, after the second's reflection in which he decided not to say, "Mind your own damn business," he suddenly told her about Sabine. He handed over Sabine, the slut, the innocent, the admirer of her own body, the good-natured, the stupid, the avaricious, the maker and seeker of love. The first woman he had spent a whole night with became an anecdote. He said, "Finally, she met an Arab prince. I mean a real one, in skirts. Jewelled dagger. He gave her some crappy bracelets that probably came from Hong Kong. She was excited. Every time you'd see her she'd be trying to write him a letter. But she made an awful mistake. When he left Berlin she said, 'Well, *shalom*.' She thought it was a kind of Middle Eastern '*Ciao*.' You know what the Arab said? He said, 'That's not exactly us.'" Ramsay's laughter was loud.

"And that wiped her out as a wife for you? Her *bêtise*?"

"I'm not looking for a *wife*." He wondered if she knew he

was twenty and would have to live for a long time on grants and on the allowance his father gave him.

"Creative men should marry young. It stabilizes them."

What was she getting at? He looked at her calm profile, at her competent hands. She had the habit of opening and closing her hands as she drove, and slightly lifting her foot, so that the car, for a fraction of time, had to drive itself — through never long enough to take them off the road. He muttered about affinities and someone whose interests, whose mind and background . . .

"That's not marriage," said Katharine impatiently. "You didn't sleep with Sabine for her mind and background. Moser did his best work after he married me. I brought him back to the country, where he belonged. I made his life calm and easy, and kept him close to nature."

Owing to a mistake in time, he was having a conversation with a very young girl who was somehow old enough to be his mother.

"I would have thought that anything Moser did was separated from nature," he said. "He would have been what he was in a hotel room. In jail."

"Without the wind in the trees and the larks?"

Ramsay reflected that these had probably been a nuisance. Katharine's letters had been intelligent; she had used another vocabulary. If she had talked about the wind and larks, he would never have come. "I've explained it all wrong," he said, though he thought he had not. "I mean that everything he did was intellectual. He was divorced from nature by intention. Now do you see?"

"Nothing can be divorced from nature and survive." She looked angry, creased suddenly. He saw how she would be fifteen years from now. "Look at what has happened to music. To painting. It is the fault of people like you."

He should have let it go, but he was angry too. Who was she to attack him? She had invited him here; he had not arrived like a baby on the doorstep. When the old man died, Ramsay had written a polite and thoughtful letter to his widow, in care of the Swiss nation, and had been surprised to receive a warm embrace of an answer, in English. *She* had kept on writing; *she* had — the fine, and humorous, and courageous hospital nurse. (He forgot how it had pleased him, for once in his life, to play up to a situation, to pretend it was not over his head, to show off his opinions, pretending all the while to be diffident — to gather favor, to charm.)

If, at this moment, she was thinking, You're not what I expected, she was to blame. She was ignorant of music. She was the persistent artists' friend who inspires nothing but a profound lack of gratitude. He was feeling it now. He said, "Painters learn to paint by looking at pictures, not at hills and valleys, and musicians listen to music, not the wind in the trees. Everything Moser said and wrote was unnatural. It was unnatural because he was sophisticated." Her head shot round, and to her blazing eyes he said, bewildered, "It is a compliment."

They drove on in a silence that presently became unbearable. "Very soon it's too late," his mother had remarked, of quarrels. Her staccato letter jumped through his mind: "I said if you can't take a holiday when I need one I had better go without you. I shall go where there are plenty of men, I promise you that. He said, Go where you like, my darling. I said, A woman like me shouldn't travel alone. I must have bitched up my life. He had the gall to say, All right I agree you've bitched it up but it wasn't all my fault. I was driving and I felt his crippled existence beside me and I thought mine might not be better. The weather is beautiful as it always is in Montreal when he is being impossible. There must be more accidents more murders more nervous breakdowns more hell in October and June. Where was I? Oh yes. When I got out of the car I saw he was crying. Pity for himself? Guilt over me?"

All at once Katharine parked sharply. Reaching behind her for a basket of empty bottles that had been rattling on the floor, she said (smiling to show they were friends again), "Is it true you have never seen a spring?" In an evil grotto a trickle of water squeezed out of the rock. A mossy stone pipe rested on the edge of a very old bathtub and dispensed a stream that overflowed the tub and ran deviously along a bed of stones, under a stone bridge, and out of sight. They stood, she worshipping, he blinking merely, each crowned with a whirling wreath of gnats. "I *own* this source," she said, and to his horror she immersed the bottles one by one in the tub. She filled each with typhoid fever, conjunctivitis, amoebic dysentery, blood poisoning, and boils. She capped them, smiling all the while, and put them back dripping in the basket; the basket was packed in the car, and they drove away.

Night after night he fought flies, midges, mosquitoes, and moths, most of which expired on his pillow or on the white bedsheet. They seemed determined to perish upon a white expansion — some mountaintop of their own insect literature and mythology — instead of going and dying in a corner where Ramsay need never see them again. One night a dying fly got in his wastebasket and thrashed and buzzed. Every time he thought it stopped it began again. At luncheon next day he told how it had kept him awake.

"All you had to do was squash it," said Anne. She was tall, and still growing. She had looked at him intently. The others seemed to concur — piggy Peggy (whom he had just interrupted) and Katharine and her friend Nanette Stein.

"Shut up," said the cook's little boy, but they turned to English now, putting a stop to Peggy's recital, in creeping French, of a visit she had made three days before to the market at Vevey. She rushed into English too: "There was nothing Swiss in Vivey, you know, nothing but vigitables." They were all sick of her. She was Anne's guest, but Anne had left her once again for the whole morning. "Time went so fast when you were away," Peggy went on calmly. "Goodness, it was half past ten before I knew *when* it was. I washed my green woolly

and I wrote Mummy and Phyllis and I went for a lovely walk."
A barely perceptible collective sigh went round the table, a
collective breath of boredom. "I went farther and farther,
straight on and up and on. The road was so steep! I thought,
What if I should slip and fall? What a long way it would be!
And so I turned and came back. I saw a herd of lovely Jersey
cows, each wearing a bill, and I thought, How lovely! The
biggest cow had the biggest bill, and the smallest one had the
smallest bill. They made heavenly music."

"Bell?" said Nanette.

"Yes, bill," said the crimson child. "I thought, Goodness,
why haven't I got a camera here?"

"I would have lent you a camera," Nanette said. "For such
an original photograph."

Peggy's flush now seemed merely gratitude that the subject
had been taken up. "If they don't move the cows, I could find
them again easily."

"Aren't you afraid, going out alone among a herd?" said
Nanette. She seemed subordinate, playing up to the others,
and Ramsay wondered exactly what her role had been when
the old man was alive.

"Not of cows, no, but actually as I went up and up I was
thinking of that English lady who was waylaid and killed on a
lonely road in Switzerland. It was near here."

"Never in Switzerland," said Nanette.

"And then there was that other one, a younger one. I
remember it. You know, knocked down and bashed about.
I'm sure it was here. I thought, Well, there's no use hanging
about here waiting for *that*."

"Men do attack girls," said Anne suddenly. The rest were
uneasy, for now the ridiculous obsession had shifted from
Peggy, who was a joke, to Anne, whom they were expected to
take seriously. Peggy had touched an apprehension so deeply
shared by the women that Ramsay felt himself in league with
the cook's child, and suspected of something. For some
reason, confirmation that she had been in danger made Peggy

cheerful. She passed around a trunk key found on the road half an hour away from the house. No one claimed it, and so she dropped the key back in the pocket of her blazer and went skipping out of the house and across the lawn, fat and maddening, with Anne behind her. The others sat smoking, watching the pair through the dining-room window.

"I hope her holiday is a success this time," said Katharine gravely.

"It never will be," said Nanette. "This is as successful as life can ever be for that girl — going to stay with a friend and talking twaddle."

Katharine waited until she and Ramsay were alone. "I want to ask you something," she said. "A great favor. Would you be nice to Nanette? Pay attention to her? She's a lost, unhappy creature. She was a bright young pianist, though you wouldn't know it now. Moser encouraged her. Do you notice how Anne ignores her? About two years ago Nanette began writing to Anne, who wasn't quite thirteen. What could I do? Anne had often seen her here. But I didn't understand why Nanette should write every day to a child half her age." Moser was too old to be bothered. What Katharine had done, she said, was slip into her daughter's room and find Nanette's letters. Anne had gone out early. She found the letters easily; Anne had her father's Swiss neatness. She saved programs, menus, anything to do with herself. There was a narcissism about Anne . . .

"What happened?"

But Katharine would not be rushed. Her own upbringing, she said, had risen like a wave. She felt watched by her own mother, who would never have done such a thing. She almost put the letters back.

This, Ramsay thought, was a lie. Katharine had sat on her daughter's bed, like her mother before her, like his mother pursuing his father, and read methodically, smoothing the pages on her knee. What Katharine saw, she said (holding up thumb and finger joined, to show with what distaste she had invaded Anne's life, and how revolting the letters were), made her see that the correspondence must stop. She drove to Ascona to have a word with Nanette, who was discovered sharing a cottage with a gendarme Englishwoman. She described that too: the rage, the tears, the abject guilt. Katharine looked tolerant and sad.

"What's Nanette doing here now?"

"But she's a friend — an excellent person. Besides, Anne has outgrown her. I sent Anne to a school where her letters are surveyed. She needed English, and her manners wanted straightening out."

Reflecting on Anne's treatment of Peggy, he thought the school wanting. And he still did not see why Nanette should be here, in the house.

He started to write to someone back home, "Honest to God, the *radar* around here," but tossed it in his basket. When it disappeared from the basket, he remembered something his father had said about women's curiosity: "You can't leave a thing around. They *uncrumple* everything."

Nanette Stein was a slight woman of twenty-seven, with a small, squashed face and a fringe of curly hair that seemed to start up from the middle of her forehead. She watched Ramsay eating his breakfast, and asked fierce questions about the racial problem in America. She told him that when an African concert tour had been organized for her (and a lot of work it had been, Katharine put in, letting Ramsay know who had been the influence behind it), she had been asked to leave South Africa. She had been shunned by British women in Northern Rhodesia. She was proud of it. Music was a waste of time when you saw the condition of the world.

Katharine, shelling peas under a large hat, seemed grave and interested, and nodded without committing herself. Nanette had gone to Barcelona just to help a strike once. She had been arrested and conducted to the frontier. When she saw the mounted policemen, the horses, something in her, a revolt against injustice (she brought her fist down on the table, remembering), made her scream and curse and fling herself against them, pummelling the horses, swearing at the police.

"I know, they say you made a lot of noise," said Katharine mildly.

Ramsay's mind snapped off; he tuned them out. He could see how this would appeal to an extremely bright girl of twelve or thirteen. Katharine might have been wrong. Nanette had perhaps been proselyting impersonally, politically.

"I decided never to touch a piano again," said Nanette.

No one touched a piano here. He had expected it to be the house of music, but he heard only the very light quarrelling of women. The music room with its records and library of scores might have been surrounded with vines and brambles. Nothing had been added for years. When he asked Nanette to play for him one evening (his way of answering Katharine's request to be nice to her), she fetched a tape recorder and they sat in the garden listening to her repeating one movement of a Haydn concerto. When she stumbled she said "*Merde*," and that was the clearest part of the tape. He thanked her when she turned the machine off.

"It's about three years old," she said. "I was trying to make something decent for Katharine."

"Does she like music?"

Nanette looked completely scandalized, as if he had been angling for gossip. She scowled and said, "I don't know what either of them liked, finally. He was old when I met him. He came to a concert in Lausanne. It meant a lot to me. He never came out anymore. It was known he hated crowds and towns. If you wanted to play for him, you had to come up here, and then you might get a telegram at the last minute telling you not to come. He had something like asthma. Some days he lay gasping — there." She pointed to the chair where Ramsay sat. "He sat with a shawl over his knees, looking down at the lights of towns he never went to. I'd played the Prokofieff Second. I hardly dared ask what he thought. He said, 'Very pretty, my

child, very pretty.' Pretty! It's so Swiss — everything is *joli*. But
she fascinated me. She was in green, in a dress like a sari, with
the black hair, and the eyes. I felt like a little provincial. She
had so much more than anyone, and he was fine-looking,
still. I never had seen a couple like them and never will again.
And then she called me and said, 'We would like to see you
again.' Oh, they were such a couple. People fell in love with
them. And Moser — of course, he stopped doing anything
here. All that wild grass was bad for his asthma. But *before*! He
was a conductor and a teacher and . . ."

"I know."

"Look at them now. Look at your hero, Jekel, in Berlin.
What does he write? A ten-minute opus every other year."

"Not my hero — my teacher." Ramsay was secretly reassured. He admired his teacher but did not mind hearing him
attacked.

"My mother thinks activity is genius," he said, and smiled.

"He was a bit dotty at the end," said Nanette, trusting
Ramsay. She walked beside him with the docility of a
little dog. As they passed the kitchen — Nanette staring
straight before her and talking in a low voice — Ramsay
turned and saw the face of the cook, which was frightened and
haggard, and so exhausted that, although her eyes met
Ramsay's, she did not see he was there. The kitchen was on
the north side of the house, under a long balcony; a single
light above the stove had already been turned on, and the cook
moved toward it and became saffron-colored. "They dote on
her little boy and spoil him," Ramsay said to himself, "but I
have never even been told the cook's name."

"He was a bit touched, at the end," Nanette said. "He was
fond of Peggy in a senile way, but she was so stupid she didn't
seem to notice she was being pawed. He would offer to buy her
presents, and she would simper and say no. Katharine was
deathly afraid the child would tell her mother. That's why

she's asked her back now; she wants to show it is a normal household."

"Did Moser like living here?"

"It was his house."

"You don't feel he lived here. That piano . . ."

"He didn't need a piano. He used to go for walks and be lost or tired, and then he would get some farmer to ring her. She was always rushing off in the car to bring him home. She would find him sitting in a hot kitchen, and he would get in the car smelling of cabbages and cooked fat. His clothes reeked of farm kitchens, but that isn't to say he felt at home there either. He was never comfortable with country people. He would sit with his hands on his walking stick, waiting for Katharine. Katharine was foreign-looking, but she got to them. She would sit down, and she would just begin telling about herself and her bees, never asking questions. Why, I've seen farmers come to help her get a swarm back, and you know they don't bother about each other, let alone strangers. As for him, oh, presently he began to hate walking. And the doctor said he had to walk, he had so much wrong with him. She had to coax him out, bribe him with caramels — because he wasn't supposed to have them and they were a treat. 'Just one ten-minute walk,' I've heard her say, 'ten out, ten back, twenty minutes in all,' but he was too muddled to count. It was along here." She meant the path where stones were now hurting Ramsay's feet. He also was supposed to exercise, but he hated it. He trudged on with Nanette, counting ten out, ten back, twenty minutes in all. She plunged her hands in the pockets of her leather coat. Her Aberdeen Angus hair seemed to him touching. Old maid at twenty-seven, older than Katharine, she let her hands pull at the shape of her coat.

The old man was dragged for a walk along this road, Ramsay reflected, looking at the silken grasses he did not care to identify, though he knew they were not alike. Like Moser, he craved anything sweet. He would have gone to the village, but if he asked for the car, Katharine would know. She would have driven him, without reproach, but he did not want her to know. Ramsay saw the old man on a bench on this stony road with smuggled chocolate in his mouth. He broke off only one square and let it melt slowly. If the old man had chocolate, then he would look at anything she wanted — at fields and chalets catching the strong evening sunlight, and clouds going pink, and one cloud pressing like a headache on a peak. If he walked to the village — but that was impossible, he never would again, for it was thirty-five minutes down, even on the shortcut by the tracks, and nearly fifty back, because it was so steep. Perhaps she thought he was meditating here on the bench. He was huddled into his cape because the evening was suddenly cold. His intellect dissolved, his mind was like water, his powers centered only on the things to eat he was forbidden to have.

"This is where the picture was taken," Ramsey said, stopping before the bench. "The old man, with Katharine beside him. Now I know why he looked in exile. He had to go for walks, and he couldn't eat what he wanted. Like a kid."

Nanette looked at the bench too. "Everyone in music is childish," she said. "Our mothers stand beside us when we practice, from the age of four."

"Somebody has to."

"Musicians live between their mothers and their confessors, forever and ever. If they lose them, they find substitutes. They invent them. *Marry* them. They marry one or the other. Always two in their lives, you'll notice. The mother and the confessor."

"No, it is not childish," Ramsay was saying to himself. "I know that *I* am not childish, I am older than my parents, but sometimes, even when I am not hungry . . ." He stopped; it was too secret. Then, crossing his mind, unsummoned, came "cruelty." It was only a word, a tag on a tree; it was like Katharine's voice saying "larch," "spruce," "acacia."

"He should have been in a city," said Ramsay. "It's as simple as that. That mania he had for collecting, even. It's a clue. They are all things you use in cities — pieces of metal, paper clips."

"A simple case of thrift," said Nanette. "Very Swiss."

He looked down at her face. "Where's your home?" he said. "Where are you from?"

"I've told you. Ascona." Her face seemed smaller all at once. "All right. From Vienna. Before that, Poland. Now you know everything. If you want the whole truth, the real truth, he didn't like foreigners. He made horrible jokes about Jews in front of me, to see if I would laugh." All Nanette had done was apply a new name, just as Katharine had said grass was millet. Ramsay would see her now wearing a tag. They heard cowbells from the valley. "Katharine thinks they sound like Oriental music," she said, smiling miserably.

"Shows how much she knows about that."

But she would not follow up what she had been saying. Without meaning to, he had made her unhappy. She talked as if they had only just met, and began all over again about the racial question in the United States.

R amsay had accepted the old man's bed, but the bath repelled him. He was glad when, one day, the taps ran nothing but rust and he was obliged to share one of the bathrooms in the house. He came into an early-morning house, with the cook stirring and the little boy eating bread on the stairs, and Nanette, encountered in the hall, wearing a striped bathrobe. Nanette had left the room full of steam and lavender. Wet washcloths festooned the tub. He removed a wire hanger holding six stockings, and, just before he turned the shower on, he listened to church bells and to thunder. Ten minutes later the lawn was obliterated by gray smoke. The tree where Pip had hunted was still. Over the thunderclap came more bells, as if to silence the sky. The wind rose all in a moment, and the first drops of rain were flung against the house. By the time he had finished shaving, soft silent rain fell from a bright sky. The air was cold. Birds sang, but the strongest sound was a brook. Now a voice covered it — Katharine's voice, complaining about last night's supper. "The soup was out of a can, the hamburger was cooked black, and I don't call half a slice of tinned pineapple on a bit of rusk a pudding. It really is unfair — I take the boy over entirely. I keep him out of the kitchen. You've got nothing to do but the meals. As for the salad, there was too much vinegar *and* too much oil. I don't know how you manage to have too much of both."

In the room where the young girls slept, light came through flimsy curtains. Ramsay, coming into the room, saw Peggy hunched, sheet up to her forehead, tufts of coarse fair hair showing like bristles. Her pillows were on the floor. Anne lay with a leg and an arm and a small breast outside the blanket. On the pillow a wreath of dead wild flowers was half crushed by her head. Her brown smooth face was lightly oiled. Watching the sleeping girl, he knew what he could be capable of, provided she loathed him, or was frightened of him. Better fear than hate. When he touched Anne her breathing changed; he thought he saw a gleam between her lashes. Watching, she made no move. She was waiting to see what could happen. Outside, Katharine called, "Pip, Pip!," beating her hands. Peggy awoke and, with a rapidity he would never have thought possible in the dull girl, sat up and looked. There they were, Anne cold and excited, her heart like a machine under his hand, and Ramsay the vivisectionist, and poor Peggy, who had been in love.

To amuse Ramsay, Katharine now organized excursions. She took them to restaurants where they lunched sitting on balconies brilliant with roses, where she ordered the food with frowning care, putting on her glasses to read the menu, suggesting and planning for them all. She had noticed that he was greedy. She watched him, sagely and fondly. She had wakened something — perhaps only a craving for strawberries and cream — she later intended to curb. Nanette looked at her, and at Ramsay, and began having headaches, and finally dropped out of their party altogether. She looked dark and wretched when she was left behind. "The truth is, she gets carsick," said Katharine, as if some other excuse had been offered and was a lie. The young girls looked through Ramsay and round him and not much at each other. They played an acquisitive game called Take It Home and fought over museums, ancient jewelry, ski lifts, whole restaurants, a view, a horse, other people's cars, but stopped short of people. Peggy was pink with joy at being included, but Ramsay knew that she, and not Anne, had been scared to death that morning in their bedroom.

After these excursions he was stiff and sore, and could hardly move his arms and legs at night or turn in bed. His memory of each day was of eating and drinking beer on blowy terraces and of parasols knocked down by wind. Katharine took him to see a famous church treasure, and to Zurchers for tea, where they sat next to Noël Coward, and to Lausanne for an exhibition of French sculpture and painting. She brought the cook's child this time, and the two girls went to a movie. Katharine wore her glasses, and looked at the catalogue in her hand before examining any of the paintings. The two men of the household walked one on each side of her. Ramsay, shut up in a series of large rooms full of paintings, rid of three out of four of the women, began to breathe.

"These Impressionists," he began. "They seem kind of tied to their wives, you know what I mean. They were limited to their wives' gardens. You feel they all had something wrong with them and that the wife was waiting with a cup of tea and some medicine." Katharine glanced at him. That had been her role, and she knew that he knew it.

"Sit down, Douglas," she said, suggesting the circular sofa in the middle of the room. "You must be tired, after all this walking around. There is nothing more tiring than looking at things that don't interest one."

Ramsay found himself sitting and looking at the headless statue of an adolescent girl. He looked at the small breasts, slightly down-pointed. The hips were wider than the chest, the legs columns. A piece of bronze, he told himself. No one had ever been like that. He put Anne's head on the bronze neck, and presently was conscious of being watched. It was the boy, who was running round and round the sofa. The little boy circled closer. He sat down, and Ramsay smiled into what seemed an open face. The child breathed something difficult to hear. He pointed at Ramsay (and he had to bring his hand all the way from a far place to do so; he liked great gestures). He breathed again — something that sounded like "Idiot."

"What?"

"Idiot," the child said. The index finger still pointed; the arm was a soft arc.

"Who?"

"*Vous.*"

Ramsay stared down at him in fury and outrage. "Idiot, am I? What do you think you are? You supposed to be clever?"

The child did not understand English, but he understood the tone. A mistake had been made; he had been bolder than he intended. "You, for instance," said Ramsay. "What are you supposed to be? *Tu n'es pas un peu idiot?*"

"*Moi, je suis gentil,*" said the child, sliding off the sofa and beginning to back away. His face trembled. He said "*zentil,*" but this evidence of his age — his inability to pronounce some letters — did not endear him to Ramsay, who rushed on, "You're a rude little bastard. *Gentil!* You're a little bastard, that's what you are."

From the safety of Katharine, the child looked boldly back. What a fool I've been, Ramsay thought. Of course the child had not remarked he was looking at the statue of an adolescent girl and thinking spellbound thoughts about Anne.

"Peggy wants to go back to England," said Katharine, and sighed.

"But she hates her family," Nanette protested.

"She may not know she does."

"She's fourteen and old enough to admit that her father isn't a god and her mother an angel," said Nanette.

"That is true." Katharine bowed her head with simulated meekness.

Anne appeared, with wet hair plastered on her cheeks. She washed it daily. She was struggling with a pullover. "Are you talking about me?" she said as her head emerged. "I thought I heard my name. Peggy is packing, by the way." She plunged down on the grass at their feet and said, "We've decided she's leaving because I've been so awful to her."

"I shall speak to her," Katharine said, looking oddly like the woman Ramsay had imagined before he ever saw her.

"I have been awful to her," said Anne. "You won't make her change her mind."

"It is the same story every time she comes here," said Katharine. "That wretched girl always threatens to leave because of some nonsense she has imagined. It used to be —" Nanette stopped her. "Now it is Anne she complains of," Katharine said.

"I want to see you alone," said Anne to her mother casually, "when you've finished with Peggy."

Katharine was already walking across the lawn, in her striped dress, in an old, large straw hat, with all her bracelets rattling. Throughout this exchange Ramsay might as well have been invisible. The group was disintegrating. The cook's child no longer came to lunch. Ramsay could observe all he liked now, for there was no one to catch him at it. Even the old man's phantom had vanished. Ramsay no longer saw or felt him, demanding chocolate, querulous and lost, too cosseted, smothered, destroyed. "Yesterday," said Nanette's small radio, "was the hottest twenty-second of June since 1873." Ramsay isolated three birds by sound; one asking a question, one cackling derisively, one talking to itself in a conversational tone.

Picked out in the headlights, a badger crossed the road, steadily, like an enormous dachshund. It turned and looked into the lights, and Ramsay, sitting next to Katharine, experienced the revulsion he felt in the presence of animals and wild creatures in particular. They had taken Peggy to the airport at Geneva and there — as at the exhibition of French paintings — he had felt completely himself and at home.

Back at the chalet was the incomprehensible language of birds, and the cat with its savage nature, and the cannibal magpies, the cannibal jays.

"If we park here, the car will be in shade tomorrow," he said.

"No, the trees are on the wrong side," Katharine said.

"There must be some shade, no matter which side they're on."

"You would have thought that after years of this, they would either have enlarged the garage," Ramsay remarked to himself, "or built another, or figured out which side of the trees received the morning sun." The car lights were put out, and flashlights distributed. Larch branches pressed on the car windows, white in the night. Katharine sat as the others — Anne and Nanette — got out. Ramsay, holding the door for her, shone his flashlight on her face.

"Do you think much about that girl in Berlin?" she said.

No. He thought of his mother in a camel-hair coat, her legs thrust out, staring straight before her. He said, "Most of the time I never think about her."

"Anne had a conversation with me today," she said. His stomach contracted; his hands were without strength. He released the switch of the pocket light. "Never mind about it," said Katharine. "There's a moon. Anne wants to go to Ascona with Nanette this week. She wants to stay all July. She and Peggy have funny holidays — school in August."

"Are you letting her?"

"Why not?" she said, without looking at him. "She wants to get away from home, which is normal. I told her she could go wherever she liked. She is old enough. I can't . . ."

You can't read her mail forever, he thought.

"What are your plans, Douglas? You can stay as long as you like, I feel there have been too many people around. We've never had a real conversation, have we? I'm afraid you'll have to put up with my cooking in July. I've fired the cook."

The cuckoo, at daybreak, was an interruption to his sleep. He saw the notes — not as notes of music but as a new kind of shorthand. He did not know enough of the shorthand to read the notes, or enough of the new language of reply. He dreamed that everyone was skeletal, while he had got enormously fat. He got up and dressed — by flashlight, to avoid doing battle with insects — and packed, not caring much what he left behind, and stepped out into the garden. Across the front of the house was a carved inscription, naming the builder, and giving a date — 1780 — and reminding Ramsay, or anyone who stopped to read it, that death waits for life. The motto did not belong to this chalet but came from another region. Katharine had bought it and put it there about a year before Moser's last stroke. The chalet — like a bison, like a bear — watched him slip and slide down the path with his two suitcases. He sat down in the station shelter in a state of such lunatic joy at his deliverance that presently he was close to tears.

At the pension he went to in Montreux, a tall, dignified woman wearing a white apron greeted Ramsay. His cases were put in an ice-cold room with a linoleum floor. He looked through the north window at another pension, then at the varnished bed, the eiderdown, the table, and the clean, un-ironed checked cloth. A small Buddha, the only ornament in the room, sat on the chest of drawers. Ramsay picked him up, but no matter how he tried he could not catch Buddha's eye.

"That was left behind," the woman said, "by a Professor Doctor. The meal hours are eight, twelve, and seven. Breakfast in your room will be fifty centimes more. With the prices we charge we cannot afford extras." From the kitchen came a crash of plates and loud cursing. When that died away he heard the soft silent crunching, like silkworms feeding, that came from the dining room, where the others were all at breakfast.

The first thing he unpacked was the unopened box of caramels: Caramels à la crème de Gruyères. He tangled with the Scotch Tape and pulled the box open. It's only fudge, he thought. He did not know what he had been expecting. He ate half the box — Moser's legacy — and felt sick, and drank tap water. "Good thing I left," he told himself, realizing indignantly what he had been driven to. By now they would know he had gone. He had left them up there with the cat and the cannibals. He was down where there were signs of life and work. He found one of the signs in a drawer, left by the Professor Doctor — a drawing of a naked and faceless woman wearing a pearl necklace. At ten he went to a film and watched a pretty German girl mixed up with some man who looked like a toad. But they were all so comfortable and so well dressed, and their problems were real problems, such as money lost and found. He could not sit in the cinema forever, but first things first: his room in the students' residence in Berlin was taken by someone else until July. He said, "Look here, Katharine, I'm not interested in weather and the color of the sky. I hate knowing what the weather is. I don't know what you mean by having inner resources. Are you supposed to recite poems from memory while the whole world dissolves into fog, goes away, and stays gone?" He blinked at the sleepy noon streets, the petunias in tubs, the brown balconies with washing under the eaves. He bought a newspaper and saw a prime minister wearing a miner's helmet. In the middle of the front page, boxed to show its importance, was this:

LES PREMIÈRES FRAMBOISES
Les premières framboises mûrissent
sur la rive droite de la vallée.

He translated everything except *"mûrissent,"* which he could have sworn he had never seen before. He substituted for it "have exploded," which gave the item some stature. He did not know what he was doing here, unless he was waiting for Katharine to come and find him. In the pension dining room he was the victim of provincial staring, because of his youth and his limp. There came the memory of the months he had spent after his accident completely at the mercy of other people, depending on nurses and resenting it. He had always been active, had lived on decisions; he remembered how his parents had respected him, let him make his own choices about what he would study and the life he would lead. He ate steadily grated carrots, meat, potatoes, wet salad, gray bread. A bowl of custard was placed beside him. He spooned some of it onto his plate, where it ran everywhere. Since the orgy of caramels sweets disgusted him. He dreaded the mattress in his room, but it was only for a night. In the morning he would take the train to Zurich and from there fly to Berlin. His room there was taken, and his girl had vanished — she was too old for him anyway. "Listen, Sabine," he had said, "is the guy really a prince?" No, only his bodyguard. But I ruined it anyway with *'shalom.'*" Ramsay laughed. "Is not funny," Sabine said. She showed him what remained of the railway station where both her parents were killed. "Who cares?" she said, meaning "Do you?"

Two days later he was still there. He looked at the sky, the blue on the horizon, the gray, then the pink. When he entered his room, mist arose outside the window as if it had been lying waiting for him to approach. One night in the dining room he started up from the table, thinking she had come. Katharine in her silk dress could save him from everything mediocre, commonplace, vile, and poor. The room was filled with solemn English couples; the women wore heavy white shoes and yards of stoles. Katharine might enter this room, warm and inquisitive, as if it were a new experience. It was not new: "He used to go for walks and be lost or tired, and then he would get some farmer to ring her." In the pension dining room, television accompanied their supper. Chairs were arranged so that everyone faced in the same direction. A girl who looked like Sabine lay on a piano and sang. Every few seconds, though the song continued without interruption, the girl wore different clothes. Now she stood with her hand on the pianist's shoulder; he looked up into her eyes, and the pair posed that way. The screen went blank, but the sound continued. They listened to a chorus from *West Side Story*, in a foreign language. Everyone looked at the empty, glowing screen, across which sticks and marbles moved, ran together, parted. Faces were lifted, for the set was high on a corner shelf. Again he thought Katharine had arrived. Nothing had happened. The screen had not changed, and the sound was nearly gone.

Early in July, in his old room in Berlin, Ramsay opened the letters that had been kept for his return. There was a letter from Katharine, written at the end of May, that must have arrived the day he departed for Switzerland. The great conductor's widow wrote that now the rain had stopped. She had seen young Italians in spotless shirts hanging about waiting for the cinemas to open — their Sundays were sad. On the promenades, by the lake, in the towns, couples are strolling. The sky changes color; the girls' white skirts are flattened against their legs. The lake is harsh-looking. The wind shakes the trees. Flower petals are strewn on the grass, and it is like the end of a season instead of the beginning. This was a letter written before she had ever met him. He felt buoyant and lightheaded tearing it to shreds. He was amazed at how simple it became. He was not sure if he had left Sabine, for example, or if she had rejected him. She had said, "Oh, I like you, but now is enough," spitting grape seed into her palm; but Ramsay had his ticket to Switzerland, bought that very day. What his father would like would be to start again, to arrive at Bonaventure, but how can he? The station is no longer there. "Lamb of God, Sheep of God," sings a woman, and the Sally Ann band is nearby. Very attractive, very nostalgic, he said to the remains of Katharine's letter, but what about the pension and the smell of mediocrity? What about your cook in the kitchen, with frightened eyes? We drove slowly, because Katharine had seen a white orchid somewhere. Did anyone dare say this was a waste of time? The orchid was a straggly poor thing with sparse anemic flowers . . . Surely he had passed a test safely and shown he was immune to the inherited blight?

Only afterward did he think that he might be mistaken, but that day, the day he arrived in Berlin, he was triumphant because he sat with his back to the window and did not know or care what the weather was like outside.

VIRUS X

1

A bunch of holly hanging upside down at the entrance to her hotel was the first thing Lottie Benz saw in all of Paris that seemed right to her. Even a word like "hotel" was subject to suspicion, since it was attached to a black façade in no way distinguished from the rest of the street. The people walking on the street did not look as if they had sisters or brothers or childhood friends, and their clothes and haircuts in no manner indicated to her a station in life. The New Look had spread from this place, but none of the women appeared to have given it a thought. As for the men, alike in their gray raincoats, only their self-absorbed but inquisitive faces kept them from seeming unemployed. Lottie, whose mother had made the dress she was wearing from a Vogue pattern, could have filled the back seat of her taxi with polka dots, the skirt was so wide. Stepping down, she shook order into the polka dots and her mother's ankle-length Persian-lamb coat, lent for the voyage. That was when she saw the holly. Even as the taxi-driver plucked every bit of change from her outstretched hand, she turned to this one familiar thing. A city that knew about holly would know about Christmas, true winter, everything.

That day, which was Tuesday, December 9, 1952, was laid on with a light brush. The street had been cut out of charcoal-colored paper with extremely fine scissors. Lottie had come here out of a tempest of snow. She drew a breath of air that seemed mild — her first breath of Paris. It swept into her lungs and was immediately converted into iron. She withdrew her hand, relieved of its francs, and pressed it against her chest.

Two boys passed her, walking in step, without a glance at Lottie stranded, the taxi grinding out and away, or the bags the driver had dumped upon the curb. One boy said to the other, in an American accent, "If people depress you, why do you bother seeing them?" The iron weight shifted as she bent to pick up her suitcases. An old man in porter's uniform watched Lottie through the frosted glass door. His eye appeared as part of the pattern of lilies etched on the glass, and then his nose. He consented to hold open the door. Lottie offered him a tip, which he pocketed. She had been advised to tip for consideration, however slight, no matter how discourteously shown. In a place where Americans were said to be hated because of the Korean War, she intended to put up a show for her own country, which was Canada. She smiled. The hotel, or France, personified by the woman at the desk with frizzy red hair, did not care. Lottie conveyed with a second smile that it was of no importance.

For the first time in her life she was compelled to put her name to a police questionnaire. Bending over the form, she wrote "Charlotte Maria," and wanted to put "Lottie" in brackets, but there was no room. Her home address — the Princess Pat Apartments, in Winnipeg — also seemed to want explaining. She could have written reams of explanation about everything, had there been space. She imagined a policeman reading her answers attentively. Next to "Profession" she wrote "none yet." The woman with frizzy hair made her cross this out and write "student" in its place. Lottie gave up the questionnaire, and with it her new blue passport.

Three messages awaited her. First, a letter from her mother, written four days before Lottie left home. Though sent with loving intention, so that Lottie would have news the instant she arrived, it contained no news. As for Kevin, he had cabled, "MISS YOU ALREADY LOVE," a few hours after her plane took off. Supposing he discovered twenty hours later that he did not miss her at all? She examined the cable gravely. The last message was from a girl named Vera Rodna. It welcomed Lottie to Paris, and gave a telephone number. Upstairs, in her ice-cold, beige-colored hotel room, Lottie tore all three messages across, then found there was no wastebasket.

A sunbeam revealed dust on the window and dust on the floor but, curiously, none in the air. (Perhaps in this place they deliberately allowed dust to settle. Was this better? Better for Lottie — for her asthma, her chronic bronchitis, her fragile lungs?) The bed, the cupboard containing a washbasin, the wardrobe that contained one bent wire hanger were all clean. There were no pillows, window shades, towels, or drinking glass. There were any number of mirrors, however, evenly shaded with dust, and velvet curtains that she accepted as luxurious.

Wondering why she was noticing so much, checking herself lest she become introspective or moody, she remembered that this was the first time she had ever been anywhere alone. The notes she was taking mentally were for future letters — the first to Dr. Keller, her thesis director, the second most likely for Kevin. She unpacked her new cake of Palmolive, her toothbrush, her unworn dressing gown with rose-pink petal neckline. A hot bath, she learned, from a notice posted on the back of the door, would cost three hundred and sixty francs, which was more than a dollar. Lottie was to live on a Royal Society scholarship, supplied out of Canadian funds frozen abroad. Any baths from now on would be considered pampering. She intended to profit from this winter of opportunities, and was grateful to her country for having provided it, but in no sense did she desire to change or begin a new life.

By Sunday the weather in the street was the weather of spring. The iron of the first breath had disintegrated, vaporized. At the bottom of her lungs was a pool of mist. She reminded herself that back home the day had not begun. The city she had left was under snow, ransacked by wind, and on the dark side of the globe. She was not homesick.

Vera Rodna, whose message had so quickly been turned into paper scrap, came to the hotel one day when Lottie was visiting the "Mona Lisa." She left a new letter, this time asking Lottie to come to lunch, and she indicated the restaurant with a great X on a map. *"Une jeune fille très élégante,"* the frizzy redhead down at the desk remarked. Lottie had to smile at that. No one here could know that Vera was only a girl from Winnipeg who had flunked out of high school and, on a suspicion of pregnancy, been shipped abroad to an exile without glamor. Some of the men in her family called themselves Rodney, and at least one was in politics. End syllables had been dropped from the name in any case, to make it less specifically Ukrainian. Vera had big hands and feet, a slouching walk, a head of blond steel wool. The nose was large, the eyes green and small. She played rough basketball, but also used to be seen downtown, Sunday-dressed, wearing ankle-strap shoes. Vera had made falsies out of a bra and gym socks — there were boys could vouch for it. In cooking class it turned out that she thought creamed carrots were made with real cream. She didn't know what white sauce was because they had never eaten it at home. That spoke volumes for the sort of home it must be.

Lottie accepted Vera's invitation, though there was no real reason for them to meet. Having been raised in the same city did not give them a common past. Attempting to impose a past, beginning with a meal in a restaurant, Vera would not establish herself as a friend from home, if that was what she was trying to do. But Vera, being Ukrainian, and probably no moron in spite of her scholastic and morals records, would have enough sense to know this.

The restaurant was an Italian place on the Rue Bonaparte. Wavy, sooty dust masked the wall paintings except for a corner where someone had been at work with a sponge. There Vera waited, backed up by frothing geraniums and blue-as-laundry-bluing seas. Ashes, Sunday papers, spilled cigarettes, and bread crumbs gave her table the look of an unswept floor. Vera's eyes tore over Lottie, head to foot, gardenia hat to plastic overshoes. She said, in a full voice that all at once became familiar and a second later had never been forgotten, "Well, this is great. Sit down."

"This is very nice," said Lottie neutrally.

"It's not bad. I've tried most of them."

Lottie had not meant the restaurant but the occasion of their meeting. Vera began to wave at a waiter and also to talk. She sloshed wine from a bottle that was nearly empty into a glass that seemed none too clean, and pushed this at Lottie. "Some rich bastard's Chambertin," she said. "Might as well lap up the dregs."

Lottie lifted the glass and sipped, and put it down forever, having shown she was game. She said, "How did you know I was in Paris, Vera?"

"My mother, from my sister Frannie. Fran's in your father's math-and-Latin. She's smart — makes up for me."

The name Frannie Ronda conveyed nothing, and Lottie accepted with some pride and some melancholy that she was now part of an older crowd.

"By the way, what are you doing here, exactly?" Vera asked. She was dressed in a black-and-brown checked cape, and a wool hat pulled straight down to her eyebrows. She may have been quite smart by local standards, which undoubtedly she knew about by now, but Lottie could not help thinking how hunkie she looked. Vera's crocheted gloves fell off the table. Her hands looked as if they could easily deal with the oilier parts of a motorbike. "Whadja say?" said Vera, after fishing round for her gloves.

"I *said*, Vera, that my *professor*, Dr. *Keller*, is *from* Alsace, and that's the reason I'm going there. My thesis is about the integration of minority groups without a loss of ethnic characteristics."

"Come again?" Vera's elbows were planted in ashes and crumbs. She turned from Lottie to deal with the waiter, and ordered an unknown something on Lottie's behalf.

"Like at home," Lottie said, when the waiter had left. "Vera, you do know. That's the strength of Canada, that it hasn't been a melting pot. Everybody knows that. The point is, I'm taking it as a good thing. Alsace is an example in an older civilization. With Dr. Keller's contacts in Strasbourg . . . Vera, don't stare just on purpose; I do find it unpleasant. I'll give you a simple example. Take the Poles." Delicacy with regard to Vera's possible feelings prevented her saying Ukrainians. "The Poles paint traditional Easter eggs. Right? They stop doing it in the States after one generation, two at most. In Canada they never stop. Now do you see?"

Vera was listening to this open-mouthed. Lottie felt she had sounded stupid, yet the idea, a favorite of Dr. Keller's, was not stupid at all. She knew it was a theory, but she was taking it for granted that it could be applied. If it could not, let Vera prove it. Vera closed her mouth, drew her lips in between her teeth, let go her breath, and when all that was accomplished said, "You crazy or something?"

"Think whatever you like."

"Do you even know what a minority is?"

"I ought to," said Lottie, and she took the bread and began peeling off the crust, after cracking its surface with her nails.

"You don't. It was always right to be what *you* are."

"Oh, was it, now?"

An explanation for Lottie's foolishness suddenly brightened Vera's face. She clasped her hands, her big mechanic's hands, and cried, "Keller's in love with you! He's meeting you in Alsace."

"He's got a wife and everything. Children, I mean. Honestly, Vera!"

"I think everybody's in love," said Vera, and indeed looked as if she thought so. "Who is it, then? Still Kevin?"

"Yes, still."

"You're going to be away, in Alsace or someplace? That's taking a chance." She seemed to be fumbling over something in her mind, perhaps a memory of Kevin. "I guess you needn't worry," she said. "You've kept him on the string since you were sixteen. You'll bring it off."

"What do you mean, Vera, 'bring it off'?"

Vera looked as if Lottie should know what she meant. A platter of something strange was placed between them. Vera dug into a bone full of marrow, extricated the marrow, and spread it over a mound of rice. It might have been dog food.

"Delicious," said Vera with her mouth full. "Know one thing I remember, Lottie? You used to choose the meals at home, and your brothers had to eat whatever you happened to like. That's what they told around, anyway."

Lottie, surprised at Vera's knowing about this, said, "Everybody favors girls."

"Boy, my father didn't," said Vera. "He kind of respects me now though. Your father used to scare me even more than my own. His voice was just a squeak when he got mad. You could hear every word, but the voice was up around the ceiling. When he told my father I wasn't college material, and not even high-school material, his voice sounded artificial. You take after him a little, but your voice just gets slower and slower. Your father was a fine man, all the same. Old Captain Hook."

Mr. Benz had been called Captain Hook by his pupils, but there was a further matter, which Vera did not mention — Captain von Hook. That was an old wartime joke. You would have thought the mean backwash of war could never have reached them there, in the middle of another country.

Lottie said with slow care, "How is your brother, Vera, the one who went into politics? Wasn't there some kind of row about him? Honest Stan Rodney?"

"Honest slob. Listen, what are you doing over Christmas? I'm going to Rome. I've got this friend there. He's from home, but you don't know him. He's a Pole. Far as I know, he doesn't paint any Easter eggs. I used to think he was a spy, but he turned out to be a teacher. Slav lit. *When* he's working. Boy, the trouble *he* gets into." Vera's admiration for the trouble made her go limp. "Do you want to do something in Paris before I go? See a play or something? You've been up the Eiffel Tower, I suppose. I like going up and looking down. You see this shadow like a kind of basket, when there's any sun. There's Versailles and that. Euh, Fontainebleau . . . boring. Katherine Mansfield's grave, how about that? Remember Miss Pink? She fed us old Mansfield till it ran out of our ears. She's buried around Fontainebleau. Mansfield is, not Miss Pink." Vera laughed with her mouth wide.

"She was my favorite author until I specialized," said Lottie primly. "Then, I'm sorry to say, I had to restrict my reading."

Vera dug into her rice as if looking for treasure. "Right," she said. "We'll go out to the grave." Lottie consented to nothing of the kind.

Vera must have mistaken Lottie's silent refusal, for the next Saturday, at half past ten, she turned up while Lottie was still in bed.

Lottie had been out with a cousin of Kevin's, who worked at the Embassy. He had made her pay for her own drinks, as if they were still students having cafeteria coffee. Lottie was puzzled by the bar he took her to, full of youngish American men, and even more by the hateful, bitter singer at the piano. Kevin's cousin seemed to feel that she had no right to criticize anything, having only just arrived, though he himself never stopped complaining. His landlord was swindling him; he was sick of dark rooms and gas heaters. He blamed Paris for its size. Until now he had lived in a house, never in a flat. His accent shot from one extreme of broad vowels to the opposite. He did not want to sound American but looked it. In the bar full of crew cuts, he matched any one of them except in assurance. Toward the end of the night, he began bemoaning his own Canadian problems of national identity, which Lottie thought a sign of weakness in a man. Moreover, she learned nothing new. What he was telling her was part of Dr. Keller's course in Winnipeg Culture Patterns. She had wasted the government's money and her own time.

Vera said she was leaving for Rome, which she called Roma, any minute. Slumped over an ashtray on the foot of Lottie's bed, she urged an excursion to Fontainebleau. It was a lovely sunny day — just the weather for visiting graveyards. Sleepy and pale, caught with curlers in her hair, Lottie rose and dressed, turning her back. Vera scarcely allowed her time to brush her teeth. They were doomed to catch, and they caught, the Lyon noon express. The train was filled with *hommes d'affaires,* who had all the seats. Lottie stood crushed against a window, looking at the backs of towns. She was cold, and speechless with hunger. After Melun she began to feel calmer, and less hungry and unwashed. Trees such as she had never seen before, and dense with ivy, met and glided apart in the window light. Touching the windows, she felt a thin cool film of sunlight. The ivy shone and suddenly darkened, as if a shutter had been swung to. Lottie forgot she had asthma, chronic colds, low blood pressure, and that Vera would regret this.

"I always thought I was going to die at the same age as Mansfield," she remarked to Vera. "I may still."

"Not the same way."

"At my age, you already know what you're going to die of." Lottie was thirteen months older than Vera, who would be twenty-one in February. Unspecified illnesses of a bronchial nature had kept Lottie out of school for months on end. A summer grippe only last August had prevented her coming over here in September.

"You used to wear those hand-smocked dresses," Vera suddenly chose to recall.

"A friend of Mother's made them," said Lottie, and closed a door on that with her tone of voice. Though ignominiously clothed then, she had been small for her age, and almost unnoticeable in the classes of children younger than herself. She skipped grades, catching up, passing, but no one praised her. They said Captain Hook had helped.

Vera explained her commitment to Mansfield, which was an old crush on Miss Pink. It had led Vera to read this one writer when she never read anything else, or wanted to. Now that she was away from the Miss Pinks of this world, she read all the time.

Lottie's transparent reflection was ivy green. "Do you think I look weak?" she asked, meaning that she wanted her health kept in mind.

Vera, who was tall, caught Lottie's face at an angle Lottie had never seen. "Weak, in a way," she said, "but not frail." Lottie's reflection went smug. Vera, squinting down and sideways, looked as if she thought weakness could not account for everything.

When they alighted at the station, Vera consulted a taxi-driver, whose head was a turtle's between muffler and cap. Showing off in French, she seemed to think the driver would think she was French and take them to a gem of a restaurant. Lottie felt cold and proud. She would not mention her low blood pressure. Actually, she was supposed to drink tea or coffee almost the minute she wakened; her mother usually brought it to her in bed. She had never fainted, but that was not to say she never would. Their driver rushed them up a dirt road and abandoned them before a billboard upon which was painted in orange "RESTAURANT — BAR — DOLLARS ACCEPTED — PARKING."

"We aren't going to like it," said Vera. "He took you for an American." Nevertheless, she rushed Lottie onward, through a room where an American soldier slept in a leather armchair, past a bar where more soldiers sat as if Saturday drinking were a cheerless command, and into a totally empty dining room that smelled of eggs frying. Not empty: out of the dim corner where he was counting empty bottles came the proprietor of the place, unshaven, clad in an American gabardine. His thick eyelids drooped; he had already seen enough of Vera and Lottie. Vera was tossing her scarf and her cape and saying chummily, "Just an omelette, really — we aren't at all hungry," and then they were in a small room, and the door to the room shut behind them. Here ashes and orange peel spilled out of a cold grate. Three tables pushed against the wall were barricaded behind armchairs, an upright piano, dining chairs, and a cheval glass. The two girls pulled a table and chairs clear and sat down. Lottie had a view of a red clay tennis court strung with Christmas lights. She turned to see what Vera was staring at. Another table was taken, but the noise and confusion coming from it at first seemed part of the chaos in the room. Lottie now saw two American soldiers and two adolescent girls who might be their wives. One of the girls, the prettier of the two, cried out, "But tell me now, am I talking loud? Because I sound to myself like I am talking loud." The laughter from the others was a kettledrum, and Lottie and Vera displayed their first pathetic complicity: "We aren't Yanks," said the look they exchanged.

Dissociating herself and perhaps Lottie from the noisy four, Vera gave their waitress a great smile and a skyrocket of French. "On n'a que ça, les Américains," said the waitress, shrugging. Vera's flashy French, her flashy good will did not endear her. Lottie watched the waitress's face and understood; she didn't like them, either. When Vera praised the small neat lighter she kept in her apron pocket, the waitress said, "C'est un briquet, tout simplement." She served a tepid omelette on cold plates and disappeared into a more interesting region, whence came the sound of men's voices. Lottie and Vera sat on, forgotten.

Vera said, "There should be a thing on the table you could hit that would go cling, cling."

"A bell," said Lottie, taken in. "The thing is a bell."

"*I* know. I was showing you how Al talks." Smoking, Vera told about walks in Roma and meals when she and her Polish friend from home had nothing to eat but hard-as-a-rock cheese. Once, he gave his share to a dog.

"Are you hard up for money, Vera?" Lottie did not mean by this she had any to lend.

"No, not really. But I sort of am when I'm with him. I pretend not to have any at all and live the way he does." Vera was bored; she was always quickly bored. Blowing smoke all over Lottie, she began defending the four Americans. "You've never seen how abominable Canadians can be."

Americans could be trained to set an example, Lottie insisted. They should be loved. Who was to blame if they were not?

Vera mashed her cigarette out on her plate. "D'you know how Canadian soldiers used to cut the Germans' throats?" she said. "Al showed me. You push the helmet like this," and she reached across quick as a snake and pressed the long helmet Lottie Benz would have been wearing had she been a soldier into the nape of her neck and drew her forefinger under Lottie's chin.

Lottie understood that an attempt had been made against her life and that she was safe. She said, "I love my country, Vera, and even if I didn't I wouldn't run it down."

"I'm not running it down. I'm telling you stories."

The bill was nineteen hundred francs. Vera said it was grossly excessive. "They took you for an American," she said. "It's those damned overshoes."

The air outside smelled of earth and eternally wet leaves, as though this place were unmindful of seasons. At the end of a walled lane the walled graveyard was a box. The sky (the sun was covered up now) was the lid. Lottie was still disturbed by Vera's attack. She knew if you show nothing, eventually you feel nothing; presently, feeling nothing, she was just herself, a visitor here — not a guest, because she was paying her way. She walked a pace or two behind Vera, who had taken on a serious and rather reproachful air, sniffing at rusty iron crosses, shaking her head beside a fresh grave covered over with planks. At the only plot of grass in the cemetery, she stopped and announced that this was it. A brownish shrub had been clipped so that it neatly surrounded a stone bench. Someone — now, in December — had planted a border of yellow pansies. Vera, stalking dramatically in her cape, left Lottie to think her thoughts. A restless pilgrim, she slashed at weeds with her handbag and all at once called, "It's not where you are, Lottie. It's over here." Lottie rose slowly from the bench, where she had not been thinking about Katherine Mansfield but simply nursing her several reasons for not feeling well. Where Vera stood, a block of polished granite weighed upon a block still larger. The base was cemented to the ground.

"'Katherine Mansfield,'" Vera droned. "'Wife of John Middleton Murry. 1888–1923. But I tell you, my lord fool, out of this nettle, danger, we pluck this flower, safety.' Well, I don't know what *that* means. Another thing I wish you'd tell me — what is that awful china rose doing there instead of real flowers? It's so puritan. You can't just abandon people that way, under all that granite. It's less than love. It's just considering your own taste."

"She is not abandoned, Vera; she is buried."

The orator heard only herself. "The stone is even moss-resistant," she said. But no, for the first wash of green crept up the granite step and touched a capital "M."

Lottie, whose ears might have been deaf to everything but Vera until now, heard other sounds — a rooster crowing, a sudden rush of motors somewhere, a metallic clanging that certainly had to do with troops. Vera planted one foot upon the step and with more effort than seemed needed removed the rose. She tossed it aside; it landed in the tall grass of another grave. Then she picked a handful of yellow pansies and strewed them where the rose had been. Like all gestures, it seemed to Lottie suspect.

L ottie need never have seen Vera again after this. Vera
departed for Rome, having first turned out her bureau
drawers and left at Lottie's hotel a number of things she did
not require. Lottie still had not looked up all the people to
whom she had been given introductions. She woke up early
each day wondering whom she would be seeing that night.
Despite Vera's remark about overshoes, she went on wearing
hers, and she wore her hats — the gardenia bandeau, the
feather toque with veil, the suède beret — even though
people turned and smiled and stared. Lottie told her new
acquaintances that she had only just arrived and was eager to
get to Strasbourg, where the university library contained
everything she wanted; but she made no move to go. One
mild rainy night, like a night in April displaced, a couple she
had talked to on the plane from Canada invited her to the
Comédie-Caumartin to see Danièle Delorme in an Ibsen
revival. The theatre reminded Lottie of Vera, although she
could not think why. It was stuffy and hot, and had been
redecorated, and it smelled of paint. "We may get a headache from this," Lottie warned. The new friends, whose
name was Morrow, thought she had said something remarkable about the play. The Morrows were dressed as if they had
not planned to spend the evening together — he in tweeds
and flannel, she in a sleeveless black dress with layers of silk
fringe overlapping down the skirt. The bracelets on her arm
jangled. Her hair was short (it had been long on the plane)
and pushed behind the ears. They had both changed since
the journey, but nothing about them seemed definite. Lottie
thought they were not wearing their clothes from home but
new outfits they were trying for effect.

Soon after the lights went down, a quarrel began in the
audience. Groans and hisses and shouts of "*Mal élevé!*"
covered the actors' voices, and the curtains had to be drawn.
The actors tried again, and got on safely until one of them said

how hot it was, upon which the audience began to laugh, a spectator shouted, *"Oui, en effet!"* and threats were exchanged, though no one was struck. Baited by the public, the actors seemed to Lottie too intimate, too involved. She lost the thread of the story and became self-conscious, as though *she* were on the stage.

Languidly, the Morrows glanced about as if they knew people, or expected to know them soon. "I can't imagine why she revived it," Mrs. Morrow said during the interval.

"The sets are dull," said the husband. "The rest of the cast is weak."

Lottie said, "We had better stuff than this in Winnipeg; we had these really good actors from England, and the audience knows how to behave." Why should that make the Morrows so distant, all at once?

The husband was the first to unbend. Forgiving Lottie for her provincialism, he described the play he was over here to write — a murder, and several people who are really all one person. The several persons are either the victim, or the murderer, or a single witness. It was all the same thing.

"What will you be doing apart from that?" said Lottie.

"Nothing. That is what I *am* doing."

There was something fishy about him. He was too old to be a student, yet clearly wasn't working. Did he have money, or what?

"What do you think Ibsen did apart from that?" said the wife, turning her big black-rimmed eyes on Lottie. She held her elbow in one hand and a cigarette holder in the other.

"Nobody knows," said Lottie. "Anyway, goodness, we're none of us Ibsen."

When Lottie called the Morrows at their hotel a day later, Mrs. Morrow said that Lottie was not to take this personally but she and her husband were working hard — she was typing for him — and her husband did not want to spend too much time with Canadians over here. Lottie was not offended. It confirmed her suspicion of fishiness. Nevertheless, she did want to be with someone familiar at Christmas, and so was not displeased when she found a telegram from Vera. The telegram said, "MEET YOU ALSACE SEE LETTER." The letter came two days later. Pages long, it told where and how they were to meet, although not why.

2

Vera was dressed this time in a purple skirt and sweater she said had come from a five-and-ten in Rome. She stood idly, hand on one hip, in the lobby of their hotel while Lottie filled out a questionnaire for the police of Colmar. If her answers varied by so much as a spelling mistake from the answers she had given in Paris, she was sure she would be summoned for an explanation. Vera's hair was thick and straight and blonder than it had been. "Didn't I have a good idea about Christmas?" she said.

"It seemed like a good idea," said Lottie, in the tone of one only prudently ready for anything.

"You couldn't of done any work over Christmas anyway."

"But why Colmar, Vera?"

"You'll see enough of Strasbourg. You might as well look at something else." Lottie let Vera link an arm through hers and guide her out of the hotel into a light-blue evening. The shape of what seemed to be a street of very old houses was outlined in colored lights. Near a church someone had propped a ladder and climbed into a spruce tree to hang tinsel balls. The spire of the church had been lighted as well, but halfheartedly, as if the electrician in charge had run out of light bulbs. Lottie thought, I have not sent Kevin a cable for Christmas.

In the restaurant Vera chose for their dinner that night, she was loud and too confident, and Lottie felt undervalued. She had submitted to a wearing journey from Paris, with a change of trains at Strasbourg. From Strasbourg to Colmar she stood,

her luggage in everyone's way, until she saw a city in a plain as
flat as home, and understood this to be her destination. This
much she let Vera know. What she did not say was how she had
without a trace of fatigue left her luggage in the station at
Strasbourg and gone out to find the cathedral. It was an important element of her thesis, for both Catholic and Protestant
services were held inside; also, Dr. Keller had said something
about an astronomical clock he admired. Flocks of bicycles
swooped at Lottie, more unnerving than the screaming cabs of
Paris. She heard German. Once, she was unable to get directions in French. When the first words of German crossed her
lips, she thought they would remain, engraven, to condemn
her. Speaking the secret language, she spoke in the name of
unknown Grandmother Benz, whom she was said to resemble.
The cathedral seemed to right itself before her — frosty, chalky,
pink and trembling in the snowy air. A brown swift river divided
that part of the city from the station. True Christmas was praised
in shopwindows, with wine and nuts and candied peel. A
gingerbread angel with painted paper face and paper wings cried
of home — not of Winnipeg but of a vestigial ceremony, never
mentioned as German, never confirmed as Canadian. The
Paris promise of Christmas had been nonsense — all but the
holly outside the hotel, and one night someone stole even that.
The cold air and certain warm memories tinged her cheeks
pink. She saw herself without disapproval in a glass. Sometimes
strangers smiled. They were not smiling meanly at her overshoes or her hat. None of this was Vera's business.

Vera chewed on a drumstick, and told what had happened
in Rome. She had found her friend Al Wiczinski living with a
French family in a crummy unheated palazzo. He was adored
by the daughter of the family, aged seventeen, and also by her
father. Al was just too nice to people. But he was coming to
Alsace. ("Coincidence, eh, Lottie?") A college had been
opened for refugees in Strasbourg, and Al had been offered a
teaching job. Politics, in a way, said Vera, but mostly the
culture racket. After all, teaching Slav lit to a bunch of Slavs

was what, culture or politics? Radio Free Europe was running the place. Lottie had never heard of it. Vera glanced at her oddly. Al had been told that he could obtain the visa he needed in Colmar more easily than in Strasbourg, and had sent Vera on to see what she could do. In theory, Al was not allowed to live along any frontier, especially this one.

"Why not?"

"Don't ask me. Ask the police."

"I don't see why a Canadian should have any trouble," said Lottie.

"He's only sort of Canadian," said Vera. "If you ask me, I don't think he should have a passport. I mean, he sort of picks on the place."

"You can't be sort of Canadian. If he is, he doesn't have to be in trouble anywhere."

"Oh, come off it, Lottie," said Vera, smiling at her. "Suppose you had to explain what you were doing here this very minute, what would you say?"

Lottie gave up. Sulking and pale, she let Vera glance at her several times but would not say what the matter was. She thought she had been taken in.

After dinner they walked beside a black gelatinous canal in which stood, upside down, a row of crooked houses. Lottie said, "Sometimes I think I've got no brains."

"You've got brains, all right," said Vera.

"No." Out of the protective dark she spoke to upside-down houses. "I've got a good memory. I can remember anything. But I've never worked on my own."

Lottchen. When she stuffed her mouth full of candy, her mother knew it had been taken without permission, but the boys were scolded instead of the little girl. Why? Oh, yes — they had put her up to it. Captain von Hook told them what he thought of it, in a high and frightening voice. He was meant to be principal of his school, but after 1939 his career was blocked.

The promenade along the canal ended Lottie's first evening in Alsace. She and Vera parted in the hotel lobby — Vera was

going to stay and converse with total strangers in the bar —
and without waiting to see if this was all right with Lottie she
kissed her good night.

On the morning of Christmas Eve, Vera rose at seven and,
after shaking Lottie awake, dragged her — cold, stunned,
already weary — into streets where pale lamps flickered and
aboard a bus filled with pale people asleep. They rolled into
dark hills, which, as the day lightened, became blotter green.
Lottie was not yet accustomed to steep hills and valleys; she
wanted them to be more beautiful than they were. Desolate,
she shut her eyes, believing herself close to a dead faint. She
heard a girl cry, *"C'est épouvantable,"* but it was only because
an elderly Alsatian peasant could not speak French. In the
town of Munster, they descended before a shuttered hotel.
The dining room was closed, glacial — Lottie had a glimpse of
stacked chairs. In the kitchen a maid was ironing sheets, while
another fed two little boys bread in the shape of men with
pointed heads and feet. Vera ordered red wine and cheese for
breakfast, and asked the price of rooms. Lottie wondered why.
The wine stung and burned, the cheese made her lips swell.
One day she would tell Vera about her low blood pressure,
and how her temperature was often lower than normal, too,
and she would let Vera understand how selfish and thoughtless
she had been. On their way out through the courtyard, Vera
banged on a door marked *"Pissoir."* Lottie walked on. "You'll
have to get over being fussy," Vera remarked. Lottie affected
not to hear. She concentrated on the view of Munster, smoke
and blue in a hollow. Above the town a blue gap broke open
the metal sky. They set off downhill over wet earth and
melting snow. Lottie walked easily in her comic overshoes,
but Vera was pitched forward by the heels on her Italian shoes.
They saw no one except a troop of little boys in sabots and
square blue caps who engulfed them, fell silent, giggled after
they had gone by. A snowball struck the back of Vera's cape.
The boy who had thrown it wore rimless glasses and was
absolutely cross-eyed. "Brat," said Lottie, who did not care for

children. But Vera laughed back at him and put out her tongue.

They missed the bus they ought to have taken back to Colmar and had a three-hour wait. Vera pretended it had been planned that way. Tugging at Lottie, she made for a café. Here a Christmas tree gave off fragrance in waves, like a hyacinth. Radio Stuttgart offered them carols. Vera ate a mountain of sauerkraut and ham and sausage and drank a bottle of white wine. "Poor old Al, he's got no one but me, and here it is Christmas Eve!" she said gaily.

Elbows on table, head in her hands, Lottie read a newspaper. "Pinay has resigned," she said.

"No skin off my nose," said Vera.

"It'll skin theirs. He was keeping the franc up." Hearing the carols on the radio, Lottie wished she were religious. It might take her mind off such things as high finance, her own health, and scholarship.

"You know about exchange and all that," said Vera. "I just know when I can't afford to do what I want."

"May I ask, Vera, what you live on?"

"My family, for the moment. But Frannie and my brother Joe will both be in college in about a year and then I'll have to be on my own. The family can't keep all three of us."

"It's good of them to keep you now," said Lottie. "You don't work or anything."

"They get me instead of a holiday in California. I'm their luxury."

"Don't they think you should work?"

"They haven't said," said Vera, grinning. "I'm waiting for the right suggestion. You know where I was this time last year? In Rome. I'd just met Al."

"You've been away a long time," Lottie said. "I could never stay away that long."

"Who wants you to?"

The trouble with Vera was that she was indifferent. She had made Lottie come all the way to Colmar, with a complicated change of trains, and had tramped her up and down the rainy slopes on Christmas Eve, just so that she, Vera, would not feel lonely. Vera whistled with the radio, stopped, and said, "I had a little girl."

"I don't understand you. Oh, I'm sorry. I do."

"She's been adopted."

Lottie said stiffly, "I'm sure she's in a good home."

"I dream she's following me. In the dream I'm not like me. I look like Michèle Morgan. I dream I'm leading her through woods and holding branches so they won't snap back in her face. She could be dead. When it's raining like it was this afternoon, she could be outside, with nobody looking after her."

The only protection Lottie had received until now in her native country was an implicit promise that no one would ever talk this way.

"The family were over here a couple of times. Nothing's changed. They still say, 'Why don't you do something about your hair?' They don't seem to think I'll ever come back, or want to. The doctor who looked after the adoption kept writing to them, '*Il faut lui trouver un bon mari.*' Instead of doing that, they put me in a sort of convent school, and I nearly died. You don't know how it was over here four, five years ago. Now they let me do what I like. I'll find a *mari* if I feel like it. If I don't, too bad for them." Vera at this moment looked despairingly plain.

"It's a sad sort of life for you, Vera. You've been on your own since you were what — seventeen?"

"You feeling sorry for me?"

Feeling sorry had not occurred to Lottie; she was astonished that Vera would think it possible. Feeling sorry would have meant she was not minding her own business. Vera had certainly been away a long time. Otherwise she would never have supposed such a thing.

The next morning at breakfast, in a coffee shop Vera liked because the *croissants* were stuffed with almond paste,

Lottie gave Vera her Christmas present — a leather case that would hold a pack of Gauloises. Vera had nothing for Lottie. She turned the case over in her hand, as if wondering what the occasion was. Lottie, slightly embarrassed, picked up from the leather seat beside her a folded, harsh-looking tract. She spread it on the glass-topped table. It was cheaply printed. In German, it informed its finder that "in the mountains" a Separatist movement that seemed to have died had only been sleeping. Recent injustices had warmed it to life.

"I know all about this," said Vera importantly, snatching it away. Her political eye looked for the printer, and she was triumphant pointing out that the name was absent, which proved that the tract was from a clandestine press.

"Of course," said Lottie, puzzled. "Who else would print it? That's what it's about, a clandestine movement. What I don't understand is, what do they want to separate from?"

"France, you dope," said Vera.

"I know all that," said Lottie, in her slowest voice. "I'm only trying to say that if there are people here who don't want to belong to France, then my proposition doesn't hold water. The idea is, these people are supposed to be loyal but still keep their national characteristics."

"There aren't many. Just a couple of nuts."

"There mustn't even be one."

"It's your own fault for inventing something and then trying to stick people in it." Vera talked, rather rambled on, until the arrival of hot chocolate and *croissants*, when she began to stuff her mouth. Lottie folded the tract with care. A few minutes later she was once more rattling around inside a bus, headed now for Kaysersberg. "Good place for Christmas," Vera decreed, consulting but not sharing a green guidebook she kept in the pocket of her cape.

"You said Colmar was a good place for Christmas!" Lottie said. Vera took no notice of this.

Kaysersberg might have been chewed by rats. The passage of armies seven years ago still littered the streets. They walked away from here and over fields toward another town Vera said would be better. The sun was warm on Lottie's back, and her mother's Persian-lamb coat was a suit of armor. Beside the narrow road, vines tied to sticks seemed to be sliding uphill. It was a trick of the eye. Another illusion was the way the mountains moved: they rose and collapsed, soft-looking, green, purple, charcoal, deserting Lottie when she turned her head. All at once a vineyard fell away, and there for one minute, spread before her, was the plain of the Rhine, strung with glistening villages, and a church steeple here and there poking through the mist. Across the river were dark clouds or dark hills. She could not see where they joined the horizon or where they rose from the plain. So this was the place she loathed and craved, and never mentioned. It was the place where her mother and father had been born, and which they seemed unable to imagine, forgive, or describe.

"Well, that's Germany," said Vera. "I'll have to go over one of these days and get my passport stamped. They didn't stamp it when I came in from Italy, and it has to be done every three months."

Lottie wished she were looking at a picture and not a real place. She wished she were a child and could *pretend* it was a picture. "I'll never go there!" she said.

They walked on and entered Riquewihr in a soft wash of mud that came over the tops of Vera's shoes. "Three stars in the book," said Vera, not even trying to be jaunty anymore. "God, what a tomb! You expect people here to come crawling out of their huts covered with moss and weeds."

"But you've been here, Vera? You said you had been all over."

"I haven't been exactly here. I thought it would be nice for you for Christmas."

Lottie considered briefly the preposterous thought that Vera had not been trying to wear her out but to entertain her. Suddenly, as if it were Lottie's fault, Vera began to complain about the way streets had been in Winnipeg when Vera's mother was a girl. Where Vera's mother had lived, there hadn't been any sidewalks; there were wooden planks. If Vera's mother stepped off a plank, she was likely to lose her overshoe in the gumbo mud. In the good part of town, on Wellington Crescent, there were no pavements either, but for a different reason. When Ukrainian children were taken across the city on digestive airings, after Sunday lunch, to look at Wellington Crescent houses — when their parents had at last lost the Old Country habit of congregating in public parks and learned the New World custom of admiring the houses of people more fortunate than they were — the children, wondering at the absence of sidewalks, were told that people here had always had carriages and then motorcars and had never needed to walk.

Vera was passionate over a past she knew nothing about. It was just her mother's folklore. Vera's mother, Lottie now learned, had washed in snow water. Vera herself could remember snow carried into the house and melted on the kitchen stove.

"Well, then, your father moved the whole family, I suppose," said Lottie, remembering Winnipeg Culture Patterns with Dr. Keller.

"That's right," said Vera, without inflection. "To your part of town."

Lottie had still not sent the Christmas cable to Kevin. Could she send it from here? It was early morning in Winnipeg — scarcely dawn.

L ottie intended to set off for Strasbourg the instant Christmas was over, but Vera gained another day. In the morning they went to see a movie called *Das Herz Einer Frau*, subtitled *Ich Suche Eine Mutti* — an incredibly sad story about a laundress and her little boy. Lottie, exasperated, turned to say something but saw that Vera was wiping tears. Later, she and Vera boldly entered a police station, where

Vera asked questions on Al's behalf. Lottie sat staring at a sign: *"C'est CHIC de parler Français!" "Chic"* was in red.

It was plain that Vera's plans had gone wrong; Al's arrival should have coincided with Lottie's going. Vera did not want to go off to Strasbourg in case he came here, and she did not want Lottie to desert her. She coaxed from Lottie one more excursion, this time not far away. After a mercifully short bus trip, they walked under pines. In these woods, so tame, so gardened, that Lottie did not know what to call them, they stumbled on a ruin covered with moss and ivy. "It is part of the Maginot Line, I think," said Vera.

Lottie, frantic with being where she did not want to be, turned from her and cried, "Is that what it is? The Maginot Line? No wonder they lost the war."

"Is that what Dr. Keller taught you? Why do you think one piece is all of everything?"

"What else can you do?" said Lottie. The mist carried in her lungs since Paris darkened and filled her chest. "You don't understand, Vera. I'm not strong physically. That's what I meant that day on the train, when you said 'weak, not frail.' I *am* frail, and I have to do this thesis on my own. I have to choose my own books and work with people I've never met before. I've never used a strange library. You've made me walk a lot. I've got this very low blood pressure. One day my heart might just stop."

"Yes, well, it was a mistake," said Vera. She folded her arms under her cape and kicked at the Maginot Line instead of kicking herself, or Al, or Lottie.

3

The advantage of Strasbourg over any other place was that Lottie here had a warm room. In a hotel on the Quai des Bateliers, discovered by Vera, she unpacked the notes and files. She could see the spire of the cathedral, encased in scaffolding, rosy and buoyed up on plain air. Chimes and bells evenly punctuated her days and nights. Every night, at a dark foggy hour, she heard strange tunes — tunes that seemed to be trying to escape from between two close parallel lines. The sound came from a shack full of Arabs, across from the hotel, on the bank of a canal. In the next room but one, Lottie had a neighbor, a man who typed. The empty room between them was a sounding box. She heard him talking to himself sometimes and walking about. His step was quick. Vera was also on this floor, at the end of a corridor papered with lettuce-sized roses. Her room gave onto nothing of interest, and her window sill was already a repository for bread, butter, dime-store knives, and old newspapers.

On January 9th, a month to the day after her arrival in France, Lottie wrote her first long letter to Kevin. The post-cards she had sent from Paris and Colmar said, "I am working hard," which was not so, and "It is terribly cold," and "I'm saving it up to tell you when I get back." Her real letters to him were those she composed in her head and was too shy to write. She could imagine him listening to anything she had to tell him but not reading what she wrote. "I went to the opening of the European Assembly in a new prefab building that already looks like a shack, looks left over from the war," she wrote, hoping that this would be a letter of such historical importance he would keep it in a folder. "A sign said that anyone showing approval *or* disapproval would be thrown out. There were hardly any visitors, and I did not have the feeling that history was being made. It was all dry and dull. I listened to the translators through the headphones, but it was more of a strain than just hearing an unknown language. Sort of English-English and bored French. M. Spaak was not there, because he had rheumatism (at least that's what I understood) and just when this was announced I felt the start of a chill and had to rush out and home in a cab. I was shaking so much in my fur coat that Vera was frightened. It's not serious" — she felt her beginning going off the rails — "but I've got a chill and a fever and a bad cough and a pain in my chest and a sore throat. Vera has bought me some pills full of codeine. Vera believes in sweat. A dog that belongs to this hotel, name of Bonzo, came in to see me. I gave him a piece of stale bread and he took it under the bed, with his legs and tail sticking out flat. It suddenly occurred to me today that there is no such thing as sociology. When you are a sociologist, all you can do is teach more of the same, and every professor has his own idea about what it is. Vera says that if I were studying the integration of Indians, which never happened anyway, it would not be called sociology. Vera will take this out to mail."

Lottie could eat nothing until the next day, when, mostly to pacify Vera, she picked at a helping of macaroni and gravy. Vera sat at Lottie's clean table and proceeded to make a mess of it. She drank beer out of a bottle and, when she had drunk all she wanted, poured the rest in the washbasin. "Do you mind the smell?" she asked, too late, peering down. Vera was already on a first-name basis with the whole hotel, and particularly friendly with the man who typed. He was an elderly madman, who had only a week before been released from the mental ward of a military hospital.

"What do you type?" Vera had asked him.

"Poems," he replied, looking at her with one eye. (The other was glass.)

Vera read aloud from *France-Soir* to Lottie, who disliked being read to. "*Le trentième anniversaire de la mort de Katherine Mansfield est célébré aujourd'hui à Avon.*"

"They'll see I got rid of that china rose," said Vera, very pleased.

In the night, Lottie spat blood. It looked bright and pure, like a chip of jewel. She had coughed enough to rupture a small blood vessel. Out of childhood came recollections of monumental nosebleeds, and of the whole family worried. As if to confirm the memory, Vera came bustling in, for all the world like Lottie's mother. She found Lottie lying across the bed with her head hanging back. She closed the window, then covered Lottie with the eiderdown. Lottie was irritated. "I need lots and lots of air," she said. Being irritated brought on an attack of coughing and pain. Vera began opening and closing windows again.

Lottie wanted to write to Kevin, "My coldness to Vera frightens me. She came in again now and was sweet and kind, and I thought I would scream. She smelled of the bar downstairs in the hotel where she likes to hang out eating stale chips and talking to men. She sat on the bed and stroked my pillow saying, 'Isn't there anything I can do for you?' She seems lost and lonely because Al hasn't turned up. She offers all the kindness she can in exchange for something I don't want to give because I can't spare it. A grain of love? Maybe the Pole, Al, is hell. It is not my fault. I shrank into myself, cold, cold. We are all like that. So are you, Kevin. Finally I said, 'Vera, would you mind awfully opening the window?' and she aired the room (she likes doing that) and held her cape so as to protect me from the draft. She looked around for something else to do. 'I'll go and complain about that washbasin,' she said. 'Yes, do go,' I said. I wanted to be left alone. She felt it, and went away looking as if she would never understand why."

This composed, but not written, Lottie dragged herself from her bed and down the rose-papered hall to Vera's room, on an impulse, to say something like "You were kind," but Vera's door was locked. She thought she heard Vera whispering to someone — or else she heard the curtains moving, or the rustle of the papers Vera kept on her window sill.

"Even when I am nice to Vera," she finished the letter, "it doesn't mean anything, because I don't honestly like her."

Vera had complained about the washbasin and then proceeded to the post office to collect her mail. She and Lottie were both using poste restante, because they thought the Quai des Bateliers was temporary. Lottie wanted to get into a students' residence where she would meet interesting people, and Vera was waiting for Al. He was in Paris now — he seemed to be approaching in stages and halts, like a traveller in an earlier century — and had sent, along with his photograph, a letter full of requests and instructions. Lottie looked at a round face and enormous dark eyes with fixed, staring pupils. He seemed drugged or startled. "His eyes are blue," said Vera. "They look dark with that fancy lighting. I've been out to the refugee college, asking around. He's got it all wrong. It's only a dorm. They go to the university for classes. It sounded funny in the first place, teaching Slav lit to Slavs. Maybe he's found something else to do. Or not to do, more like it. He's got in with some Poles who live outside Paris and do weaving. They may also have prayer and patriotic evenings. Right Wing Bohemia," said Vera, looking down her large nose, "lives in the country and weaves its own skirts. *You* know." Over Lottie's cringing mind crept the fear that Vera might be some sort of radical. Ukrainians were extreme one way or another. You would have to know which of the Uke papers Vera's parents subscribed to, and even that wouldn't help unless you could read the language. "Get this," said Vera, and, adopting a manner Lottie assumed must be Al's, she read aloud, "'You cannot imagine what a change it is for me — yesterday *le grand luxe* in Roma, today here. But I must say, even though I have the palate of a gourmet, I find nothing wrong with the cooking.'"

"He just doesn't sound Canadian," Lottie said.

"In the evening the old man came to my room," composed Lottie, introducing the old man to Kevin without warning. "He stood in the doorway, with his battered face and his one eye, and said, 'I am going to write a poem about Canada in honor of you and your friend Mademoiselle Vera. In which city is there a street called Saint-Jean-Louis?'"

"In the first place," Lottie had said earnestly, "is there any such saint?"

"Could it be in Winnipeg?" the old man said.

"No, Quebec." She recalled crooked streets, and one street where the houses were frozen and old; over the top of a stone wall had bloomed a cold spring tree . . . But I was never in Quebec, she remembered next.

There was no transition from day to night. She heard him typing, like someone dropping china beads one by one. She coughed, and put the pillow over her face. If he comes in and talks about the poem again, she thought, it might make me homesick. If something made me homesick I might cry and that could break the fever. If something could make me homesick, I would go home and not wait for someone to come and fetch me. But when she wanted to think of home, she thought of a church in Quebec, and a dark recess where the skull of General Montcalm, preserved by Ursuline nuns, and exposed by them, rested in a gold-and-glass cage. But I have never seen it — someone described it to me. It has nothing to do with home. Her eyes filled with tears, but not of home-sickness.

A mounting litter of paper handkerchiefs and empty yoghurt jars spilled out of the paper carton Vera had put beside Lottie's bed. "À *quoi bon?*" said the hotel maid when Lottie asked her to empty the box. The maid was not obliged to clean a room unless the tenant went out. It was a rule. Bribed, she said she would see about the washbasin but nothing more.

Lottie wanted to give the old man something better than an imaginary street for his poem, but now the idea of a city she had not seen obscured her memory. "What, do you mean you were never there?" he might ask if she told him she had never been to Quebec. "It was a tremendous excursion," she would have to say. "Nobody over here knows how far it was, or how much it would have cost," and tears of self-pity followed the others.

Bonzo, the hotel dog, stole under the bed and tore to pieces a box of matches. Lottie had lost her voice. She whispered, "Bad dog!" and "You'll make yourself very sick!" and on her hands and knees retrieved a slimy piece of wood. She had a high fever now. She knew it by the trouble she had getting back into bed — she could not judge its height — and she saw it reflected on the face of the nurse who had been summoned by Vera. The nurse, a peasant girl in a soiled head scarf, twin sister to the maid in appearance, told Lottie what her temperature was, in a disapproving voice. It was in centigrade and meant nothing.

"*Ma voisine!*" cried the old man, standing in the hall. "It is very warm outside, so warm that one can go out without a coat."

"Good," whispered Lottie. She heard him go out into the bitter day, perhaps without a coat.

She felt well enough to go on with her letter to Kevin: "My neighbor does exercises in the doorway to show me how spry he is. At the end of each one he hops up and stands at attention, giving just one small disciplined bound in place. He is like someone who has done these things for years in a row with other men — in a jail, or a military hospital, or a prison camp, or the Army, or a mental home. In any one, or two, or three . . ."

Lottie and the old man shared a view. At night they heard the iron chimes of the cathedral. At dawn they could see the pink spire briefly red. Inside the cathedral, Death struck the hours in Dr. Keller's clock, and at noon Our Lord blessed in turn each of the Apostles. Every noon — or, rather, at half past twelve, for the clock was half an hour off — the betrayal was announced by a mechanical cock flapping stiff wings. One night the neighbor typed all night, and, talking loudly to himself, went to bed before six, the hour at which the whole clumsy performance of the clock — chariots, pagan deities, signs of the zodiac, days of the week, Christ and the Apostles, the betrayal — finished its round. Lottie understood that night and day were done for before time from home could overtake them. She was dislocated, perhaps forever, like the clock.

The nurse returned next day with a doctor, who said, "It is a little fever."

"What kind?" Lottie asked. Her teeth were chattering. "What about my nosebleeds?"

"A little simple cough. You take yourself too seriously." He wrote out a prescription for three kinds of remedy, which were all patent medicines. Two of the three Vera had already bought. Lottie composed for Kevin: "I imagined — because with a fever you don't know where imagination begins and a dream leaves off — that my mad neighbor had to repaint the outside of the high school. I said, 'Can't the parishioners afford to hire someone?' Isn't it funny, my thinking it was a church?"

Her health improved; she got dressed and walked along the river, with Vera beside her. At the post office was a letter from Kevin, and for Vera a receipt from American Express in Rome for five hundred lire she had left as a deposit for forwarding her mail. This Vera misread as five hundred dollars she had received from home, and even when Lottie pointed out the error she continued to prattle on about what she was going to do with the money. She would take Lottie south! They would visit Al Wiczinski in Paris! Laughing, she picked up a glove someone had dropped on the pavement and put it in her pocket. Lottie was suddenly wildly angry about the glove, as if all the causes Vera had ever given for anger were pale compared with this particular offense. She walked back to the hotel, trembling with weakness and fury, and plotting some sort of obscure revenge.

The letter she had from Kevin began, "I'm fine. Sorry you aren't feeling well." She put it away with the Separatist tract found in the coffee shop. They were documents to be analyzed.

Vera said, "Listen, Lottie, I'm hard up for the moment. No, don't look scared. I'll just pawn something. If you've got anything you could lend me to pawn, that would be great."

"Kevin," Lottie thought she would write, "this morning I bundled all my trinkets into a scarf of Vera's — Granny's pearl and sapphire earrings I can't wear because my ears aren't pierced, and my cameo, which turned out to be worth nothing — and I went with Vera, who was whistling and singing and not worried at all. I had to leave my passport, because they said they were giving me a lot of money — fifteen thousand francs, which I handed to Vera, who took it as if it were a gift. She paid her hotel bill. In the afternoon, she forgot where the money came from and what it was for, and she invited me with a grand air to the Kléber, a big café like a railway station. We drank three thousand and fifty francs' worth of kümmel. Vera also invited the mad party from down the hall. He said he could read English and had been reading the love letters of Mark Twain. The band wore red coats and played 'L'Amour Est un Bouquet de Violettes.' Everywhere you go, you hear that played. The waiters were reading newspapers; there were high ceilings and trays of beer and enormous pretzels. Vera sang with the band. I wonder if I shall ever get my passport back."

Whatever Lottie's fever had been, it had worn itself down to bouts of coughing. Her head was stuffed with felt. When she looked at her old notes or tried to read anything, her eyes shut of their own accord. Without her passport she could not collect her mail. Why had Vera not given up her own? Because, said Vera, astonished at the question, then she would not have been able to get *her* mail, and, as she was expecting money from home, she needed it.

Lottie began to be worried about money. She had spent more than ever planned for on medicines, on the doctor and nurse, on the Christmas holiday in Colmar, which now seemed wild, wine-drenched.

On a cold, foggy winter Saturday, when she could hope for nothing in the post, and could not shake off her cough or rid herself of her pallor, the newspapers finally mentioned an epidemic of grippe that was sweeping through Europe. The symptoms resembled those of pneumonia. The popular name for it was Virus X. There had been two new deaths in Clermont-Ferrand. "Why do they always tell about what happens in Clermont-Ferrand?" said Vera.

She had received three hundred dollars from home. Without making a particular point of it, or showing any gratitude, she returned the fifteen thousand francs. "What I never did understand," she said, as if discussing ancient history, "was why you didn't just take your own money and unpawn your stuff and get your passport back."

Lottie could not make sense of that. The passport had been tied up by Vera, and only Vera could undo the knot.

Vera had also received a birthday box from her sister-in-law, the wife of Honest Stan. It contained aspirin, Life Savers, two cards of snap fasteners, colored ribbon, needles, thread, a bottle of vitamin pills, Band-Aids, and Ivory soap. One aspirin was missing in each tin. "She sends me old clothes sometimes," said Vera, groping at the bottom of the box. "She's from a good old United Empire Loyalist family, true-blue Tory, one-hundred-per-cent Anglo-Saxon taste in clothes." Lottie felt obscurely offended, as if her own taste had been impugned. Kevin was probably Irish, but, being Protestant, he counted as English. Remembering that Vera was a nut who collected lost gloves, Lottie ranged herself and Kevin on the side of Honest Stan's wife. "There," said Vera, with satisfaction, and pulled out a summer frock of blue voile sprigged with roses. It had puffed sleeves and reached midway between Vera's hip and knee. Vera opened the window, shook out the dress, and sent it off. The dress, picked up by the wind, rose and then floated down. The Arab music had begun — it accompanied a certain dark hour of the day — and Vera said the dress was dancing to it.

On Sunday, when the sky was full of bells, and the snow along the canals a blue that was nearly white, Lottie walked with Vera, believing that this was spring. Upon the water was the swift circle of a flight of birds. When the girls looked up from the reflection, the birds were white dots in the sky. Bridges, bare trees, and cobbles passed them, and Lottie, walking on a treadmill, was all at once drenched in sweat, and trembling, and had to lean on Vera's arm. Put to bed, she lay limp, mute, her mouth dry, her hands burning. There was a new electric pain in her lungs. In her mind she wrote to

Kevin, "My thesis is a mess. I haven't done any work, and here it is past the middle of January. Most of the things Keller let me think weren't true . . ."

The firemen's band marching beneath the window played a fat, German-sounding military air. She was like a wooden toy apart at the joints, scattered to the four corners of the room. Each of the pieces was marred. Yet by evening she was suddenly better. She got up again and walked with Vera in the cold, snowy night, dragging Bonzo on the end of a rope. She thought, but did not say, that it was the most beautiful night she had ever seen. She admired, in silence, the lamps in the brown canals and in the icy branches above. Suddenly Vera snatched Bonzo's rope and, cape flying, ran like a streak. Vera could be perfectly happy with or without Al, probably with or without Lottie. The important thing was feeling free, and never being alone.

Only one letter was waiting at the post office when Lottie turned up, passport in hand. Kevin wrote, "A funny-looking girl called Rose Perry has been around this winter. Some friend of yours introduces us saying we have a lot in common because she is a sociologist, like you, and also high Anglican, though I don't know why that gives us something in common. She's around thirty, red hair, funny-looking — I already said that. She's from England, either taking some other degree or just picking up material on the white-collar class in the prairie provinces for her own fun. Now, why couldn't you have done just that and never left home? Rose says the integration idea isn't new. She's been having a hungry winter. Her scholarship isn't a hell of a lot, and it's in pounds, not dollars. We've had her over to the house."

He likes her, and I know why, Lottie thought. Because she is English. His family will look after her, feed her, find her a place to stay. If I were having a hungry winter, I would be the immigrants' child who hadn't made it. I wouldn't dare have a hungry winter.

The sun shone — a pale sunlight, the first of 1953. Vera

climbed up the spire of the cathedral while Lottie waited below — two hundred-odd steps of winding stone to a snowy platform where pigeons hopped on the ledge, and where eighteenth-century tourists had carved the record of their climb. Up there, Vera heard the piercing screams of a schoolyard full of children. She went up a smaller and older-seeming spiral to the very top, above the cathedral bells, which she could see through windows carved in stone. Ice formed on the soles of her shoes. She was mystically moved, she declared, by the appearance of the bells, which seemed to hang over infinite space.

Walking in Vera's shadow, Lottie thought, I should never have seen her after that trip to Fontainebleau.

The days were lighter and longer. The rivers and canals became bottle green, and the delicate trees beside them were detached from fog. Vera and Lottie went often to the Grande Taverne de Kléber. When Lottie had enough kümmel to drink, Vera made sense. On one brilliantly sunny day, two girls came in the Kléber laughing the indomitable laughter of girls proving they can be friends, and Lottie said, "Look, Vera, that is like you and me." Presently they got up and changed cafés, moving by this means four streets nearer the hotel. The table here was covered with someone's cigarette ash — someone who had been here for a long time. There was in the air, with the smell of beer and fresh coffee, a substance made up of old conversations. The windows were black and streaked with melted snow. Each rivulet reflected the neon inside.

"Let's go over to Germany," Vera said for the second time. "It's nothing — just another bus ride. Maybe a train this time. All I have to do is get my passport stamped and come right back. It's just like crossing a road."

"Not for me it isn't."

Falling asleep that night, Lottie heard, pounding outside her window, a steam-driven machine the Arab workers had somehow got their hands on but could not operate. They sounded as if they were cursing each other. The sounds of Strasbourg were hard and ugly sometimes: trams and traffic, and in the night drunken people shouting the thick dialect.

"Lottie, wake up," Vera said.

Lottie thought she was in a café and that the waitress had said, "If you fall asleep here, I shall call the police." The room was full of white snow light, and Lottie was still clothed, under the eiderdown. Someone had taken off her shoes. She saw a bunch of anemones, red and blue, in a glass on the edge of the hopelessly plugged washbasin. "The nut next door brought us each a bunch of them," said Vera. She was bright and dressed, wearing tangerine lipstick that made her mouth twice as big as it should have been. "You know what time it is? One o'clock. Boy, do you look terrible! Al's just called from Paris. I wonder who paid for *that*? I thought he was calling because it's my twenty-first birthday, but he's just lonely. He wants me to come. I said, 'Why are we always doing something for *your* good? You've already left me stranded in Alsace.' I don't think he ever intended to come. He said. 'You know I need you, but I leave it up to you.' It's this moral-pressure business. Would it work with you?"

"Yes," said Lottie. She lay with her eyes open, imagining Strasbourg empty. How would she go alone to the post office?

"I hate letting him down. He's been through a lot."

"Then go."

"I don't think I should leave you. You look worse than when you had Virus X."

"We'll go out and drink to your birthday," Lottie said. "I'll look better then."

Walking again, crossing rivers and canals, they saw a man in a canoe. The water was green and thick and still. Along the banks the trees seemed bedded out, like the pansies in the graveyard. How rough and shaggy woods at home seemed now! Nothing there was ever dry underfoot until high summer, and then in a short time the ground was boggy again.

"I always felt I had less right to be Canadian than you, even though we've been there longer," Vera said. "I've never understood that coldness. I know you aren't English, but it's all the same. You can be a piece of ice when you want to. When you walked into the restaurant that day in Paris, I felt cold to the bone."

The canoe moved without a sound.

In a *brasserie* opposite the cathedral, where they celebrated Vera's coming of age, smoke lay midway between floor and ceiling, a motionless layer of blue. "I only want one thing for my birthday and there it is," said Vera, pointing to a player piano. Rolls were fed to the piano ("Poet and Peasant," the overture to "William Tell," "Vienna Blood") and not only did the piano keys rise and fall but the circle of violins, upside down, as if reflected, revolved and ground out spirited melodies. Two little lamps with spangled shades decorated the instrument, which the waitress said was German and very old. That reminded Lottie, and she said, "I'll go with you tomorrow, if you want to, to get your passport stamped."

"It's not Moscow, for God's sake," said Vera. "It's only over there."

They stayed after everyone else had gone, and the smoke and the smell of pork and cabbage grew cold. They drank kümmel and made perfect sense.

"But Vera" — Lottie tried to be serious — "what are you going to *do* now that you are twenty-one?"

"I don't know. Find out why one aspirin was missing from each tin."

When they reached the hotel, drunk on friendship and with nothing to worry about but what to do with the rest of the day, Kevin was there. He sat with his habitual patience, in the hotel lobby, wearing his overcoat, reading a stained, plastic-covered, and over-confident bar list — the hotel served only coffee and chips and beer. He was examining the German and

French columns of the menu with equal forbearance; he understood neither, and probably had no desires.

One day, she would become accustomed to Kevin, Lottie said to herself; stop seeing him, as she had nearly grown used to mountains. She thought, crazily, that if it had been Dr. Keller or any other man here to take her away, she would have clung to his hands and wept all over them. He looked so reassuring. She thought, A conservative Canadian type, and the words made her want to marry him. The confidence he assumed for them both let her know that if she had not worked on her thesis it was Dr. Keller's fault; he had prepared her badly. If she had been taken ill, it was because of a virus no one had ever heard of at home. When she saw the shapeless overcoat and the rubbers over his shoes that would make people laugh in Paris, she did not care, and she was happy because he could not read anything but English. That was the way he had to be.

"We can't talk here," she said. "Come upstairs."

"Is it all right?"

"Oh, *they* don't care."

He followed her up the stairs. He was ill at ease. He was worried about the hotel detectives.

"It's a lovely room, Kevin. Wait till you see the view, like a Flemish painting. And so warm. They leave the heat on all night. In Paris . . ."

From the doorway, looking around, he took in the half-drained basin with its greasy rim, the carton she used as a wastebasket, her underthings drying on a wire hanger, the table covered with a wine-stained cloth, the unmade bed. Lottie thought he was admiring her anemones. "My crazy neighbor gave them to me," she said. "The old boy from the military hospital. The one who's been writing the poem for Vera and me."

"No," said Kevin. "You never mentioned him. You mentioned this Vera just once. Then you stopped writing."

"I wrote all the time."

"I never got the letters. One of mine was returned. I guess the mail system here isn't exactly up to date."

"It must have been returned when I was too sick to go to the post office. You have to show your passport."

"I know, but I got just this one letter. If Vera hadn't been writing and telling your mother not to worry, I'd have been over before. It was a long time of nothing — not even a card for Christmas. Vera said how hard you were working, how busy." He left the door ajar but consented to sit on the unmade bed. "So, when I got the chance of a free hop to Zurich, a press flight . . ." He looked as if he would never grow old. The lines in his face might deepen, that was all. "I knew you'd had this flu. That can take a lot out of you."

"Yes. It was good of you to come and see how I was. How long can you stay?"

"One, two days. I don't want to interfere with your work."

Vera had said, "You've kept him on the string since you were sixteen. You'll bring it off." Ah, but it was one thing to be sixteen, pretty but modest, brilliant but unassuming. Her frail health had been slightly in her favor then. She had made the mistake of going away, and she had let Kevin discover he could get on without her. She held his hands and pretended to be as conscious as he was of the half-open door. They had never been as alone as at this moment and might never be again. They were almost dangerously on the side of friendship. If she began explaining everything that had taken place, from the moment she saw the holly in Paris and filled out her first police questionnaire, then they might become very good friends indeed, but would probably never marry.

"What I would like, Kevin — I don't know if you'll think it's a good idea — would be to go back with you. If I stay here, I'll get pneumonia. It's a good thing you came. Vera was killing me."

"Her letters didn't sound like it. Who is she, anyway?"

"A girl from home. A Ukrainian. She got in trouble, and they sent her away. Forget Vera."

"They could have just sent her to Minneapolis," said Kevin.

"Too close," said Lottie. "She might have slipped back."

"I guess you'll be glad to get out of here," said Kevin, as the bells struck the hour. He left her and returned to the hotel near the station, where he had taken a room. He could not rid himself of the fear that there might be detectives.

As she had promised, Lottie accompanied Vera to Germany. Kevin was with them. Once her passport was stamped, Vera thought she would go to Paris and help Al out of whatever predicament he was in, perhaps for the last time. "I liked it in Rome, where it was sort of crazy, but Paris is cold and dirty, and now he's twenty-six," said Vera.

"You mean, he should settle down," said Kevin, not making of it a question, and without asking what Vera imagined her help to Al could consist of.

Vera was hypocritically meek with Kevin, though she smiled when he said "Ukarainian," in five syllables. Lottie saw that if Vera had for one moment wavered, if she had considered going home because Lottie was leaving, the voice from home saying "Ukarainian" had reminded her of what the return would be. That was Vera's labyrinth. Lottie was on her way out. Kevin held Lottie's hand when Vera wasn't looking. He was friendly toward Vera, but protective of Lottie, which was the right imbalance. Lottie guessed he had made up his mind.

They walked on a coating of slush and ice — they had left the sun and the rivers on the other side.

In a totally gray village nothing stirred. Beyond it, on the dirty, icy highway by some railway tracks, they came upon a knot of orphans and a clergyman. The two groups passed each other without a glance. In a moment the children were out of sight. Answering a remark of Kevin's, Vera said they were ten or eleven years old, and unlikely to remember the air raids eight years ago. The sky was low and looked unwashed. On the horizon the dark blue mountains were so near now that Lottie saw where they rose from the plain. "Appenweier" — that was the name of the place. It was like those mysterious childhood railway journeys that begin and end in darkness.

"Are you girls by any chance going anyplace in particular?" said Kevin.

They turned and looked at him. No, they were just walking. Vera was not even leading the way.

"Well, I'm sorry then," said Kevin, "but as the saying goes, I've had it," and he marched them to the bombed station, and onto a train, and so back to France.

If that was Germany, there was nothing to wait for, expect, or return to. She had not crossed a frontier but come up to another limit.

Vera packed some things and left some, and departed for Paris. She and Lottie did not kiss, and Vera left the hotel without looking back. Her room — because it was cheaper — was instantly taken over by the mad neighbor. Kevin spent the evening, supperless, and part of the night with Lottie. Vera also must have been an inhibiting factor for him, Lottie decided — not just the phantom detectives. He might have taken Lottie to his hotel, which was more comfortable, but he thought it would look funny. They had given Vera a day's start. Kevin and Lottie were leaving for Zurich in the morning, and from Zurich flying home. Lottie did not think this night would give her a claim on Kevin, but when she woke, at an hour she could not place — woke because the Arabs were quarrelling outside the window, got up to shut the window and, in the dark, comb her hair — she thought that a memory of it could. Vera had left a parcel of food. If she had not been afraid of disturbing Kevin, she would have spread it on the table and eaten a meal — salami, pickles, butter, and bread, half a bottle of Sylvaner.

Kevin now rose, obsessed by what the people who owned the hotel might be supposing. He smoked a cigarette, refused the wine, and put on his clothes. He and Lottie were to meet next morning at the station; there was some confusion about the time. Kevin remarked, with a certain pride, that as far as he was concerned it was now around seven at night. He had brought a travelling clock to lend to Lottie so that she could wake up in plenty of time to pack. He set it for six, and placed the clock where she could reach it.

Lottie made a list not of what she was taking but of what she was leaving behind: food, wilted anemones, medicine, all Vera's residue as well as her own. The hotel maid would have a full day of it, and could not get away with saying "À quoi bon?" Lottie could not make herself believe that someone else would be sleeping in this room and that there would be no trace of Lottie and Vera anywhere. She rose before the alarm rang, and stood at the window with the curtain in her hand. She composed, "Last night, just at the end of the night, the sky and the air were white as milk. Snow had fallen and a thick low fog lay in the streets and on the water, filling every crack between the houses. The cathedral bells were iron and muffled in snow. I heard drunks up and down the sidewalk most of the night."

This could not be a letter to Kevin; he was there, across the city, and had never received any of the others. It was not a letter to anyone. There was no sense to what she was doing. She would never do it again. That was the first of many changes.

IN YOUTH
IS PLEASURE

My father died, then my grandmother; my mother was left, but we did not get on. I was probably disagreeable with anyone who felt entitled to give me instructions and advice. We seldom lived under the same roof, which was just as well. She had found me civil and amusing until I was ten, at which time I was said to have become pert and obstinate. She was impulsive, generous, in some ways better than most other people, but without any feeling for cause and effect; this made her at the least unpredictable and at the most a serious element of danger. I was fascinated by her, though she worried me; then all at once I lost interest. I was fifteen when this happened. I would forget to answer her letters and even to open them. It was not rejection or anything so violent as dislike but a simple indifference I cannot account for. It was much the way I would be later with men I fell out of love with, but I was too young to know that then. As for my mother, whatever I thought, felt, said, wrote, and wore had always been a positive source of exasperation. From time to time she attempted to alter the form, the outward shape at least, of the creature she thought she was modelling, but at last she came to the conclusion there must be something wrong with the clay. Her final unexpected upsurge of attention coincided with my abrupt unconcern: one may well have been the reason for the other.

It took the form of digging into my diaries and notebooks and it yielded, among other documents, a two-year-old poem, Kiplingesque in its rhythms, entitled "Why I Am a Socialist." The first words of the first line were "You ask . . .," then came a long answer. But it was not an answer to anything she'd wondered. Like all mothers — at least, all I have known — she was obsessed with the entirely private and possibly trivial matter of a daughter's virginity. Why I was a Socialist she rightly conceded to be none of her business. Still, she must have felt she had to say something, and the something was "You had better be clever, because you will never be pretty." My response was to take — take, not grab — the poem from her and tear it up. No voices were raised. I never mentioned the incident to anyone. That is how it was. We became, presently, mutually unconcerned. My detachment was put down to the coldness of my nature, hers to the exhaustion of trying to bring me up. It must have been a relief to her when, in the first half of Hitler's war, I slipped quietly and finally out of her life. I was now eighteen, and completely on my own. By "on my own" I don't mean a show of independence with Papa-Mama footing the bills; I mean that I was solely responsible for my economic survival and that no living person felt any duty toward me.

On a bright morning in June I arrived in Montreal, where I'd been born, from New York, where I had been living and going to school. My luggage was a small suitcase and an Edwardian picnic hamper — a preposterous piece of baggage my father had brought from England some twenty years before; it had been with me since childhood, when his death turned my life into a helpless migration. In my purse was a birth certificate and five American dollars, my total fortune, the parting gift of a Canadian actress in New York, who had taken me to see *Mayerling* before I got on the train. She was kind and good and terribly hard up, and she had no idea that apart from some loose change I had nothing more. The birth certificate, which testified I was Linnet Muir, daughter of Angus and of Charlotte, was my right of passage. I did not own a passport and possibly never had seen one. In those days there was almost no such thing as a "Canadian." You were Canadian-born, and a British subject, too, and you had a third label worth no consular reality, like the racial tag that on Soviet passports will make a German of someone who has never been to Germany. In Canada you were also whatever your father happened to be, which in my case was English. He was half Scot, but English by birth, by mother, by instinct. I did not feel a scrap British or English, but I was not an American either. In American schools I had refused to salute the flag. My denial of that curiously Fascist-looking celebration, with the right arm stuck straight out, and my silence when the others intoned the trusting ". . . and justice for all" had never been thought offensive, only stubborn. Americans then were accustomed to gratitude from foreigners but did not demand it; they quite innocently could not imagine any country fit to live in except their own. If I could not recognize it, too bad for me. Besides, I was not a refugee — just someone from the backwoods. "You got schools in Canada?" I had been asked. "You got radios?" And once, from a teacher, "What do they major in up there? Basket-weaving?"

My travel costume was a white piqué jacket and skirt that must have been crumpled and soot-flecked, for I had sat up all night. I was reading, I think, a novel by Sylvia Townsend Warner. My hair was thick and long. I wore my grandmother's wedding ring, which was too large, and which I would lose before long. I desperately wanted to look more than my age, which I had already started to give out as twenty-one. I was travelling light; my picnic hamper contained the poems and journals I had judged fit to accompany me into my new, unfettered existence, and some books I feared I might not find again in clerical Quebec — Zinoviev and Lenin's *Against the Stream*, and a few beige pamphlets from the Little Lenin Library, purchased second hand in New York. I had a picture of Mayakovsky torn out of *Cloud in Trousers* and one of Paddy Finucane, the Irish R.A.F. fighter pilot, who was killed the following summer. I had not met either of these men, but I approved of them both very much. I had abandoned my beloved but cumbersome anthologies of American and English verse, confident that I had whatever I needed by heart. I knew every word of Stephen Vincent Benét's "Litany for Dictatorships" and "Notes to be Left in a Cornerstone," and the other one that begins:

They shot the Socialists at half-past five
In the name of victorious Austria . . .

I could begin anywhere and rush on in my mind to the end. "Notes . . ." was the New York I knew I would never have again, for there could be no journeying backward; the words "but I walked it young" were already a gate shut on a part of my life. The suitcase held only the fewest possible summer clothes. Everything else had been deposited at the various war-relief agencies of New York. In those days I made symbols out of everything, and I must have thought that by leaving a tartan skirt somewhere I was shedding past time. I remember one of those wartime agencies well because it was full of Canadian matrons. They wore pearl earrings like the Duchess of Kent's and seemed to be practicing her tiny smile. Brooches pinned to their cashmere cardigans carried some daft message about the Empire. I heard one of them exclaiming, "You don't expect me, a Britisher, to drink tea made with tea bags!" Good plain girls from the little German towns of Ontario, christened probably Wilma, Jean, and Irma, they had flowing eighteenth-century names like Georgiana and Arabella now. And the Americans, who came in with their arms full of every stitch they could spare, would urge them, the Canadian matrons, to stand fast on the cliffs, to fight the fight, to slug the enemy on the landing fields, to belt him one on the beaches, to keep going with whatever iron rations they could scrape up in Bronxville and Scarsdale; and the Canadians half-shut their eyes and tipped their heads back like Gertrude Lawrence and said in thrilling Benita Hume accents that they would do that — indeed they would. I recorded "They're all trained nurses, actually. The Canadian ones have a good reputaiton. They managed to marry these American doctors."

Canada had been in Hitler's war from the very beginning, but America was still uneasily at peace. Recruiting had already begun; I had seen a departure from New York for Camp Stewart in Georgia, and some of the recruits' mothers crying and even screaming and trying to run alongside the train. The recruits were going off to drill with broomsticks because there weren't enough guns; they still wore old-fashioned headgear and were paid twenty-one dollars a month. There was a song about it: "For twenty-one dollars a day, once a month." As my own train crossed the border to Canada I expected to sense at once an air of calm and grit and dedication, but the only changes were from prosperous to shabby, from painted to unpainted, from smiling to dour. I was entering a poorer and a curiously empty country, where the faces of the people gave nothing away. The crossing was my sea change. I silently recited the vow I had been preparing for weeks: that I would never be helpless again and that I would not let anyone make a decision on my behalf.

When I got down from the train at Windsor Station, a man sidled over to me. He had a cap on his head and a bitter Celtic face, with deep indentations along his cheeks, as if his back teeth were pulled. I thought he was asking a direction. He repeated his question, which was obscene. My arms were pinned by the weight of my hamper and suitcase. He brushed the back of his hand over my breasts, called me a name, and edged away. The murderous rage I felt and the revulsion that followed were old friends. They had for years been my reaction to what my diaries called "their hypocrisy." "They" was a world of sly and mumbling people, all of them older than myself. I must have substituted "hypocrisy" for every sort of aggression, because fright was a luxury I could not afford. What distressed me was my helplessness — I who had sworn only a few hours earlier that I'd not be vulnerable again. The man's gaunt face, his drunken breath, the flat voice which I assigned to the graduate of some Christian Brothers teaching establishment haunted me for a long time after that. "The man at Windsor Station" would lurk in the windowless corridors of my nightmares; he would be the passenger, the only passenger, on a dark tram. The first sight of a city must be the measure for all second looks.

But it was not my first sight. I'd had ten years of it here — the first ten. After that, and before New York (in one sense, my deliverance), there had been a long spell of grief and shadow in an Ontario city, a place full of mean judgments and grudging minds, of paranoid Protestants and slovenly Catholics. To this day I cannot bear the sight of brick houses, or of a certain kind of empty treeless street on a Sunday afternoon. My memory of Montreal took shape while I was there. It was not a random jumble of rooms and summers and my mother singing "We've Come to See Miss Jenny Jones," but the faithful record of the true survivor. I retained, I rebuilt a superior civilization. In that drowned world, Sherbrooke Street seemed to be glittering and white; the vision of a house upon that street was so painful that I was obliged to banish it from the memorial. The small hot rooms of a summer cottage became enormous and cool. If I say that Cleopatra floated down the Chateauguay River, that the Winter Palace was stormed on Sherbrooke Street, that Trafalgar was fought on Lake St. Louis, I mean it naturally; they were the natural backgrounds of my exile and fidelity. I saw now at the far end of Windsor Station — more foreign, echoing, and mysterious than any American station could be — a statue of Lord Mount Stephen, the founder of the Canadian Pacific, which everyone took to be a memorial to Edward VII. Angus, Charlotte, and the smaller Linnet had truly been: this was my proof; once upon a time my instructions had been to make my way to Windsor Station should I ever be lost and to stand at the foot of Edward VII and wait for someone to find me.

I have forgotten to say that no one in Canada knew I was there. I looked up the number of the woman who had once been my nurse, but she had no telephone. I found her in a city directory, and with complete faith that "O. Carette" was indeed Olivia and that she would recall and welcome me I took a taxi to the east end of the city — the French end, the poor end. I was so sure of her that I did not ask the driver to wait (to take me where?) but dismissed him and climbed two flights of dark-brown stairs inside a house that must have been built soon after Waterloo. That it was Olivia who came to the door, that the small gray-haired creature I recalled as dark and towering had to look up at me, that she unhesitatingly offered me shelter all seem as simple now as when I broke my fiver to settle the taxi. Believing that I was dead, having paid for years of Masses for the repose of my heretic soul, almost the first thing she said to me was *"Tu vis?"* I understood *"Tu es ici?"* We straightened it out later. She held both my hands and cried and called me *belle et grande. Grande* was good, for among American girls I'd seemed a shrimp. I did not see what there was to cry for; I was here. I was as naturally selfish with Olivia as if her sole reason for being was me. I stayed with her for a while and left when her affection for me made her possessive, and I think I neglected her. On her deathbed she told one of her daughters, the reliable one, to keep an eye on me forever. Olivia was the only person in the world who did not believe I could look after myself. Where she and I were concerned I remained under six.

Now, at no moment of this remarkable day did I feel anxious or worried or forlorn. The man at Windsor Station could not really affect my view of the future. I had seen some of the worst of life, but I had no way of judging it or of knowing what the worst could be. I had a sensation of loud, ruthless power, like an enormous waterfall. The past, the part I would rather not have lived, became small and remote, a dark pinpoint. My only weapons until now had been secrecy and insolence. I had stopped running away from schools and situations when I finally understood that by becoming a name in a file, by attracting attention, I would merely prolong my stay in prison — I mean, the prison of childhood itself. My rebellions then consisted only in causing people who were physically larger and legally sovereign to lose their self-control, to become bleached with anger, to shake with such temper that they broke cups and glasses and bumped into chairs. From the malleable, sunny child Olivia said she remembered, I had become, according to later chroniclers, cold, snobbish, and presumptuous. "You need an iron hand, Linnet." I can still hear that melancholy voice, which belonged to a friend of my mother's. "If anybody ever marries you he'd better have an iron hand." After today I would never need to hear this, or anything approaching it, for the rest of my life.

And so that June morning and the drive through empty, sunlit, wartime streets are even now like a roll of drums in my mind. My life was my own revolution — the tyrants deposed, the constitution wrenched from unwilling hands; I was, all by myself, the liberated crowd setting the palace on fire; I was the flags, the trees, the bannered windows, the flower-decked trains. The singing and the skyrockets of the 1848 I so trustingly believed would emerge out of the war were me, no one but me; and, as in the lyrical first days of any revolution, as in the first days of any love affair, there wasn't the whisper of a voice to tell me, "You might compromise."

If making virtue of necessity has ever had a meaning it must be here: for I was independent *inevitably*. There were good-hearted Americans who knew a bit of my story — as much as I wanted anyone to know — and I hoped I would swim and not drown, but from the moment I embarked on my journey I went on the dark side of the moon. "You seemed so sure of yourself," they would tell me, still troubled, long after this. In the cool journals I kept I noted that my survival meant nothing in the capitalist system; I was one of those not considered to be worth helping, saving, or even investigating. Thinking with care, I see this was true. What could I have turned into in another place? Why, a librarian at Omsk or a file clerk at Tomsk. Well, it hadn't happened that way; I had my private revolution and I settled in with Olivia in Montreal. Sink or swim? Of course I swam. Jobs were for the having; you could pick them up off the ground. Working for a living meant just what it says — a brisk necessity. It would be the least important fragment of my life until I had what I wanted. The cheek of it, I think now; penniless, sleeping in a shed room behind the kitchen of Olivia's cold-water flat, still I pointed across the wooden balustrade in a long open office where I was being considered for employment and said, "But I won't sit there." Girls were *there*, penned in like sheep. I did not think men better than women — only that they did more interesting work and got more money for it. In my journals I called other girls "coolies." I did not know if life made them bearers or if they had been born with a natural gift for giving in. "Coolie" must have been the secret expression of one of my deepest fears. I see now that I had an immense conceit; I thought I occupied a world other people could scarcely envision, let alone attain. It involved giddy risks and changes, stepping off the edge blindfolded, one's hand on nothing more than a birth certificate and a five-dollar bill. At this time of sitting in judgment I was earning nine dollars a week (until I was told by someone that the local minimum wage was twelve, on which I left for greener fields) and washing my white piqué skirt at night and ironing at dawn, and coming home at all hours so I could pretend to Olivia I had dined. Part of this impermeable sureness that I needn't waver or doubt came out of my having lived in New York. The first time I ever heard people laughing in a cinema was there. I can still remember the wonder and excitement and amazement I felt. I was just under fourteen and I had never heard people expressing their feelings in a public place in my life. The easy reactions, the way a poignant moment caught them, held them still — all that was new. I had come there straight from Ontario, where the reaction to a love scene was a kind of unhappy giggling, while the image of a kitten or a baby induced a long flat "Aaaah," followed by shamed silence. You could imagine them blushing in the dark for having said that — just that "Aaaah." When I heard that open American laughter I thought I could be like these people too, but had been told not to be by everyone, beginning with Olivia: "*Pas si fort*" was something she repeated to me so often when I was small that my father had made a tease out of it, called "passy four." From a tease it became oppressive too: "For the love of God, Linnet, passy four." What were these new people? Were they soft, too easily got at? I wondered that even then. Would a dictator have a field day here? Were they, as Canadian opinion had it, vulgar? Perhaps the notion of vulgarity came out of some incapacity on the part of the refined. Whatever they were, they couldn't all be daft; if they weren't I probably wasn't either. I supposed I stood as good a chance of being miserable here as anywhere, but at least I would not have to pretend to be someone else.

Now, of course there is much to be said on the other side; people who do not display what they feel have practical advantages. They can go away to be killed as if they didn't mind; they can see their sons off to war without a blink. Their upbringing is intended for a crisis. When it comes, they behave themselves. But it is murder in everyday life — truly murder. The dead of heart and spirit litter the landscape. Still, keeping a straight face makes life tolerable under stress. It makes *public* life tolerable — that is all I am saying; because in private people still got drunk, went after each other with bottles and knives, rang the police to complain that neighbors were sending poison gas over the transom, abandoned infant

children and aged parents, wrote letters to newspapers in favor
of corporal punishment, with inventive suggestions. When I
came back to Canada that June, at least one thing had been
settled: I knew that it was all right for people to laugh and cry
and even to make asses of themselves. I had actually known
people like that, had lived with them, and they were fine,
mostly — not crazy at all. That was where a lot of my
confidence came from when I began my journey into a new
life and a dream past.

M y father's death had been kept from me. I did not know
its exact circumstances or even the date. He died when
I was ten. At thirteen I was still expected to believe a fable
about his being in England. I kept waiting for him to send for
me, for my life was deeply wretched and I took it for granted
he knew. Finally I began to suspect that death and silence can
be one. How to be sure? Head-on questions got me nowhere. I
had to create a situation in which some adult (not my mother,
who was far too sharp) would lose all restraint and hurl the
truth at me. It was easy: I was an artist at this. What I had not
foreseen was the verbal violence of the scene or the effect it
might have. The storm that seemed to break in my head, my
need to maintain the pose of indifference ("What are you
telling me for? What makes you think I care?") were such a
strain that I had physical reactions, like stigmata, which
doctors would hopelessly treat on and off for years and which
vanished when I became independent. The other change was
that if anyone asked about my father I said, "Oh, he died."
Now, in Montreal, I could confront the free adult world of
falsehood and evasion on an equal footing; they would be
forced to talk to me as they did to each other. Making
appointments to meet my father's friends — Mr. Archie
McEwen, Mr. Stephen Ross-Colby, Mr. Quentin Keller — I
left my adult name. "Miss Muir." These were the men who
eight, nine, ten years ago had asked, "Do you like your

school?" — not knowing what else to say to children. I had
curtsied to them and said, "Good night." I think what I wanted
was special information about despair, but I should have
known that would be taboo in a place where "like" and "don't
like" were heavy emotional statements.

Archie McEwen, my father's best friend, or the man I
mistook for that, kept me standing in his office on St. James
Street West, he standing too, with his hands behind his back,
and he said the following — not reconstructed or approximate
but recalled, like "The religions of Ancient Greece and Rome
are extinct" or "O come, let us sing unto the Lord":

"Of course, Angus was a very sick man. I saw him walking
along Sherbrooke Street. He must have just come out of
hospital. He couldn't walk upright. He was using a stick.
Inching along, his hair had turned gray. Nobody knew where
Charlotte had got to, and we'd heard you were dead. He
obviously wasn't long for this world either. He had too many
troubles for any one man. I crossed the street because I didn't
have the heart to shake hands with him. I felt terrible."

Savage? Reasonable? You can't tell, with those minds.
Some recent threat had scared them. The Depression was too
close, just at their heels. Archie McEwen did not ask where I
was staying or where I had been for the last eight years; in fact,
he asked only two questions. In response to the first I said,
"She is married."

There came a gleam of interest — distant, amused: "So she
decided to marry him, did she?"

My mother was highly visible; she had no secrets except
unexpected ones. My father had nothing but. When he asked,
"Would you like to spend a year in England with your Aunt
Dorothy?" I had no idea what he meant and I still don't. His
only brother, Thomas, who was killed in 1918, had not been
married: he'd had no sisters, that anyone knew. Those English
mysteries used to be common. People came out to Canada
because they did not want to think about the Thomases and
Dorothys anymore. Angus was a solemn man, not much of a

smiler. My mother, on the other hand — I won't begin to describe her, it would never end — smiled, talked, charmed anyone she didn't happen to be related to, swam in scandal like a partisan among the people. She made herself the central figure in loud, spectacular dramas which she played with the houselights on; you could see the audience too. That was her mistake; they kept their reactions, like their lovemaking, in the dark. You can imagine what she must have been in this world where everything was hushed, muffled, disguised: she must have seemed all they had by way of excitement, give or take a few elections and wars. It sounds like a story about the old and stale, but she and my father had been quite young eight and ten years before. The dying man creeping along Sherbrooke Street was thirty-two. First it was light chatter, then darker gossip, and then it went too far (*he* was ill and he couldn't hide it; *she* had a lover and didn't try); then suddenly it became tragic, and open tragedy was disallowed. And so Mr. Archie McEwen could stand in his office without a trace of feeling on his narrow Lowland face — not unlike my father's in shape — he could say, "I crossed the street."

Stephen Ross-Colby, a bachelor, my father's painter chum: the smell of his studio on St. Mark Street was the smell of a personal myth. I said timidly, "Do you happen to have anything of his — a drawing or anything?" I was humble because I was on a private, personal terrain of vocation that made me shy even of the dead.

He said, "No, nothing. You could ask around. She junked a lot of his stuff and he junked the rest when he thought he wouldn't survive. You might try . . ." He gave me a name or two. "It was all small stuff," said Ross-Colby. "He didn't do anything big." He hurried me out of the studio for a cup of coffee in a crowded place — the Honey Dew on St. Catherine Street, it must have been. Perhaps in the privacy of his studio I might have heard him thinking. Years after that he would try to call me "Lynn," which I was never was, and himself "Steve." He'd come into his own as an artist by then, selling wash drawings of Canadian war graves, sun-splashed, wisteria-mauve, lime-green, with drifts of blossom across the name of the regiment; gained a reputation among the heartbroken women who bought these impersonations, had them framed — the only picture in the house. He painted the war memorial at Caen. ("Their name liveth forever.") His stones weren't stones but mauve bubbles — that is all I have against them. They floated off the page. My objection wasn't to "He didn't do anything big" but to Ross-Colby's way of turning the dead into thistledown. He said, much later, of that meeting, "I felt like a bastard, but I was broke, and I was afraid you'd put the bite on me."

Let me distribute demerits equally and tell about my father's literary Jewish friend, Mr. Quentin Keller. He was older than the others, perhaps by some twelve years. He had a whispery voice and a long pale face and a daughter older than I. "Bossy Wendy" I used to call her when, forced by her parents as I was by mine, Bossy Wendy had to take a whole afternoon of me. She had a room full of extraordinary toys, a miniature kitchen in which everything worked, of which all I recall her saying is "Don't touch." Wendy Keller had left Smith after her fresh-man year to marry the elder son of a Danish baron. Her father said to me, "There is only one thing you need to know and that is that your father was a gentleman."

Jackass was what I thought. Yes, Mr Quentin Keller was a jackass. But he was a literary one, for he had once written a play called *Forbearance*, in which I'd had a role. I had bounded across the stage like a tennis ball, into the arms of a young woman dressed up like an old one, and cried my one line: "Here I am, Granny!" Of course, he did not make his living fiddling about with amateur theatricals; thanks to our meeting I had a good look at the inside of a conservative architect's private office — that was about all it brought me.

What were they so afraid of, I wondered. I had not yet seen that I was in a false position where they were concerned; being "Miss Muir" had not made equals of us but lent distance. I thought they had read my true passport, the invisible one we all carry, but I had neither the wealth nor the influence a provincial society requires to make a passport valid. My credentials were lopsided: the important half of the scales was still in the air. I needed enormous collateral security — fame, an alliance with a powerful family, the power of money itself. I remember how Archie McEwen, trying to place me in some sensible context, to give me a voucher so he could take me home and show me to his wife, perhaps, asked his second question: "Who inherited the —?"

"The what, Mr. McEwen?"

He had not, of course, read "Why I Am a Socialist." I did not believe in inherited property. "Who inherited the —?" would not cross my mind again for another ten years, and then it would be a drawer quickly opened and shut before demons could escape. To all three men the last eight years were like minutes; to me they had been several lives. Some of my confidence left me then. It came down to "Next time I'll know better," but would that be enough? I had been buffeted until now by other people's moods, principles, whims, tantrums; I had survived, but perhaps I had failed to grow some outer skin it was now too late to acquire. Olivia thought that; she was the only one. Olivia knew more about the limits of nerve than I did. Her knowledge came out of the clean, swept, orderly poverty that used to be tucked away in the corners of cities. It didn't spill out then, or give anyone a bad conscience. Nobody took its picture. Anyway, Olivia would not have sat for such a portrait. The fringed green rug she put over her treadle sewing machine was part of a personal fortune. On her mantelpiece stood a copper statuette of Voltaire in an armchair. It must have come down to her from some robustly anticlerical ancestor. "Who is he?" she said to me. "You've been to school in a foreign country." "A governor of New France," I replied. She knew Voltaire was the name of a bad man and she'd have thrown the figurine out, and it would have made one treasure less in the house. Olivia's maiden name was Ouvrardville, which was good in Quebec, but only really good if you were one of the rich ones. Because of her maiden name she did not want anyone ever to know she had worked for a family; she impressed this on me delicately — it was like trying to understand what a dragonfly wanted to tell. In the old days she had gone home every weekend, taking me with her if my parents felt my company was going to make Sunday a very long day. Now I understood what the weekends were about; her daughters, Berthe and Marguerite, for whose sake she worked, were home from their convent schools Saturday and Sunday and had to be chaperoned. Her relatives pretended not to notice that Olivia was poor or even that she was widowed, for which she seemed grateful. The result of all this elegant sham was that Olivia did not say, "I was afraid you'd put the bite on me," or keep me standing. She dried her tears and asked if there was a trunk to follow. No? She made a pot of tea and spread a starched cloth on the kitchen table and we sat down to a breakfast of toast and honey. The honey tin was a ten-pounder decorated with bees the size of hornets. Lifting it for her, I remarked, *"C'est collant,"* a word out of a frozen language that started to thaw when Olivia said, *"Tu vis?"*

On the advice of her confessor, who was to be my rival from now on, Olivia refused to tell me whatever she guessed or knew, and she was far too dignified to hint. Putting together the three men's woolly stories, I arrived at something about tuberculosis of the spine and a butchery of an operation. He started back to England to die there but either changed his mind or was too ill to begin the journey; at Quebec City, where he was to have taken ship, he shot himself in a public park at five o'clock in the morning. That was one version; another was that he died at sea and the gun was found in his luggage. The revolver figured in all three accounts. It was an officer's weapon from the Kaiser's war, that had belonged to his brother. Angus kept it at the back of a small drawer in the tall chest used for men's clothes and known in Canada as a highboy. In front of the revolver was a pigskin stud box and a

pile of ironed handkerchiefs. Just describing that drawer dates
it. How I happen to know the revolver was loaded and how I
learned never to point a gun even in play is another story. I
can tell you that I never again in my life looked inside a drawer
that did not belong to me.

I know a woman whose father died, she thinks, in a concentration camp. Or was he shot in a schoolyard? Or hanged or
thrown in a ditch? Were the ashes that arrived from some
eastern plain his or another prisoner's? She invents different
deaths. Her inventions have become her conversation at
dinner parties. She takes on a child's voice and says, "My
father died at Buchenwald." She chooses and rejects elements of the last act; one avoids mentioning death, shooting,
capital punishment, cremation, deportation, even fathers.
Her inventions are not thought neurotic or exhibitionist but
something sanctioned by history. Peacetime casualties are not
like that. They are lightning bolts out of a sunny sky that
strike only one house. All around the ashy ruin lilacs blossom, leaves gleam. Speculation in public about the disaster
would be indecent. Nothing remains but a silent, recurring
puzzlement to the survivors: Why here and not there? Why
this and not that? Before July was out I had settled his fate in
my mind and I never varied; I thought he had died of
homesickness; sickness for England was the consumption, the
gun, the everything. "Everything" had to take it all in, for
people in Canada then did not speak of irrational endings to
life, and newspapers did not print that kind of news: this was
because of the spiritual tragedy for Catholic families, and
because the act had long been considered a criminal one in
British law. If Catholic feelings were spared it gave the
impression no one but Protestants ever went over the edge,
which was unfair; and so the possibility was eliminated, and
people came to a natural end in a running car in a closed
garage, hanging from a rafter in the barn, in an icy lake with

a canoe left to drift empty. Once I had made up my mind, the whole story somehow became none of my business: I had looked in a drawer that did not belong to me. More, if I was to live my own life I had to let go. I wrote in my journal that "they" had got him but would not get me, and after that there was scarcely ever a mention.

My dream past evaporated. Montreal, in memory, was a leafy citadel where I knew every tree. In reality I recognized nearly nothing and had to start from scratch. Sherbrooke Street had been the dream street, pure white. It was the avenue poor Angus descended leaning on a walking stick. It was a moat I was not allowed to cross alone; it was lined with gigantic spreading trees through which light fell like a rain of coins. One day, standing at a corner, waiting for the light to change, I understood that the Sherbrooke Street of my exile — my Mecca, my Jerusalem — was this. It had to be; there could not be two. It was *only* this. The limitless green where in a perpetual spring I had been taken to play was the campus of McGill University. A house, whose beauty had brought tears to my sleep, to which in sleep I'd returned to find it inhabited by ugly strangers, gypsies, was a narrow stone thing with a shop on the ground floor and offices above — if that was it, for there were several like it. Through the bare panes of what might have been the sitting room, with its deep private window seats, I saw neon striplighting along a ceiling. Reality, as always, was narrow and dull. And yet what dramatic things had taken place on this very corner: Once Satan had approached me — furry dark skin, claws, red eyes, the lot. He urged me to cross the street and I did, in front of a car that braked in time. I explained, "The Devil told me to." I had no idea until then that my parents did not believe what I was taught in my convent school. (Satan is not bilingual, by the way; he speaks Quebec French.) My parents had no God and therefore no Fallen Angel. I was scolded for lying, which was a thing my father detested, and which my mother regularly did but never forgave in others.

Why these two nonbelievers wanted a strong religious education for me is one of the mysteries. (Even in loss of faith they were unalike, for he was ex-Anglican and she was ex-Lutheran and that is not your same atheist — no, not at all.) "To make you tolerant" was a lame excuse, as was "French," for I spoke fluent French with Olivia, and I could read in two languages before I was four. Discipline might have been one reason — God knows, the nuns provided plenty of that — but according to Olivia I did not need any. It cannot have been for the quality of the teaching, which was lamentable. I suspect that it was something like sending a dog to a trainer (they were passionate in their concern for animals, especially dogs), but I am not certain it ever brought me to heel. The first of my schools, the worst, the darkest, was on Sherbrooke Street too. When I heard, years later, it had been demolished, it was like the burial of a witch. I had remembered it penitentiary size, but what I found myself looking at one day was simply a very large stone house. A crocodile of little girls emerged from the front gate and proceeded along the street — white-faced, black-clad, eyes cast down. I knew they were bored, fidgety, anxious, and probably hungry. I should have felt pity, but at eighteen all that came to me was thankfulness that I had been correct about one thing throughout my youth, which I now considered ended: time had been on my side, faithfully, and unless you died you were always bound to escape.

BETWEEN
ZERO AND ONE

When I was young I thought that men had small lives of their own creation. I could not see why, born enfranchised, without the obstacles and constraints attendant on women, they set such close limits for themselves and why, once the limits had been reached, they seemed so taken aback. I could not tell much difference between a man aged thirty-six, about, and one forty or fifty; it was impossible to fix the borderline of this apparent disappointment. There was a space of life I used to call "between Zero and One" and then came a long mystery. I supposed that men came up to their wall, their terminal point, quite a long way after One. At that time I was nineteen and we were losing the war. The news broadcast in Canada was flatly optimistic, read out in the detached nasal voices de rigueur for the CBC. They were voices that seemed to be saying. "Good or bad, it can't affect *us*." I worked in a building belonging to the federal government — it was a heavy Victorian structure of the sort that exists on every continent, wherever the British thought they'd come to stay. This one had been made out of the reddish-brown Montreal stone that colors, in memory, the streets of my childhood and that architects have no use for now. The office was full of old soldiers from one war before: Ypres (pronounced "Wipers") and Vimy Ridge were real, as real as this minute, while Singapore, Pearl Harbor, Voronezh were the stuff of fiction. It seemed as if anything that befell the young, even dying, was bound to be trivial.

"Half of 'em'll never see any fighting," I often heard. "Anyway not like in the trenches." We did have one veteran from the current war — Mac Kirkconnell, who'd had a knock on the head during his training and was now good for nothing except civilian life. He and two others were the only men under thirty left in the place. The other two were physical crocks, which was why they were not in uniform (a question demented women sometimes asked them in the street). Mr. Tracy had been snow-blinded after looking out of a train window for most of a sunny February day; he had recovered part of his sight but had to wear mauve glasses even by electric light. He was nice but strange, infirm. Mr. Curran, reputed to have one kidney, one lung, and one testicle, and who was the subject of endless rhymes and ditties on that account, was not so nice: he had not wanted a girl in the office and had argued against my being employed. Now that I was there he simply pretended that he had won. There were about a dozen other men — older, old. I can see every face, hear every syllable, which evoked, for me, a street, a suburb, a kind of schooling. I could hear just out of someone's saying to me, "Say, Linnet, couja just gimme a hand here, please?" born here, born in Glasgow; immigrated early, late; raised in Montreal, no, farther west. I can see the rolled shirtsleeves, the braces, the eyeshades, the hunched shoulders, the elastic armbands, the paper cuffs they wore sometimes, the chopped-egg sandwiches in waxed paper, the apples, the oatmeal cookies ("Want any, Linnet? If you don't eat lunch nobody'll marry you"), the thermos flasks. Most of them lived thinly, paying for a bungalow, a duplex flat, a son's education: a good Protestant education was not to be had for nothing then. I remember a

day of dark spring snowstorms, ourselves reflected on the black
windows, the pools of warm light here and there, the green-
shaded lamps, the dramatic hiss and gurgle of the radiators
that always sounded like the background to some emotional
outburst, the sudden slackening at the end of the afternoon
when every molecule of oxygen in the room had turned into
poison. Assistant Chief Engineer Macaulay came plodding
softly along the wintry room and laid something down on my
desk. It was a collection of snapshots of a naked woman
prancing and skipping in what I took to be the back yard of his
house out in Cartierville. In one she was in a baby carriage
with her legs spread over the sides, pretending to drink out of
an infant's bottle. The unknown that this represented was
infinite. I also wondered what Mr. Macaulay wanted — he
didn't say. He remarked, shifting from foot to foot, "Now,
Linnet, they tell me you like modern art." I thought then, I
think now, that the tunnel winters, the sudden darkness that
April day, the years he'd had of this long green room, the
knowledge that he would die and be buried "Assistant Chief
Engineer Grade II" without having overtaken Chief Engineer
McCreery had simply snapped the twig, the frail matchstick in
the head that is all we have to keep us sensible.

   Bertie Knox had a desk facing mine. He told the other men
I'd gone red in the face when I saw Macaulay's fat-arsed wife.
(He hadn't seen *that* one; I had turned it over, like a bad card.)
The men teased me for blushing, and they said, "Wait till you
get married, Linnet, you haven't done with shocks." Bertie
Knox had been in this very office since the age of twelve. The
walls had been a good solid gray then — not this drawing-
room green. The men hadn't been pampered and coddled
either. There wasn't even a water cooler. You were fined for
smoking, fined for lateness, fined for sick leave. He had
worked the old ten-hour day and given every cent to his
mother. Once he pinched a dime of it and his mother went for
him. He locked himself in a cupboard. He mother took the
door off its hinges and beat him blue with a wooden hanger.

During the Depression, married, down to half pay, four kids in the house, he had shovelled snow for twenty cents an hour. "And none the worse for it," he would always wind up. Most of the men seemed to have been raised in hardship by stern, desperate parents. What struck me was the good they thought it had done them (I had yet to meet an adult man with a poor opinion of himself) and their desire to impose the same broken fortunes on other people, particularly on the young — though not their own young, of course. There was a touch of sadness, a touch of envy to it, too. Bertie Knox had seen Mr. Macaulay and Mr. McCreery come in as Engineers Grade II, wet behind the ears, puffed up with their new degrees, "just a couple more college punks." He said that engineering was the world's most despised profession, occupied mainly by human apes. Instead of a degree he had a photograph of himself in full kilt, Highland Light Infantry, 1917; he had gone "home," to a completely unknown Old Country, and joined up there. "Will you just look at that lad?" he would plead. "Do they come like him today? By God, they do not!" Bertie Knox could imitate any tone and accent, including mine. He could do a CBC announcer droning, "The British have ah taken ah Tobruk," when we knew perfectly well the Germans had. (One good thing about the men was that when anything seemed hopeless they talked nonsense. The native traits of pessimism and constant grumbling returned only when there was nothing to grumble about.) Bertie Knox had a wooden leg, which he showed me; it was dressed in a maroon sock with clocks up the sides and a buckled garter. He had a collection of robust bawdy songs — as everyone (all the men, I mean) had in Canada, unless they were pretending — which I copied in a notebook, verse upon verse, with the necessary indications: Tune — "On, Wisconsin!" Tune — "Men of Harlech," Tune — "We Gather Together to Ask the Lord's Blessing." Sometimes he took the notebook and corrected a word here and there. It doesn't follow that he was a cheerful person. He laughed a lot but he never smiled. I don't think he liked anyone, really.

The men were statisticians, draftsmen, civil engineers.
Painted on the frosted glass of the office door was

REVIEW AND DEVELOPMENT
RESEARCH AND EXPANSION
OF
WARTIME INDUSTRY
"REGIONAL AND URBAN"

The office had been called something else up until September, 1939; according to Bertie Knox they were still doing the
same work as before, and not much of it. "It looks good," he
said. "It sounds good. What is its meaning? Sweet buggerall."
A few girls equipped with rackety typewriters and adding
machines sat grouped at the far end of the room, separated
from the men by a balustrade. I was the first woman ever
permitted to work on the men's side of this fence. A pigeon
among the cats was how it sometimes felt. My title was "aide."
Today it would be something like "trainee." I was totally
unqualified for this or any other kind of work and had been
taken on almost at my own insistence that they could not do
without me.

"Yes, I know all about that," I had replied, to everything.

"Well, I *suppose* it's all right," said Chief Engineer. The
hiring of girls usually fell to a stout grim woman called
"Supervisor," but I was not coming in as a typist. He had never
interviewed a girl before and he was plainly uncomfortable,
asking me questions with all the men straining to hear. There
were no young men left on account of the war, and the office
did need someone. But what if they trained me, he said, at
great cost and expense to the government, and what if I then
did the dreadful thing girls were reputed to do, which was to go
off and get married? It would mean a great waste of time and
money just when there was a war on.

I was engaged, but not nearly ready for the next step. In any
case, I told him, even if I did marry I would need to go on

working, for my husband would more than likely be sent overseas. What Chief Engineer did not know was that I was a minor with almost no possibility of obtaining parental consent. Barring some bright idea, I could not do much of anything until I was twenty-one. For this interview I had pinned back my long hair; I wore a hat, gloves, earrings, and I folded my hands on my purse in a conscious imitation of older women. I did not mind the interview, or the furtively staring men. I was shy, but not self-conscious. Efforts made not to turn a young girl's head — part of an education I had encountered at every stage and in every sort of school — had succeeded in making me invisible to myself. My only commercial asset was that I knew French, but French was of no professional use to anyone in Canada then — not even to French Canadians; one might as well have been fluent in Pushtu. Nevertheless I listed it on my application form, along with a very dodgy "German" (private lessons between the ages of eight and ten) and an entirely impudent "Russian": I was attending Russian evening classes at McGill, for reasons having mainly to do with what I believed to be the world's political future. I recorded my age as twenty-two, hoping to be given a grade and a salary that would correspond. There were no psychological or aptitudes tests; you were taken at your word and lasted according to performance. There was no social security and only the loosest sort of pensions plan; hiring and firing involved no more paperwork than a typed letter — sometimes not even that. I had an unmistakably Montreal accent of a kind now almost extinct, but my having attended school in the United States gave me a useful vagueness of background.

And so, in an ambience of doubt, apprehension, foreboding, incipient danger, and plain hostility, for the first time in the history of the office a girl was allowed to sit with the men. And it was here, at the desk facing Bertie Knox's, on the only uncomfortable chair in the room, that I felt for the first time that almost palpable atmosphere of sexual curiosity, sexual resentment, and sexual fear that the presence of a woman can create where she is not wanted. If part of the resentment vanished when it became clear that I did not know what I was doing, the feeling that women were "trouble" never disappeared. However, some of the men were fathers of daughters, and they quickly saw that I was nothing like twenty-two. Some of them helped me then, and one man, Hughie Pryor, an engineer, actually stayed late to do some of my work when I fell behind.

Had I known exactly what I was about, I might not have remained for more than a day. Older, more experienced, I'd have called it a dull place. The men were rotting quietly until pension time. They kept to a slow English-rooted civil-service pace; no one wasted office time openly, but no one produced much, either. Although they could squabble like hens over mislaid pencils, windows open or shut, borrowed triangles, special and sacred pen nibs used for tracing maps, there was a truce about zeal. The fact is that I did not know the office was dull. It was so new to me, so strange, such another climate, that even to flow with the sluggish tide draining men and women into the heart of the city each day was a repeated experiment I sensed, noted, recorded, as if I were being allowed to be part of something that was not really mine. The smell of the building was of school — of chalk, dust, plaster, varnish, beeswax. Victorian, Edwardian, and early Georgian oil portraits of Canadian captains of industry, fleshed-out pirate faces, adorned the staircase and halls — a daily reminder that there are two races, those who tread on people's lives, and the others. The latest date on any of the portraits was about 1925: I suppose photography had taken over. Also by then the great fortunes had been established and the surviving pirates were retired, replete and titled, usually to England. Having had both French and English schooling in Quebec, I knew that these pink-cheeked marauders were what

English-speaking children were led to admire (without much hope of emulation, for the feast was over). They were men of patriotism and of action; we owed them everything. They were in a positive, constructive way a part of the Empire and of the Crown; this was a good thing. In a French education veneration was withheld from anyone except the dead and defeated, ranging from General Montcalm expiring at his last battle to a large galaxy of maimed and crippled saints. Deprivation of the senses, mortification of mind and body were imposed, encouraged, for phantom reasons — something to do with a tragic past and a deep fear of life itself. Montreal was a city where the greater part of the population were wrapped in myths and sustained by belief in magic. I had been to school with little girls who walked in their sleep and had visions; the nuns who had taught me seemed at ease with the dead. I think of them even now as strange, dead, punishing creatures who neither ate nor breathed nor slept. The one who broke one of my fingers with a ruler was surely a spirit without a mind, tormented, acting in the vengeful driven way of homeless ghosts. In an English school visions would have been smartly dealt with — cold showers, the parents summoned, at the least a good stiff talking to. These two populations, these two tribes, knew nothing whatever about each other. In the very poorest part of the east end of the city, apparitions were commonplace; one lived among a mixture of men and women and their imaginings. I would never have believed then that anything could ever stir them from their dark dreams. The men in the portraits were ghosts of a kind, too; they also seemed to be saying, "Too late, too late for you," and of course in a sense so it was: it was too late for anyone else to import Chinese and Irish coolie labor and wring a railway out of them. That had already been done. Once I said to half-blind Mr. Tracy, "Things can't just stay this way."

"Change is always for the worse" was his reply. His own father had lost all his money in the Depression, ten years before; perhaps he meant that.

I climbed to the office in a slow reassuring elevator with iron grille doors, sharing it with inexpressive women and men — clearly, the trodden on. No matter how familiar our faces became, we never spoke. The only sound, apart from the creaking cable, was the gasping and choking of a poor man who had been gassed at the Somme and whose lungs were said to be in shreds. He had an old man's pale eyes and wore a high stiff collar and stared straight before him, like everyone else. Some of the men in my office had been wounded, too, but they made it sound pleasant. Bertie Knox said he had hobbled on one leg and crutches in the 1918 Allied victory parade in Paris. According to him, when his decimated regiment followed their Highland music up the Champs-Élysées, every pretty girl in Paris had been along the curb, fighting the police and screaming and trying to get at Bertie Knox and take him home.

"It was the kilts set 'em off," said Bertie Knox. "That and the wounds. And the Jocks played it up for all they was worth, bashing the very buggery out of the drums." "Jocks" were Scots in those days — nothing more.

Any mention of that older war could bring the men to life, but it had been done with for more than twenty years now. Why didn't they move, walk, stretch, run? Each of them seemed to inhabit an invisible square; the square was shared with *my* desk, *my* graph paper, *my* elastic bands. The contents of the square were tested each morning: The drawers of my own desk — do they still open and shut? My desk lamp — does it still turn on and off? Have my special coat hanger, my favorite nibs, my drinking glass, my calendar, my children's pictures, my ashtray, the one I brought from home, been tampered with during the night? Sometimes one glimpsed another world, like an extra room ("It was my young daughter made my lunch today" — said with a dismissive shrug, lest it be taken for boasting) or a wish outdistanced, reduced, shrunken, trailing somewhere in the mind: "I often thought I wanted . . ." "Something I wouldn't have minded having . . " Easily angry, easily offended, underpaid, at the mercy of accidents — an illness in the family could wipe out a life's savings — still they'd have resisted change for the better. Change was double-edged; it might mean improving people with funny names, letting them get uppity. What they had instead were marks of privilege — a blind sureness that they were superior in every way to French Canadians, whom in some strange fashion they neither heard nor saw (a lack of interest that was doubly and triply returned); they had the certainty they'd never be called on to share a washroom or a drawing board or to exchange the time of day with anyone "funny" (applications from such people, in those days, would have been quietly set aside); most important of all, perhaps, they had the distinction of the individual hand towel. These towels, as stiff as boards, reeking of chloride bleach, were distributed once a week by a boy pushing a trolley. They were distributed to men, but not even to *all* men. The sanctioned carried them to the washroom, aired and dried them on the backs of chairs, kept them folded in a special drawer. Assimilated into a male world, I had one too. The stenographers and typists had to make do with paper towels that scratched when new and dissolved when damp. Any mistake or oversight on towel day was a source of outrage; "Why the bejesus do I get a torn one three times running? You'd think I didn't count for anything round here." It seemed a true distress; someday some simple carelessness might turn out to be the final curse; they were like that prisoner of Mussolini, shut up for life, who burst into tears because the soup was cold. When I received presents of candy I used to bring them in for the staff; these wartime chocolates tasted of candlewax but were much appreciated nonetheless. I had to be careful to whom I handed the box first: I could not begin with girls, which I'd have thought natural, because Supervisor did not brook interruptions. I would transfer the top layer to the lid of the box for the girls, for later on, and then consider the men. A trinity of them occupied glass cubicles. One was diabetic; another was Mr. Tracy, who, a gentle alcoholic, did not care for sweets; and the third was Mr. Curran. Skipping all three I would start with

Chief Engineer McCreery and descend by way of Assistant
Chief Engineers Grade I and then II — I approached them by
educational standards, whose with degrees from McGill and
Queen's — Queen's first — to, finally, the technicians. By
that time the caramels and nougats had all been eaten and
nothing left but squashy orange and vanilla creams nobody
liked. Then, then, oh God, who was to receive the affront of
the last chocolate, the one reposing among crumbs and fluted
paper casings? Sometimes I was cowardly and left the box
adrift on a drawing board with a murmured "Pass it along,
would you?"

I was deeply happy. It was one of the periods of inexplicable
grace when every day is a new parcel one unwraps, layer on
layer of tissue paper covering bits of crystal, scraps of words in
a foreign language, pure white stones. I spent my lunch hours
writing in notebooks, which I kept locked in my desk. The
men never bothered me, apart from trying to feed me little
pieces of cake. They were all sad when I began to smoke — I
remember that. I could write without hearing anyone, but
poetry was leaving me. It was not an abrupt removal but like a
recurring tide whose high-water mark recedes inch by inch.
Presently I was deep inland and the sea was gone. I would
mourn it much later; it was such a gentle separation at the
time that I scarcely noticed. I had notebooks stuffed with
streets and people: my journals were full of "but what he *really*
must have meant was . . ." There were endless political
puzzles I tried to solve by comparing one thing with another,
but of course nothing matched; I had not lost my adolescent
habit of private, passionate manifestos. If politics were nothing
but chess — Mr. Tracy's ways of sliding out of conviction — K
was surely Social Justice and Q Extreme Morality. I was
certain of this, and that after the war — unless we were
completely swallowed up, like those Canadian battalions at
Hong Kong — K and Q would envelop the world. Having no
one to listen to, I could not have a thought without writing it
down. There were pages and pages of dead butterflies, wings

without motion or lift. I began to ration my writing, for fear I would dream through life as my father had done. I was afraid I had inherited a poisoned gene from him, a vocation without a gift. He had spent his own short time like a priest in charge of a relic, forever expecting the blessed blood to liquefy. I had no assurance I was not the same. I was so like him in some ways that a man once stopped me in front of the Bell Telephone building on Beaver Hall Hill and said, "Could you possibly be Angus Muir's sister?" That is how years telescope in men's minds. That particular place must be the windiest in Montreal, for I remember dust and ragged papers blowing in whirlpools and that I had to hold my hair. I said, "No, I'm not," without explaining that I was not his sister but his daughter. I had heard people say, referring to me but not knowing who I was, "He had a daughter, but apparently she died." We couldn't *both* be dead. Having come down on the side of life, I kept my distance. Writing now had to occupy an enormous space. I had lived in New York until a year before and there were things I was sick with missing. There was no theatre, no music; there was one museum of art with not much in it. There was not even a free public lending library in the sense of the meaning that would have been given the words "free public lending library" in Toronto or New York. The municipal library was considered a sinister joke. There was a persistent, apocryphal story among English Canadians that an American philanthropic foundation (the Carnegie was usually mentioned) had offered to establish a free public lending library on condition that its contents were not to be censored by the provincial government of Quebec or by the Catholic Church, and that the offer had been turned down. The story may not have been true but its persistence shows the political and cultural climate of Montreal then. Educated French Canadians summed it up in shorter form: their story was that when you looked up "Darwin" in the card index of the Bibliothèque de Montréal you found "See anti-Darwin." A Canadian actress I knew in New York sent me the first published text of *The Skin of Our Teeth*. I wrote imploring her to tell me everything about the production — the costumes, the staging, the voices. I've never seen it performed — not read it since the end of the war. I've been told that it doesn't hold, that it is not rooted in anything specific. It was then; its Ice Age was Fascism. I read it the year of Dieppe, in a year when "Russia" meant "Leningrad," when Malta could be neither fed nor defended. The Japanese were anywhere they wanted to be. Vast areas of the world were covered with silence and ice. One morning I read a little notice in the *Gazette* that Miss Margaret Urn would be taking auditions for the Canadian Broadcasting Corporation. I presented myself during my lunch hour with *The Skin of Our Teeth* and a manuscript one-act play of my own, in case. I had expected to find queues of applicants but I was the only one. Miss Urn received me in a small room of a dingy office suite on St. Catherine Street. We sat down on opposite sides of a table. I was rendered shy by her bearing, which had a headmistress quality, and perplexed by her accent — it was the voice any North American actor will pick up after six months of looking for work in the West End, but I did not know that. I opened *The Skin of Our Teeth* and began to read. It was floating rather than reading, for I had much of it by heart. When I read "Have you milked the mammoth?" Miss Urn stopped me. She reached over the table and placed her hand on the page.

"My dear child, what is this rubbish?" she said.

I stammered, "It is a . . . a play in New York."

Oh, fool. The worst thing to say. If only I had said, "Tallulah Bankhead," adding swiftly, "London, before the war." Or, better, "An Edwardian farce. Queen Alexandra, deaf though she was, much appreciated the joke about the separation of 'm' and 'n'." "A play in New York" evoked a look Canada was making me familiar with: amusement, fastidious withdrawal, gentle disdain. What a strange city to have a play in, she might have been thinking.

"Try reading this," she said.

I shall forget everything about the war except that at the worst point of it I was asked to read *Dear Octopus*. If Miss Urn had never heard of Thornton Wilder I had never heard of Dodie Smith. I read what I took to be a parody. Presently it dawned on me these were meant to be real people. I broke up laughing because of Sabina, Fascism, the Ice Age that was perhaps upon us because of the one-act play still in my purse. She took the book away from me and closed it and said I would, or would not, be hearing from her.

Now there was excitement in the office: a second woman had been brought in. Mrs. Ireland was her name. She had an advanced degree in accountancy and she was preparing a doctorate in some branch of mathematics none of the men were familiar with. She was about thirty-two. Her hair was glossy and dark; she wore it in braids that became a rich mahogany color when they caught the light. I admired her hair, but the rest of her was angry-looking — flushed cheeks, red hands and arms. The scarf around her throat looked as though it had been wound and tied in a fury. She tossed a paper on my desk and said, "Check this. I'm in a hurry." Chief Engineer looked up, looked at her, looked down. A play within the play, a subplot, came to life; I felt it exactly as children can sense a situation they have no name for. In the afternoon she said, "Haven't you done that yet?" She had a positive, hammering sort of voice. It must have carried as far as the portraits in the hall. Chief Engineer unrolled a large map showing the ministry resources of eastern Canada and got behind it. Mrs. Ireland called, to the room in general, "Well, is she supposed to be working for me or isn't she?" Oh? I opened the bottom drawer of my desk, unlocked the middle drawer, began to pack up my personal affairs. I saw that I'd need a taxi: I had about three pounds of manuscripts and notes, and what seemed to amount to a wardrobe. In those days girls wore white gloves to work; I had two extra pairs of these, and a makeup kit, and extra shoes. I began filling my wastebasket with superfluous cargo. The room had gone silent: I can still see Bertie Knox's ratty little eyes judging, summing up, taking the measure of this new force. Mr. Tracy, in his mauve glasses, hands in his pockets, came strolling out of his office; it was a sort of booth, with frosted-glass panels that did not go up to the ceiling. He must have heard the shouting and then the quiet. He and Mr. Curran and Mr. Elwitt, the diabetic one, were higher in rank than Chief Engineer, higher than Office Manager; they could have eaten Supervisor for tea and no one would dare complain. He came along easily — I never knew him to rush. I remember now that Chief Engineer called him "Young Tracy," because of his father; "Old Tracy" — the real Tracy, so to speak — was the one who'd gone bust in the Depression. That was why Young Tracy had this job. He wasn't all that qualified, really; not so different from me. He sat down on Bertie Knox's desk with his back to him.

"Well, Bolshie," he said to me. This was a long joke: it had to do with my political views, as he saw them, and it was also a reference to a character in an English comic called "Pip and Squeak" that he and I had both read as children — we'd discussed it once. Pip and Squeak were a dog and a penguin. They had a son called Wilfred, who was a rabbit. Bolshie seemed to be a sort of acquaintance. He went around carrying one of those round black bombs with a sputtering fuse. He had a dog, I think — a dog with whiskers. I had told Mr. Tracy how modern educators were opposed to "Pip and Squeak." They thought that more than one generation of us had been badly misled by the unusual family unit of dog, penguin, and rabbit. It was argued that millions of children had grown up believing that if a dog made advances to a female penguin she would produce a rabbit. "Not a *rabbit*," said Mr. Tracy reasonably. "*Wilfred*."

I truly liked him. He must have thought I was going to say something now, if only to rise to the tease about "Bolshie," but I was in the grip of that dazzling anger that is a form of snow blindness, too. I could not speak, and and anyway didn't want to. I could only go on examining a pencil to see if it was company property or mine — as if that mattered. "Are you taking the day off or trying to leave me?" he said. I can feel that tense listening of men pretending to work. "I was looking over your application form," he said. "D'you know that your father knew my father? Yep. A long time ago. My father took it into his head to commission a mural for a plant in Sorel. Brave thing to do. Nobody did anything like that. Your father said it wasn't up his street. Suggested some other guy. My old man took the *two* of them down to Sorel. Did a lot of clowning around, but the Depression was just starting, so the idea fell through. My old man enjoyed it, though."

"Clowning around" could not possibly have been my father, but then the whole thing was so astonishing. "I should have mentioned it to you when you first came in," he said, "but I didn't realize it myself. There must be a million people called Muir; I happened to be looking at your form because apparently you're due for a raise." He whistled something for a second or two, then laughed and said, "Nobody ever quits around here. It can't be done. It upsets the delicate balance between labor and government. You don't want to do that. What do you want to do that for?"

"Mr. Curran doesn't like me."

"Mr. Curran is a brilliant man," he said, "Why, if you knew Curran's whole story you'd" — he paused — "you'd stretch out the hand of friendship."

"I've been asking and asking for a chair that doesn't wobble."

"Take the day off," he said. "Go to a movie or something. Tomorrow we'll start over." His life must have been like that. "You know, there's a war on. We're all needed. Mrs. Ireland has been brought here from . . ."

"From Trahnah," said Mrs. Ireland.

"Yes, from Toronto, to do important work. I'll see something gets done about that chair."

He stood up, hands in his pockets, slouching, really; gave an affable nod all round. The men didn't see; their noses were almost touching their work. He strolled back to his glass cubicle, whistling softly. The feeling in the room was like the sight of a curtain raised by the wind now sinking softly.

"Oh, Holy Hannah!" Mrs. Ireland burst out. "I thought this was supposed to be a wartime agency!"

No one replied. *My father knew your father. I'll see something gets done about that chair.* So that is how it works among men. To be noted, examined, compared.

Meanwhile I picked up the paper she'd tossed on my desk hours before and saw that it was an actuarial equation. I waited until the men had stopped being aware of us and took it over and told her I could not read it, let alone check it. It had obviously been some kind of test.

She said, "Well, it was too much to hope for. I have to single-handedly work out some wartime overtime pensions plan taking into account the cost of living and the earnest hope that the Canadian dollar won't sink." And I was to have been her assistant. I began to admire the genius someone — Assistant Chief Engineer Macaulay, perhaps — had obviously seen in me. Mrs. Ireland went on, "I gather after this little comic opera we've just witnessed that you're the blue-eyed girl around here." (Need I say that I'd hear this often? That the rumor I was Mr. Tracy's mistress now had firm hold on the feminine element in the room — though it never gained all the men — particularly on the biddies, the two or three old girls loafing along to retirement, in comfortable corsets that gave them a sort of picket fence around the middle? That the obscene anonymous notes I sometimes found on my desk — and at once unfairly blamed on Bertie Knox — were the first proof I had that prolonged virginity can be the mother of invention?) "You can have your desk put next to mine," said Mrs. Ireland. "I'll try to dig some good out of you."

But I had no intention of being mined by Mrs. Ireland. Remembering what Mr. Tracy had said about the hand of friendship I told her, truthfully, that it would be a waste for her and for me. My name was down to do documentary-film work, for which I thought I'd be better suited; I was to be told as soon as a vacancy occurred.

"Then you'll have a new girl," I said. "You can teach her whatever you like."

"*Girl?*" She could not keep her voice down, ever. "There'll not be a girl in this office again, if I have a say. Girls make me sick, sore, and weary."

I thought about that for a long time. I had believed it was only because of the men that girls were parked like third-class immigrants at the far end of the room — the darkest part, away from the windows — with the indignity of being watched by Supervisor, whose whole function was just that. But there, up on the life raft, stepping on girls' fingers, was Mrs. Ireland, too. If that was so, why didn't Mrs. Ireland get along with the men, and why did they positively and openly hate her — openly especially after Mr. Tracy's extraordinary and instructive sorting out of power?

"What blinking idiot would ever marry *her?*" said Bertie Knox. "Ten to one she's not married at all. Ireland must be her maiden name. She thinks the 'Mrs.' sounds good." I began to wonder if she was not a little daft sometimes: she used to talk to herself; quite a lot of it was about me.

"You can't run a wartime agency with *that* going on," she'd say loudly. "That" meant poor Mr. Tracy and me. Or else she would declare that it was unpatriotic of me to be drawing a man's salary. Here I think the men agreed. The salary was seventy-five dollars a month, which was less than a man's if he was doing the same work. The men had often hinted it was a lot for a girl. Girls had no expenses; they lived at home. Money paid them was a sort of handout. When I protested that I had the same expenses as any bachelor and did not live at home, it was countered by a reasonable "Where you live is up to you." They looked on girls as parasites of a kind, always being taken to restaurants and fed by men. They calculated the cost of probable outings, even to the Laura Secord chocolates I might be given, and rang the total as a casual profit to me. Bertie Knox used to sing, "I think that I shall never see a dame refuse a meal that's free." Mrs. Ireland said that all this money would be better spent on soldiers who were dying, on buying war bonds and plasma, on the purchase of tanks and Spitfires. "When I think of parents scrimping to send their sons to college!" she would conclude. All this was floods of clear water; I could not give it a shape. I kept wondering what she expected me to *do*, for that at least would throw a shadow on the water, but then she dropped me for a time in favor of another crusade, this one against Bertie Knox's singing. He had always sung. His voice conveyed rakish parodies of hymns and marches to every corner of the room. Most of the songs were well known; they came back to us from the troops, were either simple and rowdy or expressed a deep skepticism about the war, its aims and purposes, the way it was being conducted, and about the girls they had left at home. It was hard to shut Bertie Knox up: he had been around for a long time. Mrs. Ireland said she had not had the education she'd had to come here and listen to foul language. Now absolutely and flatly forbidden by Chief Engineer to sing any ribald song *plainly*, Bertie Knox managed with umptee-um syllables as best he could. He became Mrs. Ireland's counterpoint.

"I know there's a shortage of men," Mrs. Ireland would suddenly burst out.

"Oh umptee tum titty," sang Bertie Knox.

"And that after this war it will be still worse . . ."

"Ti umpty dum diddy."

"There'll hardly be a man left in the world worth his salt . . ."

"Tee umpty tum tumpty."

"But what I do not see . . ."

"Tee diddle dee dum."

"Is why a totally unqualified girl . . ."

"Tum tittle umpty tumpty."

"Should be subsidized by the taxpayers of this country . . ."

"Pum pum tee umpty pumpee."

"Just because her father failed to paint . . ."

"Oh umpty tumpty tumpty."

"A mural down in . . ."

"Tee umpty dum dum."

"Sorel."

"Tum tum, oh, dum dum, oh, pum pum, oh, oh, uuuum."

"Subsidized" stung, for I worked hard. Having no training I had no shortcuts. There were few mechanical shortcuts of any kind. The engineers used slide rules, and the machines might baffle today because of their simplicity. As for a computer, I would not have guessed what it might do or even look like. Facts were recorded on paper and stored in files and summarized by doing sums and displayed in some orderly fashion on graphs. I sat with one elbow on my desk, my left hand concealed in my hair. No one could see that I was counting on my fingers, in units of five and ten. The system by twelves would have finished me; luckily no one mentioned it. Numbers were a sunken world; they were a seascape from which perfect continents might emerge at any minute. I never saw more than their outline. I was caught on Zero. If zero meant Zero, how could you begin a graph on nothing? How could anything under zero be anything but Zero too? I spoke to Mr. Tracy: What occupied the space between Zero and One? It must be something arbitrary, not in the natural order of numbers. If One was solid ground, why not begin with One? Before One there was what? Thin air? Thin air must be Something. He said kindly, "Don't worry your head," and if I had continued would certainly have added, "Take the day off." Chief Engineer McCreery often had to remind me, "But we're not *paying* you to think!" If that was so, were we all being paid not to think? At the next place I worked things were even worse. It was another government agency, called Dominion Film Center — my first brush with the creative life. Here one was handed a folded thought like a shapeless school uniform and told, "There, wear that." Everyone had it on, regardless of fit. It was one step on: "We're not paying you to think about whatever you are thinking." I often considered approaching Mrs. Ireland, but she would not accept even a candy from me, let alone a question. "There's a war on" had been her discouraging refusal of a Life Saver once.

The men by now had found out about her husband. He had left school at Junior Fourth (Grade Seven) and "done nothing to improve himself." He was a Pole. She was ashamed of having a name that ended in "ski" and used her maiden name; Bertie Knox hadn't been far off. Thinking of it now, I realize she might not have been ashamed but only aware that the "ski" name on her application could have relegated it to a bottom drawer. Where did the men get their information, I wonder. Old "ski" was a lush who drank her paycheck and sometimes beat her up; the scarves she wound around her neck were meant to cover bruises.

That she was unhappily married I think did not surprise me. What impressed me was that so many of the men were too. I had become engaged to be married, for the third time. There was a slight overlapping of two, by which I mean that the one in Halifax did not know I was also going to marry the one from the West. To the men, who could not follow my life as closely as they'd have wanted — I gave out next to nothing — it seemed like a long betrothal to some puppy in uniform, whom they had never seen, and whose Christian name kept changing. One of my reasons for discretion was that I was still under age. Until now I had been using my minority as an escape hatch, the way a married man will use his wife — for "Ursula will never divorce" I substituted "My mother will never consent." Once I had made up my mind I simply began looking for roads around the obstacle; it was this search, in fact, that made me realize I must be serious. No one, no one at all, knew what I was up to, or what my entirely apocryphal emancipation would consist of; all that the men knew was that

this time it did look as if I was going through with it. They took
me aside, one after the other, and said, "Don't do it, Linnet.
Don't do it." Bertie Knox said, "Once you're in it, you're in it,
kiddo." I can't remember any man ever criticizing his own
wife — it is something men don't often do, anywhere — but
the warning I had was this: marriage was a watershed that
transformed sweet, cheerful, affectionate girls into, well, their
own mothers. Once a girl had caught (their word) a husband
she became a whiner, a snooper, a killjoy, a wet blanket, a
grouch, and a bully. What I gleaned out of this was that it
seemed hard on the men. But then even Mrs. Ireland, who
never said a word to me, declared, "I think it's terrible." She
said it was insane for me to marry someone on his way
overseas, to tie up my youth, to live like a widow without a
widow's moral status. Why were she and I standing together,
side by side, looking out the window at a gray sky, at pigeons,
at a streetcar grinding up the steep street? We could never
possibly have stood close, talking in low voices. And yet there
she is; there I am with Mrs. Ireland. For once she kept her
voice down. She looked out — not at me. She said the worst
thing of all. Remembering it, I see the unwashed
windowpane. She said, "Don't you girls ever know when
you're well off? Now you've got no one to lie to you, to belittle
you, to make a fool of you, to stab you in the back." But we
were different — different ages, different women, two lines of
a graph that could never cross.

Mostly when people say "I know exactly how I felt" it can't
be true, but here I am sure — sure of Mrs. Ireland and the
window and of what she said. The recollection has something
to do with the blackest kind of terror, as stunning as the bolts of
happiness that strike for no reason. This blackness, this
darkening, was not wholly Mrs. Ireland, no; I think it had to
do with the men, with squares and walls and limits and
numbers. How do you stand if you stand upon Zero? What
will the passage be like between Zero and One? And what will
happen at One? Yes, what will happen?

VARIETIES OF EXILE

I n the third summer of the war I began to meet refugees. There were a large numbers of them in Montreal — to me a source of infinite wonder. I could not get enough of them. They came straight out of the twilit Socialist-literary landscape of my reading and my desires. I saw them as prophets of a promised social order that was to consist of justice, equality, art, personal relations, courage, generosity. Each of them — Belgian, French, Catholic German, Socialist German, Jewish German, Czech — was a book I tried to read from start to finish. My dictionaries were films, poems, novels, Lenin, Freud. That the refugees tended to hate one another seemed no more than a deplorable accident. Nationalist pigheadedness, that chronic, wasting, and apparently incurable disease, was known to me only on Canadian terms and I did not always recognize its symptoms. Anything I could not decipher I turned into fiction, which was my way of untangling knots. At the office where I worked I now spent my lunch hour writing stories about people in exile. I tried to see Montreal as an Austrian might see it and to feel whatever he felt. I was entirely at home with foreigners, which is not surprising — the home was all in my head. They were the only people I had met until now who believed, as I did, that our victory would prove to be a tidal wave nothing could stop. What I did not know was how many of them hoped and expected their neighbors to be washed away too.

I was nineteen and for the third time in a year engaged to be married. What I craved at this point was not love, or romance, or a life added to mine, but conversation, which was harder to find. I knew by now that a man in love does not necessarily have anything interesting to say: If he has, he keeps it for other men. Men in Canada did not talk much to women and hardly at all to young ones. The impetus of love — of infatuation, rather — brought on a kind of conversation I saw no reason to pursue. A remark such as "I can't live without you" made the speaker sound not only half-witted to me but almost truly, literally, insane. There is a girl in a Stefan Zweig novel who says to her lover, "Is that all?" I had pondered this carefully many years before, for I supposed it had something unexpected to do with sex. Now I gave it another meaning, which was that where women were concerned men were satisfied with next to nothing. If every woman was a situation, she was somehow always the same situation, and what was expected from the woman — the situation — was so limited it was insulting. I had a large opinion of what I could do and provide, yet it came down to "Is that all? Is that all you expect?" Being promised to one person after another was turning into a perpetual state of hesitation and refusal: I was not used to hesitating over anything and so I supposed I must be wrong. The men in my office had warned me of the dangers of turning into a married woman; if this caution affected me it was only because it coincided with a misgiving of my own. My private name for married women was Red Queens. They looked to me like the Red Queen in *Through the Looking-Glass*, chasing after other people and minding their business for them. To get out of the heat that summer I had taken a room outside Montreal in an area called simply "the Lakeshore." In those days the Lakeshore was a string of verdant towns with next to no traffic. Dandelions grew in the pavement cracks. The streets were thickly shaded. A fragrance I have never forgotten of mown grass and leaf smoke drifted from yard to yard. As I walked to my commuters' train early in the morning I saw kids still in their pajamas digging holes in the lawns and Red Queen wives wearing housecoats. They stuck their heads out of screen doors and yelled instructions — to husbands, to children, to dogs, to postmen, to a neighbor's child. How could I be sure I wouldn't sound that way — so shrill, so discontented? As for a family, the promise of children all stamped with the same face, cast in the same genetic mold, seemed a cruel waste of possibilities. I would never have voiced this to anyone, for it would have been thought unnatural, even monstrous. When I was very young, under seven, my plan for the future had been to live in every country of the world and have a child in each. I had confided it; with adult adroitness my listener led me on. How many children? Oh, one to a country. And what would you do with them? Travel in trains. How would they go to school? I hate schools. How will they learn to read and write, then? They'll know already. What would you live on? It will all be free. That's not very sensible, is it? Why not? As a result of this idyll, of my divulgence of it, I was kept under watch for a time and my pocket money taken away lest I save it up and sail to a tropical island (where because of the Swiss Family Robinson I proposed to begin) long before the onset of puberty. I think no one realized I had not even a nebulous idea of how children sprang to life. I merely knew two persons were required for a ritual I believed had to continue for nine months, and which I imagined in the nature of a long card game with mysterious rules. When I was finally "told" — accurately, as it turned out — I was offended at being asked to believe something so unreasonable, which could not be true because I had never come across it in books. This trust in the printed word seems all the more remarkable when I remember that I thought children's books were written by other children. Probably at nineteen I was still dim about relevant dates, plain facts, brass tacks, consistent reasoning. Perhaps I was still hoping for magic card games to short-circuit every sort of common sense — common sense is only an admission we don't know much. I know that I wanted to marry this third man but that I didn't want to be anybody's Red Queen.

The commuters on the Montreal train never spoke much to each other. The mystifying and meaningless "Hot enough for you?" was about the extent of it. If I noticed one man more than the anonymous others it was only because he looked so hopelessly English, so unable or unwilling to concede to anything, even the climate. Once, walking a few steps behind him, I saw him turn into the drive of a stone house, one of the few old French-Canadian houses in that particular town. The choice of houses seemed to me peculiarly English too — though not, of course, what French Canadians call "English," for that includes plain Canadians, Irish, Swedes, anything you like not natively French. I looked again at the house and at the straight back going along the drive. His wife was on her knees holding a pair of edging shears. He stopped to greet her. She glanced up and said something in a carrying British voice so wild and miserable, so resentful, so intensely disagreeable that it could not have been the tag end of a morning quarrel; no, it was the thunderclap of some new engagement. After a second he went on up the walk, and in another I was out of earshot. I was persuaded that he had seen me; I don't know why. I also thought it must have been humiliating for him to have had a witness.

Which of us spoke first? It could not have been him and it most certainly could not have been me. There must have been a collision, for there we are, speaking, on a station platform. It is early morning, already hot. I see once again, without surprise, that he is not dressed for the climate.

He said he had often wondered what I was reading. I said I was reading "all the Russians." He said I really ought to read

Arthur Waley. I had never heard of Arthur Waley. Similar signalling takes place between galaxies rushing apart in the outer heavens. He said he would bring me a book by Arthur Waley the next day.

"Please don't. I'm careless with books. Look at the shape this one's in." It was the truth. "All the Russians" were being published in uniform edition with flag-red covers, on grayish paper, with microscopic print. The words were jammed together; you could not have put a pin between the lines. It was one of those cheap editions I think we were supposed to be sending the troops in order to cheer them up. Left in the grass beside a tennis court *The Possessed* now curved like a shell. A white streak ran down the middle of the shell. The rest of the cover had turned pink. That was nothing, he said. All I needed to do was dampen the cover with a sponge and put a weight on the book. *The Wallet of Kai Lung* had been to Ceylon with him and had survived. Whatever bait "Ceylon" may have been caught nothing. Army? Civil Service? I did not take it up. Anyway I thought I could guess.

"You'd better not bring a book for nothing. I don't always take this train."

He had probably noticed me every morning. The mixture of reserve and obstinacy that next crossed his face I see still. He smiled, oh, not too much: I'd have turned my back on a grin. He said, "I forgot to . . . Frank Cairns."

"Muir. Linnet Muir." Reluctantly.

The thing is, I knew all about him. He was, one, married and, two, too old. But there was also three: Frank Cairns was stamped, labelled, ticketed by his tie (club? regiment? school?); by his voice, manner, haircut, suit; by the impression he gave of being stranded in a jungle, waiting for a rescue party — from England, of course. He belonged to a species of British immigrant known as remittance men. Their obsolescence began on 3 September 1939 and by 8 May 1945 they were extinct. I knew about them from having had one in the family. Frank Cairns worked in a brokerage house — he told me later — but he probably did not need a job, at least not for a living. It must have been a way of ordering time, a flight from idleness, perhaps a means of getting out of the house.

The institution of the remittance man was British, its genesis a chemical structure of family pride, class insanity, and imperial holdings that seemed impervious to fission but in the end turned out to be more fragile than anyone thought. Like all superfluous and marginal persons, remittance men were characters in a plot. The plot began with a fixed scene, an immutable first chapter, which described a powerful father's taking umbrage at his son's misconduct and ordering him out of the country. The pound was then one to five dollars, and there were vast British territories everywhere you looked. Hordes of young men who had somehow offended their parents were shipped out, golden deportees, to Canada, South Africa, New Zealand, Singapore. They were reluctant pioneers, totally lacking any sense of adventure or desire to see that particular world. An income — the remittance — was provided on a standing banker's order, with one string attached: "Keep out of England." For the second chapter the plot allowed a choice of six crimes as reasons for banishment: Conflict over the choice of a profession — the son wants to be a tap-dancer. Gambling and debts — he has been barred from Monte Carlo. Dud checks — "I won't press a charge, sir, but see that the young rascal is kept out of harm's way." Marriage with a girl from the wrong walk of life — "Young man, you have made your bed!" Fathering an illegitimate child: ". . . and broken your mother's heart." Homosexuality, if discovered: too grave for even a lecture — it was a criminal offense.

This is the plot of the romance: this is what everyone repeated and what the remittance man believed of himself. Obviously, it is a load of codswallop. A man legally of age could marry the tattooed woman in a circus, be arrested for check-bouncing or for soliciting boys in Green Park, be obliged to recognize his by-blow and even to wed its mother, become a ponce or a professional wrestler, and still remain where he was born. All he needed to do was eschew the remittance and tell his papa to go to hell. Even at nineteen the plot was a story I wouldn't buy. The truth came down to something just as dramatic but boring to tell: a classic struggle for dominance with two protagonists — strong father, pliant son. It was also a male battle. No son was ever sent into exile by his mother, and no one has ever heard of a remittance *woman*. Yet daughters got into scrapes nearly as often as their brothers. Having no idea what money was, they ran up debts easily. Sometimes, out of ignorance of another sort, they dared to dispose of their own virginity, thus wrecking their value on the marriage market and becoming family charges for life. Accoucheurs had to be bribed to perform abortions; or else the daughters were dispatched to Austria and Switzerland to have babies they would never hear of again. A daughter's disgrace was long, expensive, and hard to conceal, yet no one dreamed of sending her thousands of miles away and forever: on the contrary, she became her father's unpaid servant, social secretary, dog walker, companion, sick nurse. Holding on to a daughter, dismissing a son were relatively easy: it depended on having tamely delinquent children, or a thunderous personality no child would dare to challenge, and on the weapon of money — bait or weapon, as you like.

Banished young, as a rule, the remittance man (the RM, in my private vocabulary) drifted for the rest of his life, never quite sounding or looking like anyone around him, seldom raising a family or pursuing an occupation (so much for the "choice of profession" legend) — remote, dreamy, bored. Those who never married often became low-key drunks. The remittance was usually ample without being handsome, but enough to keep one from doing a hand's turn; in any case few remittance men were fit to do much of anything, being well schooled but half educated, in that specifically English way, as well as markedly unaggressive and totally uncompetitive, which would have meant early death in the New World for anyone without an income. They were like children waiting for the school vacation so that they could go home, except that at home nobody wanted them: the nursery had been turned into a billiards room and Nanny dismissed. They were parted from mothers they rarely mentioned, whom in some way they blended with a Rupert Brooke memory of England, of the mother country, of the Old Country as everyone at home grew old. Often as not the payoff, the keep-away blackmail funds, came out of the mother's marriage settlement — out of the capital her own father had agreed to settle upon her unborn children during the wear and tear of Edwardian engagement negotiations. The son disgraced would never see more than a fixed income from this; he was cut off from a share of inheritance by his contract of exile. There were cases where the remittance ended abruptly with the mother's death, but that was considered a bad arrangement. Usually the allowance continued for the exile's lifetime and stopped when he died. No provision was made for his dependents, if he had them, and because of his own subject attitude to money he was unlikely to have made any himself. The income reverted to his sisters and brothers, to an estate, to a cat-and-dog hospital — whatever his father had decreed on some black angry day long before.

Whatever these sons had done their punishment was surely a cruel and singular one, invented for naughty children by a cosmic headmaster taking over for God: they were obliged to live over and over until they died the first separation from home, and the incomparable trauma of rejection. Yes, they were like children, perpetually on their way to a harsh school; they were eight years of age and sent "home" from India to childhoods of secret grieving among strangers. And this wound, this amputation, they would mercilessly inflict on their own children when the time came — on sons always, on daughters sometimes — persuaded that early heartbreak was right because it was British, hampered only by the financial limit set for banishment: it costs money to get rid of your young.

And how they admired their fathers, those helpless sons! They spoke of them with so much admiration, with such a depth of awe: only in memory can such voices still exist, the calm English voice on a summer night — a Canadian night so alien to the speaker — insisting, with sudden firmness, with a pause between words, "My . . . father . . . once . . . said . . . to . . . me . . ." and here would follow something utterly trivial, some advice about choosing a motorcar or training a dog. To the Canadian grandchildren the unknown grandfather was seven foot tall with a beard like George V, while the grandmother came through weepy and prissy and not very interesting. It was the father's Father, never met, never heard, who made Heaven and earth and Eve and Adam. The father in Canada seemed no more than an apostle transmitting a paternal message from the Father in England — the Father of us all. It was, however, rare for a remittance man to marry, rarer still to have any children; how could he become a father when he had never stopped being a son?

If the scattered freemasonry of offspring the remittance man left behind, all adult to elderly now, had anything in common it must have been their degree of incompetence. They were raised to behave well in situations that might never occur, trained to become genteel poor on continents where even the concept of genteel poverty has never existed. They were brought up with plenty of books and music and private lessons, a nurse sometimes, in a household where certain small luxuries were deemed essential — a way of life that, in North America at least, was supposed to be built on a sunken concrete base of money; otherwise you were British con men, a breed of gypsy, and a bad example.

Now, your remittance man was apt to find this assumption quite funny. The one place he would never take seriously was the place he was in. The identification of prominent local families with the name of a product, a commodity, would be his running joke: "The Allseeds are sugar, the Bilges are coal, the Cumquats are cough medicine, the Doldrums are coffins, the Earwigs are saucepans, the Fustians are timber, the Grindstones are beer." But his young, once they came up against it, were bound to observe that their concrete base was the dandelion fluff of a banker's order, their commodity nothing but "life in England before 1914," which was not negotiable. Also, the constant, nagging "What does your father really *do*?" could amount to persecution.

"Mr. Bainwood wants to know what you do."

"Damned inquisitive of him."

Silence. Signs of annoyance. Laughter sometimes. Or something silly: "What do *you* do when you aren't asking questions?"

No remittance man's child that I know of ever attended a university, though care was taken over the choice of schools. There they would be, at eighteen and nineteen, the boys wearing raincoats in the coldest weather, the girls with their hair ribbons and hand-knits and their innocently irritating English voices, well read, musical, versed in history, probably because they had been taught that the past is better than now, and somewhere else better than here. They must have been the only English-Canadian children to speak French casually, as a matter of course. Untidy, unpunctual, imperially tactless, they drifted into work that had to be "interesting," "creative," never demeaning, and where — unless they'd had the advantage of a rough time and enough nous to draw a line against the past — they seldom lasted. There was one in every public-relations firm, one to a radio station, two to a publisher — forgetting appointments, losing contracts, jamming typewriters, sabotaging telephones, apologizing in accents it would have taken elocution lessons to change, so strong had been paternal pressure against the hard Canadian "r," not to mention other vocables:

"A-t-e is *et*, darling, not ate."

"I can't say *et*. Only farmers say it."

"Perhaps here, but you won't always be here."

Of course the children were guilt-drenched, wondering which of the six traditional crimes they ought to pin on their father, what his secret was, what his past included, why he had been made an outcast. The answer was quite often "Nothing, no reason," but it meant too much to be unravelled and knit up. The saddest were those unwise enough to look into the families who had caused so much inherited woe. For the family was often as not smaller potatoes than the children had thought, and their father's romantic crime had been just the inability to sit for an examination, to stay at a university, to handle an allowance, to gain a toehold in any profession, or even to decide what he wanted to do — an ineptitude so maddening to live with that the Father preferred to shell out forever rather than watch his heir fall apart before his eyes. The male line, then, was a ghost story. A mother's vitality would be needed to create ectoplasm, to make the ghost offspring visible. Unfortunately the exiles were apt to marry absentminded women whose skirts are covered with dog hairs — the drooping, bewildered British-Canadian mouse, who counts on tea leaves to tell her "what will happen when Edward goes." None of us is ever saved entirely, but even an erratic and alarming maternal vitality could turn out to be better than none.

Frank Cairns was childless, which I thought wise of him. He had been to Ceylon, gone back to England with a stiff case of homesickness disguised as malaria, married, and been shipped smartly out again, this time to Montreal. He was a neat, I think rather a small, man, with a straight part in his hair and a quick, brisk walk. He noticed I was engaged. I did not reply. I told him I had been in New York, had come back about a year ago, and missed "different things." He seemed to approve. "You can't make a move here," he said more than once. I was not sure what he meant. If he had been only the person I have described I'd have started taking an earlier train to be rid of him. But Frank Cairns was something new, unique of his kind, and almost as good as a refugee, for he was a Socialist. At least he said he was. He said he had never voted anywhere but that if he ever in the future happened to be in England when there was an election he would certainly vote Labour. His Socialism did not fit anything else about him, and seemed to depend for its life on the memory of talks he'd once had with a friend whom he described as brilliant, philosophical, farseeing, and just. I thought, Like Christ, but did not know Frank Cairns well enough to say so. The nonbeliever I had become was sometimes dogged by the child whose nightly request had been "Gentle Jesus, meek and mild, look upon a little child," and I sometimes got into ferocious arguments with her, as well as with other people. I was too curious about Frank Cairns to wish to quarrel over religion — at any rate not at the beginning. He talked about his friend without seeming able to share him. He never mentioned his name. I had to fill in the blank part of this conversation without help; I made the friend a high-ranking civil servant in Ceylon, older than anyone — which might have meant forty-two — an intellectual revolutionary who could work the future out on paper, like arithmetic.

Wherever his opinions came from, Frank Cairns was the first person ever to talk to me about the English poor. They seemed to be a race, different in kind from other English. He showed me old copies of *Picture Post* he must have saved up from the Depression. In our hot summer train, where everyone was starched and ironed and washed and fed, we considered slum doorways and the faces of women at the breaking point. They looked like Lenin's "remnants of nations" except that there were too many of them for a remnant. I thought of my mother and her long preoccupation with the fate of the Scottsboro Boys. My mother had read and mooned and fretted about the Scottsboro case, while I tried to turn her attention to something urgent, such as that my school uniform was now torn in three places. It is quite possible that my mother had seldom seen a black except on railway trains. (If I say "black" it is only because it is expected. It was a rude and offensive term in my childhood and I would not have been allowed to use it. "Black" was the sort of thing South Africans said.) Had Frank Cairns actually seen those *Picture Post* faces, I wondered. His home, his England, was every other remittance man's — the one I called "Christopher-Robin-land" and had sworn to keep away from. He hated Churchill, I remember, but I was used to hearing that. No man who remembered the Dardanelles really trusted him. Younger men (I am speaking of the handful I knew who had any opinion at all) were not usually irritated by his rhetoric until they got into uniform.

Once in a book I lent him he found a scrap of paper on which I had written the title of a story I was writing, "The Socialist RM," and some scrawls in, luckily, a private shorthand of mine. A perilous moment: "remittance man" was a term of abuse all over the Commonwealth and Empire.

"What is it?" he asked, "Resident Magistrate?"

"It might be Royal Marine. Royal Mail. I honestly don't remember. I can't read my own writing sometimes." The last sentence was true.

His Socialism was unlike a Czech's or a German's; though he believed that one should fight hard for social change, there was a hopelessness about it, an almost moral belief that improving their material circumstances would get the down-trodden nowhere. At the same time, he thought the poor *were* happy, that they had some strange secret of happiness — the way people often think all Italians are happy because they have large families. I wondered if he really believed that a man with no prospects and no teeth in his head was spiritually better off than Frank Cairns and why, in that case, Frank Cairns did not let him alone with his underfed children and his native good nature. This was a British left-wing paradox I was often to encounter later on. What it seemed to amount to was leaving people more or less as they were, though he did speak about basic principles and the spread of education. It sounded dull. I was Russian-minded; I read Russian books, listened to Russian music. After Russia came Germany and Central Europe — that was where the real mystery and political excitement lay. His Webbs and his Fabians were plodding and gray. I saw the men with thick mustaches, wearing heavy boots, sharing lumpy meals with moral women. In the books he brought me I continued to find his absent friend. He produced Housman and Hardy (I could not read either), Siegfried Sassoon and Edmund Blunden, H. G. Wells and Bernard Shaw. The friend was probably a Scot — Frank Cairns admired them. The Scots of Canada, to me, stood for all that was narrow, grasping, at a standstill. How I distrusted those granite bankers who thought it was sinful to smoke! I was wrong, he told me. The true Scots were full of poetry and political passion. I said, "Are you sure?" and turned his friend into a native of Aberdeen and a graduate from Edinburgh. I also began a new notebook: "Scottish Labour Party. Keir Hardie. Others." This was better than the Webbs but still not as good as Rosa Luxemburg.

It was Frank Cairns who said to me, "Life has no point," without emphasis, in response to some ignorant assumption of mine. This was his true voice. I recall the sidelong glance, the lizard's eye that some men develop as they grow old or when they have too much to hide. I was no good with ages. I cannot place him even today. Early thirties, probably. What else did he tell me? That "Scotch" was the proper term and "Scots" an example of a genteelism overtaking the original. That unless the English surmounted their class obsessions with speech and accent Britain would not survive in the world after the war. His remedy (or his friend's) was having everyone go to the same schools. He surprised me even more by saying, "I would never live in England, not as it is now."

"Where, then?"

"Nowhere. I don't know."

"What about Russia? They all go to the same schools."

"Good Lord," said Frank Cairns.

He was inhabited by a familiar who spoke through him, provided him with jolting outbursts but not a whole thought. Perhaps that silent coming and going was the way people stayed in each other's lives when they were apart. What Frank Cairns was to me was a curio cabinet. I took everything out of the cabinet, piece by piece, examined the objects, set them down. Such situations, riddled with ambiguity, I would blunder about with for a long time until I learned to be careful.

The husband of the woman from whom I rented my summer room played golf every weekend. On one of those August nights when no one can sleep and the sky is nearly bright enough to read by, I took to the back yard and found him trying to cool off with a glass of beer. He remembered he had offered to give me golf lessons. I did not wish to learn, but did not say so. His wife spoke up from a deck chair: "You've never offered to teach me, I notice." She then compounded the error by telling me everyone was talking about me and the married man on the train. The next day I took the Käthe Kollwitz prints down from the walls of my room and moved back to Montreal without an explanation. Frank Cairns and I met once more that summer to return some books. That was all. When he called me at my office late in November, I said, "Who?"

He came into the coffee shop at Windsor Station, where I was waiting. He was in uniform. I had not noticed he was good-looking before. It was not something I noticed in men. He was a first lieutenant. I disapproved: "Couldn't they make you a private?"

"Too old," he said. "As it is I am too old for my rank." I thought he just meant he might be promoted faster because of that.

"You don't look old." I at once regretted this personal remark, the first he had heard from me. Indeed, he had shed most of his adult life. He must have seemed as young as this when he started out to Ceylon. The uniform was his visa to England; no one could shut him away now. His face was radiant, open: he was halfway there. This glimpse of a purpose astonished me; why should a uniform make the change he'd been unable to make alone? He was not the first soldier I saw transfigured but he was the first to affect me.

He kept smiling and staring at me. I hoped he was not going to make a personal remark in exchange for mine. He said, "That tam makes you look, I don't know, Canadian. I've always thought of you as English. I still think England is where you might be happy."

"I'm happy here. You said you'd never live there."

"It would be a good place for you," he said. "Well, well, we shall see."

He would see nothing. My evolution was like freaky weather then: a few months, a few weeks even, were the equivalent of long second thoughts later on. I was in a completely other climate. I no longer missed New York and "different things." I had become patriotic. Canadian patriotism is always anti-American in part, and feeds upon anecdotes. American tourists were beginning to arrive in Montreal looking for anything expensive or hard to find in the United States; when they could not buy rationed food such as meat and butter, or unrationed things such as nylon stockings (because they did not exist), they complained of ingratitude. This was because Canada was thought to be a recipient of American charity and on the other end of Lend-Lease. Canadians were, and are, enormously touchy. Great umbrage had been taken over a story that was going around in the States about Americans who had been soaked for black-market butter in Montreal; when they got back across the border they opened the package and found the butter stamped "Gift of the American People." This fable persisted throughout the war and turned up in print. An American friend saw it in, I think, Westbrook Pegler's column and wrote asking me if it was true. I composed a letter I meant to send to the *New York Times*, demolishing the butter story. I kept rewriting and reshaping it, trying to achieve a balance between crippling irony and a calm review of events. I never posted it, finally, because my grandmother appeared to me in a dream and said that only fools wrote to newspapers.

Our coffee was tepid, the saucers slopped. He complained, and the waitress asked if we knew there was a war on. "Christ, what a bloody awful country this is," he said.

I wanted to say, Then why are you with a Canadian regiment? I provided my own answer: They pay more than the Brits. We were actually quarrelling in my head, and on such a mean level. I began to tear up a paper napkin and to cry.

"I have missed you," he remarked, but quite happily; you could tell the need for missing was over. I had scarcely thought of him at all. I kept taking more and more napkins out of the container on the table and blotting my face and tearing the paper up. He must be the only man I ever cried about in a public place. I hardly knew him. He was not embarrassed, as a Canadian would have been, but looked all the happier. The glances we got from other tables were full of understanding. Everything gave the wrong impression — his uniform, my engagement ring, my tears. I told him I was going to be married.

"Nonsense," he said.

"I'm serious."

"You seem awfully young."

"I'll soon be twenty." A slip. I had told him I was older. It amazed me to remember how young I had been only the summer before. "But I won't actually be a married woman," I said, "because I hate everything about them. Another thing I won't be and that's the sensitive housewife — the one who listens to Brahms while she does the ironing and reads all the new books still in their jackets."

"No, don't be a sensitive housewife," he said.

He gave me *The Wallet of Kai Lung* and *Kai Lung's Golden Hours*, which had been in Ceylon with him and had survived.

D id we write to each other? That's what I can't remember. I was careless then; I kept moving on. Also I really did, that time, get married. My husband was posted three days afterward to an American base in the Aleutian Islands — I have forgotten why. Eight months later he returned for a brief embarkation leave and then went overseas. I had dreaded coming in to my office after my wedding for fear the men I worked with would tease me. But the mixture of war and separation recalled old stories of their own experiences, in the First World War. Also I had been transformed into someone with a French surname, which gave them pause.

"Does he — uh — speak any French?"

"Not a word. He's from the West." Ah. "But he ought to. His father is French." Oh.

I had disappeared for no more than four days, but I was Mrs. Something now, not young Linnet. They spoke about me as "she", and not "Linnet" or "the kid." I wondered what they saw when they looked at me. In every head bent over a desk or a drawing board there was an opinion about women; expressed, it sounded either prurient or coarse, but I still cannot believe that is all there was to it. I know I shocked them profoundly once by saying that a wartime ditty popular with the troops, "Rock me to sleep, Sergeant-Major, tuck me in my little bed," was innocently homosexual. That I could have such a turn of thought, that I could use such an expression, that I even knew it existed seemed scandalous to them. "You read too damned much," I was told. Oddly enough, they had never minded my hearing any of the several versions of the song, some of which were unspeakable; all they objected to was my unfeminine remark. When I married they gave me a suitcase, and when I left for good they bought me a Victory

Bond. I had scrupulously noted every detail of the office, and the building it was in, yet only a few months later I would walk by it without remembering I had ever been inside, and it occurs to me only now that I never saw any of them again.

I was still a minor, but emancipated by marriage. I did not need to ask parental consent for anything or worry about being brought down on the wing. I realized how anxious I had been once the need for that particular anxiety was over. A friend in New York married to a psychiatrist had sent me a letter saying I had her permission to marry. She did not describe herself as a relative or state anything untrue — she just addressed herself to whom it may concern, said that as far as *she* was concerned I could get married, and signed. She did not tell her husband, in case he tried to put things right out of principle, and I mentioned to no one that the letter was legal taradiddle and carried about as much weight as a library card. I mention this to show what essential paperwork sometimes amounts to. My husband, aged twenty-four, had become my legal guardian under Quebec's preposterous Napoleonic law, but he never knew that. When he went overseas he asked me not to join any political party, which I hadn't thought of doing, and not to enlist in the Army or the Air Force. The second he vanished I tried to join the Wrens, which had not been on the list only because it slipped his mind. Joining one of the services had never been among my plans and projects — it was he who accidentally put the idea in my head. I now decided I would turn up overseas, having made it there on my own, but I got no further than the enlistment requirements, which included ". . . of the white race only." This barrier turned out to be true of nearly all the navies of the Commonwealth countries. I supposed everyone must have wanted it that way, for I never heard it questioned. I was only beginning to hear the first rumblings of hypocrisy on our side — the right side; the wrong side seemed to be guilty of every sin humanly possible except simulation of virtue. I put the blame for the racial barrier on Churchill, who certainly *knew*, and had known since the First

World War; I believed that Roosevelt, Stalin, Chiang Kai-shek, and de Gaulle did not know, and that should it ever come to their attention they would be as shocked as I was.

Instead of enlisting I passed the St. John Ambulance first-aid certificate, which made me a useful person in case of total war. The Killed-Wounded-Missing columns of the afternoon paper were now my daily reading. It became a habit so steadfast that I would automatically look for victims even after the war ended. The summer of the Scottish Labour Party, Keir Hardie, and Others fell behind, as well as a younger, discarded Linnet. I lighted ferocious autos-da-fé. Nothing could live except present time. In the ever-new present I read one day that Major Francis Cairns had died of wounds in Italy. Who remembers now the shock of the known name? It was like a flat white light. One felt apart from everyone, isolated. The field of vision drew in. Then, before one could lose consciousness, vision expanded, light and shadow moved, voices pierced through. One's heart, which had stopped, beat hard enough to make a room shudder. All this would occupy about a second. The next second was inhabited by disbelief. I saw him in uniform, so happy, halfway there, and myself making a spectacle of us, tearing a paper napkin. I was happy for him that he would never need to return to the commuting train and the loneliness and be forced to relive his own past. I wanted to write a casual letter saying so. One's impulse was always to write to the dead. Nobody knew I knew him, and in Canada it was not done to speak of the missing. I forgot him. He went under. I was doing a new sort of work and sharing a house with another girl whose husband was also overseas. Montreal had become a completely other city. I was no longer attracted to refugees. They were going through a process called "integrating." Some changed their names. Others applied for citizenship. A refugee eating cornflakes was of no further interest. The house I now lived in contained a fireplace, in which I burned all my stories about Czech and German anti-Fascists. In the picnic hamper I used for storing journals and notebooks I found a manila envelope marked "Lakeshore." It contained several versions of "The Socialist RM" and a few other things that sounded as if they were translated from the Russian by Constance Garnett. I also found a brief novel I had no memory of having written, about a Scot from Aberdeen, a left-wing civil servant in Ceylon — a man from somewhere, living elsewhere, confident that another world was entirely possible, since he had got it all down. It had shape, density, voice, but I destroyed it too. I never felt guilt about forgetting the dead or the living, but I minded about that one manuscript for a time. All this business of putting life through a sieve and then discarding it was another variety of exile; I knew that even then, but it seemed quite right and perfectly natural.

VOICES
LOST IN SNOW

Halfway between our two great wars, parents whose own early years had been shaped with Edwardian firmness were apt to lend a tone of finality to quite simple remarks: "Because I say so" was the answer to "Why?," and a child's response to "What did I just tell you?" could seldom be anything but "Not to" — not to say, do, touch, remove, go out, argue, reject, eat, pick up, open, shout, appear to sulk, appear to be cross. Dark riddles filled the corners of life because no enlightenment was thought required. Asking questions was "being tiresome," while persistent curiosity got one nowhere, at least nowhere of interest. How much has changed? Observe the drift of words descending from adult to child — the fall of personal questions, observations, unnecessary instructions. Before long the listener seems blanketed. He must hear the voice as authority muffled, a hum through snow. The tone has changed — it may be coaxing, even plaintive — but the words have barely altered. They still claim the ancient right-of-way through a young life.

"Well, old cock," said my father's friend Archie McEwen, meeting him one Saturday in Montreal. "How's Charlotte

taking life in the country?" Apparently no one had expected
my mother to accept the country in winter.

"Well, old cock," I repeated to a country neighbor, Mr.
Bainwood. "How's life?" What do you suppose it meant to me,
other than a kind of weathervane? Mr. Bainwood thought it
over, then came round to our house and complained to my
mother.

"It isn't blasphemy," she said, not letting him have much
satisfaction from the complaint. Still, I had to apologize. "I'm
sorry" was a ritual habit with even less meaning than "old
cock." "Never say that again," my mother said after he had
gone.

"Why not?"

"Because I've just told you not to."

"What does it mean?"

"Nothing."

It must have been after yet another "nothing" that one
summer's day I ran screaming around a garden, tore the heads
off tulips, and — no, let another voice finish it; the only
authentic voices I have belong to the dead: ". . . then she *ate*
them."

It was my father's custom if he took me with him to visit a
friend on Saturdays not to say where we were going. He was
more taciturn than any man I have known since, but that
wasn't all of it; being young, I was the last person to whom
anyone owed an explanation. These Saturdays have turned
into one whitish afternoon, a windless snowfall, a steep street.
Two persons descend the street, stepping carefully. The child,
reminded every day to keep her hands still, gesticulates wildly
— there is the flash of a red mitten. I will never overtake this
pair. Their voices are lost in snow.

We were living in what used to be called the country and is
now a suburb of Montreal. On Saturdays my father and I
came in together by train. I went to the doctor, the dentist, to

my German lesson. After that I had to get back to Windsor Station by myself and on time. My father gave me a boy's watch so that the dial would be good and large. I remember the No. 83 streetcar trundling downhill and myself, wondering if the watch was slow, asking strangers to tell me the hour. Inevitably — how could it have been otherwise? — after his death, which would not be long in coming, I would dream that someone important had taken a train without me. My route to the meeting place — deviated, betrayed by stopped clocks — was always downhill. As soon as I was old enough to understand from my reading of myths and legends that this journey was a pursuit of darkness, its terminal point a sunless underworld, the dream vanished.

Sometimes I would be taken along to lunch with one or another of my father's friends. He would meet the friend at Pauzé's for oysters or at Drury's or the Windsor Grill. The friend would more often than not be Scottish- or English-sounding, and they would talk as if I were invisible, as Archie McEwen had done, and eat what I thought of as English food — grilled kidneys, sweetbreads — which I was too finicky to touch. Both my parents had been made wretched as children by having food forced on them and so that particular torture was never inflicted on me. However, the manner in which I ate was subject to precise attention. My father disapproved of the North American custom that he called "spearing" (knife laid on the plate, fork in the right hand). My mother's eye was out for a straight back, invisible chewing, small mouthfuls, immobile silence during the interminable adult loafing over dessert. My mother did not care for food. If we were alone together, she would sit smoking and reading, sipping black coffee, her elbows used as props — a posture that would have called for instant banishment had I so much as tried it. Being constantly observed and corrected was like having a fly buzzing around one's plate. At Pauzé's, the only child, perhaps the only female, I sat up to an oak counter and ate oysters quite neatly, not knowing exactly what they were and certainly not that they were alive. They were served as in "The Walrus and the Carpenter," with bread and butter, pepper and vinegar. Dessert was a chocolate biscuit — plates of them stood at intervals along the counter. When my father and I ate alone, I was not required to say much, nor could I expect a great deal in the way of response. After I had been addressing him for minutes, sometimes he would suddenly come to life and I would know he had been elsewhere. "Of course I've been listening," he would protest, and he would repeat by way of proof the last few words of whatever it was I'd been saying. He was seldom present. I don't know where my father spent his waking life: just elsewhere.

What was he doing alone with a child? Where was his wife? In the country, reading. She read one book after another without looking up, without scraping away the frost on the windows. "The Russians, you know, the Russians," she said to her mother and me, glancing around in the drugged way adolescent readers have. "They put salt on the window sills in winter." Yes, so they did, in the nineteenth century, in the boyhood of Turgenev, of Tolstoy. The salt absorbed the moisture between two sets of windows sealed shut for half the year. She must have been in a Russian country house at that moment, surrounded by a large Russian family, living out vast Russian complications. The flat white fields beyond her imaginary windows were like the flat white fields she would have observed if only she had looked out. She was myopic; the pupil when she had been reading seemed to be the whole of the eye. What age was she then? Twenty-seven, twenty-eight. Her husband had removed her to the country; now that they were there he seldom spoke. How young she seems to me now — half twenty-eight in perception and feeling, but with a husband, a child, a house, a life, an illiterate maid from the village whose life she confidently interfered with and mismanaged, a small zoo of animals she alternately cherished and forgot; and she was the daughter of such a sensible, truthful, pessimistic woman — pessimistic in the way women become when they settle for what actually exists.

Our rooms were not Russian — they were aired every day and the salt became a great nuisance, blowing in on the floor. "There, Charlotte, what did I tell you?" my grandmother said. This grandmother did not care for dreams or for children. If I sensed the first, I had no hint of the latter. Out of decency she kept it quiet, at least in a child's presence. She had the reputation, shared with a long-vanished nurse named Olivia, of being able to "do anything" with me, which merely meant an ability to provoke from a child behavior convenient for adults. It was she who taught me to eat in the Continental way, with both hands in sight at all times upon the table, and who made me sit at meals with books under my arms so I would learn not to stick out my elbows. I remember having accepted this nonsense from her without a trace of resentment. Like Olivia, she could make the most pointless sort of training seem a natural way of life. (I think that as discipline goes this must be the most dangerous form of all.) She was one of three godparents I had — the important one. It is impossible for me to enter the mind of this agnostic who taught me prayers, who had already shed every remnant of belief when she committed me at the font. I know that she married late and reluctantly; she would have preferred a life of solitude and independence, next to impossible for a woman in her time. She had the positive voice of the born teacher, sharp manners, quick blue eyes, and the square, massive figure common to both lines of her ancestry — the West of France, the North of Germany. When she said "There, Charlotte, what did I tell you?" without obtaining an answer, it summed up mother and daughter both.

My father's friend Malcolm Whitmore was the second godparent. He quarrelled with my mother when she said something flippant about Mussolini, disappeared, died in Europe some years later, though perhaps not fighting for Franco, as my mother had it. She often rewrote other people's lives, providing them with suitable and harmonious endings. In her version of events you were supposed to die as you'd lived. He would write sometimes, asking me, "Have you been confirmed yet?" He had never really held a place and could not by dying leave a gap. The third godparent was a young woman named Georgie Henderson. She was my mother's choice, for a long time her confidante, partisan, and close sympathizer. Something happened, and they stopped seeing each other. Georgie was not her real name — it was Edna May. One of the reasons she had fallen out with my mother was that I had not been called Edna May too. Apparently, this had been promised.

Without saying where we were going, my father took me along to visit Georgie one Saturday afternoon.

"You didn't say you were bringing Linnet" was how she greeted him. We stood in the passage of a long, hot, high-ceilinged apartment, treading snow water into the rug.

He said, "Well, she is your godchild, and she has been ill."

My godmother shut the front door and leaned her back against it. It is in this surprisingly dramatic pose that I recall her. It would be unfair to repeat what I think I saw then, for she and I were to meet again once, only once, many years after this, and I might substitute a lined face for a smooth one and tough, large-knuckled hands for fingers that may have been delicate. One has to allow elbowroom in the account of a rival: "She must have had something" is how it generally goes, long after the initial "What can he see in her? He must be deaf and blind." Georgie, explained by my mother as being the natural daughter of Sarah Bernhardt and a stork, is only a shadow, a tracing, with long arms and legs and one of those sightly puggy faces with pulled-up eyes.

Her voice remains — the husky Virginia-tobacco whisper I associate with so many women of that generation, my parents' friends; it must have come of age in English Montreal around

1920, when girls began to cut their hair and to smoke. In middle life the voice would slide from low to harsh, and develop a chronic cough. For the moment it was fascinating to me — opposite in pitch and speed from my mother's, which was slightly too high and apt to break off, like that of a singer unable to sustain a long note.

It was true that I had been ill, but I don't think my godmother made much of it that afternoon, other than saying, "It's all very well to talk about that now, but I was certainly never told much, and as for that doctor, you ought to just hear what Ward thinks." Out of this whispered jumble my mother stood accused — of many transgressions, certainly, but chiefly of having discarded Dr. Ward Mackey, everyone's doctor and a family friend. At the time of my birth my mother had all at once decided she liked Ward Mackey better than anyone else and had asked him to choose a name for me. He could not think of one, or rather, thought of too many, and finally consulted his own mother. She had always longed for a daughter, so that she could call her after the heroine of a novel by, I believe, Marie Corelli. The legend so often repeated to me goes on to tell that when I was seven weeks old my father suddenly asked, "What did you say her name was?"

"Votre fille a frôlé la phtisie," the new doctor had said, the one who had now replaced Dr. Mackey. The new doctor was known to me as Uncle Raoul, though we were not related. This manner of declaring my brush with consumption was worlds away from Ward Mackey's "subject to bilious attacks." Mackey's objections to Uncle Raoul were neither envious nor personal, for Mackey was the sort of bachelor who could console himself with golf. The Protestant in him truly believed those other doctors to be poorly trained and superstitious, capable of recommending the pulling of teeth to cure tonsillitis, and of letting their patients cough to death or perish from septicemia just through Catholic fatalism.

What parent could fail to gasp and marvel at Uncle Raoul's announcement? Any but either of mine. My mother could invent and produce better dramas any day; as for my father, his French wasn't all that good and he had to have it explained. Once he understood that I had grazed the edge of tuberculosis, he made his decision to remove us all to the country, which he had been wanting a reason to do for some time. He was, I think, attempting to isolate his wife, but by taking her out of the city he exposed her to a danger that, being English, he had never dreamed of: this was the heart-stopping cry of the steam train at night, sweeping across a frozen river, clattering on the ties of a wooden bridge. From our separate rooms my mother and I heard the unrivalled summons, the long, urgent, uniquely North American beckoning. She would follow and so would I, but separately, years and desires and destinations apart. I think that women once pledged in such a manner are more steadfast than men.

"*Frôler*" was the charmed word in that winter's story; it was a hand brushing the edge of folded silk, a leaf escaping a spiderweb. Being caught in the web would have meant staying in bed day and night in a place even worse than a convent school. Charlotte and Angus, whose lives had once seemed so enchanted, so fortunate and free that I could not imagine lesser persons so much as eating the same kind of toast for breakfast, had to share their lives with me, whether they wanted to or not — thanks to Uncle Raoul, who always supposed me to be their principal delight. I had been standing on one foot for months, now, midway between *frôler* and *falling into*, propped up by a psychosomatic guardian angel. Of course I could not stand that way forever; inevitably my health improved and before long I was declared out of danger and then restored — to the relief and pleasure of all except the patient.

"I'd like to see more of you than eyes and nose," said my godmother. "Take off your things." I offer this as an example of unnecessary instruction. Would anyone over the age of three prepare to spend the afternoon in a stifling room wrapped like a mummy in outdoor clothes? "She's smaller than she looks," Georgie remarked, as I began to emerge. This authentic godmother observation drives me to my only refuge, the insistence that she must have had something — he could not have been completely deaf and blind. Divested of hat, scarf, coat, overshoes, and leggings, grasping the handkerchief pressed in my hand so I would not interrupt later by asking for one, responding to my father's muttered "Fix your hair," struck by the command because it was he who had told me not to use "fix" in that sense, I was finally able to sit down next to him on a white sofa. My godmother occupied its twin. A low table stood between, bearing a decanter and glasses and a pile of magazines and, of course, Georgie's ashtrays; I think she smoked even more than my mother did.

On one of these sofas, during an earlier visit with my mother and father, the backs of my dangling feet had left a smudge of shoe polish. It may have been the last occasion when my mother and Georgie were ever together. Directed to stop humming and kicking, and perhaps bored with the conversation in which I was not expected to join, I had soon started up again.

"It doesn't matter," my godmother said, though you could tell she minded.

"Sit up," my father said to me.

"I am sitting up. What do you think I'm doing?" This was not answering but answering back; it is not an expression I ever heard from my father, but I am certain it stood like a stalled truck in Georgie's mind. She wore the look people put on when they are thinking, Now what are you spineless parents going to do about that?

"Oh, for God's sake, she's only a child," said my mother, as though that had ever been an excuse for anything.

Soon after the sofa-kicking incident she and Georgie moved into the hibernation known as "not speaking." This, the lingering condition of half my mother's friendships, usually followed her having said the very thing no one wanted to hear, such as "Who wants to be called Edna May, anyway?"

Once more in the hot pale room where there was nothing to do and nothing for children, I offended my godmother again, by pretending I had never seen her before. The spot I had kicked was pointed out to me, though, owing to new slip-covers, real evidence was missing. My father was proud of my quite surprising memory, of its long backward reach and the minutiae of detail I could describe. My failure now to shine in a domain where I was naturally gifted, that did not require lessons or create litter and noise, must have annoyed him. I also see that my guileless-seeming needling of my godmother was a close adaptation of how my mother could be, and I attribute it to a child's instinctive loyalty to the absent one. Giving me up, my godmother placed a silver dish of mint wafers where I could reach them — white, pink, and green, overlapping — and suggested I look at a magazine. Whatever the magazine was, I had probably seen it, for my mother subscribed to everything then. I may have turned the pages anyway, in case at home something had been censored for children. I felt and am certain I have not invented Georgie's disappointment at not seeing Angus alone. She disliked Charlotte now, and so I supposed he came to call by himself, having no quarrel of his own; he was still close to the slighted Ward Mackey.

My father and Georgie talked for a while — she using people's initials instead of their names, which my mother would not have done — and they drank what must have been sherry, if I think of the shape of the decanter. Then we left and went down to the street in a wood-panelled elevator that had sconce lights, as in a room. The end of the afternoon had a particular shade of color then, which is not tinted by distance or enhancement but has to do with how streets were lighted. Lamps were still gas, and their soft gradual blooming at dusk made the sky turn a peacock blue that slowly deepened to marine, then indigo. This uneven light falling in blurred pools gave the snow it touched a quality of phosphorescence, beyond which were night shadows in which no one lurked.

There were few cars, little sound. A fresh snowfall would lie in the streets in a way that seemed natural. Sidewalks were dangerous, casually sanded; even on busy streets you found traces of the icy slides children's feet had made. The reddish brown of the stone houses, the curve and slope of the streets, the constantly changing sky were satisfactory in a way that I now realize must have been aesthetically comfortable. This is what I saw when I read "city" in a book; I had no means of knowing that "city" one day would also mean drab, filthy, flat, or that city blocks could turn into dull squares without mystery.

We crossed Sherbrooke Street, starting down to catch our train. My father walked everywhere in all weathers. Already mined, colonized by an enemy prepared to destroy what it fed on, fighting it with every wrong weapon, squandering strength he should have been storing, stifling pain in silence rather than speaking up while there might have been time, he gave an impression of sternness that was a shield against suffering. One day we heard a mob roaring four syllables over and over, and we turned and went down a different street. That sound was starkly terrifying, something a child might liken to the baying of wolves.

"What is it?"

"Howie Morenz."

"Who is it? Are they chasing him?"

"No, they like him," he said of the hockey player admired to the point of dementia. He seemed to stretch, as if trying to keep every bone in his body from touching a nerve; a look of helplessness such as I had never seen on a grown person gripped his face and he said this strange thing: "Crowds eat me. Noise eats me." The kind of physical pain that makes one seem rat's prey is summed up in my memory of this.

When we came abreast of the Ritz-Carlton after leaving Georgie's apartment, my father paused. The lights within at that time of day were golden and warm. If I barely knew what "hotel" meant, never having stayed in one, I connected the lights with other snowy afternoons, with stupefying adult conversation (Oh, those shut-in velvet-draped unaired low-voice problems!) compensated for by creamy bitter hot choco-late poured out of a pink-and-white china pot.

"You missed your gootay," he suddenly remembered. Established by my grandmother, "goûter" was the family word for tea. He often transformed French words, like putty, into shapes he could grasp. No, Georgie had not provided a goûter, other than the mint wafers, but it was not her fault — I had not been announced. Perhaps if I had not been so disagreeable with her, he might have proposed hot chocolate now, though I knew better than to ask. He merely pulled my scarf up over my nose and mouth, as if recalling something Uncle Raoul had advised. Breathing inside knitted wool was delicious — warm, moist, pungent when one had been sucking on mint candies, as now. He said, "You didn't enjoy your visit much."

"Not very," through red wool.

"No matter," he said. "You needn't see Georgie again unless you want to," and he walked on. He must have been smarting, for he liked me to be admired. When I was not being admired I was supposed to keep quiet. "You needn't see Georgie again" was also a private decision about himself. He was barely thirty-one and had a full winter to live after this one — little more. Why? "Because I say so." The answer seems to speak out of the lights, the stones, the snow; out of the crucial second when inner and outer forces join, and the environment becomes part of the enemy too.

Ward Mackey used to mention me as "Angus's precocious pain in the neck," which is better than nothing. Long after that afternoon, when I was about twenty, Mackey said to me, "Georgie didn't play her cards well where he was concerned. There was a point where if she had just made one smart move she could have had him. Not for long, of course, but none of us knew that."

What cards, I wonder. The cards have another meaning for me — they mean a trip, a death, a letter, tomorrow, next year.

I saw only one move that Saturday: my father placed a card face up on the table and watched to see what Georgie made of it. She shrugged, let it rest. There she sits, looking puggy but capable. Angus waiting, the precocious pain in the neck turning pages, hoping to find something in the *National Geographic* harmful for children. I brush in memory against the spiderweb: what if she had picked up, remarking in her smoky voice, "Yes, I can use that"? It was a low card, the kind that only a born gambler would risk as part of a long-term strategy. She would never have weakened a hand that way; she was not gambling but building. He took the card back and dropped his hand, and their long intermittent game came came to an end. The card must have been the eight of clubs — "a female child."

THE DOCTOR

Who can remember now a picture called "The Doctor"? From 1891, when the original was painted, to the middle of the Depression, when it finally went out of style, reproductions of this work flowed into every crevice and corner of North America and the British Empire, swamping continents. Not even "The Angelus" supplied as rich a mixture of art and lesson. The two people in "The Angelus" are there to tell us clearly that the meek inherit nothing but seem not to mind; in "The Doctor" a cast of four enacts a more complex statement of Christian submission or Christian pessimism, depending on the beholder: God's Will is manifested in a dying child, Helpless Materialism in a baffled physician, and Afflicted Humanity in the stricken parents. The parable is set in a spotless cottage; the child's bed, composed of three chairs, is out of a doll's house. In much of the world — the world as it was, so much smaller than now — two full generations were raised with the monochrome promise that existence is insoluble, tragedy static, poverty endearing, and heavenly justice a total mystery.

It must have come as a shock to overseas visitors when they

discovered "The Doctor" incarnated as an oil painting in the Tate Gallery in London, in the company of other Victorian miseries entitled "Hopeless Dawn" and "The Last Day in the Old Home." "The Doctor" had not been divinely inspired and distributed to chasten us after all, but was the work of someone called Sir Luke Fildes — nineteenth-century rationalist and atheist, for all anyone knew. Perhaps it was simply a scene from a three-decker novel, even a joke. In museum surroundings — classified, ticketed — "The Doctor" conveyed a new instruction: Death is sentimental, art is pretense.

Some people had always hated "The Doctor." My father, for one. He said, "You surely don't want *that* thing in your room."

The argument (it became one) took place in Montreal, in a house that died long ago without leaving even a ghost. He was in his twenties, to match the century. I had been around about the length of your average major war. I had my way but do not remember how; neither tears nor temper ever worked. What probably won out was his wish to be agreeable to Dr. Chauchard, the pediatrician who had given me the engraving. My father seemed to like Chauchard, as he did most people — just well enough — while my mother, who carried an uncritical allegiance from person to person, belief to belief, had recently declared Chauchard to be mentally, morally, and spiritually without fault.

Dr. Chauchard must have been in his thirties then, but he seemed to me timeless, like God the Father. When he took the engraving down from the wall of his office, I understood him to be offering me a portrait of himself. My mother at first refused it, thinking I had asked; he assured her I had not, that he had merely been struck by my expression when I looked at the ailing child. "*C'est une sensible,*" he said — an appraisal my mother dismissed by saying I was as tough as a boot, which I truly believe to have been her opinion.

What I was sensitive to is nearly too plain to be signalled: the dying child, a girl, is the heart of the composition. The parents are in the shadow, where they belong. Their function is to be sorry. The doctor has only one patient; light from a tipped lampshade falls on her and her alone.

The street where Dr. Chauchard lived began to decline around the same time as the popularity of "The Doctor" and is now a slum. No citizens' committee can restore the natural elegance of those gray stone houses, the swept steps, the glittering windows, because, short of a miracle, it cannot resurrect the kind of upper-bourgeois French Canadians who used to live there. They have not migrated or moved westward in the city — they have ceased to exist. The handful of dust they sprang from, with its powerful components of religion and history, is part of another clay. They were families who did not resent what were inaccurately called "the English" in Montreal; they had never acknowledged them. The men read a newspaper sometimes, the women never. The women had a dark version of faith for private drama, a family tree to memorize for intellectual exercise, intense family affection for the needs of the heart. Their houses, like Dr. Chauchard's, smelled of cleanness as if cleanness were a commodity, a brand of floor wax. Convents used to have that smell; the girls raised in them brought to married life an ideal of house-keeping that was a memory of the polished convent corridor, with strict squares of sunlight falling where and as they should. Two sons and five daughters was the average for children; Simone, Pauline, Jeanne, Yvonne, and Louise the feminine names of the decade. The girls when young wore religious medals like golden flower petals on thin chains, had positive torrents of curls down to their shoulder blades, and came to children's parties dressed in rose velvet and white stockings, too shy to speak. Chauchard, a bachelor, came out of this world, which I can describe best only through its girls and women.

His front door, painted the gloomy shade my father called Montreal green, is seen from below, at an angle — a bell too high for me during the first visits, a letter box through which I called, "Open the door; *c'est moi*," believing still that *moi*

would take me anywhere. But no one could hear in any
language, because two vestibules, one behind the other, stood
in the way. In the first one overshoes dripped on a mat, then
came a warmer place for coats. Each vestibule had its door,
varnished to imitate the rings of a tree trunk, enhanced by a
nature scene made of frosted glass; you unbuckled galoshes
under herons and palm trees and shed layers of damp wool
under swans floating in a landscape closer to home.

Just over the letter box of the green door a large, beautifully
polished brass plate carried, in sloped writing:

> Docteur Raoul Chauchard
> Spécialiste en Médecine Infantile
> Ancien Externe et Interne
> des Hôpitaux de Paris
> Sur Rendez-vous

On the bottom half of the plate this information was repeated
in English, though the only English I recall in the waiting
room was my mother's addressed to me.

He was not Parisian but native to the city, perhaps to the
street, even to the house, if I think of how the glass-shaded
lamps and branched chandeliers must have followed an
evolution from oil to kerosene to gas to electricity without
changing shape or place. Rooms and passages were papered
deep blue fading to green (the brighter oblong left by the
removal of "The Doctor" was about the color of a teal), so that
the time of day indoors was winter dusk, with pools of light like
uncurtained windows. An assemblage of gilt-framed pictures
began between the heron and swan doors with brisk scenes of
Biblical injustice — the casting-out of Hagar, the swindling of
Esau — and moved along the hall with European history:
Vercingetorix surrendering to the Romans, the earthquake at
Lisbon, Queen Victoria looking exactly like a potato pancake
receiving some dark and humble envoy; then, with a light over
him to mark his importance, Napoleon III reviewing a

regiment from a white horse. (The popularity of "Napoléon" as a Christian name did not connect with the first Bonaparte, as English Canadians supposed — when any thought was given to any matter concerning French Canadians at all — but with his nephew, the lesser Bonaparte, who had never divorced or insulted the Pope, and who had established clerical influence in the saddle as firmly as it now sat upon Quebec.) The sitting-room-converted-to-waiting-room had on display landmarks of Paris, identified in two languages:

Le Petit Palais — The Petit Palais
Place Vendôme — Place Vendôme
Rue de la Paix — Rue de la Paix

as if the engraver had known they would find their way to a wall in Montreal.

Although he had trained in Paris, where, as our English doctor told my mother, leeches were still sold in pharmacies and babies died like flies, Chauchard was thought modern and forward-looking. He used the most advanced methods imported from the United States, or, as one would have said then, "from Boston," which meant both stylish and impeccably right. Ultraviolet irradiation was one, recommended for building up delicate children. I recall the black mask tied on, and the danger of blindness should one pull it off before being told. I owe him irradiation to the marrow and other sources of confusion: it was he who gave my mother the name of a convent where Jansenist discipline still had a foot on the neck of the twentieth century and where, as an added enchantment, I was certain not to hear a word of English. He never dreamed, I am sure, that I would be packed off there as a boarder from the age of four. Out of goodness and affection he gave me books to read — children's stories from nineteenth-century France which I hated and still detest. In these oppressive stories children were punished and punished hard for behavior that seemed in another century, above all on another continent, natural and right. I could never see the right-and-wrong over which they kept stumbling and only much later recognized it in European social fiddle-faddle — the trivial yardsticks that measure a man's character by the way he eats a boiled egg. The prose was stiff, a bit shrill, probably pitched too high for a North American ear. Even the bindings, a particularly ugly red, were repellent to me, while their gilt titles lent them the ceremonial quality of school prizes. I had plenty of English Victorian books, but the scolding could be got over, because there was no unfairness. Where there was, it was done away with as part of the plot. The authors were on the side of morality but also of the child. For a long time I imagined that most of my English books had been written by other children, but I never made that mistake with French: I saw these authors as large, scowling creatures with faces as flushed with crossness as the books' covers. Still, the books were presents, therefore important, offered without a word or a look Dr. Chauchard would not have bestowed on an adult. They had been his mother's; she lived in rooms at the top of the house, receiving her own friends, not often mingling with his. She must have let him have these treasures for a favored patient who did not understand the courtesy, even the sacrifice, until it was too late to say "Thank you." Another child's name — his mother's — was on the flyleaf; I seldom looked at it, concentrated as I was on my own. It is not simply rhetoric to say that I see him still — Fildes profile, white cuff, dark sleeve, writing the new dedication with a pen dipped in the blue inkwell, hand and book within the circle cast by the lamp on his desk. At home I would paste inside the front cover the plate my father had designed for me, which had "Linnet: Her Book" as ex libris, and the drawing of a stream flowing between grassy banks — his memory of the unhurried movement of England, no reflection of anything known to me in Quebec

— bearing a single autumn leaf. Under the stream came the lines

> Time, Time which none can bind
> While flowing fast leaves love
>   behind.

The only child will usually give and lend its possessions easily, having missed the sturdy training in rivalry and forced sharing afforded by sisters and brothers, yet nothing would have made me part willingly with any of the grim red books. Grouped on a special shelf, seldom opened after the first reading, they were not reminders but a true fragment of his twilit house, his swan and heron doors, Napoleon III so cunningly lighted, "Le Petit Palais — The Petit Palais," and, finally, Dr. Chauchard himself at the desk of his shadowy room writing *"Pour ma chère petite Linnet"* in a book that had once belonged to another girl.

Now, how to account for the changed, stern, disapproving Chauchard who in that same office gave me not a book but a lecture beginning "Think of your unfortunate parents" and ending "You owe them everything; it is your duty to love them." He had just telephoned for my father to come and fetch me. "How miserable they would be if anything ever happened to you," he said. He spoke of my *petit Papa* and my *petite Maman* with that fake diminution of authority characteristic of the Latin tongues which never works in English. I sat on a chair still wearing outdoor clothes — navy reefer over my convent uniform, HMS *Nelson* sailor hat held on by a black elastic — neither his patient nor his guest at this dreadful crisis, wondering, What does he mean? For a long time now my surprise visits to friends had been called, incorrectly, "running away." Running away was one of the reasons my parents gave when anyone asked why I had been walled up in such a severe school at an early age. Dr. Chauchard, honored by one of my visits, at once asked his office nurse, "Do her parents know she's here?" Women are supposed to make dangerous patients for bachelor doctors; besotted little girls must seem even worse. But I was not besotted; I believed we were equals. It was he who had set up the equality, and for that reason I still think he should have invited me to remove my coat.

The only thing worth remarking about his dull little sermon is that it was in French. French was his language for medicine; I never heard him give an opinion in English. It was evidently the language to which he retreated if one became a nuisance, his back to a wall of white marble syntax. And when it came to filial devotion he was one with the red-covered books. Calling on my parents, not as my doctor but as their friend, he spoke another language. It was not merely English instead of French but the private dialect of a younger person who was playful, charming, who smoked cigarettes in a black-and-silver holder, looking round to see the effect of his puns and jokes. You could notice then, only then, that his black-currant eyes were never still.

The house he came to remained for a long time enormous in memory, though the few like it still standing — "still living," I nearly say — are narrow, with thin, steep staircases and close, high-ceilinged rooms. They were the work of Edinburgh architects and dated from when Montreal was a Scottish city; it had never been really English. A Saturday-evening gathering of several adults, one child, and a couple of dogs created a sort of tangle in the middle of the room — an entwining that was surely not of people's feet: in those days everyone sat straight. The women had to, because their girdles had hooks and stays. Men sat up out of habit, probably the habit of prosperity; the Depression created the physical slump, a change in posture to match the times. Perhaps desires and secrets and second thoughts threading from person to person, from bachelor to married woman, from mother of none to somebody's father, formed a cat's cradle — matted, invisible, and quite dangerous. Why else would Ruby, the latest homesick underpaid Newfoundland import, have kept tripping up as she lurched across the room with cups and glasses on a tray?

Transformed into jolly Uncle Raoul (his request), Dr. Chauchard would arrive with a good friend of his, divorced Mrs. Erskine, and a younger friend of both, named Paul-Armand. Paul-Armand was temporary, one of a sequence of young men who attended Mrs. Erskine as her bard, her personal laureate. His role did not outlive a certain stage of artless admiration; at the first sign of falling away, the first mouse squeak of disenchantment from him, a replacement was found. All of these young men were good-looking, well brought up, longing to be unconventional, and entirely innocent. Flanked by her pair of males, Mrs. Erskine would sway into the room, as graceful as a woman can be when she is boned from waist to thigh. She would keep on her long moleskin coat, even though like all Canadian rooms this one was vastly overheated, explaining that she was chilly. This may have been an attempt to reduce the impression she gave of general largeness by suggesting an inner fragility. Presently the coat would come off, revealing a hand-woven tea-cozy sort of garment — this at a time when every other woman was showing her knees. My mother sat with her legs crossed and one sandal dangling. Her hair had recently been shingled; she seemed to be groping for its lost comfortable warmth. Other persons, my father apart, are a dim choir muttering, "Isn't it past your bedtime?" My father sat back in a deep, chintz-covered chair and said hardly anything except for an occasional "Down" to his dogs.

In another season, in the country, my parents had other friends, summer friends, who drank Old-Fashioneds and danced to gramophone records out on the lawn. Winter friends were mostly coffee drinkers, who did what people do between wars and revolutions — sat in a circle and talked about revolutions and wars. The language was usually English, though not everyone was native to English. Mrs. Erskine commanded what she called "*good* French" and rather liked displaying it, but after a few sentences, which made those who could not understand French very fidgety and which annoyed the French Canadians present exactly in the way an affected accent will grate on Irish nerves, she would pick her way back to English. In mixed society, such little of it as existed, English seemed to be the social rule. It did not enter the mind of any English speaker that the French were at a constant disadvantage, like a team obliged to play all their matches away from home. Dr. Chauchard never addressed me in French here, not even when he would ask me to recite a French poem learned at my convent school. It began, "If I were a fly, Maman, I would steal a kiss from your lips." The nun in charge of memory work was fiddly about liaison, which produced an accidentally appropriate *"Si j'étaiszzzzzzzune mouche, Maman."* Dr. Chauchard never seemed to tire of this and may have thought it a reasonable declaration to make to one's mother.

It was a tactless rhyme, if you think of all the buzzing and stealing that went on in at least part of the winter circle, but I could not have known that. At least not consciously. Unconsciously, everyone under the age of ten knows everything. Under-ten can come into a room and sense at once everything felt, kept silent, held back in the way of love, hate, and desire, though he may not have the right words for such sentiments. It is part of the clairvoyant immunity to hypocrisy we are born with and that vanishes just before puberty. I knew, though no one had told me, that my mother was a bit foolish about Dr. Chauchard; that Mrs. Erskine would have turned cartwheels to get my father's attention but that even cartwheels would have failed; that Dr. Chauchard and Mrs. Erskine were somehow together but never went out alone. Paul-Armand was harder to place; too young to be a parent, he was a pest, a tease to someone smaller. His goading was never noticed, though my reaction to it, creeping behind his chair until I was in a position to punch him, brought an immediate response from the police: "Linnet, if you don't sit down I'm afraid you

will have to go to your room." "If" and "I'm afraid" meant
there was plenty of margin. Later: "Wouldn't you be happier if
you just went to bed? No? Then get a book and sit down and
read it." Presently, "Down, I said, sit down; did you hear what
I've just said to you? I said, sit down, *down*." There came a
point like convergent lines finally meeting where orders to
dogs and instructions to children were given in the same voice.
The only difference was that a dog got "Down, damn it," and,
of course, no one ever swore at me.

This overlapping in one room of French and English, of
Catholic and Protestant — my parents' way of being, and so to
me life itself — was as unlikely, as unnatural to the Montreal
climate as a school of tropical fish. Only later would I discover
that most other people simply floated in mossy little ponds
labelled "French and Catholic" or "English and Protestant,"
never wondering what it might be like to step ashore; or
wondering, perhaps, but weighing up the danger. To be out of
a pond is to be in unmapped territory. The earth might be flat;
you could fall over the edge quite easily. My parents and their
friends were, in their way, explorers. They had in common a
fear of being bored, which is a fear one can afford to nourish in
times of prosperity and peace. It makes for the most ruthless
kind of exclusiveness, based as it is on the belief that anyone
can be the richest of this or cleverest of that and still be the
dullest dog that ever barked. I wince even now remembering
those wretched once-only guests who were put on trial for a
Saturday night and unanimously condemned. This heart-
lessness apart, the winter circle shared an outlook, a kind of
humor, a certain vocabulary of the mind. No one made any of
the standard Montreal statements, such as "What a lot of
books you've got! Don't tell me you've read them," or "I hear
you're some kind of artist. What do you really *do*?" Explorers
like Dr. Chauchard and Mrs. Erskine and my mother and the
rest recognized each other on sight; the recognition cut
through disguisements of class, profession, religion, language,
and even what polltakers call "other interests."

Once you have jumped out of a social enclosure, your eye is bound to be on a real, a geographical elsewhere; theirs seemed to consist of a few cities of Europe with agreeable-sounding names like Vienna and Venice. The United States consisted only of Boston and Florida then. Adults went to Florida for therapeutic reasons — for chronic bronchitis, to recover from operations, for the sake of mysterious maladies that had no names and were called in obituaries "a long illness bravely borne." Boston seemed to be an elegant little republic with its own parliament and flag. To English Montreal, cocooned in that other language nobody bothered to learn, the rest of the continent, Canada included, barely existed; travellers would disembark after long, sooty train trips expressing relief to be in the only city where there were decent restaurants and well-dressed women and where proper English could be heard. Elsewhere, then, became other people, and little groups would form where friends, to the tune of vast mutual admiration, could find a pleasing remoteness in each other. They resembled, in their yearnings, in their clinging together as a substitute for motion, in their craving for "someone to talk to," the kind of marginal social clans you find today in the capitals of Eastern Europe.

I was in the dining room cutting up magazines. My mother brought her coffee cup in, sat down, and said, "Promise me you will never be caught in a situation where you have to compete with a younger woman."

She must have been twenty-six at the very most; Mrs. Erskine was well over thirty. I suppose she was appraising the amount of pickle Mrs. Erskine was in. They had become rivals. With her pale braids, her stately figure, her eyes the color of a stoneware teapot, Mrs. Erskine seemed to me like a white statue with features painted on. I had heard my mother praising her beauty, but for a child she was too large, too still. "Age has its points," my mother went on. "The longer your life goes on, the more chance it has to be interesting. Promise me that when you're thirty you'll have a lot to look back on."

My mother had on her side her comparative youth, her quickness, her somewhat giddy intelligence. She had been married, as she said, "for ever and ever" and was afraid nothing would ever happen to her again. Mrs. Erskine's chief advantage over my mother — being unmarried and available — was matched by an enviable biography. "Ah, don't ask me for my life's story now," she would cry, settling back to tell it. When the others broke into that sighing, singing recital of cities they went in for, repeating strings of names that sounded like sleigh bells (Venice, London, Paris, Rome), Mrs. Erskine would narrow her stoneware eyes and annihilate my mother with "But Charlotte, I've *been* to all those places, I've *seen* all those people." What, indeed, hadn't she seen — crown princes dragged out of Rolls-Royces by cursing mobs, duchesses clutching their tiaras while being raped by anarchists, strikers in England kicking innocent little Border terriers.

". . . And as for the Hun*ga*rians and that Béla *Kun*, let me tell *you* . . . tore the uniforms right off the Red Cross *nurses* . . . made them dance the Charleston naked on top of *street*cars . . ."

"Linnet, wouldn't you be better off in your room?"

The fear of the horde was in all of them; it haunted even their jokes. "Bolshevik" was now "Bolshie," to make it harmless. Petrograd had been their early youth; the Red years just after the war were still within earshot. They dreaded yet seemed drawn to tales of conspiracy and enormous might. The English among them were the first generation to have been raised on *The Wind in the Willows*. Their own Wild Wood was a dark political mystery; its rude inhabitants were still to be tamed. What was needed was a leader, a Badger. But when a Badger occurred they mistrusted him, too; my mother had impressed on me early that Mussolini was a "bad, wicked man." Fortunate Mrs. Erskine had seen "those people" from legation windows; she had, in another defeat for my mother, been married twice, each time to a diplomat. The word "diplomat" had a greater cachet then than it has now. Earlier in the century a diplomat was believed to have attended universities in more than one country, to have two or three languages at his disposal and some slender notion of geography and history. He could read and write quite easily, had probably been born in wedlock, possessed tact and discretion, and led an exemplary private life. Obviously there were no more of these paragons then than there might be now, but fewer were needed, because there were only half as many capitals. Those who did exist spun round and round the world, used for all they were worth, until they became like those coats that outlast their buttons, linings, and pockets: your diplomat, recalled from Bulgaria, by now a mere warp and woof, would be given a new silk lining, bone buttons, have his collar turned, and, after a quick reading of Norse myths, would be shipped to Scandinavia. Mrs. Erskine, twice wedded to examples of these freshened garments, had been everywhere — everywhere my mother longed to be.

"My *life*," said Mrs. Erskine. "Ah, Charlotte, don't ask me to tell you everything — you'd never believe it!" My mother asked, and believed, and died in her heart along with Mrs. Erskine's first husband, a Mr. Sparrow, shot to death in Berlin by a lunatic Russian refugee. (Out of the decency of his nature Mr. Sparrow had helped the refugee's husband emigrate accompanied by a woman Mr. Sparrow had taken to be the Russian man's wife.) In the hours that preceded his "going," as Mrs. Erskine termed his death, Mr. Sparrow had turned into a totally other person, quite common and gross. She had seen exactly how he would rise from the dead for his next incarnation. She had said, "Now, then, Alfred, I think it has been a blissful marriage but perhaps not blissful enough. As I am the best part of your karma, we are going to start all over again in another existence." Mr. Sparrow, in his new coarse, uneducated voice, replied, "Believe you me, Bimbo, if I see you in another world, this time I'm making a detour." His last words — not what every woman hopes to hear, probably, but nothing in my mother's experience could come ankle-high to having a husband assassinated in Berlin by a crazy Russian. Mr. Erskine, the second husband, was not quite so interesting, for he merely "drank and drank and *drank*," and finally, unwittingly, provided grounds for divorce. Since in those days adultery was the only acceptable grounds, the divorce ended his ambitions and transformed Mrs. Erskine into someone déclassée; it was not done for a woman to spoil a man's career, and it was taken for granted that no man ever ruined his own. I am certain my mother did not see Mr. Sparrow as an ass and Mr. Erskine as a soak. They were men out of novels — half diplomat, half secret agent. The natural progress of such men was needed to drag women out of the dullness that seemed to be woman's fate.

There was also the matter of Mrs. Erskine's French: my mother could read and speak it but had nothing of her friend's intolerable fluency. Nor could my mother compete with her special status as the only English and Protestant girl of her generation to have attended French and Catholic schools. She had spent ten years with the Ursulines in Quebec City (languages took longer to learn in those days, when you were obliged to start by memorizing all the verbs) and had emerged with the chic little Ursuline lisp.

"Tell me again," my entranced mother would ask. "How do you say 'squab stuffed with sage dressing'?"

"Charlotte, I've told you and told you. *'Pouthin farthi au thauge.'*"

"Thankth," said my mother. Such was the humor of that period.

For a long time I would turn over like samples of dress material the reasons why I was sent off to a school where by all the rules of the world we lived in I did not belong. A sample that nearly matches is my mother's desire to tease Mrs. Erskine, perhaps to overtake her through me: if she had been unique in her generation, then I would be in mine. Unlikely as it sounds today, I believe that I was. At least I have never met another, just as no French-Canadian woman of my period can recall having sat in a classroom with any other English-speaking Protestant disguised in convent uniform. Mrs. Erskine, rising to the tease, warned that convents had gone downhill since the war and that the appalling French I spoke would be a handicap in Venice, London, Paris, Rome; if the Ursuline French of Quebec City was the best in the world after Tours, Montreal French was just barely a language.

How could my mother, so quick and sharp usually, have been drawn in by this? For a day or two my parents actually weighed the advantages of sending their very young daughter miles away, for no good reason. Why not even to France? "You know perfectly well why not. Because we can't afford it. Not that or anything like it."

Leaning forward in her chair as if words alone could not convince her listener, more like my mother than herself at this moment, Mrs. Erskine with her fingertips to her cheek, the other hand held palm outward, cried, "Ah, Angus, don't ask me for my life's story now!" This to my father, who barely knew other people had lives.

My father made this mysterious answer: "Yes, Frances, I do see what you mean, but I have a family, and once you've got children you're never quite so free."

There was only one child, of course, and not often there, but in my parents' minds and by some miracle of fertility they had produced a whole tribe. At any second this tribe might rampage through the house, scribbling on the wallpaper, tearing up books, scratching gramophone records with a stolen diamond brooch. They dreaded mischief so much that I can only suppose them to have been quite disgraceful children.

"What's Linnet up to? She's awfully quiet."

"Sounds suspicious. Better go and look."

I would be found reading or painting or "building," which meant the elaboration of a foreign city called Marigold that spread and spread until it took up a third of my room and had to be cleared away when my back was turned upon which, as relentless as a colony of beavers, I would start building again. To a visitor Marigold was a slum of empty boxes, serving trays, bottles, silver paper, overturned chairs, but these were streets and houses, churches and convents, restaurants and railway stations. The citizens of Marigold were cut out of magazines: Gloria Swanson was the Mother Superior, Herbert Hoover a convent gardener. Entirely villainous, they did their plotting and planning in an empty cigar box.

Whatever I was doing, I would be told to do something else immediately: I think they had both been brought up that way. "Go out and play in the snow" was a frequent interruption. Parents in bitter climates have a fixed idea about driving children out to be frozen. There was one sunken hour on January afternoons, just before the street lamps were lighted, that was the gray of true wretchedness, as if one's heart and stomach had turned into the same dull, cottony stuff as the sky; it was attached to a feeling of loss, of helpless sadness, unknown to children in other latitudes.

I was home weekends but by no means every weekend. Friday night was given to spoiling and rejoicing, but on Saturday I would hear "When does she go back?"

"Not till tomorrow night."

Ruby, the homesick offshore import, sometimes sat in my room, just for company. She turned the radiator on so that you saw a wisp of steam from the overflow tap. A wicker basket of mending was on her lap; she wiped her eyes on my father's socks. I was not allowed to say to anyone "Go away," or anything like it. I heard her sniffles, her low, muttered grievances. Then she emerged from her impenetrable cloud of Newfoundland gloom to take an interest in the life of Marigold. She did not get down on the floor or in the way, but from her chair suggested some pretty good plots. Ruby was the inspirer of "The Insane Stepmother," "The Rich, Selfish Cousins," "The Death from Croup of Baby Sister" ("Is her face

blue yet?" "No; in a minute"), and "The Broken Engagement," with its cast of three — rejected maiden, fickle lover,
and chaperon. Paper dolls did the acting, the voices were ours.
Ruby played the cast-off fiancée from the heart: "Don't chew
men ever know what chew want?" Chaperon was a fine bossy
part: "That's enough, now. Sit down: I said, *down.*"

My parents said, "What does she see in Ruby?" They were
cross and jealous. The jealousness was real. They did not drop
their voices to say "When does she go back?" but were alert to
signs of disaffection, and offended because I did not crave their
company every minute. Once, when Mrs. Erskine, a bit of a
fool probably, asked, "Who do you love best, your father or
your mother?" and I apparently (I have no memory of it)
answered, "Oh, I'm not really dying about anybody," it was
recalled to me for a long time, as if I had set fire to the
curtains or spat on the Union Jack.

"Think of your unfortunate parents," Dr. Chauchard had
said in the sort of language that had no meaning to
me, though I am sure it was authentic to him.

When he died and I read his obituary, I saw there had been
still another voice. I was twenty and had not seen him since
the age of nine. "The Doctor" and red-covered books had been
lost even before that, when during a major move from
Montreal to a house in the country a number of things that
belonged to me and that my parents were tired of seeing
disappeared.

There were three separate death notices, as if to affirm that
Chauchard had been three men. All three were in a French
newspaper; he neither lived nor died in English. The first was
a jumble of family names and syntax: "After a serene and
happy life it has pleased our Lord to send for the soul of his
faithful servant Raoul Étienne Chauchard, piously deceased
in his native city in his fifty-first year after a short illness
comforted by the sacraments of the Church." There followed a

few particulars — the date and place of the funeral, and the names and addresses of the relatives making the announcement. The exact kinship of each was mentioned: sister, brother-in-law, uncle, nephew, cousin, second cousin.

The second obituary, somewhat longer, had been published by the medical association he belonged to; it described all the steps and stages of his career. There were strings of initials denoting awards and honors, ending with: "Dr. Chauchard had also been granted the Medal of Epidemics (Belgium)." Beneath this came the third notice: "The Arts and Letters Society of Quebec announces the irreparable loss of one of its founder members, the poet R. É. Chauchard." R. É. has published six volumes of verse, a book of critical essays, and a work referred to as "the immortal 'Progress,'" which did not seem to fall into a category or, perhaps, was too well known to readers to need identification.

That third notice was an earthquake, the collapse of the cities we build over the past to cover seams and cracks we cannot account for. He must have been writing when my parents knew him. Why they neglected to speak of it is something too shameful to dwell on; he probably never mentioned it, knowing they would believe it impossible. French books were from France; English books from England or the United States. It would not have entered their minds that the languages they heard spoken around them could be written, too.

I met by accident years after Dr. Chauchard's death one of Mrs. Erskine's ex-minnesingers, now an elderly bachelor. His name was Louis. He had never heard of Paul-Armand, not even by rumor. He had not known my parents and was certain he had never accompanied Dr. Chauchard and Mrs. Erskine to our house. He said that when he met these two he had been fresh from a seminary, aged about nineteen, determined to live a life of ease and pleasure but not sure how to begin. Mrs. Erskine had by then bought and converted a farmhouse south of Montreal, where she wove carpets, hooked rugs, scraped and waxed old tables, kept bees, and bottled tons of pickled beets, preparing for some dark proletarian future should the mob — the horde, "those people" — take over after all. Louis knew the doctor only as the poet R. É. of the third notice. He had no knowledge of the Medal of Epidemics (Belgium) and could not explain it to me. I had found "Progress" by then, which turned out to be R. É.'s diary. I could not put faces to the X, Y, and Z that covered real names, nor could I discover any trace of my parents, let alone of *ma chère petite Linnet*. There were long thoughts about Mozart — people like that.

Louis told me of walking with Mrs. Erskine along a snowy road close to her farmhouse, she in a fur cape that came down to her boot tops and a fur bonnet that hid her braided hair. She talked about her unusual life and her two husbands and about what she now called "the predicament." She told him how she had never been asked to meet Madame Chauchard *mère* and how she had slowly come to realize that R. É. would never marry. She spoke of people who had drifted through the predicament, my mother among them, not singling her out as someone important, just as a wisp of cloud on the edge of the sky. "Poor Charlotte" was how Mrs. Erskine described the thin little target on which she had once trained her biggest guns. Yet "poor Charlotte" — not even an X in the diary, finally — had once been the heart of the play. The plot must have taken a full turning after she left the stage. Louis became a new young satellite, content to circle the powerful stars, to keep an eye on the predicament, which seemed to him flaming, sulphurous. Nobody ever told him what had taken place in the first and second acts.

Walking, he and Mrs. Erskine came to a railway track quite far from houses, and she turned to Louis and opened the fur cloak and said, smiling, *"Viens voir Mrs. Erskine."* (Owing to the Ursuline lisp this must have been "Mitheth Erthkine.") Without coyness or any more conversation she lay down — he said "on the track," but he must have meant near it, if you think of the ties. Folded into the cloak, Louis at last became part of a predicament. He decided that any further experience could only fall short of it, and so he never married.

In this story about the cloak Mrs. Erskine is transmuted from the pale, affected statue I remember and takes on a polychrome life. She seems cheerful and careless, and I like her for that. Carelessness might explain her unreliable memory about Charlotte. And yet not all that careless: "She even knew the train times," said Louis. "She must have done it before." Still, on a sharp blue day, when some people were still in a dark classroom writing "*abyssus abyssum invocat*" all over their immortal souls, she, who had been through this and escaped with nothing worse than a lisp, had the sun, the snow, the wrap of fur, the bright sky, the risk. There is a raffish kind of nerve to her, the only nerve that matters.

For that one conversation Louis and I wondered what our appearance on stage several scenes apart might make us to each other: if A was the daughter of B, and B rattled the foundations of C, and C, though cautious and lazy where women were concerned, was commited in a way to D, and D was forever trying to tell her life's story to E, the husband of B, and E had enough on his hands with B without taking on D, too, and if D decided to lie down on or near a railway track with F, then what are A and F? Nothing. Minor satellites floating out of orbit and out of order after the stars burned out. Mrs. Erskine reclaimed Dr. Chauchard but he never married anyone. Angus reclaimed Charlotte but he died soon after. Louis, another old bachelor, had that one good anecdote about the fur cloak. I lost even the engraving of "The Doctor," spirited away quite shabbily, and I never saw Dr. Chauchard again or even tried to. What if I had turned up one day, aged eighteen or so, only to have him say to his nurse, "Does anyone know she's here?"

When I read the three obituaries it was the brass plate on the door I saw and "Sur Rendez-vous." That means no dropping in." After the warning came the shut heron door and the shut swan door and, at another remove, the desk with the circle of lamplight and R. É. himself, writing about X, Y, Z, and Mozart. A bit humdrum perhaps, a bit prosy, not nearly as good as his old winter Saturday self, but I am sure that it was his real voice, the voice that transcends this or that language. His French-speaking friends did not hear it for a long time (his first book of verse was not sold to anyone outside his immediate family), while his English-speaking friends never heard it at all. But I should have heard it then, at the start, standing on tiptoe to reach the doorbell, calling through the letter box every way I could think of, "I, me." I ought to have heard it when I was still under ten and had all my wits about me.

WITH
A CAPITAL T

For Madeleine and Jean-Paul Lemieux

In wartime, in Montreal, I applied to work on a newspaper. Its name was *The Lantern*, and its motto, "My light shall shine," carried a Wesleyan ring of veracity and plain dealing. I chose it because I thought it was a place where I would be given a lot of different things to do. I said to the man who consented to see me, "But not the women's pages. Nothing like that." I was eighteen. He heard me out and suggested I come back at twenty-one, which was a soft way of getting rid of me. In the meantime I was to acquire experience; he did not say of what kind. On the stroke of twenty-one I returned and told my story to a different person. I was immediately accepted; I had expected to be. I still believed, then, that most people meant what they said. I supposed that the man I had seen that first time had left a memorandum in the files: "To whom it may concern — Three years from this date, Miss Linnet Muir will join the editorial staff." But after I'd been working for a short time I heard one of the editors say, "If it hadn't been for the god-damned war we would never have hired even one of the god-damned women," and so I knew.

In the meantime I had acquired experience by getting married. I was no longer a Miss Muir, but a Mrs. Blanchard. My husband was overseas. I had longed for emancipation and independence, but I was learning that women's autonomy is like a small inheritance paid out a penny at a time. In a journal I kept I scrupulously noted everything that came into my head about this, and about God, and about politics. I took it for granted that our victory over Fascism would be followed by a sunburst of revolution — I thought that was what the war was about. I wondered if going to work for the capitalist press was entirely moral. "Whatever happens," I wrote, "it will be the Truth, nothing half-hearted, the Truth with a Capital T."

The first thing I had to do was write what goes under the pictures. There is no trick to it. You just repeat what the picture has told you like this:

"Boy eats bun as bear looks on."

The reason why anything has to go under the picture at all is that a reader might wonder, "Is that a bear looking on?" It looks like a bear, but that is not enough reason for saying so. Pasted across the back of the photo you have been given is a strip of paper on which you can read: "Saskatoon, Sask. 23 Nov. Boy eats bun as bear looks on." Whoever composed this knows two things more than you do — a place and a time.

You have a space to fill in which the words must come out even. The space may be tight; in that case, you can remove "as" and substitute a comma, though that makes the kind of terse statement to which your reader is apt to reply, "So what?" Most of the time, the Truth with a Capital T is a matter of elongation: "Blond boy eats small bun as large bear looks on."

"Blond boy eats buttered bun . . . " is livelier, but unscrupulous. You have been given no information about the butter. "Boy eats bun as hungry bear looks on," has the beginnings of a plot, but it may inspire your reader to protest: "The boy must be a mean sort of kid if he won't share his food

with a starving creature." Child-lovers, though less prone to
fits of anguish than animal-lovers, may be distressed by the
word "hungry" for a different reason, believing "boy" subject to
attack from "bear." You must not lose your head and type,
"Blond bear eats large boy as hungry bun looks on," because
your reader may notice, and write a letter saying, "Some of
you guys around there think you're pretty smart, don't you?"
while another will try to enrich your caption with, "Re your
bun write-up, my wife has taken better pictures than that in
the very area you mention."

At the back of your mind, because your mentors have
placed it there, is an obstruction called "the policy factor."
Your paper supports a political party. You try to discover what
this party has had to say about buns and bears, how it intends
to approach them in the future. Your editor, at golf with a
member of parliament, will not want to have his game upset
by: "It's not that I want to interfere but some of that bun stuff
seems pretty negative to me." The young and vulnerable
reporter would just as soon not pick up the phone to be told,
"I'm ashamed of your defeatist attitude. Why, I knew your
father! He must be spinning in his grave!" or, more effectively,
"I'm telling you this for your own good — I think you're
subversive without knowing it."

Negative, defeatist and subversive are three of the things you
have been cautioned not to be. The others are seditious,
obscene, obscure, ironic, intellectual and impulsive.

You gather up the photo and three pages of failed captions,
and knock at the frosted glass of a senior door. You sit down
and are given a view of boot soles. You say that the whole
matter comes down to an ethical question concerning information and redundancy; unless "reader" is blotto, can't he see
for himself that this is about a boy, a bun, and a bear?

Your senior person is in shirtsleeves, hands clasped behind
his neck. He thinks this over, staring at the ceiling; swings his
feet to the floor; reads your variations on the bear-and-bun
theme; turns the photo upside-down. He tells you patiently,

that it is not the business of "reader" to draw conclusions. Our subscribers are not dreamers or smart alecks; when they see a situation in a picture, they want that situation confirmed. He reminds you about negativism and obscuration; advises you to go sit in the library and acquire a sense of values by reading the back issues of *Life*.

The back numbers of *Life* are tatty and incomplete, owing to staff habits of tearing out whatever they wish to examine at leisure. A few captions, still intact, allow you to admire a contribution to pictorial journalism, the word "note":

"American flag flies over new post office. Note stars on flag."

"GI waves happily from captured Italian tank. Note helmet on head."

So, "Boy eats bun as bear looks on. Note fur on bear." All that can happen now will be a letter asking, "Are you sure it was a bun?"

From behind frosted-glass doors, as from a leaking intellectual bath, flow instructions about style, spelling, caution, libel, brevity, and something called "the ground rules." A few of these rules have been established for the convenience of the wives of senior persons and reflect their tastes and interests, their inhibitions and fears, their desire to see close friends' pictures when they open to the social page, their fragile attention span. Other rules demand that we pretend to be independent of British foreign policy and American commerce — otherwise our readers, discouraged, will give up caring who wins the war. (Soon after victory British foreign policy will cease to exist; as for American commerce, the first grumbling will be heard when a factory in Buffalo is suspected of having flooded the country with defective twelve-inch pie tins.) Ground rules maintain that you must not be flippant about the Crown — an umbrella term covering a number of high-class subjects, from the Royal Family to the nation's judicial system — or about our war effort or, indeed, our reasons for making any effort about anything. Religions, in particular those observed by decent Christians, are not up for debate. We may, however, describe and denounce marginal sects whose puritanical leanings are even more dizzily slanted than our own. The Jehovah's Witnesses, banned as seditious, continue to issue inflammatory pamphlets about Jesus; patriotic outrage abounds over this. The children of Witnesses are beaten up in public schools for refusing to draw Easter bunnies. An education officer, interviewed, declares that the children's obstinate observance of the Second Commandment is helping Hitler. Everyone knows that the Easter bunny, along with God and Santa Claus, is on our side.

To argue a case for the children is defeatist; to advance reasons against their persecution is obscure. Besides, your version of the bunny conflict may be unreliable. Behind frosted-glass doors lurk male fears of female mischief. Women, having no inborn sense of history, are known to invent absurd stories. Celebrated newspaper hoaxes (perpetrated by men, as it happens) are described to you, examples of irresponsible writing that have brought down trusting editors. A few of these stories have been swimming, like old sea turtles, for years now, crawling ashore wherever British possessions are still tinted red on the map. "As the niece of the Governor-General rose from a deep curtsey, the Prince, with the boyish smile that has made him the darling of five continents, picked up a bronze bust of his grandmother and battered Lady Adeline to death" is one version of a perennial favorite.

Privately, you think you could do better. You will never get the chance. The umpires of ground rules are nervous and watchful behind those doors. Wartime security hangs heavy. So does the fear that the end of hostilities will see them turfed out to make way for war correspondents wearing nonchalant mustaches, battered caps, carelessly-knotted white scarves, raincoats with shoulder tabs, punctuating their accounts of Hunnish atrocities perceived at Claridges and the Savoy with "Roger!" and "Jolly-oh!" and "Over to you!"

Awaiting this dreadful invasion the umpires sit, in shirt-sleeves and braces, scribbling initials with thick blue pencils. "NDG" stands for "No Damned Good." (Clairvoyant, you will begin to write "NBF" in your journal meaning "No Bloody Future.") As a creeping, climbing wash of conflicting and contradictory instructions threatens to smother you, you discover the possibilities of the quiet, or lesser, hoax. Obeying every warning and precept, you will write, turn in, and get away with, "Dressed in shoes, stockings and hat appropriate to the season, Mrs. Horatio Bantam, the former Felicity Duck-pond, grasped the bottle of champagne in her white-gloved hand and sent it swinging against the end of HMCS *Make-weight* that was nearest the official party, after which, swaying slightly, she slid down the ways and headed for open waters."

A s soon as I realized that I was paid about half the salary men were earning, I decided to do half the work. I had spent much of my adolescence as a resourceful truant, evolving the good escape dodges that would serve one way and another all my life. At *The Lantern* I used reliable school methods. I would knock on a glass door — a door that had nothing to do with me.

"Well, Blanchard, what do you want?"

"Oh, Mr. Watchmaster — it's just to tell you I'm going out to look something up."

"What for?"

"An assignment."

"Don't tell *me*. Tell Amstutz."

"He's organizing fire-drill in case of air-raids."

"Tell Cranach. He can tell Amstutz."

"Mr. Cranach has gone to stop the art department from striking."

"*Striking?* Don't those buggers know there's a war on? I'd like to see Accounting try that. What do they want now?"

"Conditions. They're asking for conditions. Is it all right if I go now, Mr. Watchmaster?"

"You know what we need around here, don't you? One German regiment. Regiment? What am I saying? *Platoon.* That'd take the mickey out of 'em. Teach them something about hard work. Loving your country. Your duty. Give me one trained German sergeant. I'd lead him in. 'O.K. — you've been asking for this!' Ratatatat. You wouldn't hear any more guff about conditions. What's your assignment?"

"The Old Presbyterians. They've decided they're against killing people because of something God said to Moses."

"Seditious bastards. Put 'em in work camps, the whole damned lot. All right, Blanchard, carry on."

I would go home, wash my hair, listen to Billie Holiday records.

"Say, Blanchard, where the hell were you yesterday? Seventy-nine people were poisoned by ham sandwiches at a wedding party on Durocher Street. The sidewalk was like a morgue."

"Actually, I just happened to be in Mr. Watchmaster's office. But only for a minute."

"Watchmaster's got no right to ask you to do anything. One of these days I'm going to close in on him. I can't right now — there's a war on. The only good men we ever had in this country were killed in the last one. Look, next time Watchmaster gets you to run his errands, refer it to Cranach. Got that? All right, Blanchard, on your way."

No good dodge works forever.
    "Oh, Mr. Watchmaster, I just wanted to tell you I'm going out for an hour or two. I have to look something up. Mr. Cranach's got his door locked, and Mr. Amstutz had to go home to see why his wife was crying."

"Christ, what an outfit. What do you have to look up?"

"What Mussolini did to the Red Cross dogs. It's for the 'Whither Italy?' supplement."

"You don't need to leave the building for that. You can get all you want by phone. You highbrows don't even know what a phone is. Drop around Advertising some time and I'll show you down-to-earth people using phones as working instruments. All you have to do is call the Red Cross, a veterinarian, an Italian priest, maybe an Italian restaurant, and a kennel. They'll tell you all you need to know. Remember what Churchill said about Mussolini, eh? That he was a fine Christian gentleman. If you want my opinion, whatever those dogs got they deserved."

I nterviews were useful; you could get out and ride around in taxis and waste hours in hotel lobbies reading the new American magazines, which were increasingly difficult to find.

"I'm just checking something for *The Lantern* — do you mind?"

"Just so long as you don't mar the merchandise. I've only got five *Time*, three *Look*, four *Photoplay* and two *Ladies' Home*. Don't wander away with the *Esquire*. There's a war on."

Once I was sent to interview my own godmother. Nobody knew I knew her, and I didn't say. She was president of a committee that sent bundles to prisoners-of-war. The committee was launching an appeal for funds; that was the reason for the interview. I took down her name as if I had never heard it before: Miss Edna May Henderson. My parents had called her "Georgie," though I don't know why.

I had not seen my godmother since I was eight. My father had died, and I had been dragged away to be brought up in different cities. At eighteen, I had summoned her to a telephone: "It's Linnet," I said. "I'm here, in Montreal. I've come back to stay."

"Linnet," she said. "Good gracious me." Her chain-smoker's voice made me homesick, though it could not have been for a place — I was in it. Her voice, and her particular Montreal accent, were like the unexpected signatures that underwrite the past: If this much is true, you will tell yourself, then so is all the rest I have remembered.

She was too busy with her personal war drive to see me then, though she did ask for my phone number. She did not enquire where I had been since my father's death, or if I had anything here to come back to. It is true that she and my mother had quarrelled years before; still, it was Georgie who had once renounced in my name "the devil and all his works, the vain pomp and glory of the world, with all covetous desires of the same, and carnal desires of the flesh." She might have been curious to see the result of her bizarre undertaking, but a native canny Anglo-Montreal prudence held her still.

I was calling from a drugstore; I lived in one room of a cold-water flat in the east end. I said, "I'm completely on my own, and entirely self-supporting." That was so Georgie would understand I was not looking for help; at all events, for nothing material.

I realize now how irregular, how fishy even, this must have sounded. Everybody has a phone, she was probably thinking. What is the girl trying to hide?

"Nothing" would have been the answer. There seemed no way to connect. She asked me to call her again in about a month's time, but of course I never did.

My godmother spent most of her life in a block of granite designed to look like a fortress. Within the fortress were sprawling apartments, drawn to an Edwardian pattern of high ceilings, dark corridors, and enormous kitchens full of pipes. Churches and schools, banks and prisons, dwellings and railway stations were part of an imperial convallation that wound round the globe, designed to impress on the minds of indigenous populations that the builders had come to stay. In Georgie's redoubt, the doorman was shabby and lame; he limped beside me along a gloomy passage as far as the elevator, where only one of the sconce lights fixed to the panelling still worked. I had expected someone else to answer my ring, but it was Georgie who let me in, took my coat, and indicated with a brusque gesture, as if I did not know any English, the mat where I was to leave my wet snowboots. It had not occurred to me to bring shoes. Padding into her drawing room on stockinged feet, I saw the flash photograph her memory would file as further evidence of Muir incompetence; for I believe to this day that she recognized me at once. I was the final product, the last living specimen of a strain of people whose imprudence, lack of foresight, and refusal to take anything seriously had left one generation after another unprepared and stranded, obliged to build life from the ground up, fashioning new materials every time.

My godmother was tall, though not so tall as I remembered. Her face was wide and flat. Her eyes were small, deep-set, slightly tilted, as if two invisible thumbs were pulling at her temples. Her skin was as coarse and lined as a farm woman's; indifference to personal appearance of that kind used to be a matter of pride.

Her drawing room was white, and dingy and worn-looking. Curtains and armchairs needed attention, but that may have been on account of the war: it had been a good four years since anyone had bothered to paint or paper or have slipcovers made. The lamps were blue-and-white, and on this winter day already lighted. The room smelled of the metallic central heating of old apartment buildings, and of my godmother's Virginia cigarettes. We sat on worn white sofas, facing each other, with a table in between.

My godmother gave me Scotch in a heavy tumbler and pushed a dish of peanuts towards me, remarking in that harsh evocative voice, "Peanuts are harder to find than Scotch now." Actually, Scotch was off the map for most people; it was a civilian casualty, expensive and rare.

We were alone except for a Yorkshire terrier, who lay on a chair in the senile sleep that is part of dying.

"I would like it if Minnie could hang on until the end of the war," Georgie said. "I'm sure she'd like the victory parades and the bands. But she's thirteen, so I don't know."

That was the way she and my parents and their friends had talked to each other. The duller, the more earnest, the more literal generation I stood for seemed to crowd the worn white room, and to darken it further.

I thought I had better tell her straightaway who I was, though I imagined she knew. I did not intend to be friendly beyond that, unless she smiled. And even there, the quality of the smile would matter. Some smiles are instruments of repression.

Telling my new name, explaining that I had married, that I was now working for a newspaper, gave an accounting only up to a point. A deserted continent stretched between us, cracked and fissured with bottomless pits over which Georgie stepped easily. How do you deal with life? her particular Canadian catechism asked. By ignoring its claims on feeling. Any curiosity she may have felt about such mysteries as coincidence and continuity (my father was said to have been the love of her life; I was said to resemble him) had been abandoned, like a game that was once the rage. She may have been unlucky with games, which would explain the committee work; it may be dull, but you can be fairly sure of the outcome. I often came across women like her, then, who had no sons or lovers or husbands to worry about, and who adopted the principle of the absent, endangered male. A difference between us was that, to me, the absence and danger had to be taken for granted; another was that what I thought of as men, Georgie referred to as "boys." The rest was beyond my reach. Being a poor judge of probabilities, she had expected my father to divorce. I was another woman's child, foolish and vulnerable because I had lost my dignity along with my boots; paid to take down her words in a notebook; working not for a lark but for a living, which was unforgivable even then within the shabby fortress. I might have said, "I am innocent," but she already knew that.

My godmother was dressed in a jaunty blue jacket with a double row of brass buttons, and a pleated skirt. I supposed this must be the costume she and her committee wore when they were packing soap and cigarettes and second-hand cheery novels for their boys over there in the coop. She told me the names of the committee women, and said, "Are you getting everything down all right?" People ask that who are not used to being interviewed. "They told me there'd be a picture," she complained. That explained the uniform.

"I'm sorry. He should be here now."

"Do you want me to spell those names for you?"

"No. I'm sure I have them."

"You're not writing much."

"I don't need to," I said. "Not as a rule."

"You must have quite a memory."

She seemed to be trying to recall where my knack of remembering came from, if it was inherited, wondering whether memory is of any use to anyone except to store up reasons for discord.

We gave up waiting for the photographer. I stood stork-like in the passage, pulling on a boot. Georgie leaned on the wall, and I saw that she was slightly tight.

"I have four godchildren," she said. "People chose me because I was an old maid, and they thought I had money to leave. Well, I haven't. There'll be nothing for the boys. All my godchildren were boys. I never liked girls."

She had probably been drinking for much of the day, on and off; and of course there was all the excitement of being interviewed, and the shock of seeing me: still, it was a poor thing to say. Supposing, just supposing, that Georgie had been all I had left? My parents had been perfectly indifferent to money — almost pathologically so, I sometimes thought. The careless debts they had left strewn behind and that I kept picking up and trying to settle were not owed in currency.

Why didn't I come straight out with that? Because you can't — not in that world. No one can have the last retort, not even when there is truth to it. Hints and reminders flutter to the ground in overheated winter rooms, lie stunned for a season, are reborn as everlasting grudges.

"Goodbye, Linnet," she said.

"Goodbye."

"Do you still *not* have a telephone?" No answer. "When will it come out?" She meant the interview.

"On Saturday."

"I'll be looking for it." On her face was a look I took to mean anxiety over the picture, and that I now see to have been mortal terror. I never met her again, not even by accident. The true account I wrote of her committee and its need for public generosity put us at a final remove from each other.

I did not forget her, but I forgot about her. Her life seemed silent and slow and choked with wrack, while mine moved all in a rush, dislodging every obstacle it encountered. Then mine slowed too; stopped flooding its banks. The noise of it abated and I could hear the past. She had died by then — thick-skinned, chain-smoking survivor of the regiment holding the fort.

I saw us in the decaying winter room, saw the lamps blazing coldly on the dark window panes; I heard our voices: "Peanuts are harder to find than Scotch now." "Do you send parcels to Asia, or just to Germany?"

What a dull girl she is, Georgie must have thought; for I see, now, that I was seamless, and as smooth as brass; that I gave her no opening.

When she died, the godsons mentioned in her will swarmed around for a while, but after a certain amount of scuffling with trustees they gave up all claim, which was more dignified for them than standing forlorn and hungry-looking before a cupboard containing nothing. Nobody spoke up for the one

legacy the trustees would have relinquished: a dog named
Minnie, who was by then the equivalent of one hundred and
nineteen years old in human time, and who persisted so
unreasonably in her right to outlive the rest of us that she had
to be put down without mercy.